SLAYER OF SPACE
QUAZAR
BOOK ONE OF THE ORBITAL MISSIONS

ARCADIUS MAZE

Quazar
Book One of the Orbital Missions
Copyright © 2023 by Arcadius Maze

All rights reserved. No part of this publication may be reproduced, distributed, or transmitted in any form or by any means, including photocopying, recording, or other electronic or mechanical methods, without the prior written permission of the author, except in the case of brief quotations embodied in critical reviews and certain other non-commercial uses permitted by copyright law.

Tellwell Talent
www.tellwell.ca

ISBN
978-0-2288-9233-5 (Hardcover)
978-0-2288-9234-2 (Paperback)
978-0-2288-9232-8 (eBook)

This first book is dedicated to my parents: Bill and Louise.

I owe you so much – even all the words in the world cannot repay what you have done for me.

For all of the time you have invested in me – I thank you!

TABLE OF CONTENTS

Prologue: The Gambit Galaxy, Nova Martia vii

Chapter 1:   A Few Wrong Choices 1
Chapter 2:   Sleet Sheets 13
Chapter 3:   Shot to Hell 31
Chapter 4:   Black Holes and Darker Issues 57
Chapter 5:   Adrift 73
Chapter 6:   Weapons at the Ready 87
Chapter 7:   The Galactic Post 101
Chapter 8:   Stonesend 123
Chapter 9:   Falling Together 151
Chapter 10: A Cold, Sharp Hello 169
Chapter 11: Prime Station Alpha 185
Chapter 12: Two Steps Forward 217
Chapter 13: Insignificance 233
Chapter 14: Meeting 261
Chapter 15: Rotations 279

Chapter 16: Roustabout's	287
Chapter 17: Cause and Effect	315
Chapter 18: A Healthy Admission	335
Chapter 19: Lures	351
Chapter 20: Haze of Lies	381
Chapter 21: Crumpled Space	395
Chapter 22: Mondo	413

PROLOGUE

The Gambit Galaxy, Nova Martia
Year 2475

My floater skimmed upon the red, dusty plains of Daedalia at a truly dizzying speed. It would have been alarming, but those barren plains failed to give my journey some form of perspective.

"Brant Zenith." The robotic voice from my floater wafted through the cabin like a misshaped gong. "Sign in for your upcoming classes."

The voice was as cold as the space above my head, and as it spoke my name I felt a sense of detachment from the vessel I travelled upon. Nonetheless I quickly typed out my name on a flat-screened keyboard.

I was ten Earth years of age, no older than a medium-aged bottle of apple-infused rum. I sat beneath the vessel's domed ceilings, staring off into the stars as if they were the eyes of the angels themselves. I couldn't pull my young, quizzical mind away from all the adventures the stars foretold for the lucky travellers and explorers already out there.

I had been born in Daedalia Prime, capital city on Nova Martia, to human parents. As far as planets went, Nova Martia was eerily similar to Mars, although it was located in the Gambit Galaxy, far from the Earth where my parents had grown up. They had moved to Nova Martia only a few years before my birth.

Life beneath the capital's energy dome was a good one. The terraformation of Nova Martia hadn't created a true second Earth, of course, as the first human explorers of this nook of space had hoped, but it had allowed for its inhabitants to spend hours each day in the free open air surrounded by a technologically advanced city filled with dozens of species.

As I rocketed across the dusty red plains at speeds above two hundred kilometres per hour, maintaining an altitude of just about a metre, I noticed the blur of natural stone walls begin to form around me. They reminded me of small toes and fingers of stone jutting through the sand on a beach, random and artful all at once.

My young gaze drifted over the floater's interior. The command screen, beneath the crystal dome, displayed holographic images which surrounded me in a ring. Every direction I looked allowed me to perceive readouts about the terrain, the floater's speed, and distance to my destination, to name but a few of the vehicle's functions.

I looked upon the dome and toggled the heads-up display to describe which stars I was peering at. The HUD fed my imagination, able to fill in the details of any star or planet I could spy at any given moment. If my love of space hadn't been born during these floater voyages across the surface of Nova Martia, it was certainly well nurtured here.

I deeply enjoyed my weekly shuttle rides to and from Gravitas Mons, the planet's largest volcano, and Daedalia Prime, its largest city. The trips were peaceful and gave me all the time a ten-year-old needed to dwell on his thoughts—which, if I were being honest, mostly concerned laser blasters, robots, and space exploration.

I was alone on this particular voyage, as I had been many times before. There were so many floaters available for public transportation that passengers could often ride in their own shuttles if they chose to travel after-hours. Most floaters, except for those few military vehicles, operated according to an autonomous program, with every detail of the voyage predetermined before I'd even stepped foot aboard. This sometimes bothered me. I had half a mind to try jury-rigging the vessel, thus taking command of my future and all the adventures I could reach upon it.

But like a good human, I respected my superiors and did as I was told, restraining myself to the realm of my imagination. I didn't wish to disappoint my parents. Even though I didn't get to see them often, I still wished to make them proud of me.

Gravitas Mons loomed into view, its immense, steeply sloped sides daunting to behold. I knew we were now within a hundred kilometres of the continent-sized volcano. I had always dreamed about life inside the volcano, fending off battles from the notorious Nova Martians I had heard lived deep beneath the surface.

Nova Martians were a relative enigma on the planet, strange as that thought seemed. Not many, perhaps a dozen, had been discovered by explorers throughout the past one hundred fifty years of human habitation. They tended to live deep beneath the planet's crust, as they had for thousands of years. I had heard they were made of stone, or iron… or possibly even clay. I'd also heard they were large and could be fierce. But this, too, I didn't know from firsthand experience.

My lack of education on the topic made my mind run wild. I had a vivid imagination. I dreamed of being the first child to slay such massive creatures en masse. I could see it clearly in my mind, stumbling upon a Nova Martian in the dark, murky mining tunnels kilometres beneath the surface, accidentally interrupting a horde of these beasts tearing into a hapless group of human workers. Armed with my trusty blaster, always at the ready, I would happily save everyone from certain doom, blasting holes in these Nova Martians' rigid bodies.

My mind drifted through childhood reveries, only dimly aware that I was twenty minutes out from Gravitas Mons where I would meet my classmates for our weekly subterranean excursions.

I was jarred from my pleasant daydreams as the floater abruptly lifted with an ear-splitting crash, spinning me across the vessel's interior. The vessel must have impacted something, knocking it off the pocket of energy and dense air that ordinarily kept it afloat. The crash flipped the floater off its axis of gravity. I lurched hard, flipping upside-down so quickly that I felt certain I was going to die.

For a few long, drawn-out moments, I saw the stars spin, the inky black sky and red soil jockeying back and forth in my field of vision. The floater flipped too many times to count; the low force of gravity and speed at which we'd been travelling didn't allow the dangerous accident to end quickly.

When next I opened my eyes, the spinning had finally stopped, and I breathed deeply in relief. My floater had been torn apart, and behind me the wreckage had left a long gouge in the red earth. Above me, the floater's crystal dome had been split down the middle in an arc wider than my body.

But at least I was alive and upright.

I wasn't dressed for the open air, so I was beyond lucky that we were in the warmest months of the year. The temperature was hardly balmy, but it was reasonable enough for me to walk through the damp sand in my light school-issued jacket.

I stepped out of the remains of the floater, amazed and relieved to realize that the dense energy pocket in the vehicle's cabin had been activated the moment the vessel's gyros had been triggered. During the crash, my body had been locked in place, prevented from falling. I'd been held safe like that until the last moments when the vessel had split upon a rocky crag at the base of a foothill.

Floater accidents were so rare on Nova Martia as to be nearly unheard of. All I could think about was how glad I was that these safety features had kept me alive.

Gravitas Mons loomed over me, all at once foreboding yet seemingly eager for me to return to it. The stars and the planet's large moons provided just enough light for me to take in the surreal terrain. As the dust settled, having been stirred up from the accident, my vision grew clearer. The sand around me looked something like butter, carved smoothly by a knife around the crash site.

My hands shook and I didn't know if it was from fear of dying or being lost in the middle of the fearsome red plains. I knew I would need the supplies which had been kept in the floater's core, now strewn widely across the surface.

I began walking back through the wreckage and found it to have been tossed further than anticipated. Due to assisted gravity fields in the inhabited regions of the planet, gravity was always within one or two percent of Earth normal. But out here in the middle of nowhere, the low gravity was my friend. I could hop along quicker than I ever could have in the cities.

I took protracted steps, as we had been taught in school. They had heavily reinforced in us basic skills of survival. Even at the age of ten, I knew well enough to look for the compartment that housed my emergency bag. Within that bag I would find food, water, and, perhaps most importantly, my travel suit; the suit could be energized to keep the wearer warm and provide protection from the periodic sandstorms.

My footfalls landed metres apart and I sped along at nearly thirty kilometres per hour. I was both light and nimble as I searched the wreckage for my belongings. But the damage was extensive, and it was difficult to determine what each piece of debris had once been.

After a few minutes, I managed to find a damaged portion of the floater that I presumed still held my emergency supplies. It had crumpled as though having been struck by a boulder.

This made me wonder about what had gone wrong to begin with. The floater's course and speed had been predetermined days earlier, just as satellites and unmanned drones constantly engaged in terrain assessment all over Nova Martia. Whatever my vessel had struck couldn't have been on my planned course… unless the vessel's computers had malfunctioned.

I edged into the wreckage as it lay at an angle against a crag of volcanic glass and stone. I placed my foot upon the formation's side and pulled free my backpack.

What happened next even I couldn't have imagined.

The craggy rock began to move! The formation grew taller and shook the ground. The floater's hull flipped off the side of the reddish-black stone and tumbled away violently, stirring up fresh dust with each roll.

I jumped back in surprise as the craggy stone moved toward me.

For all my dreaming, the truth is that I had no idea if I was the least amount brave. I was about to find out.

The stone began to twist, and with a bolt of fear I realized that it wasn't the chunk of Nova Martian rock I had believed it to be. It was, in fact, a living being. It was a Nova Martian!

Descriptions of Nova Martians were vague and often differed greatly depending on who was speaking. But I had come to learn that they were large and red as the desert sands.

The Nova Martian leaned heavily, reaching out for me. I jumped back but didn't run, as I am both thankful and proud to say. Instead I searched for some type of weapon with which to protect myself from this beast. I looked down at my feet and grabbed the first thing I could find: an odd black stone about the size of a bowling ball. Its edges were just jagged enough to give me fingerholds as I lifted it above my head, ready to throw.

No matter how hard I wish I could forget what happened next, I fear I never will.

The red, cratered creature raised a pair of appendages I recognized as arms and dropped upon its stony knees. I could see at this point that it had a face not so dissimilar from those of other humanoids. Its face was chiselled stone and it looked almost buffed to a sheen, like a marble countertop. Below two dull grey eyes rested a small protrusion that seemed a bit like a nose, although the nostrils weren't positioned quite right.

I stood in place, the black stone held high, unable to understand its actions. Would it be braver to throw the stone or remain still? I didn't have time to answer, for the Nova Martian began to speak.

"Please. Do not."

I faltered in place, as motionless as the remains of the floater. I simply waited. I couldn't determine whether I was more scared or intrigued.

"Please."

I was struck by the silky-smooth tone of the towering creature's voice. It had a heart-breaking quality to it. Whatever I had expected such a monster to sound like, this wasn't it.

It remained on its knees and began to shake violently. This sound was more like the one I might have expected—gruesome, like the smashing together of rocks. The creature's shudders didn't threaten me, but I felt alarmed. It seemed to be experiencing an earthquake.

Before I could decide what to do next, the Nova Martian collapsed hard upon the sand.

I lowered the stone to my waist and stepped closer. The creature barely moved; its only sign of life was to shift its weight to better peer up at me. Its dull grey eyes made me hurt inside, but I didn't know why.

"Please. Do not hurt."

I held the stone out in front of me like a protective shield in case it attacked. It never did. Instead I began to wonder how it was possible that this creature could speak English.

Regardless, I decided that I wouldn't hurt it.

Looking down, I realized that I still carried my makeshift weapon. I was about to toss it away when the Nova Martian cried out in pain.

"No! Please do not!"

Alarmed once more, I grasped the stone more tightly. Something was very wrong.

At my age, I didn't understand anything of Nova Martian anatomy. This was no surprise, since most people didn't even believe the beings existed. But I watched grey sludge leak from a jagged split on the side of its head. The substance looked, to me, like blood.

Please do not. The words rang through my head, more like a choir of angels than a lumbering beast.

As I took a step closer, it reached out to me. This time, instead of freezing, I knelt, loosening my grip on the stone. In fact, I was about to drop the stone when it began to move in my hands. Startled, I looked down and saw two red slits open in its dark surface.

This was no boulder, I realized, but rather a small lifeform! Could it be that this stone was actually a baby Nova Martian?

Without hesitating, I handed the baby to the Nova Martian. I had seen enough nature shows from Earth to recognize the actions of a mother.

"You're hurt," I said.

Her dull grey eyes shone with relief. She tried to edge away from me, but I could see that she had very little strength.

I didn't know what else to do but remain close by and keep watch over the mother and child. There were a few perceptible differences between them, apart from size. The mother's stone skin, if it could be called skin, was red and extremely thick. Small, rounded horns grew out from the sides of her temples. Her face was angular, with a bulbous protrusion for a jaw.

Her offspring's face, on the other hand, was small and round, and I could see the start of similar horns. The biggest difference, of course, was the colour; this child was obsidian, apart from its red eyes which glowed like embers.

I looked around, feeling the panic of being alone and unable to help the two creatures.

It took me a few moments to realize that help should have come by now. The instant the floater had gone off-course, the attendants at the Gravitas Mons station would have noticed the break in routine. And yet about ten minutes had passed without any assistance.

Looking away from the Nova Martians, I turned my attention back to the wreckage, which was far beyond repair. I would have no choice but to wait for help.

And so I waited.

Eventually I noticed the lights of drones approaching from the west, no doubt the first signs of a search party. I no longer feared for my life, but that didn't mean the dread of the situation had altogether deserted me.

Periodically, the Nova Martian mother had taken to shaking uncontrollably. When the shaking visibly worsened, I reached out to her instinctively, not knowing what to do. She seemed to extend her arms towards me in a rigid movement. Blackish tendrils spider webbed over her hands and fingers, and I sensed she was somehow acting to keep her precious cargo safe.

She picked up her stone baby, lifted it in her gigantic hands, and lowered it into my waiting arms. I looked down at the infant. Was it staring up at me? Was that the hint of a grin appearing on its face?

I do not know if Nova Martians can communicate telepathically, but it seemed to me that the mother was effecting a sort of sad farewell. The painful expression in her grey eyes would be impossible for me to forget.

Stone infant held uncertainly in my arms, I watched as the mother closed her eyes. Her body ceased its violent shaking and began to sink into the red sand. I tried to reach for her, to offer some aid, but her enormous weight pulled her away from me.

By the time she had fully submerged, her form was difficult to distinguish from the rest of the red plain. She was gone. But at last the lights from the search parties grew nearer.

CHAPTER ONE

A Few Wrong Choices

Peering down upon my doom, I, Captain Brant Zenith always suspected that one day my vast skills may not measure up to the demands of my bold ego. I realized that this may be the day, for in approximately ten seconds I was likely going to die.

In my left hand I held my recently acquired smooth-action laser pistol. Its dual barrel, dark metal chassis glowed from the intense heat. The damage inside the weapon was compressing the already volatile gases, causing the temperature to rise too quickly for me to control. The deep auburn glow emanating from the pistol's side was a sure sign of my impending death. It was beginning to sear my palm, burning more deeply with each moment I held onto it. It emitted a faintly sweet smell.

In my right hand I held a spano-gripper, about the size of a screwdriver. I was using it to open the pistol's side valve—to vent the gas which was now expanding so quickly that it threatened to explode in my face. Such an explosion would tear through me and beyond, ripping a massive hole in *Orbital*'s side.

I feared there just wasn't enough time.

I was standing in my pathetically small quarters, so it may not have been such an injustice if the weapon did explode. But it would have been a travesty for my meagre crew. They were few in number but good people. They didn't deserve to perish from such a happenstance, and I wouldn't let it happen.

When the pistol's internal temperature hit one thousand degrees, the contraption began to whir. The sound of a siren erupted from God knows where, causing me to give up my jury-rigging efforts and throw the valuable weapon in the air perhaps two metres in front of my face.

I sighed, saying goodbye to the pistol. I'd hardly gotten the chance to get to know her.

Activating my wristband communicator, I noted on its screen the date: April 28, 2500. I initiated the black rift setting. This relatively new and costly technology was my only chance. I pointed the communicator at the thrown pistol drifting in front of me, then slapped my hands together. A burst of energy emitted from the communicator as the energy of the black rift surrounded the weapon's destructive force.

Begone!

In the same instant, the pistol exploded and then disappeared from view, only to reappear outside the ship.

It all happened so fast. The detonation beyond the ship crashed into *Orbital*. I should have been able to look out the window to see clearly as the brilliant coalescent orange hues beat down upon the hull, but I wasn't quick enough to discard all the energy. The force of the interior explosion sent me flying two metres through the air, slamming me backward into the opposite wall.

With the tiniest amount of good fortune, I dropped unconscious upon my mattress.

As I slept, my dreams came fast, and in a surprisingly concise arrangement. My mind shifted back in time approximately twenty-four hours to a moment when I'd been ensconced in a blue spacesuit while walking along the outer hull of the ship. It was the most peaceful experience a person could ask for, the only sound that of my breathing, the only sight that of darkness and stars that dared to burn through the blackness of space.

I stood midway down the ship's less-than-sleek, turkey-shaped body. The spaceship I commanded, *Orbital,* was motionless. Behind me, the titan planet Arberus blazed like a supernova. Its rings presented a unique opportunity—one I would have been a fool to ignore.

Arberus fell into the Militia Space Fleet's territory. It was one of many millions of planets in our meagre stretch of the sprawling Gambit Galaxy, which humanity had reached two hundred fifty years earlier.

Bathed in the light of Arberus, I observed upon *Orbital*'s burnished exterior a multitude of nicks and notches. Through the faintly glowing blue lens of my helmet's visor, I stepped carefully over the metal rods that led one-third of the way from stern to bow. The deep gash I encountered upon *Orbital*'s surface near the energy transfer chutes would have been profoundly worrying if not for the fact that it had probably happened more than a hundred years ago. There was no easy way to know the precise timeframe.

The only thing that held my ship together was probably prayer, but *Orbital* had been my home for the past five godawful years. I sighed, trying to ignore the deep feelings of regret that welled up in me.

I walked forward about fifty steps and came to the bulbous glass dome around the front of the ship. Within the dome, I saw someone moving around—Bog. He was a constant reminder to me of that fateful day on Nova Martia two decades earlier. Having grown up together since the crash that had ended his mother's life,

I had found him to be the closest thing to a brother I could ever hope to have.

This made him a perfect accomplice in the current, slightly illegal endeavour. At the moment, the remainder of my crew were off duty, their shifts at least four hours away.

I leaned over and linked my tether cable to a metal loop near the dome. Next, I pulled out a blue bag and flat-edged trowel, then got to work. For other captains, it may have been embarrassing to be forced to scrape scourge barnacles from one's hull, but not me.

The scrape-and-snag technique was gruesome at first, yet I found with just the right flip of the wrist, with just the correct momentum, the little buggers easily detached. The work was slow but rewarding; soon I would have an entire bag full of the small, clawed space creatures.

But that's where that part of my dream ended. Still lying unconscious on my bed, my mind drifted to the next memory in my vision.

I found myself this time on Omicron One—specifically, the gambling den known as Inferno's. From my seat, I looked around the casino, illuminated almost entirely by the garish screens of digital slot machines. The walls and floor were otherwise dull, so as not to draw anyone's attention from the bright advertisements of sporting and gaming events from across the Gambit Galaxy.

Perhaps five metres above my head, I spotted the small red dots of a centipede drone, the casino's primary method of maintaining order on the floor. Their magnetic limbs held to the ceiling perfectly, allowing them to scamper about and keep a robotic eye on all the bar's occupants. The drones kept the establishment running smoothly. I smiled; everyone was safer because of those things.

I sat on the far side of the casino, alone at a private table encircled by an elongated booth. Hovering above the centre of the table glowed a three-dimensional holographic display that showed the odds and allowed customers to place wagers on the hour's main event in the duelling den.

A duelling den was typically found in seedier space bars, a place where a pair of adversaries could line up across from one another, ready to turn and fire. The last man standing was the victor, as were the lucky customers who had bet on him.

This particular duelling den wasn't located onsite. It was found in a drinking establishment known as Roustabout's, one of the most popular places to exact legal revenge upon one's enemy.

I watched as the combatants lined up, ready to step away from each other. I quickly placed my bet, not too invested in either duellist. I just wanted to have a little fun.

After my wager was placed, I looked up as a stout figure clunked down directly across the booth from me. It was Barnaby, a contact I had known for years who specialized in procuring less-than-scrupulous items. He was small for his race and age; a bulbous nose sat in the middle of his pewter-coloured face, although it seemed to have become more bronze since the last time I'd seen him. This was the sign that a Vesuvien was nearing his biannual sleep phase.

It was the year 2500 and according to all evidence Barnaby looked like he could sleep until well past the year 2502.

I slid across the table a small sack of the scourge barnacles I had spent hours scouring from *Orbital*'s hull. He eyed them greedily, his whisker-like eyebrows bunching over his wide green eyes as he squinted at the barnacles.

I looked away, noting about three dozen other patrons gathered around the gambling machines and tables in various states of celebration or remorse. Such was the nature of gambling.

But I hadn't come here to gamble. I had come to make a deal, and Barnaby had seemed trustworthy enough the past four times we'd done business together.

Of course, that didn't lessen my natural wariness whenever I was with him. I had heard the terrible rumours about four Ignots of Blatherly who had been nothing more than farmers searching to make a fortune; after their meeting with Barnaby, they had never been seen or heard from again.

Despite my reasonable liking for the strange space peddler, I remained on high alert. This is why I had strapped my less-than-trustworthy propulsion gun to my right leg before entering the casino. The holster's clasp was unsnapped. It would be my best chance of escape in case the shit hit the fan.

I looked down at my wristband communicator, knowing I only had an hour before I would need to return to *Orbital*. The communicator whirred, emitting a trace of smoke as it worked. What a piece of space shit!

Note to Brant Zenith: put in for a replacement communicator. This is ridiculous! Sell Orbital's *engine itself to get one.*

My communicator was perhaps the most antiquated version this quadrant of the Gambit Galaxy had seen in a century. The black-and-white screen was often full of static and I feared the thing may just crumble if I shook my wrist hard enough. Just one more thing that needed righting.

Barnaby sighed, his excitement at the sight of the barnacles turning to disappointment. "Captain Brant Zenith of *Orbital*, I thought you of all people would appreciate the value of honesty and loyalty."

As he spoke, his second and third jowls danced merrily below his pudgy face.

"What the hell are you talking about, Barnaby?" I snapped back. I didn't like his tone or the way he said my name or that of my ship. It sounded like a vague insult.

"Well, Zenith… I thought we had an understanding."

I didn't speak. Instead I just raised my eyebrow in question.

"When we spoke twelve hours ago, you assured me these were to be of the finest quality scourge." Barnaby eyed the bag of barnacles, then pointed a meaty finger into an equally meaty hand. "I see that you were incorrect in that assessment."

"I doubt that, Barnaby. I've seen enough of these blasted little hull suckers to know."

"Then how do you explain these broken aerials?" Barnaby asked, indicating the scourge—and specifically, the ring of narrow white antennae around each one.

"What kind of fool do you think I am?" I asked.

He didn't have an opportunity to answer, as at that moment we were interrupted by a casino waitress. Her feet hovered five centimetres above the floor due to her gliding boots, the bottoms of which shone blue. She carried a tray of drinks.

"Go away, now," Barnaby snapped. He closed his meaty paw and gestured with a corpulent pinkie finger. "We're busy."

Before she could huff off in that direction, I cut in.

"Now, now, Barnaby. Don't be rude." I waved the waitress to return and pointed to the drinks—notably, a frosty glass full of fruit and a divine red elixir. Ah, the heavenly Martian Breeze... "I'll even pay for your own dubious beverage, since you're in such a charming mood."

I reached out and took from the tray a bubbling concoction whose glass looked like a cauldron. As I handed it to the peddler, I noted that the drink was ice-cold.

The waitress drifted away after I handed her the payment and a nice tip.

Barnaby seemed agitated, casting a furtive glance around the casino. In fact, this was the second time I had caught him doing so. I could tell something was wrong.

I took a sweet sip of my drink. "Tell me."

"I don't know of what you ask," he replied huffily.

"You aren't yourself today, Barnaby. Explain."

I stared into his swirling green eyes; the swirling was a sign that the Vesuvien was under some form of duress.

I pulled out my propulsion gun, its wooden handle feeling comfortable between my fingers. The heavy metallic barrel clanged on the tabletop.

Barnaby followed suit and doubled down, placing two identical firearms next to my gun. Each were dual-barrelled laser pistols. Very impressive weapons indeed.

I stared Barnaby in the eyes, the tension between us growing. But I still couldn't see where it came from. The last several times we'd made a trade, the exchanges had been quick and simple, followed by a few celebratory beverages. Something was different this time; his tension made me question whether I wanted to deal with him at all.

But I really wanted the merchandise he could offer.

Our standoff didn't last long. The centipede security drone I'd noticed earlier was creeping towards us. As it approached, my hand instinctively edged closer to the handle of my gun, and in that moment I couldn't help by notice the strange, dented notch on the gun's wooden body.

I didn't have time to focus on that. Instead I eyed Barnaby's pair of laser pistols with envy.

Barnaby's eyes darted between me and the centipede drone. It was perhaps a metre long, its body made from links of metal forming a spine-like carapace. Each section of its body had four legs and a series of red-dotted cameras.

I released a deep breath and forced myself to relax. I knew how deadly these drones could be. It was legal to carry weapons into the casino, of course, and it was even legal to shoot an enemy. But it was not tolerated if you missed your mark. The bar's code of conduct was clear: do not damage casino property or harm staff, or else the security drones would mow you down. Punishment would be swift, which was an enormously strong deterrent.

"Relax, Barnaby." I pulled my hand away from my gun, an idea formulating in my mind. "I have something more to offer."

His bushy eyebrows lifted in interest. He couldn't contain his natural trader instincts.

I reached across the table for the bag containing the barnacles. As I thrust my hand inside, I felt a waft of coldness. The frigid air was visible to the eyes, like a volcano steaming before eruption. This was the result of a deep-space pellet I'd dropped into the bag a few hours ago, to keep the barnacles fresh. It was doing the trick.

Barnaby's eyes never left my hand. I wasn't wearing gloves, so I shuddered at the cold; unlike Barnaby, I didn't take to the extreme temperature all too well. Vesuviens were fortunate that way.

My hand closed around the largest of the barnacles. This one was special.

His expression changed immediately when I withdrew my hand and showed him what I held in my palm. His mouth dropped open, like a hippo ready to gobble dinner, at the sight of the bright crimson scourge in my hand.

"Is it... truly?" he asked.

I could see that all thoughts of weapons and harm had left his mind. "It is, indeed, my friend."

It was enjoyable to see him react this way. He reminded me of a child who had just discovered a new toy. I recognized that I had tapped into a very special part of the man. At this moment, I could probably ask for anything I wanted.

"I've been doing this for a long time, Mr. Zenith," he said, his breath slowing. "Only once before have I seen such a thing. It is majestic."

I knew I had him. He had never called me Mr. before.

"It truly is," I murmured, fiddling with the red barnacle. Not only was it larger than the others, but it was covered in bulbous growths. Its antennae swayed; it didn't like being in such a warm environment. I was going to have to put it back soon.

"What... what would you like, Mr. Zenith?"

"What do you have to offer?"

I could have drawn this out for several long minutes, but frankly I wanted the contents of his own bag of merchandise. It called to me.

Plus, I was very interested in what else I could get in trade. The crimson scourge was exceedingly rare, perhaps less than one in a hundred million. Few had been so lucky to discover such a crustacean.

Barnaby was in the process of reaching into his own bag of wonders when we were interrupted again. A black-clad form stepped forward from behind a nearby pillar. Whoever this was, he had found the only place in the joint where he could watch us unobserved until now.

The figure wore a duster jacket that hid its shape. His face, too, was darkly shrouded behind a hood. I assumed it must be a man, due to his height, but I couldn't be certain.

As the newcomer stepped forward, raising his weapon, Barnaby froze.

Fuck, I thought. *Now I might not get a good look at what he has to offer...*

I dropped the crimson scourge back into my bag, not even having enough time to close it properly. I grabbed the closest weapon, which turned out to be one of Barnaby's dual-action pistols.

The figure seemed to ignore me, instead focusing his attention on Barnaby. I was sure that Barnaby would be dead in the split second it would take me to get away.

At that moment, the shadowy bastard unexpectedly looked in my direction—and recognized me. I guess I could find fortune in the fact that even though I couldn't see his face, I somehow recognized something in his bearing.

He pointed the weapon at me, having found a more appealing target. I raised the laser pistol, caught between two gruesome eventualities. The first was that he was going to plug me full of god's fire if I didn't react in time. The second was that if I missed, the centipede drones would cut me down like ripened wheat.

I leaped up and flung back the table, feeling momentary regret at not having finished my Martian Breeze. I aimed the pistol with as much sureness as I could muster. But just as I was about to fire, the newcomer's weapon erupted. The attack missed its mark by centimetres. He had aimed at my torso, but instead the orange blast struck the side of the pistol, ricocheting and hitting a gaming machine a few metres behind Barnaby.

Fuck! I hadn't fired the shot, but it had technically redirected off my weapon.

I looked at the shadowy attacker and he looked back. We both recognized the situation we were in. Who would the security drones choose to punish for the damaged gaming machine?

The attacker raised his weapon to fire again when a whole platoon of centipede drones scurried towards us. A second later, I heard my attacker curse in English. A moment later, he black-rifted out of the casino completely.

I realized in that moment that our attacker was indeed a man, and probably human too.

But I didn't have time to ponder the mystery. Out of the corner of my eye, I caught Barnaby stealing away with my bag of crustaceans, including the crimson specimen. It was quite extraordinary how quickly the rotund Vesuvien could move when he was truly motivated.

I followed suit, grabbing his bag of merchandise from where it had fallen on the floor, as well as my own propulsion gun.

The only thing that saved me was the fact that the drones seemed to have taken a few seconds to review the video footage of the incident. I was thankful that they needed to be sure of who to fire upon before they incinerated the poor soul.

In that split second, I used one of the two remaining black rifts from my wristband communicator and jumped into the void. Thank the Mackmian gods of fate that my wristband communicator didn't hesitate like it typically did!

Moments later, I reappeared outside the casino, where I was able to blend into the crowds of beings all going about their merry way. Behind me, the lights flashed and whirred as some lucky customer struck it rich deep in the heart of Inferno's Casino.

CHAPTER TWO

Sleet Sheets

I awoke with my brains on fire, struggling against the weight of my eyelids. I was losing the fight. The screeching call of the intercom had awoken me, but I couldn't focus.

As I tried to sit up in bed, I heard the typical whistle and hiss of the intercom warming up to release a message. The thing was overamped, terribly antiquated, and always loud.

"What the hell now?" I yelled into my empty quarters, trying to sort out the events of the previous night. I could recall something about gunfire, gambling... an explosion...

"Captain, please report to the control hub," a voice spoke over the intercom. "You are late for your shift again."

I finally succeeded at sitting up. Although the recent past was still hazy, at least I could remember who I was—and where I was. I was the captain of *Orbital*, and these were my pathetically small quarters. More of a closet than anything else, with my clothes flung all over the floor...

Struggling to get my feet into my boots, stifling the urge to vomit, I stared at my Militia Space Fleet uniform with malice. It was grotesque, reminding me of a marching band's outfit. What kind of uniform was green and white with big damned gold tassels?

I didn't understand why it was folded nicely upon the chair. This was the second night in a row that had happened, and I couldn't account for it.

It didn't take me as long as I thought, given my disorientation, to get ready. All I needed was my weapon…

I looked over and noticed the propulsion gun resting alone on the shelf next to my chair. I grabbed for it, mistakenly squeezing the hair trigger in the process. It was unfortunately aimed at my nether regions.

Click.

A misfire. I breathed a heavy sigh of relief. Sweat pouring down my face, I thanked the Mackmian gods of fate that the gun malfunctioned every second shot. Sometimes the unreliability of *Orbital*'s equipment could be a blessing.

Not very often.

It was at this point that my foggy memory of the previous night returned. Remembering the laser pistol's explosion, I looked around for evidence of the blast. I saw only the faintest residue on the walls where the carbonized gas had touched down. I detected the faint outline of a body—my body, I realized—on the wall, where I had absorbed the worst of the detonation.

Touching the back of my head, I discovered the source of my headache. The goose egg that had formed back there was only barely covered over by my lustrous blonde locks.

Thankfully, nothing seemed too amiss this morning. The blankets had been blown back and into a corner, the edges of the fabric singed a little. Luckily the fire had burnt itself out quickly enough.

I was sad to lose the laser pistol, though. This was the fourth time in several months that I had tried to acquire a new weapon only to immediately lose it. One had been lost to theft, while a second had never functioned to begin with. Yet another had been destroyed outright.

At least I still had my blasted propulsion gun. It only worked half the time, but at least it stayed with me.

Before exiting my quarters, I glanced in the mirror—and what I saw made me cringe. I looked terrible. My eyes were bloodshot and my hair dishevelled. A damned catastrophe. I would have to put in some serious grooming after my shift ended. I shouldn't have skimped on shaving the previous day; the remaining stubble had my face resembling the rump of a Telnian cow.

Normally I cut a striking figure what with being two metres tall with sandy blonde hair and crystal blue eyes, but today I looked like the entire population of hell had run me over with a tractor.

Oh well. Still better than almost everyone else in the galaxy.

The intercom whirred to life again. "Captain, did you not hear me? You are requested at the control hub."

The voice belonged to Mara, the ship's resident ambassador, and she seemed peevish today. Or more accurately, extra peevish. I briefly wondered what her problem might be, then shrugged off my concern. Or I would have if it didn't hurt my head to shrug.

I pushed a button on my wristband communicator's readout and initiated a com link with the control hub. I received no response, but of course it hadn't worked; this was *Orbital*.

Choking down a vile oath, I set out for the control hub. On the way I heard the intercom whir again and immediately fizzle out. I swore under my breath.

"What could that woman possibly want at…" I looked down at the time readout on my wristband communicator. "Umm, two o'clock in the afternoon?"

Uh-oh. I *was* late. Later than normal, in fact.

As I marched through the ship's corridor, I suppressed the urge to vomit, but not specifically from my headache. The ship's interior made me cringe every time I looked at it. The colours scarred my retinas; mismatched reds, greens, and purples marred the walls in inconsistent patterns. And who had decided to install shag carpeting on a spaceship anyway?

One day I would like to travel back in time and kick that person square in the biscuits.

I began the curved ascent that would lead to the control hub. Rounding a corner, my head was hit with a blast of cold air. I threw my hand up in front of my face, squinting into the frigid arctic air that bombarded me. *Orbital*'s atmospheric stabilizers must be malfunctioning again. It was a sporadic phenomenon we knew to expect from time to time.

I managed to make it through the frigid hurricane before the snow began to fall. Thankfully the precipitation only lasted for a few seconds.

Upon entering the control hub, I nearly collided with Mara.

"What could you have possibly been doing to make you so late?" she demanded with a tone of incredulity. No small amount of annoyance was written on her face. I didn't even get the chance to stutter out a response before she resumed her verbal barrage. "Sometimes I wonder why my father made you captain of *Orbital* anyway."

I had pondered that same fact when I'd first taken the promotion, but I always came back to the same rationale: never underestimate the power of a firm grip on mathematics and the will to dive into any crisis headfirst without regard for consequence.

That, plus I figured the old man still valued me from when I'd served under him as a rookie, back when our work had seemed to mean something.

The truth was, I could have questioned Mara's posting to the ship as well. *Orbital* only had five crewmembers. Why did one of them have to be an ambassador? It would have been more prudent to have an engineer or medic!

It was strange to be spoken to like that from Mara. Even though she held the title of Ambassador, her true rank within the

Militia was Orbiter, the next step up from Agent, our organization's entry-level rank.

I did my best not to wobble as she and I walked further into the control hub, trying to come up with a useful response. Unable to think of a worthy comeback, I just absorbed Mara's abuse. But I wondered why she was so upset with me. It wasn't like this hadn't happened many times before.

I mustered a commanding presence as I looked at the crew, each of them standing at the ready. I found that very strange. They hadn't gathered this way in quite some time.

It occurred to me to look towards the viewscreen, and there I saw the reason for their attentiveness. On the screen was a black-and-white image of Mayer Olwen, high marshal of the Militia Space Fleet. It wasn't every day that the high marshal called.

Well, that wasn't quite true. Olwen communicated with the ship most every day, but rarely in an official capacity. Most of the time, he was calling to have a daddy-daughter chat with Mara.

I approached the main viewscreen. I didn't bother to run my hands through my undoubtedly tangled hair. Not because I didn't care what the old man thought of my appearance, but rather because he was nearly blind, even with those telescopic glasses of his.

"Captain, my boy!" Olwen chortled. "I have an urgent matter for you and your illustrious crew to handle."

Illustrious? I didn't know who he thought he was bullshitting, but I wasn't going to contradict him.

"I've already run the details by Mara and Agent Sparning over there."

Once again, I decided not to correct him. Our pilot's actual name was Agent Sybella Sparling, a fairly recent intake. So far she had proven to know her way around the ship's controls, but in truth she looked too young to fly a ship. I remembered that at one time she had been part of a program for children who were enthusiastic about working in space. I couldn't remember the program's name, though…

"It seems that the Militia has an opportunity," the high martial continued. "One we've been awaiting for some time."

"Please go on, sir."

"Yes!" he exclaimed, making me jump in surprise. If my drinking, gambling, or gunfights didn't kill me, I figured it would be a silly outburst like this.

I could tell that Olwen was excited. The wispy white strands he called hair seemed to stand on end—and not only the ones in his ears, but on his head as well.

"We have the chance to gain the allegiance of a race not well known to many here in the Gambit Galaxy," he said.

I lifted my eyebrows with some genuine interest. That did sound like a worthwhile endeavour.

"The race is known as the Mondorians," Olwen continued. "They are a small and obscure species."

"Brant remembers," Mara stated—more to remind her father than to remind me, I suspected. "We tried to bring the residents of Mondo 4 into the Militia Space Fleet years ago."

"Of course he remembers," Olwen said. "Well, it seems they have a bit of a problem pertaining to their sun. It may be vanishing! It seems… umm… a mysterious…" He groped for words.

"Situation," I muttered.

"Of course, situation." The high marshal paused imperiously. "We must help the Mondorians find their sun!"

That sounded very odd, but it intrigued me. Did we actually have a real mission? Something more than a relentless string of meaningless duties?

Although intrigued, there was something about all this that didn't quite track. If the Mondorians had turned to the fledgling Militia Space Fleet, it meant that the much larger Prime Star Force must have turned them down. That made no sense whatsoever and raised my natural paranoia and suspicion.

The Prime Star Force were our neighbours in the Gambit Galaxy, and the most powerful space organization around. Whereas the Militia Space Fleet only had three ships at the moment, including *Orbital*, Prime probably had thousands. I didn't know for sure how many, but their fleet seemed to grow every day.

In fact, of all the space organizations operating in this region of the galaxy, the Militia had to be right at the bottom. And *Orbital* was so ancient that it was only slightly younger than the institution of gravity.

But our antiquated technology wasn't my biggest concern. Perhaps worse than the spiralling lack of funds and dearth of meaningful work was the high marshal's view of the Prime Space Force. Somehow he had begun to believe that Prime was our ally. Despite having served for them himself, he seemed to have concluded that if our two organizations made an alliance, we could still the storm and create a better future for the Militia.

This was a mistake, but I couldn't convince him to see it. I'd given up trying.

"Anyway, Brant, my boy," Olwen said, "you are to make your way to Prime Station Alpha for a meeting regarding the Mondorians. Proceed there, but only after you finish your next run to the Quazar black hole. The Mackmians are still awaiting their escort."

My heart sank with the force of a graviton field. Despite the promise of a real mission in our future, it seemed there was no way out of our current contract, which amounted to little more than a garbage run.

Even worse, how was I going to avert the impending disaster that may befall me should I step foot back on Prime Station Alpha? It had been years since leaving it, but I wasn't sure what might happen when I returned. Would my previous act of defiance continue to haunt me?

Like all negative thoughts swirling through my head like a tornado, I buried this one along with the fear that rippled down my spine. I'd have to deal with all this when the time came.

The image on the viewscreen went blurry, and then dark, as the transmission ended.

My mind was a mix of conflicting emotions as I turned to face my crew. My eyes fell first on my closest friend, Bog. It was hard not to spot the security officer. His massive body was covered in a coarse black hide that more closely resembled stone than skin. At three and a half metres in height, he towered over the rest of the crew. Fearsome black horns sprouted from his temples, pointing up and ever so slightly forward.

Back when I'd held Bog in my arms all those years ago on Nova Martia, I had found it hard to imagine him growing to such proportions—even having seen his mother with my own eyes.

Bog sat precariously on the three-legged seat which served as our tactical station. Perched on a such a little chair, he reminded me of a clown bear pedalling a tiny bike.

"What do you think?" I asked.

Bog stood up and crossed his arms, pondering the question. When he wrapped his large stony arms tight to his body, he appeared almost spherical.

"Could be something," he rumbled. "Or nothing. We'll see."

I was disappointed by this answer. I had thought I knew him well enough to believe he would find this news exciting. After all, we had grown up together, my parents agreeing to adopt him despite the strong difficulties in doing so.

Years later, he and I had been accepted to the Prime Academy together. And when I'd left to start up the Militia five years ago, he had joined me. I had always felt safer in his presence, except perhaps when he drank too much…

I looked over at Agent Sparling, a talented and secretive young woman. I felt we were fortunate to have any pilot, since flying

Orbital was a bit like steering a cannonball fired by a drunken chimp.

"What do you think?" I asked her.

A small smile grew at the edges of her mouth. "Sounds like an adventure."

I noticed her gaze drift over to Agent Lazarus Stairn, a similarly new recruit. Stairn and Sparling had joined our team only days apart, and neither had yet agreed to sign the full Militia contract. The rank of Orbiter was open to both recruits; we could hardly afford to turn down any willing applicant.

To be honest, I didn't know much about Stairn except that he annoyed the hell out of me. I think he was near my age, but he had the personality of a layer of dust. Stairn's job involved the tedious study of logistics—keeping track of inventory, people, supplies, etc. I had little appreciation for the work he performed.

I opted not to bother asking Stairn his opinion. Instead I refocused my attention on Mara.

In addition to serving as our ship's ambassador, Mara Olwen handled most communication with people off-ship. I had always found this insulting. Was I not the captain? Could I not speak for *Orbital*? But her father was, well… her father.

Everything else aside, though, I had to admit she was stunningly beautiful. Unfortunately, equal to her beauty was her distaste of me.

"What's your opinion of the Mondo 4 situation?" I asked.

"I'm excited to give it a chance," she said. "Militia Space Fleet could always use another avenue to recruits."

"Shoe's right," Bog added, throwing out his personal nickname for Mara. If it bothered Mara, she had learned to hide it years ago. "We are looking a little thin."

I decided to keep my comments to myself.

I crossed the floor and stepped into my personal office at the rear of the control hub. The door surprised me and opened just wide enough to let me through.

The dim room was improperly lit, and I tripped on something that rested unexpectedly in the middle of the chamber. I landed face-first on the floor, barely catching myself.

Oof! This wasn't going to help my headache.

Pushing myself up, I turned my head to see if anyone had noticed my fall from the control hub. Fortunately, the automatic doors seemed to have closed behind me just in time. Or at least so I hoped.

I looked down at what had tripped me up. It was Cerbot, a robot that served as *Orbital*'s answer to our chronic staff shortage. It was designed to assist in technological and engineering repairs.

Or at least it would have, if it ever fucking worked.

I raised my leg to give the robot a kick. "That's where you are, you little son of a…"

The rest of the sentence died in my mouth and I lowered my leg. I really should be practicing better anger management… or maybe it was just that my toes were still on the mend from the last time I'd tried to show Cerbot how much I appreciated him.

I gave the robot a cursory inspection and saw that he hadn't sustained any damage from my clumsiness. He stood nearly waist high when in standby mode, although he could rise up to my chest when in full operation. Most of his body was painted a dull blue, except the panels that contained his readouts and his dimly glowing blue eyes. Even with all the rust around every edge, I had to admit that the robot looked cooler than we did in our Militia uniforms.

I'd been keeping track of Cerbot's work routine to the best of my ability for reasons I couldn't be sure of. Perhaps I was just bored. So far as I could tell, he only worked two random days a week. His schedule was unpredictable.

And what he was doing in my office was beyond me.

I leaned over, picked up the little guy, and relocated him to the corner. I braced myself as I moved him across the room, careful not to strain any muscles. I remembered how heavy Cerbot had been the last time I'd picked him up.

Had he been in here to repair something? I glanced around and determined that nothing looked different or even out of place. I didn't have a great deal of prized possessions, with the exception of the massive, cylindrically shaped Zigma Bannisher gun hanging on the wall above my desk and the smaller electron gun which sat in its unique box on that same desk.

The electron gun had been a gift from Mara in the days before our first Alhalran mission. The priceless weapon was said to have been created by a mad scientist two and a half centuries ago, and I'd since learned there were fewer than ten in existence.

The weapons and Cerbot had one very important thing in common: none of them worked worth a damn.

I didn't have long to enjoy my own company before Mara stepped into the office with a certain look on her face. She had a digital document pad in her hands and was tapping her foot angrily, waiting for me to take notice of her.

I stepped back from my desk, trying my best to guess what she was scowling about this time. I wondered if it was because I had left the control hub after only a few seconds of command?

"You need to sign these," she demanded.

She handed me the pad. I could feel her eyes bore into me as I read, or pretended to read the documents. The first one was an application for us to dock with a Prime ship. We had to fill out these forms every time we came in contact with them, even when they were the ones summoning us. For that matter, we had to sign documents just to use their lavatories!

My temper always rose when I saw a document with the Prime emblem on it.

At that precise moment, I noticed Stairn waltz into the office without so much as knocking.

"Captain, I have our inventory list for the month. I would read them off to you right now." Without waiting for an answer, he began. "Six crates of C-96 cogs for Cerbot—"

"Why does he need six crates of cogs?" I blurted more angrily than I'd intended. "He doesn't work more than two days a week on the ones he has now!"

Stairn disregarded my indignant outburst and continued with his list. I ignored him and handed the pad back to Mara.

"You didn't read them, did you?" she said with irritation. "You just put your mark on them and pushed them away. Like you always do, right?"

That was all I could take at the moment. "Why on God's green earth are you so angry today?"

Mara didn't respond to my question. She just stared at me with those intense green eyes. I had a great deal of difficulty keeping my eyes locked on hers, so angry was her gaze.

"Why so angry at *me*, I mean," I amended.

I awaited another scolding, but instead she said nothing at all. We stood frozen like that for what seemed like an eternity.

All the while, Stairn continued rambling on in the background. "...three bags of lithium charges, running drastically low, sleet sheets at three percent, optimal is fifty percent..."

Why was he so impervious to my inattention?

I still couldn't take my eyes off Mara. "What the hell did I do this time?"

"You really have no idea, do you?"

She phrased it as a question, but I knew she wasn't going to tell me what was going on until I admitted something.

"Brant, did you even see what you wrote on these documents?" Her face flushed, and I realized that she had brought a couple of other pads with her.

Double shit! I definitely wasn't in the mood for another tongue-lashing.

"I signed off on them, just like you requested."

"I requested?" She stepped closer to me, angrier than ever. I could tell she wasn't going to lay off. "You didn't even read these."

I looked past her toward Stairn, still reciting his list. His eyes never looked up. I doubt he even noticed we weren't listening.

"I perused one of them," I said nonchalantly. I couldn't have cared less about all this digital paperwork. It just wasn't worth my time.

"Well, while you perused one of them, did you happen to notice that you forgot to mark an X beside the slot that stated you did *not*, in fact, wish to deposit *Orbital* into the Quazar black hole as garbage herself?"

"Uh-oh." I sighed. "I guess I skipped past that bit."

"Yes, I believe you did." She seemed to calm down a bit, although I could see now that she had a right to be angry. "Brant, that mistake could have cost us the ship."

I ran my hand through my wonderful hair. "I'm sorry, Mara. It was a simple oversight."

In response, she sat on the edge of my desk and looked intently into my eyes. I felt uncomfortable by it, for some reason. More and more, being around Mara made me uncomfortable.

"You aren't happy, Captain."

The statement stung, cutting deeper than I would have expected. It had been weeks since she and I had spoken to each other for more than a minute before raising our voices.

"Is it that obvious?"

Mara put a hand on my shoulder, taking me by surprise. "It is to me. I know you, Brant. I mean, Captain…"

I laughed derisively. I truly doubted she knew anything about me.

"You doubt it?" she asked. "You hate the present and want nothing more than to be back in your good old days of ten years ago."

What the hell was going on? Was she reading my mind?

"You believe the past is sweeter than the present, don't you?" she asked solemnly.

"Yes. Definitely." I was surprised just how much I believed it to be so. "The past is so much more certain than the future. Bleak though it is."

"The future is what you make of it."

I don't know if I scrunched my face in hearing that cliché. I hoped that I hadn't offended her, though, as she was trying to cheer me up. Even if she was failing, I owed her the respect to at least listen.

"Take heart," she added. "Time changes everything."

She stood up and left the office behind, sidestepping Stairn on her way out the door.

Watching her go, I thought more about my past—specifically, about ten years ago. Back then, my life had been the envy of everyone I knew. I had been the most promising member of Prime Star Force, and I'd deserved it. No one had worked harder than I had. I had jumped through the ranks for good reason; everyone knew I was fearless when facing the unknown. And I cared. I had truly cared about it all.

But time was like waves in the ocean. Given enough of them, they could erode even the most resolute character into something unrecognizable.

The past was gone. I was an officer of the Militia Space Fleet now.

"...one can of mustard, a jar of relish, three bags of pickles..." Stairn continued, oblivious. "...six zero-gravity flight suits, six pairs of shielded multi-functioning viewing goggles, two pairs of three-legged undergarments—"

"Wait a minute!" I cut in. "What the hell do we need three-legged undergarments for?"

Not one iota of surprise registered on Stairn's stoic face. "It's one of our categorized necessities. Therefore, we have them on the list."

"So let me get this straight. We have no engineer, we have no medic or ship's doctor, we have no repair technicians... but we have three-legged undergarments!?"

"Captain, everything has its purpose." He stopped there, as if that explained everything. He once more launched into his itemized list—

"Enough!" I barked. "We'll resume the inventory later."

I stormed out of my office and through the control hub, not even pausing as I spat out my next instructions to the crew.

"I'm going back to my quarters," I said. "We meet up with the Mackmians in three hours. No one disturb me for two hours." Before stepping into the corridor, I looked back. "And by two hours, I really mean two and a half hours."

With that, I found my way back to my quarters for some wholly needed rest. After all, I had been on duty for a solid fifty-five minutes.

Mara Olwen ducked another laser blast destined to sear through her torso. She did her best to dive and roll out of the way, just as she had watched done on the instructional videos she had purchased the last time she'd visited Prime Station Alpha.

Another laser seared past her, almost striking her directly in the face. The golden beam of light nearly took her down.

Her body slammed into one of the many crates housed in the storage bay where her training continued. The brown wooden box had the red letters "Rectus 42: Super Filling Plant Food" written on its side.

Mara turned and fired her laser pistol at the enemy figure approaching her. She missed her shot, and in return received a golden beam of light right in the centre of her torso.

"Ah, poop!" she cursed as violently as she had ever.

She hit her wristband communicator and disengaged the holographic simulation. The image of her assailant vanished, leaving her to breathe heavily in the ensuing silence. She had spent the past three months of salary to afford this simulator, but it had been worth the investment. She needed to improve her combat proficiency.

She wasn't like the captain. Captain Zenith, whom she knew well from her own studies years ago, was a marksman and gifted fighter both with and without weapons. She would never tell him so, but she envied his considerable talents with sidearms. He had won the Marksman and Sidearms Combat awards each year he had spent in the Prime Academy. It was a remarkable feat.

Her feelings towards Brant caused her confusion. She wished somehow she could be more like him. At the same time, she was also desperate for him to be more like her. She shook her head in frustration.

Mara couldn't forget those early days when she and Brant had joined the newly formed Militia Space Fleet. She had been dazzled by his charm and confidence. He'd possessed an energy and magnetism no armour could protect her against.

The Alhalran mission had changed everything. When Mara had found herself in deep danger she should have avoided, Brant had risked everything to be with her and protect her. She hadn't been able to shake the turbulent feelings she'd possessed from standing next to him while he had shielded her body with his own during their fight with the Miscrants, the swarm of foes that had gotten the jump on them.

Standing so close together, weapons in hand, Brant had been there for her when she had needed him most.

She didn't wish to spend so much time thinking about the captain, but he was all too often on her mind. But she feared the feelings weren't mutual. He possessed everything she had ever dreamed of in a mate. Unfortunately, he was well aware of his own qualities. She knew that the only thing to rival his shooting ability was his ego.

She had tried asking for his help with combat training years ago, but it had been to no avail. He had given up on her.

He was now a dark, brooding, self-destructive shell of the man she had met years ago. She knew she should move on emotionally, but how could she do that when the deep-seated feeling seemed so unshakable?

She just hoped her feelings would resolve themselves. She had *Orbital* and the Militia to worry about.

But Mara had never given up on her combat training. In fact, she'd spent each of the past five years since their mission to Alhalran either investing in herself or improving *Orbital*.

Try as she may, though, she had never gained even the least amount of proficiency with weapons. She had gotten so desperate that she'd even asked Bog for aid. And how had he responded? He'd simply told her no.

Well, that wasn't totally accurate. What had been his exact words? "Not going to happen, Shoe."

Mara disliked the nickname he had given her, but she would never let him know that.

She fully deactivated the holographic simulation and placed the weapons training projector into its own small storage container. Tomorrow would be another day to improve.

CHAPTER THREE

Shot to Hell

I dropped my weary body down onto my soft mattress with a sigh of relief. A tough shift, that had been.

I couldn't tell with clarity how long I slept, but I was awoken by a dull, hollow knocking sound. My mind groggy, I thought at first that I might have imagined it. But within scant moments I heard another thump, much louder and more intense than the first series.

I sat up in bed, realizing for the first time how truly dark it was in my quarters. This was odd because my nightlight usually glowed next to the bed. Maybe it had been destroyed when the pistol exploded?

As a third round of knocking filled the room, my pulse quickened. Something was wrong. My senses screamed to me of danger, and somehow I knew I was about to be attacked.

My heart raced and I slowed my breathing to calm myself. This wouldn't have been the first time someone had trespassed into my sleeping quarters wishing to inflict harm on me; most times they were jealous husbands or angry fathers. And sometimes they were even lawyers.

But I wondered how this someone had snuck onto *Orbital* in the past several hours. Was it the unknown assassin from Inferno's coming to finish the job? Had he followed me somehow?

As smoothly and quietly as I could, I rolled myself out from my covers and pushed my weight onto the shag carpeting. I landed on my hands and knees, head upright. My heart hammered in my chest; I could feel the pulse in my temples.

Thump-thump, thump-thump...

The acute presence of danger heightened my senses. Whoever the attacker was, he or she was moving closer.

Gracefully, I made my way toward the door. By the time I had almost reached it, I caught the glimpse of a shadowy form in the corner of my vision. I decided to keep going, hoping to fool the intruder into thinking I was about to flee. Perhaps I could lure him or her into the open and tilt the odds back in my favour.

Since the door to my quarters almost never opened automatically as it was supposed to, I was caught completely by surprise when it did—and at just the wrong moment. I flinched, momentarily blinded by the godawful light of the corridor.

That's when the intruder struck.

The dark shape swung at my head. Instinctively, I rolled out of the way. I heard a solid *thunk* as the attacker missed me and collided with the wall. I could almost feel the floor shake from the impact.

The dark shape charged for me again, but this time I was better prepared. Sidestepping, I grabbed for the first solid thing I could find—as luck would have it, my chill bar, a small metal rod, approximately one-half metre long, whose sole purpose was deep-freezing anything it touched. Being the professional space adventurer I was, I used it to chill my Martian Breeze cocktails.

The tip of the bar caught the attacker just below the armpit, freezing a patch of the creature's most sensitive skin. He was taller than I anticipated. The attacker let out a satisfying eruption of obscenities.

And that's when I recognized him.

"Bog, I think you may be too big or too fat to properly sneak into someone's quarters," I said, panting from the exertion of evasion and attack. "At the very least, I would appreciate if you would tone down your intake of Telnian beef sausages and third-rate space cologne."

I stamped my hand onto the light switch, and as the room flooded with new illumination I saw my best friend's face twist in annoyance and regret.

"I thought I did pretty well, all things considered." Bog massaged his frozen armpit with one of his monstrous black hands. "I mean, give me some blasted credit. This shithole you call your quarters isn't an easy place for a big guy like me to sneak around."

I stepped into the bathroom for a moment, taking a gander in the mirror. I still needed a shave, but I assumed time must be limited. I wetted my hair and combed the tangles out of my blonde crown.

Once back in my uniform, I left the bathroom and immediately located my propulsion gun. Then I turned to take in the sight of *Orbital*'s security officer.

Even though we had spent nearly all our lives together, I was still taken aback by his enormous frame. I figured the Militia's budget must be heavily taxed just from the cost of having to issue him such a large uniform. It was a miracle he fit into *any* uniform.

"How long did I have before you knew it was me?" he asked with a show of professional curiosity.

"About two seconds after I introduced you to the chill bar. As I said, you aren't well-suited to sneaking around in the dark."

All I received in reply was a bellowing grumble. I counted myself lucky that I was among a very small group of people who could attempt such a comment without being torn in half and eaten in two bites. He was like a brother.

"I think we should take a break from our game," I said after a moment's thought.

"Really? You only say that now because you're up by two points. Very convenient to quit when you're ahead."

"I don't much give two shits right now about winning the game. I'm tired of it… and I want a break."

And I meant it. Bog and I had been playing a version of catch-the-other-off-guard for years. Decades really. We had even incorporated our competition into our Prime training back in the day. It had seemed logical to do so. Now that we served with the Militia, though, we probably maintained the game out of simple boredom. Or Bog was tired of the empty crates I sent crashing down on his rocky head every time he let down his guard.

Our game was simple enough: just catch the other off guard and deliver a mild blow without causing any real harm. It was fun when you knew your opponent seemed nearly indestructible to most physical damage. That was no understatement. Bog could absorb most any assault without enduring true harm. Most notably, since Bog thrived in heat he could gladly absorb many types of weapons fire. But I didn't know his limits and didn't like seeing him test them.

When we exited my quarters, about two hours after I'd entered to catch some sleep, I suddenly felt very cold. Even with my Militia space boots, my feet got the chills. A coating of ice had formed over the carpet several centimetres thick; it nearly took our feet out from under us. *Orbital's* climate control had always been sketchy, but I found that the cold air generators always worked on the maximum setting.

Unfortunately, in the dead of space our ship didn't usually need help cooling down.

"You really ought to take a shovel to that," Bog said, indicating the layer of ice. "Or an ice pick. Or better yet, use that hair dryer I know you own. You know, the one you hide from everyone else."

"As captain of *Orbital*, I command that your next duty is to shut it."

The heat in my voice surprised him. "Holy shit, you're in a foul mood, aren't you? Don't worry. I'll take care of it."

At that moment, Bog opened his cavernous mouth and made a terrible sound that momentarily made me believe it could have rumbled directly out of hell itself. He narrowed his lips and released a trail of red-hot embers onto the floor. Steam whistled off the floor like a tea kettle.

"For shit's sake, be careful with that," I said. "Do you want the whole ship to melt?"

Silence hung in the air a long moment. I looked up into his big red eyes and swore I could see them well up a little.

Bog was a contradiction. If you didn't know him well, he could be downright terrifying. The skin on his massive physique was as thick as a rhino, his red eyes shone like lava, and his tusks were fearsome; two of those tusks jutted out of his mouth even when it was closed.

But beneath all this intimidation beat the heart of a true and loyal friend.

I shook my head wearily. I hadn't intended to snap at him, but the meaningless duties thrust upon us were beginning to wear thin.

"Sorry, Bog. I guess I'm a little on edge lately. Between *Orbital* being *Orbital* all the time and the personal attacks on me… well, I think I've hit a wall."

"Personal attacks?" he asked. "Why didn't you tell me about this? I'm in charge of security…"

Now I knew I had hurt his feelings.

"Well, it started months ago when we were docked at Station Woog," I explained. "I was strolling down a hallway, minding my own business, when a six-limbed Mukrian parasite jumped out of nowhere and tried to stick a burning blade of freaking death into my stomach."

"Really?"

Bog didn't seem as surprised as I thought he should have been. Now I was the one with my feelings a little hurt.

Bog squinted his burning red eyes at me. "Well, it doesn't *really* surprise me, my friend."

"Oh?" I asked, halting my walk.

"Yeah. I was there with you at Station Woog. You went into that casino looking to squander your Militia bonus at the gaming tables… and managed to piss off pretty much every creature there in the process."

"Thanks. Although squandering a paycheque worth less than a pair of socks is hardly a big deal," I replied dryly, scratching behind my ear in consideration. "Well, perhaps I was a little abrasive. Where were you that night? I don't remember seeing you."

"As it turns out, I may have met with a special someone."

"Was she hot?" I asked automatically, giving no thought to my question.

"So hot that my boots were on fire just being next to her," he said, but not as proudly as I would have expected.

"I can't blame you for that. You do like it hot." I meant that literally. Bog's body survived on extreme heat; his core temperature rested somewhere around a toasty two hundred degrees Celsius.

And I could hardly blame him for ditching me in a gambling hole when a beautiful creature came calling.

"Don't fret, my friend," he said. "It was just one attack. I would be surprised if someone hadn't gone after you that night."

"I guess so."

I started walking again and he followed. Our pace seemed to me to be overly hurried, but that was the norm whenever I was in Bog's presence. His strides were almost double the length of mine, even though he was only about fifty percent taller than me.

Bog was tall enough that he had to walk in the centre of the corridor or duck beneath the metal arches. I'd heard him bang his head and horns several times on those support arches.

In fact, those clangs and grumbles of discontent could be heard throughout the ship…

I searched through my memory, trying to dredge up details of my recent attackers.

"Since then, though, there have been twelve others," I added.

When I said this out loud, I strangely felt a little proud of the fact.

"That is impressive," he said. "Even for you."

"Thanks." I kept up my pace, not taking my eyes off the corridor ahead. On *Orbital*, it was best not to take your eyes off where you were going. "I thought the first two attacks were no big deal. I find myself in pistol fights more often than I'd like."

"Yeah. I definitely understand someone wanting to shoot you."

"Be that as it may, this is getting ridiculous. I haven't pissed off that many people recently." I hesitated, thinking back over the past few months. "Well, not that I can remember, anyway. I just wish I knew where they were all coming from. It's disconcerting."

Bog nodded sagely. "I'll look into it for you. Can you tell me more about each attack? When, where, and why? That will help narrow things down."

"As a matter of fact, I've been keeping a very detailed written account of them," I said, feeling mighty captain-like for the moment. "I've been keeping track of my days these past few months."

"You mean you're writing in a diary?" His black-ridge eyebrow lifted.

I could feel him mocking me even without looking over at him. "No, not like a diary. I just figured it was a good idea to keep a log of my duties since I became captain all those years ago."

"So you keep it all in a diary."

I was suddenly furious. "No, not a diary! Only pussies keep a diary! This is a *journal*. Captains keep journals." I pulled out a digital pad to show him my manly journal. "Look! The cover has a picture of a polar bear eating a Telnian cow."

That should have explained it all.

He looked down and chuckled.

"What's so funny?" I asked.

"I knew you were fond of wildlife, but I wouldn't really be showing off a picture of your pet Telnian cow."

When I glanced down at the pad, instead of seeing a frightful, god-fearing polar bear eating a Telnian cow, all I could see was a very pregnant Telnian cow feeding on some stalks of grass.

Ah fuck. Even the digital pads had a way of malfunctioning unexpectedly. I guess they had been aboard *Orbital* too long. I wondered if eventually even the ship's living crew might start malfunctioning for no reason. I really didn't want my ears to start smelling the air or my eyeballs to start hearing.

As I continued walking, I decided to drop the point. I initiated the transfer of the data from my pad to Bog's wristband communicator. It took a few violent shakes of the pad to make it work. I'm not sure why *Orbital* technology often worked better when it was physically abused, but I had given up trying to understand *Orbital* a long time ago.

I continued shaking the pad around until the final file had been transferred. By this time, we had been quiet for several long moments and I was beginning to recover from the diary argument.

"Aft guns are shot to hell…" he slapped me with that comment out of the blue.

I looked to him, confused by the sudden change in topic.

"…and the ballistic space torpedoes wouldn't work to save your soul," he continued.

"I suspected as much. So tell me, what *does* work?"

Bog turned his head toward me without slowing his gigantic gait. "Hull propulsion lasers. The vacuum on level three. The ale taps in the lounge. The doors on the hydroponics bay. The disco ball in my quarters…"

He launched into a lengthy, overly detailed list that reminded me of one of Stairn's annoyingly long-winded reports. My mind couldn't help but wander as I stared into the putridity that was *Orbital*'s shaggy corridor...

"IP1 is still working," Bog stated, coming to an end.

"When was the last time you used it?" I asked sceptically. I had no idea how an interactive probe like the IP1, a remote drilling device, could still be working when virtually nothing else seemed to.

Bog looked away sheepishly.

"What?" I asked, my suspicions growing.

He just looked around, avoiding my stare.

"You went asteroid fishing again?" I asked. "I thought we had all agreed not to do that anymore."

This was a pastime the big Nova Martian loved. He used to employ the IPs to test his aim as he launched them at hapless asteroids. The only problem was that when the asteroids started to spin from the impact, they brought the ill fortune of occasionally dragging *Orbital* into the fray.

He harrumphed. "You go careening after space barnacles, and I go asteroid fishing."

"Fair enough," I said. "Sorry I drifted off there... what else works aboard *Orbital*?"

"Energy barriers, shag carpet vacuum... two of the three lights in the meeting room entrance..."

He went on to mention another half-dozen or so random ship facilities and components before I cut him short.

"I meant, which *weapons* work." Once again, I didn't mean to sound so testy.

He scratched his massive chin. "Hull propulsion lasers, and that's about it."

I sighed. *Orbital* had a decent array of weapons when she was fully functional. Most of those systems hadn't worked as of five years ago—and with little funds, no mechanic, and no engineer, we were slowly being stripped of our ability to defend ourselves. The hull propulsion lasers were intended to be little more than a last-ditch defence. They didn't work at long-range and certainly weren't powerful enough to take down a ship until it was already on top of us.

"What are your feelings about our upcoming mission for the Mondorians?" I asked.

Bog shrugged. "We'll see where it leads."

His lack of interest rather offended my sense of excitement, but I let it go.

Over these past five years on board *Orbital*, I had begun to notice a pattern. The ship constantly broke down—that much was clear as daylight—but things always seemed to work just well enough to keep the crew alive.

Unfortunately, a key component of the ship that broke down most frequently was the atmospheric stabilizers. Most spacecraft used atmospheric stabilizers to keep travellers safe, and *Orbital* was no exception. The stabilizers regulated the ship to provide the correct levels of oxygen, gravity, temperature, and humidity at all times. Another key function of the stabilizers was to offset the effects of time and space when travelling at speeds greatly faster than light. Time did indeed slow down as one approached the speed of light, and it was up to the stabilizers to ensure that time didn't collapse in on itself during these voyages.

At least the breakdowns on *Orbital* were never quite as serious as the collapse of time.

After our first mission to Alhalran, though, I had decided that if we couldn't afford to fix *Orbital* properly, it was imperative that we at least learn how dire these atmospheric stabilizer failures could be. We spent time circling the most populated space routes and experienced dozens of glitches. But nothing we tried ever caused the ship to fail in a way that put our lives at risk in any overt way. The random occurrences were only ever mild to medium annoyances.

I wished that *Orbital's* atmospheric stabilizers worked like the ones on Prime's starships. Oddly, I had a great deal of experience maintaining those. Alas, I was not so lucky on *Orbital*.

One fateful day, while running headlong down a corridor towards the control hub, desperately trying to avoid what I had believed to be an imminent system failure, *Orbital's* gravity had simply given out. One moment I had been in the midst of a sprinter's dash, the next I was floating into an air supply register. I still had the crosshatched indentation in the crown of my head to prove it.

Two metres further down the corridor, the gravity had worked perfectly well, much to my chagrin. This sort of malfunction had become especially common.

Yes, it had taken me years to recognize the strange pattern of seemingly random malfunctions. I didn't know the pattern well enough to predict all future incidents, but I had developed a sixth sense, almost by intrinsic necessity, to detect when the next breakdown would manifest.

Which is why I suddenly grabbed hold of Bog and employed all my strength to shove him up the corridor.

"What the fu...!" He choked on the words as his enormous body lifted into the air and floated.

Two metres later, like clockwork, the gravity returned to normal.

"...uh, thanks," he finished, landing back on his feet. "I should have felt that coming."

I hopped forward to catch up to him. "No worries. I swear, I can almost feel when *Orbital's* going to kick up a fuss. God, I wished this damned ship would work."

"Don't kill yourself over it. It could be worse."

"Oh yeah, how?" I asked, annoyed.

Bang-bang!

We both jumped at the unexpected noise. I thought *Orbital* was about to explode right then and there… or maybe it was just wishful thinking.

We stopped in place and looked over at the lavatory door from which the sound had seemed to erupt. There was another burst of noise, followed by a muffled voice.

Turning to each other, we knew what was wrong. Yet another breakdown.

This malfunction didn't seem so serious unless you happened to be on the other side of the lavatory door. It was a single-person chamber, and in this case it seemed some poor occupant was trapped inside. Once that door sealed shut, there was no way out.

What a messed-up ship I commanded, when the most secure room in the whole facility was a lavatory.

Bog flipped off the door's lights and consequently the electromagnetic locks. A moment later Agent Sparling pushed herself out of the cramped little cubicle. She looked flushed from embarrassment.

"How was your stay?" Bog asked sarcastically.

Sparling muttered out a quick thank you, then nearly sprinted back towards her post in the control hub. We watched her dark hair sway quickly with her walk.

Moments later, we too found ourselves in the control hub. And it didn't take long before I was under attack again.

"Captain, so far today you have been more than normally truant," Stairn began, his voice irritatingly polite. He indicated his digital clipboard. "I have it recorded here. You have been five and a half hours absent for an eight-hour shift."

All eyes were upon me. At least there was humour dancing behind Bog's beet-red gaze. I tried my best to ignore Mara's stink eye.

"You are incorrect, Agent Stairn," I replied calmly. Did the air smell vaguely of dust and cotton candy today? A stranger than normal combination. "Yesterday, note that I said I would arrive fifteen minutes early for duty. Therefore, I am actually five hours and forty-two minutes truant."

"Yes," the logistics officer allowed. "That being the case, I must report that you are seventy percent truant for your shift today, which lowers your attendance to a measly forty-one percent this *Orbital* term."

I shrugged it off. "Actually, Stairn, I'm 71.25 percent truant today, which in absolute accuracy means I am at an attendance of 40.7 percent for the *Orbital* term."

I don't know for certain why I said this, since it would only paint me in an even poorer light. It might have been better to just keep quiet. But Stairn's attitude towards such menial details aggravated me, and it seemed a good opportunity to show off my mathematical prowess. One could never argue with math.

I heard Bog stifle a chuckle, and I'm pretty sure Mara was staring me down angrily. I didn't care.

As the moment passed, the order of the day seemed to settle back over us.

"Cap'n," Bog said informally, "we really need to have our weapons and armour repaired by the time we board Prime Station Alpha."

I gave Mara a meaningful look, and she understood my meaning exactly.

"I'll talk to my father," she said. "Perhaps we'll be able to afford the cost of repairs this time… with the new mission in hand…"

She glared at me a moment longer and then went back to work. It was a nice feeling to have that stink eye shift its focus for a few minutes.

"Where do we stand?" I asked, looking over my shoulder to Sparling.

"We are currently twenty-two minutes from rendezvous with the Mackmians, Captain," the pilot reported, looking more or less recovered from the lavatory incident.

"Good."

I was so tired of these garbage runs. In fact, I think the only thing lighting a fire in my mind was knowing that when we arrived at the Quazar black hole, I could jump on board the space station and meander myself down to the intergalactic post-station. About a day ago, I had received word that a package of mine had finally come in. It would be my reward for a bout of heroics I'd executed six months previous. It had taken a great deal to earn this particular shipment and its contents, if it came as promised, had the potential to change my life.

I had a nagging doubt about the validity of the package, however. The only way to find out if the promise was true would be to pick it up and open it myself.

Nevertheless, I hoped this would be our last garbage run with the Mackmians—even though I'd always liked them. Their bodies were so proportionally round that sometimes I thought God had created the whole notion of the sphere based on them. There was a certain efficiency to their shape; maybe it lent itself towards building the determination the species was so well known for. The Mackmians were extremely hard workers, punctual as all getup, and trustworthy. Three qualities that couldn't be overappreciated.

It might sound ironic to praise the Mackmians for hard work and punctuality when I couldn't seem to make it to my shifts on time. But I was happy to give credit where it was due.

I glanced at the viewscreen and noted the presence of certain star clusters that let me know we were nearing our rendezvous point with the Mackmian garbage frigate. We would escort them to the Quazar black hole, located on the edge of Militia space, close enough to the border of neutral space that it had always made perfect sense for the Mackmians to hire us on these thankless voyages.

I stepped past Mara and Sparling and lowered myself onto the captain's chair. The seat was hard as rock and it had a misplaced spring that tended to play pogo with my private parts. To make matters worse, a highly offensive wire under the right armrest gave me a jolt every now and again. Only laziness has prevented me from fixing it myself. God, I hated this seat!

"Sparling, put me in contact with the Mackmians. Data on all screens, please."

She complied immediately and I soon heard the black-and-white monitors sputter to life, alive with an array of disparate images.

One screen showed the layout of a Mackmian ship, which made me smile. Their ships were the only ones in all of space that could make someone from the Militia feel superior; they were round and bulbous, like their creators, and resembled a toilet bowl. But they worked, and they worked well.

Another screen displayed the enormous barge the Mackmians were towing this time. Data continued to pop up and revolve around the image. I was quite amazed to see that *Orbital* was actually allowing us to read privileged data; I never expected anything to work aboard our ship, so this took me entirely by surprise.

Anyway, the data told me everything I needed to know: the frigate was hauling eight million tonnes of waste. It sounded incredible, although weight meant nothing in space, of course. Once out in the cosmos, my nanny could have pushed that load with one foot in the grave.

Orbital's main viewscreen soon brought up a live video feed from the tow ship, called the *Tanslen*. I was greeted by the familiar, and wide-bodied, Captain Ambden.

"Captain, with clarity of the stars," Ambden said, his voice as gruff as any Mackmian's.

I had always found that greeting quaint and sort of misleading. It was hardly even a complete sentence.

Most important, Ambden almost seemed to be smiling at me. I'd had considerable dealings with the Mackmians, and with Ambden in particular, and only had the opportunity to witness a smile a handful of times. It was strange to behold a Mackmian smile, their four nostrils pinching inwards and making their faces look a Christmas tree. The strange effect was probably worth it, though; their sense of smell was reputedly outstanding.

"Galaxies await," I replied, completing the traditional greeting.

Ambden nodded his approval. He and I had been through this about a thousand times before. There was one time when I'd forgotten my half of the greeting, although he seemed to have gotten over that faux pas.

"I see you're carrying a Class-1a barge today," I stated in observation.

He nodded his head, a tricky endeavour since I had never been able to determine for sure whether he even had a neck.

"Are we ready to proceed?" I was anxious to be done with this garbage duty once and for all.

"We are."

"Then let us begin."

We passed through the Silas solar system at a moderate speed, not wishing to push our ships too hard. We continued our course for the better part of six hours, *Orbital* tailing the *Tanslen* by mere kilometres.

I sat back, a slight smile etched on my face throughout the journey. It had been so long since I'd cared enough to really pay attention to the sights of the Gambit Galaxy, and specifically our little sliver of space, but today I found myself able to appreciate the beauty of the universe, the luminescence of stars, the contrasting dark voids of nothingness, and the infinitude of magnificent planets. At this moment, I felt lucky to feel the miraculous nature of the galaxy, even in the context of such a pathetic mission.

Time dawdled on, however, and I began to grow bored. There was only so much stargazing I could stomach. The blurry stars eventually became monotonous, streaks of yellow and red blurring and becoming almost tedious.

"Agent Sparling," I said, breaking the long period of silence, "fire up the Corridor display."

Within seconds, the control hub was aglow with a three-dimensional holographic display. It filled the entire width of the hub's domed ceiling. The domed ceiling made a near perfect display board for the moving images. The display linked in with our main viewscreen. But again, it was very odd that any of this worked. I took it as a miraculous omen and smiled.

The lights in the control hub dimmed, allowing us to see the holographic display more clearly. Our faces were lit up like campfires by the screens below and above our heads.

The display showed a star map of this portion of the galaxy, centred upon our current position and expanding ten lightyears in every direction. As I watched, Sparling focused the map on our crew's favourite region of interest: Neutral Corridor 101.

Neutral Corridor 101 was interesting for two main reasons. First, it was a narrow channel of space that allowed any race to travel freely from one region of the Gambit Galaxy to another. Other neutral corridors were scattered strategically throughout the region, like superhighways.

The second reason? It ran more or less parallel to Militia territory. As poor as our fleet was in terms of ships, we still had rights to a region of space about one hundred by one thousand lightyears. A small area, relative to the galaxy's immensity.

From my elevated position in the captain's chair, I had an excellent vantage of the entire three-dimensional display. Agent Sparling and Mara, because of their forward positions, had to look almost straight up.

On the display, I noted *Orbital*'s position, represented by a blinking blue dot only two lightyears from the long border between Militia space and Neutral Corridor 101. I also noted the position of our two sister ships, the *Apogee* and *Perigee*. They were a long way off, soon to fall off our display entirely since we were moving in opposite directions from each other.

Other ships were shown in a variety of colours, each given its own standard to help us keep track of who was who. When the display worked especially well, the names of those ships hovered above their standards.

Again, we were lucky tonight; the names were all visible.

I stood up, trying my best not to bump my command screen, as that sometimes caused the images to shake and distort completely out of form. Once I bumped it so hard that every light in the control hub shut off.

"Well, ladies and gentlemen, who's ready for this night's round of corralling?" I asked, hardly able to contain my excitement.

Mara frowned at me. "Brant, I thought we were done with all this."

Corralling was the first in a series of games we often played to pass the time during a garbage run. It was harmless fun, really. We would all place bets on which ship currently in the Corridor would be the first to get into trouble. The winner would typically hand over menial tasks and responsibilities to the loser.

Behind me, I could hear Bog grumbling about Mara's comment to avoid the game tonight—and Agent Stairn seemed to agree with him. I wasn't surprised by Bog, but Stairn? He was typically as animated as a dried-up string of spaghetti, and even he seemed interested.

"See, Mara, the crew seems to like the idea of games before garbage," I pointed out.

"Fine." She turned her head, her straight strawberry-blonde hair swishing with the motion. "Carry on then."

"Excellent," I said. "I have dibs on the three Brunken megaships."

I looked more closely at the three-dimensional light show and pointed at three green dots flying in formation near the border of Neutral Corridor 101 and Militia space.

"No way." Bog's voice as deep as a didgeridoo. "Safe bet is on the *Doomsday* getting confronted by those Cutters. I wager two days of scrub duties."

He often liked to bet on Prime ships getting in trouble, and I couldn't blame him. And the Cutters served as a type of patrol, policing the neutral corridors to ensure the various races obeyed the interstellar rules.

"What makes you so certain?" Mara asked.

The security officer paused, then smiled at me. His black horns and tusks shimmered red ever so slightly, his subtle way of indicating excitement. He seemed to know something about the *Doomsday*.

I turned to Sparling and Stairn. "How about you, Agents?"

Sparling pointed to the Profen ship *Scientifica*, represented by a yellow dot. "This science vessel, for sure. She's been hovering around the third planet in Delda system for hours now. Definitely up to something shady."

"Accepted for two scrub duties," I said. "And Stairn, who do you chose?"

"The Shaydren vessel following *Scientifica*."

All our eyes focused on the little red blip of the Shaydren ship just before it vanished.

"Accepted, Stairn," I said. "But remember, if you can't spot it on the display arc, you can't claim victory."

The logistics officer nodded. "Understood."

We all knew that the Shaydren were the most elusive species in this part of the galaxy—that, and they were supremely dangerous. The Shaydren relied heavily on stealth, surprise, and sudden attacks. The stories I'd heard could have scared the udders off a Telnian cow.

Together we watched the display, each keeping an eye on the ships we had selected. The light show always offered entertainment, if only one had a good reason to look for it.

In the meantime, Mara seemed to be growing more interested in the game, which I was happy to see.

"Okay, fine," she said. "If I must participate, I choose that one."

We all looked intently as she stood and pointed to a lavender-coloured dot on the far side of the Corridor, near the Stig system. Lavender dots represented ships of unknown races. This particular mystery ship was perhaps two hours of travel ahead of us, probably one of the thousands of minor races that frequented the Quazar black hole.

"Okay, you all remember the rules," I said once I'd logged each of our bets into a file which we could each view on our own screens. "You'll get one point if your ship is approached by the Cutters. Two points for being detained by the Cutters."

"Or escorted away by the Cutters," Bog rumbled. "It happens."

"And you can earn five points for something more," I finished.

Something more could mean a heated altercation such as battle or total obliteration. We had witnessed it ourselves a few times over the course of five years. The Cutter ships were powerful and employed a formidable number of ships to help in their duties.

As the time passed, the game took on a more relaxed pace. We had about six hours until we reached our destination and there was no guarantee that anything interesting would happen to our chosen vessels between now and then. But anticipation was part of the fun.

I brought up some information about the Brunken ships I had selected. The lead vessel seemed to be captained by none other than the infamous Captain Borkrieg. As his image came up on my screen, I was reminded that he was a monster in every way.

"Who's that attractive fellow?" Bog asked.

I hadn't heard my friend lurch out of his feeble chair. The act typically brought to mind the sounds of wounded wildebeests rolling down rocky cliffs. I must have been too engrossed in my research to notice.

"It's Captain Borkrieg."

Bog smiled. "Big guy, huh?" I think he appreciated a healthy size, since he himself was so much larger than the average humanoid.

I scanned for more details and saw that the Brunken captain nearly matched Bog for size. That was impressive, even for a race that was said to be dumber than Telnian cow dung.

"And ruthless," Stairn chimed in.

I turned around to see the logistics officer studying Borkrieg's bio as well.

"He's a hero to the Brunken people," Stairn added. "And he's a bloody lunatic."

"So much emotion, Stairn," I teased.

"No." Stairn held up his digital clipboard. "He's literally a lunatic. And in many photos, he's literally bloody."

Mara sighed. "I guess we should do well to avoid that guy."

"It's a big galaxy," I said. "The odds of running into him are slim."

I didn't care too much about the Brunken, per se, although today I hoped they would fall into the path of the Cutters. And with any luck, perhaps they would be detained.

That said, I truly doubted the Cutters could take out a Brunken megaship, and certainly not three of them. If the Brunken were as stupid as I'd heard, though, they could choose to attack the Cutters. That would almost guarantee me a win.

As the minutes drifted on and the ships travelled on their merry way, our interest in them faded. Stairn went back to his work, his lean frame rigid as he peered down at his clipboard's small screen.

It struck me that I had never seen a single emotion cross Stairn's face. I couldn't even be sure he experienced emotions at all.

Mara and Sparling also soon returned to whatever they had been working on before I'd started up the game.

"Mara, your mystery ship is gone," Bog stated, his voice breaking the relative silence.

We all looked up again. True to his word, the lavender dot representing Mara's selection had vanished.

"Oh poop." Mara drew a deep breath as she started scanning for that ship's transponder signature—to no avail. "Double poop."

Suddenly, I sat up straight. "The *Doomsday* is being approached by the Cutters. Mara, bring up the readouts."

Despite her disappointment in losing the wager, Mara did as I asked. On the holographic display, we watched not one but four Cutter ships drift closer to the *Doomsday*. The Prime ship was armed with an intimidating array of weapons. This could get interesting.

"Its captain is Maximillian Flint," Bog reported. "He and his crew are honed like a razor."

"Sounds a lot like a specific captain I know," Mara remarked, looking directly at me.

That was hardly an insulting comparison, I thought. Flint was perhaps the most formidable officer in the entire Prime Star Force.

"They can afford to be provocative," I told her. "Us? Well, not so much."

Mara gave me a petulant smirk. "And yet that rarely seems to stop you, Captain."

The Cutters approached more closely. I figured they must be able to see each other by now. All we had to go on were the display's graphics.

"I wish we could see what's transpiring," Bog said.

We watched as the four Cutters and *Doomsday* sat more or less motionless for the next few minutes.

"Oh, for frick's sake!" Bog complained as he threw his massive arms in the air, smacking his hands on the overhead girders, nearly leaving a dent. A noisy clang echoed through the control hub—and probably down every corridor on *Orbital*.

The reason for his complaint? The Cutter ships were now drifting away from *Doomsday*. So much for the confrontation he had been hoping for!

"Well, it looks like Bog's horse is riding limp," I said.

It didn't take long for the *Doomsday* to drift out of the neutral corridor and into our very own Militia Space Fleet territory.

"As if that wasn't enough!" Bog exclaimed. "First they weasel out of a situation I had good hopes for, and now they're trespassing in our space."

"Technically, it's not trespassing." Mara turned in her seat to face him. "We have a peace treaty with Prime. They're allowed to travel through our space."

"Not much of a treaty," I said angrily. "I think the only thing we got in return was a couple of derelict ships that look like they haven't flown in two decades." I was of course referring to the only two other ships in Militia's fleet.

Mara stood her ground. "I think it's a little more than that. I was part of that negotiation."

"Well, Lieutenant Bog's ship seems to no longer be in the running," Sparling said from the pilot's position pointing up. "Anyway, the Cutters are approaching the Profen ship."

Her hands moved quickly to bring up details of the impending interception. She seemed excited by her chance at winning.

I looked over at Stairn, keenly aware that his Shaydren ship wasn't far behind the Profens. What they were doing, only God could guess.

Once again, we watched intently—but nothing seemed to happen. The Cutters simply drifted past the *Scientifica*, ignoring her altogether.

It appeared they were, in fact, more interested in the Shaydrens.

True to form, the unidentified Shaydren vessel vanished from view when the Cutters swung toward it. The Shaydrens' shroud technology was astonishing. Although there were ways to penetrate the technology, it required a great deal of effort and understanding.

I supposed the Cutters might very well have that ability.

But as I stared at the display, the four Cutter vessels simply changed direction and began to leave the area entirely.

As I looked over at Stairn, the man's dark eyes suddenly went wide. Was it my imagination or was he beginning to vibrate? His left hand gripped the copper railing that separated his station from the rest of the hub. His right hand touched his chest, just below his neckline, which seemed to be emitting a slight red glow.

I shook my head in surprise. A moment later, he had gone back to normal, his expression as still as a stone. His hands had gone back to that blasted digital clipboard he cradled like a new-born.

That was perplexing! But as I looked up at the display again, I was immediately distracted.

"Did your bird lay eggs, Mara?"

I pointed to the former location of her mystery ship. Instead of just one lavender dot, there were now three hovering in the same approximate location, very close to the black hole.

"That is curious," Mara marvelled. "I don't know what to make of it."

There wasn't much information available since none of the three ships could be identified.

Not that it mattered.

"I believe we have a winner," I said, indicating my three Brunken megaships. In the last couple of minutes, the Cutters had flown right up to the armada.

"Captain Borkrieg is launching a projectile at the nearest Cutter vessel," Mara reported from her station. "The Cutter vessel has been destroyed."

On the display, a rippling shockwave spread out from the point of the attack. The display blinked, and several points of data disappeared from view. The attack must have damaged the local spatial attenuators, which were spread throughout the Corridor to monitor ship activity. Without the attenuators, it was impossible to know what was going on.

"Well, I must thank you, ladies and gentlemen," I said.

"Yeah, yeah," Bog replied, not too happy with the way things had worked out.

Sparling turned to face me, looking so young and unassuming. "I don't know how you knew those would be the first ships to break the rules," she murmured.

"Trade secret, Agent."

The next hour passed with no excitement to speak of. As my crew checked and maintained the ship's systems, I spent the time reading a book and pondering what length of hair would best flatter my chiselled jawline.

When we finally reached the Quazar black hole, the smile dropped from my face like a hammer on anvil. It only took me a moment to process the carnage showing on the main viewscreen.

Fire was erupting out of the side of a Mackmian spacecraft. Frozen Mackmian fighter pilots were drifting about the wreckage.

Before I could react, debris from the explosion smashed into *Orbital*'s front starboard quadrant.

As I braced myself, I wondered why none of this had shown up on our scanners. Our fleet's spatial attenuators were heavily dispersed across millions of square kilometres around the Quazar black hole.

My attention turned to the space station in orbit around the black hole. It too was under attack, and I feared it was already too late. The station appeared to be all but destroyed.

CHAPTER FOUR

Black Holes and Darker Issues

I stood up from the captain's chair as *Orbital* closed in on the station—specifically, the location where refuse was usually dropped into the black hole's event horizon. My fingers clenched so hard that I could feel the fabric of my uniform strain beneath them.

Quazar was an intermediate mass black hole measuring tens of thousands of kilometres across. Its proximity to Neutral Corridor 101 ensured that it was one of the most frequented waste drop sites in the known universe. The Mackmians owned and operated the dome-shaped station orbiting the singularity.

Unfortunately, at that moment I didn't have time to take in the sights. All hell was breaking loose.

"I fear everyone aboard that station—indeed, everyone in every ship nearby—is doomed unless we do something," I said, breaking the silence. And then I came to a pivotal decision. "I'm taking *Orbital* in. You can stay at your posts, or you can leave. You still have that chance… here, now. I won't begrudge you deciding to go. Perhaps you don't have the training to conduct a battle like this. Perhaps you're not prepared. If you decide to leave, you can use the shuttle. If you leave now, you may make it to safety in time."

No one in the control hub moved a muscle. I wasn't sure if this was a good thing.

"If you stay and join me, I'll have to ask something more of you," I added. "Find a reason. Find the reason that is important enough for you to risk your life. It has to be a good enough reason to help see you through whatever we're about to face, because it may be all you have to hold onto if things go truly bad."

I looked into the eyes of each member of my meagre crew, seeing emotions in them that I hadn't witnessed in anyone in years. Fear? Something else?

Without the protective containment of the station and the five rings which encircled the event horizon, we would be facing imminent death. Near as I could tell, only one of those rings was still operational, giving off a shimmering, incandescent wave of light.

Three unknown spacecraft were flying through the debris of the station, stirring up all sorts of hell. Enormous, smoky holes had been blasted in the surface of the station, and one of the alien ships I didn't recognize was still blowing new holes every few seconds.

How long would the station last? There were normally thousands of people aboard it!

"Make your choice now," I said again when still not a single member of my crew stood up to leave.

The moment was rudely interrupted as one of those mysterious ships flashed in front of *Orbital*, letting loose a silver ball of energy. Its tiny eruptions of lightning reminded me of a million dandelion seeds being cast into the wind.

"Incoming!"

The crew braced themselves in their seats as the lightning slammed into *Orbital*, but the violent impact I'd anticipated never came. The only effect was a shimmer of silver energy that danced over the ship's hull.

Suddenly, the temperature in the control hub dropped to freezing. A gust of wind blew through the room, slamming me back into the captain's chair and rustling the tassels on my uniform. If I had to guess, the temperature must have dropped by thirty degrees. A veil of frost and snow covered every surface.

The effect only lasted for a few seconds before the air returned to normal.

"What the god-damned fuck was that?" I muttered to myself.

But of course no one had an answer.

On *Orbital*'s viewscreen, I tried to track the movement of the three enemy ships. They looked similar enough to each other that they were hard to tell apart. I felt that was terribly irresponsible of them, given my current predicament.

However, each craft sported an oblong hull with four engines protruding at thirty-degree angles. The ships weren't large, no larger than *Orbital* anyway, but they were fast. They were black and silver in colour and their engines glowed an evil shade of red. Even their weapons were visually remarkable—and if we continued trying to get in their way, I had a feeling we would learn first-hand what they were capable of.

What did they think of *Orbital*, I wondered? They were probably asking themselves what the hell this flying, featherless turkey was doing trying to sneak up behind their keisters. And true to form, this turkey lacked bite.

Hopefully this would at least make for an interesting battle. I didn't see another way out of this situation if we were going to save the inhabitants of the system.

In this moment, on the brink of battle, I realized the folly of how I'd spent the past five years. I had let my growing disgust at Militia Space Fleet sway me from all my training. As I worked to recall strategies and tactics, I felt rustier than *Orbital* herself.

I reached for my propulsion gun, but at the last minute I stayed my hand. Fidgeting with the unreliable weapon probably wasn't the best idea.

Note to Brant Zenith: buy a real gun, or at least one that won't cause bodily damage should you drop it.

Lord, I needed another drink. Instead I took a deep breath and tried to steady myself. Something told me I would need all my senses intact for this encounter.

"Sparling, give me a status report!" I yelled.

"We have three vessels in shallow orbit of the event horizon," the pilot called back, her voice so soft that I could barely make it out.

"You'll have to speak louder, Agent!" As usual, it came out more sharply than I had intended.

Before Sparling could try again, though, Mara began reading off the information on her control panel. "Captain, I can confirm that four of the five containment rings are disabled."

If the last one failed, we'd all be dead in milliseconds—not just us, but everyone on the station as well as anyone unfortunate enough to be nearby.

I quickly assessed the three enemy ships and noticed that they seemed to each have a different assignment. One was intent on shooting new holes in the defenceless station. The second ship was parked next to the final containment ring.

The third ship is the one I suddenly felt most concerned about—it was headed straight for *Orbital*, and it didn't seem happy to see us. I was only guessing, of course. I couldn't distinguish between a happy ship and an angry ship.

"Open communications to the *Tanslen*," I said.

Sparling still sounded uneasy. "Com–com–communications o–open, s–s–sir…"

"Captain Ambden," I began. "Take your cargo and book it! We'll try to keep them busy long enough for you to escape."

Mara looked back at me from her station.

I'll be damned if that isn't actually a look of approval, I thought to myself. But I didn't have time to revel in it.

Ambden appeared on the viewscreen, his round face heaving with exertion. "Captain Zenith, universe be yours."

I had no idea what the hell that meant, but it didn't matter. A moment later, his ship and attached barge sped out of view. I watched in amazement at how manoeuvrable the *Tanslen* proved to be, even carrying eight million tons of garbage.

As I watched the Mackmian ship escape, *Orbital* was rocked by enemy fire. At least the Mackmians were safely away.

I focused on the image of the third alien ship, now practically right on top of us. I also noticed that it had a red coloured banner painted on it, distinguishing it from the other two attackers.

Orbital shook again as I watched the ship release a stream of... what were they? They looked almost like raindrops, except that they unleashed hell when they impacted the hull. These misty drops of globular death seemed to be eating away at the hull. I thought we were going to lose *Orbital's* ass end altogether. For now, I could only guess at the extent of the damage.

"Evasive action!" I yelled. "Aft thrusters, maximum! Run long and steady... shimmy up in tight formation."

Mara looked first at Sparling, then at me in confusion. "Captain, I don't even know what that means."

Truth be told, I wasn't surprised. She didn't have any notable battle training, and neither did Sparling.

I rethought my strategy. "Okay. Full thrusters ahead."

"Yes, sir," Sparling replied.

Orbital shot past the enemy as effortlessly as lies out of a politician's mouth.

"Captain, sensors show hull penetrations throughout the ship," Stairn stated calmly, almost indifferently. "Decks one through five show signs of fire."

"But we only have four decks!" I yelled in aggravation, coupled with adrenaline and some small amount of panic. I wasn't used to holding so many lives from the ugly jaws of death. I hadn't been in a situation like this for a long time.

Stairn shrugged. "Internal spatial attenuators read that a fifth deck is indeed on fire."

"Oh, for God's sake," I spat out in mounting anger. I looked over at Bog. "Bog, get yourself down there and see what you can do…"

He was the best-equipped member of the crew to deal with a fire since he was impervious. Truth be told, I would have rather had him and his defensive know-how in the control hub, but we really didn't have the luxury of choice.

He started to exit the control hub.

"And be careful," I added.

My friend turned and gave me the-wink-and-the-gun gesture, which I found a little disconcerting under the circumstances. I didn't have time to ponder his smartass attitude, though, since the enemy was circling around for another attack. She was at our ten o'clock, heading straight towards us and looking mean.

We had only a moment to react.

"Port and aft thrusters to full!" I roared, hoping to avoid yet another round of that globular hail.

Orbital rocked hard as our thrusters kicked into high gear. The globules of acid—at least, that was my theory—whistled past, grazing our left flank and leaving little to no trace of damage.

I breathed a sigh of relief, even as the fingernails of my left hand dug into the soft black leather of my chair's armrest. The other hand reached impulsively for my gun.

The control hub was awash in the glow of a small army of distorted screens struggling to keep up the analytics of the battle. Amidst this visual frenzy, the enemy cruiser spun in pursuit as we rifled past them, heading for the station at near breakneck speed, hoping to gain some distance.

It hadn't been my intention to bring us closer to the first enemy vessel, though, and we found ourselves on a direct course for it.

Unlike the other ship, this one—marked with a white banner—didn't fire off globules of burning acid, but rather lightning strikes of death. It would have been breathtaking if our lives hadn't been within a hair of being extinguished.

Without warning, at least to me, Sparling veered sharply portside to avoid a strike, and in the process we struck the engine of the red-bannered ship.

I looked over at her with surprise and probably a dozen other emotions written over my ruggedly handsome face. Her quick piloting skills had undoubtedly saved our lives.

"Sorry, sir," she said quietly. "I didn't think it was a good idea to wait for the command."

"Keep them in view. Don't let them flank us."

Sparling hesitated, looking up at me with uncertainty. I had to remind myself that the Militia didn't have the luxury of being choosy with personnel. There were so few applicants. Despite her youth, Sparling clearly had the skills we needed, just not the experience.

"How do I do that, sir?" she asked.

Good question. "Just watch what they're doing. They're flying in concentric rings. Anticipate and intercept if needed. Although it may not matter now…"

The red-bannered ship fell back, ugly brown smoke billowing out of its damaged engine. We broke away and shot past the station and the white-bannered ship's electric death rays.

The intercom crackled to life and a horrible roar of thunder rumbled out of it, a sound that would have made God jump out of his socks.

"Captain, damage is pretty bad down here," Bog reported through the static in his gravelly voice. "Energy barriers are holding, but there are holes the size of a man's head right through the ship."

"My head or your head?" Stairn cut in quickly. I thought I saw him transcribe information on a digital pad. Was he really taking notes in the middle of battle?

I made eye contact with the logistics officer, surprised with the question and actions.

Death was on our heels, beside our flanks, and generally right up our asses, and Stairn chose this moment to veer into comedy? I think this was the first time he'd ever told a joke. I hadn't even been aware he had a sense of humour.

"Your god-damned head!" Bog yelled through the intercom. I could almost feel his spit on my face. "The holes are dispersed in an arc and span the entire rear end of *Orbital*. Energy barriers are holding, but readouts state that our reserves are down."

I let go of the armrest, stood, and began to pace the back of the control hub, my hand still clutching my untrustworthy weapon.

"Bog?" I asked, speaking into my wristband communicator.

I had forgotten that my communicator was basically a decorative wristband that only told me the weather within the ship... the day after it transpired. It sometimes showed the time, when I was lucky.

I stepped back over to the captain's chair and hit a button on the armrest. From it, I received a jolt of electricity from the loose wire beneath. Argh!

"Bog, see what you can to do seal off that entire section of the ship," I called. "Start floor by floor by imaginary floor. Let me know if you run into any difficulties."

There, I thought to myself. *That sounded like I knew what I was doing. I even surprise myself sometimes.*

"Captain, can you send Stairn down here?" Bog asked with some malice in his voice.

"Why?"

"I was going to use his head to plug one of the smaller holes here."

"Twelve," Stairn replied solemnly.

I turned to the logistics officer. "What?"

"Well, sir, that is the twelfth time the security officer has threatened me."

"This year?"

"No, this week. I think I'll add that to my report to the high marshal when next we see him."

There was no real fear in Stairn's voice. I had to give him credit, since Bog could have squished him into paste with his thumb and spread him over crackers if he'd wanted to.

"Stairn," Bog cut in. I could hear the tension in his voice as *Orbital*'s emergency doors strained in the background. "Why don't you add my boot up your ass as well?"

"Thirteen."

"Enough!" Mara roared.

I turned to see her busily at work running diagnostics on the final protective ring around the black hole's event horizon. Her hands were probably moving faster than *Orbital* herself was.

"We don't have a lot of time here," she said, "and you two are bickering like a couple of pregnant cows!"

Good one, Mara.

"Captain, we need to make a choice," Mara continued. "At this rate, even if our enemy leaves it alone, the final ring has less than an hour before it collapses, and the station has even less time than that."

"Plus, we need to shake this accursed fighter," I added glumly.

At least Sparling was navigating us around them, trying to steer clear of the globular fire. Fortunately for us, the pilot found more than enough debris floating around to create effective obstacles. *Orbital* was just small and agile enough to allow that.

I was extremely hopeful with Sparling. If she ever got some real combat training, *Orbital* might have a real chance—should we have a future.

It wouldn't matter, though. Even if she were to be trained by the four Mackmian gods of war and pudding, our weapons were still disgraceful. All we really had were propulsion cannons. And I suppose I might include the IP1. Bog had spent a good deal of time keeping the interactive drilling probe functional, since using it was one of his favourite pastimes.

The only way to do any damage to an enemy fighter would be to lure it into range of our propulsion cannons, but it wouldn't be enough to destroy them. As for the IP1, an enemy would have to be rendered motionless in order for us to use it.

Maybe we could force them somehow into the singularity itself. Once an object passed through the final ring, the immense gravitational pull would make escape impossible.

I ran a hand through my lustrous blonde mane, hopefully my only outward show of stress. If we tried forcing our enemy through the black hole, we'd have to make damned sure it didn't take us down right along with it.

"Ah, screw it," I said. "Sparling, I want full power to engines. Coordinates are right the hell over there!"

I pointed at our viewscreen.

"Uh, Captain?" Mara asked hesitantly.

"Just do it, Sparling." I was at least fifty percent sure I was half-correct. I wondered if my lack of recent training or practice was clouding my judgment. Ah, well. Fortune favoured the bold.

Our engines roared to full power and carried us forward on a new course, one that would take us straight into the next cruiser, the one parked near the final ring. As we hurtled towards the ship, which seemed unaware of our intentions, I noticed that it had a blue banner painted across its hull.

Perhaps the pilot of this fighter didn't believe that anyone would be crazy enough to fly straight at it, knowing that the black hole—and certain doom—awaited just a few degrees away.

I was near certain that *Orbital*'s hull could withstand a collision with this blue-bannered ship. Thanks to Bog, and perhaps me, there were times in our boring past when we had inadvertently collided with asteroids and limped away with our skin intact.

Sparling kept our course steady, and I felt everyone's nerves as they stared at me. They had good reason to be worried, but I had to go with my gut on this one. My pulse throbbed in my temple and sweat dripped down my back. Forcing myself to breathe, I scratched my fingernail against the trigger of my weapon; it was a nervous habit.

As we sped towards the blue-bannered ship with alarming speed, the white-bannered ship followed behind, shooting up a storm. The view of its weapon fire was quite mesmerizing against the backdrop of starry space. The incoming bolts of energy grazed the hull and made the deck tremble under my feet. Was it my imagination or was the ambient temperature rising due to the transfer of energy? In a way, it was a nice effect after those blizzard winds we'd felt just a few minutes ago.

In response to our approach, the blue-bannered ship finally began to move. My plan had been to ram them, but suddenly they were moving so quickly that I realized we wouldn't be able to change course in time to avoid running into the fifth and final protective ring around the event horizon. And if even the length of a leprechaun's toenail entered that ring, *Orbital* would be sucked into oblivion.

"Sparling, change course!" I yelled, grasping my armrest again.

Miraculously, Sparling succeeded in angling the ship just enough to miss the ring. We couldn't have missed it more narrowly, and indeed I thought *Orbital*'s flank had skimmed the ring's rippling surface.

A jolt went through the control hub, and we were thrown from our seats. I pulled myself back to my feet, my cheek stinging where the shoulder tassels of my uniform had whipped the skin of my face.

Everyone but Sparling was beginning to pick themselves up, in fact. Only the pilot, having thought to buckle herself into her seat, had managed to remain upright. I felt a bit sheepish, until I remembered that the captain's chair seatbelt was currently being used to hold the ship's bingo machine to the wall of the staff lounge.

Oh well. It had seemed like a decent trade-off at the time.

I checked my console and weapons screen and realized both enemy ships were running parallel to us, the white-bannered one at the six o'clock position and the blue-bannered one at three o'clock. The weapons on each glowed red, waiting to unleash the kill shot.

Things were looking bleak, but our doom hadn't been sealed quite yet.

"Sparling, edge closer to the blue ship!"

She obeyed, and in a moment we nudged closer, almost close enough to rub hulls with her. One wrong turn and our lives would be over.

I activated our propulsion laser cannons and a scope opened on the viewscreen in front of me. I grabbed the control stick which appeared from the armrest of the captain's chair and aimed at the enemy ship's most sensitive spot—its engines.

My shot missed. True to form, *Orbital*'s guidance was off. In fact, some genius had programmed the target guidance inversely! Up was down, left was right. It was very confusing.

I kept firing, and after a few tries I managed to get used to the controls.

For the better part of five seconds, waves of energy rippled out of *Orbital*'s hull cannons, landing squarely on the blue-bannered ship's second engine. I watched as its hull buckled under the stress. If only we'd had some larger ballistic or electrical dispersion weapons, my task would have been complete; the engine would have exploded, followed by the rest of the ship.

At this point, I may have even settled for a water gun filled with peanut butter.

The enemy ship altered course and pulled away, giving Sparling a little more room to manoeuvre. Its engine was still under duress, though, and the hull scorched from internal fires. She looked a bit like a recently extinguished cigar.

Now we were down to just one undamaged enemy fighter—at least in this immediate battle; I'd lost track of the red ship.

The angry fizzle of our intercom caught me by surprise.

"Decks one through five are sealed off," Bog reported, wheezing like a geriatric dinosaur with emphysema.

"Good," I shouted in relief. I'd almost forgotten about our own internal haemorrhages. "Get back to the control hub. We have a lot of work to do."

I needed to assess the situation and make some decisions. On the one hand, our hull cannons were still operational, two enemy ships were damaged, and the Mackmians seemed to be safe—for the moment. Another upside? Despite everything, *Orbital*'s captain was still a damned fine-looking man.

On the other hand, our hull cannons packed no punch, one enemy ship remained undamaged, and I had no idea how much more abuse the other two would be able to sustain. These ships were a lot nicer than mine. Even though I was reasonably certain we would survive a collision with one of them, I had to consider the possibility that ramming one might end up destroying us. And no matter how fine-looking the captain, no one ever fell in love with a corpse.

I was running out of ideas.

"Sparling, slam us into reverse," I stated as calmly as I could.

"Uh, sir?"

Acknowledging to myself that this wasn't a well-thought-out plan, I chose to bluff my way through.

"You heard me."

Mara turned to me and exhaled sharply. "Captain, that would lead to a collision with the enemy ship."

"Listen up, folks," I said. "We're outnumbered, our hull is breached, our weapons suck, and we have a station full of innocent people who need our help. Not to mention a black hole that's moments away from swallowing us like a deep dish of death."

I looked at my armrest's screen and noted our distance from the enemy ship. It was steadily pulling in close, meaning it would hardly be able to miss us the next time it fired.

"Do it now, Sparling!" I said through gritted teeth.

She followed my order.

The crew lurched forward as Sparling put our thrusters into full reverse. This time, we were ready for the sudden stop, but I held on *too* tight, causing my muscular frame to be thrown over the side of the chair.

Note to Brant Zenith: steal back the seatbelt from that bingo machine... if you survive this mess...

I allowed my body to roll with the impact, my shoulders slightly bunching as they hit the floor. Without any real effort, my roll landed me right back on my feet. I stretched and felt for damage, but none was evident.

Orbital had held up much better than I expected. The atmospheric stabilizers had worked well, suspending enough of the ship's contents so as not to do any permanent damage.

I returned to my chair and checked the ship's rear view on the monitor. *Orbital* was careening towards the blue-bannered enemy ship as it veered sharply to starboard. It seemed almost out of control.

Not until it was too late did I realize my folly. The white-bannered ship suddenly dropped in from out of nowhere, its weapons blazing. It seemed to me that it had jettisoned its damaged engine, perhaps sustaining further damage in the resulting explosion; I could see small fissures in its hull, and sparks flew from those crevices.

But we were caught in the white glow of a tractor beam, frozen in place. I was beginning to realize that escape would be impossible.

"Captain, ship is unresponsive." Even Sparling's quiet voice couldn't hide her panic. "We can't move!"

There we sat—trapped, out of weapons range, and with the blue-bannered ship bearing down on us.

"Enemy ship on intercept course in ten seconds," Mara said. "Ten... eight... six..."

Her count sounded surreal as my mind cast wildly for solutions. Only one thought came to me: why wasn't the white-bannered ship finishing us off? Unless it was immobilized too. Perhaps she had been more badly damaged than I'd thought.

"...four... two..."

Well, my pseudo-glorious career had to end sometime.

I watched our viewscreen as the blue-bannered ship covered us in that projectile acid. One shot hit the dome right above the control hub and began eating its way through the ceiling, hitting the floor. The blob fizzled through the deck, releasing an odorous vapour, then disappeared from view as it continued its descent through the ship.

I felt the first symptoms of decompression as a blast of air whistled past me. The ensuing silence was deathly eerie. Even worse, it messed up my hair.

Fortunately, the energy barriers kicked in quickly.

"Hull breaches all over the ship, Captain," Stairn reported as the enemy fighter continued its relentless fire. "Complete hull failure in one minute, at the current pace of the attack. Energy barriers are holding, but they won't last long."

Our time seemed pretty much up. Two more globs of acid were about to break through the ceiling, one of them almost directly above my head.

I looked up at the damage done to the domed ceiling, marvelling at our newly punctured sunroof.

Our final seconds ticked by, and I used the time to gaze thoughtfully at each member of my crew. Stairn looked not at all worried about our impending death, as if he and God already had a golf game scheduled for later that day. I envied the guy.

Sparling, however, was rapidly activating her controls, her hands moving in a blurred frenzy. I felt bad for not leading her to a better end.

My eyes drew towards Mara, her face flushed with fear and excitement. Never had I seen her look more beautiful and dignified. When we made eye contact, though, I couldn't read the expression in those fierce green eyes. Perhaps I should have taken more time these last five years to get to know her better, but I'd had important womanizing and drinking to attend to.

The shaking of the ship brought me out of my reverie, and I glanced down at my feet, hovering just centimetres from yet another gaping hole the size of Stairn's head. The realization seemed unimportant. *Orbital* had scant moments left.

Just as my dread fully sank in, I saw out of the corner of my eye something wholly unexpected: on the viewscreen, the *Tanslen* and its towed refuse came barrelling down on us, dropping its shroud.

The white-bannered ship, as immobile as *Orbital*, happened to sit directly in the Mackmian ship's path.

The *Tanslen* released their waste barge, veered off course, and then came to a screeching halt. The barge continued on its course, racing toward the enemy ship and hammering into the side of its hull. The fighter split in half like a pickaxe through tissue paper, instantly obliterated, the colourful explosion leaving a thousand tiny pieces of sparkling debris in its wake.

I loved when things other than *Orbital* exploded!

The barge continued directly through the final containment ring and disappeared into the Quazar black hole, exactly as it had been scheduled to do all along.

Suddenly free from the tractor beam, we were able to get underway.

At that exact moment, Bog entered the control hub and nodded in my direction before silently taking his position across from Stairn.

With that one simple effort by Captain Ambden and his Mackmian crew, *Orbital* had improbably survived. It was a good thing, too; the Gambit Galaxy surely wouldn't be able to survive the loss of Brant Zenith.

CHAPTER FIVE

Adrift

What occurred next happened so quickly and with such precision that it almost showed evidence of rehearsal. *Orbital* was hobbling a step behind the blue-bannered ship with murderous intentions when Stairn miraculously implemented a plan to keep our meagre energy barriers in place. He also worked with Bog to address our faltering power. I watched as their hands flew over the often-ill-working computers, hoping they would be successful.

If their implementations held, so too might *Orbital* remain in one piece.

As my eyes fell on the viewscreen, the enemy fighter raced ahead of us trying to escape. I was pissed. Those arrogant pricks! How dare they run before I had the chance to repay the favour?

"Agent Sparling, we must reach those bastards before they rendezvous with the red-bannered ship," I said.

Fortunately, the fighter wasn't making great speed. Even though *Orbital* was in dire straits—indeed, she looked like a dartboard—we were, in fact, making up ground.

Speed didn't turn out to be a crucial factor, in the end. The *Tanslen* swooped in and levelled its own tractor beam at the fighter, holding in place until *Orbital* was able to catch up.

I found myself mightily taken by Ambden's ship. Although it was stated in the local treaties that only security and exploration vessels could mount weapons, Ambden had still managed to hide an arsenal up his chubby sleeves.

"Sparling, circle the ship," I said with a grin on my face. Actually, I was damn near laughing. "I think it's time to humble our guests."

It was way past time that the fighter felt the business end of *Orbital*'s boot up its keister… and I was certainly looking forward to administrating said boot.

Within seconds, we came up the fighter's flank.

"Launch IP1!"

The interactive probe hadn't been designed as a weapon, of course. It was only a boring tool with automated controls, and it only worked well on an immobilized object. Like the tractored fighter, for example.

A wide grin broke out over Bog's bulky face. He loved this particular tool. "Launching the sodomizer!"

Stairn nearly spit up a mess of saliva and began coughing.

I looked over at him with an arched eyebrow. That was twice in an hour that Bog had provoked a reaction from the logistics officer. This was a monumental day indeed.

The cylindrical probe sped quickly towards the fighter, attracted to her heat. As it approached, the bow of the probe flung itself open and unleashed its inner workings. With a crackling hiss, its fiery blue laser cut into the enemy ship's hull.

"Now activate the destabilizer."

"Probe destabilizer activated," Stairn replied solemnly.

With a flash of white light, the enemy ship suddenly went dead from the inside-out. The only light visible on its surface was the faint glow of the probe inside. What a glorious sight!

"Enemy ship deactivated, Captain," Mara said, bringing up a screen full of statistics about the fighter.

"Good." With some amusement in my voice, I added, "Bog, with only three engines left, don't you think the ship looks a bit lopsided?"

The security officer responded right away. Using our hull cannons, he began blasting at the ship's fourth engine. Within a minute, it exploded in a ball of blue-green fire.

God, I loved this job sometimes.

"Engine four is kaputski, Captain," Bog said enthusiastically. I did admire the man's way with words.

Mara glanced at Bog with some dissatisfaction. "If I may, we still have a lot of problems ahead. The space station is critically damaged and the final containment ring is only minutes from failure."

I swore to myself. In my haste for revenge, I had almost forgotten the greatest danger to us all. I hated to admit that she was right.

"Open a com line to Ambden's ship."

"Communication line is open," Sparling replied.

A moment later, Ambden's image appeared on the viewscreen again.

"Captain, glad to see you return," I said.

"Just taking out the trash," the captain said. "What can I do for you now, Captain Zenith?"

I scratched my cheek, thinking my way through the situation. "We have two problems. Can you find it in your heart to take out that red-bannered enemy ship? Let's render it as helpless as a beached whale with a sprained fin and sturdy bout of constipation."

At this, he gave me another of those rare smiles. His leathery jowls crinkled. "I think I can arrange that."

"Great. Once it's done, I'll see what I can do about that final containment ring around the event horizon."

With that, the *Tanslen* shot toward the space station and the damaged ship that had continued its attack. I hoped the enemy didn't open fire on the Mackmians, but Ambden had already proved that he knew what he was doing.

Very quickly, the *Tanslen* fixed the ship with its familiar tractor beam.

I looked over at Bog, who had already brought up the controls for IP2.

"The enema is on its way, Captain," Bog stated through his pearly white tusks. He gave a quick glance to Stairn, anticipating another reaction. This time the logistics officer merely arched his eyebrow in indifference.

Bog shrugged and manipulated the probe's controls. A few seconds later, IP2 had burrowed her way into the enemy ship and rendered her useless.

With one problem temporarily resolved, I deployed my acute intellect towards figuring out how to stop the containment ring from collapsing and killing everyone in the system.

"Sparling, we need to get closer to the station and the port hub," I ordered.

The pilot reacted with skill, setting *Orbital* on a path towards the port hub, which served to relay power into the system of containment rings. Thousands of emanator markers were dispersed through those rings, suspended in precise orbits around the black hole. Even if half these markers were destroyed, the rings should continue to operate, but the port hub was vulnerable.

And that's where the final enemy ship was focusing its attack, trying to disable the hub's shields.

The port hub wasn't a large structure, but its black and silver hull was sleek enough to give it a stylish appearance. To emphasize its extreme importance, I'd always thought it should have been given something extra—perhaps some flares, or more impactful lighting, to draw travellers' attention to it. It wouldn't have taken much more than a drunken pilot to accidentally back into the thing and wreak havoc.

I supposed that's why it had been given such a strong shield matrix, but those shields were failing. The white sparks emanating from the heart of the little hub told me our time was running short. Thoughts of what would happen if it did fail scared the hell out of me.

I looked in the opposite direction from the looming black hole and saw a stream of ships trying desperately to escape from the space station. Escape was slow. Much too slow to save everyone.

"We're within twenty metres, Captain," Sparling said.

"Can we get any closer?" Mara asked, her face flushed from the emotions of the battle.

Sparling shook her head. "I cannot. The hub seems to be emitting magnetic interference. With the damage to *Orbital*, we run the risk of having our hull torn apart completely."

"Well, shit," I mumbled to myself, thinking through my options. It didn't take me long to decide.

Mara looked over at me, her face dropping as she realized what I was planning.

"You wouldn't," Mara said breathlessly.

I nodded in response to the unarticulated question.

"Bog," I said, turning toward my best friend and brother. "Follow me to the docking bay. I need to get suited up."

Bog seemed to understand perfectly what I intended. This was part of the beauty of working with someone who knew me so well.

Standing, I quickly made my way down the incline towards the exit at the back of the control hub. Bog had managed to get to the doorway a few paces ahead of me.

Mara fell into step next to me, matching me stride for stride. "Captain, are you thinking what I think you're thinking?"

"That depends on what you're thinking that I'm thinking."

"You know very well what I'm thinking!" She didn't seem happy about my decision. "You can't go out there in a propulsion suit and expect to survive. One simple mistake and your life is over."

I ignored her. She wasn't wrong. I was, in fact, going to dive into a propulsion suit and jump out into space, hoping to grab onto the hub and climb aboard. From there I would try to buy enough time for everyone to get out of the system safely.

We made our way into the docking bay, a long rectangular room with huge metallic beams crisscrossing high overhead. At the end were a pair of enormous doors large enough to allow for the shuttle to pass. The floor, thankfully, was free of shag carpeting.

I sighed in relief that the docking bay was intact, with no evidence of damage from the firefight.

A line of propulsion spacesuits hung on the wall. I happily peeled off my uniform, taking no particular care to avoid damaging the annoying shoulder tassels. Rip! Oops. I glanced at Mara and noticed the flash of disapproval in her eyes. But it was only a flash; mostly her expression was one of fear.

Truth be told, I felt very much like kissing her at that moment. Due to the urgency of the situation, I opted to keep locking eyes with her as I stripped down.

She hardly reacted at all. I had to admit I was disappointed.

I didn't have time to dwell on it, though, as Bog was preparing my propulsion suit. He had the one-piece navy outfit already in hand. I took it from him and hastily put it on, first two feet, then two legs at a time...

I held my breath as Bog brought both sides of the polymer suit together. It had an innovative design which only bound together into an airtight shell once the occupant was already inside. The melding process began just under my chin and continued down my chest, past my stomach—I sucked in my breath—and past my belly button. Afterward I checked to make sure my man bits hadn't accidentally been left outside.

"Shoe, can you hand me the helmet?" Bog asked Mara, who ignored him and instead handed the helmet directly to me.

Mara looked calmer than earlier. "Captain, please reconsider."

"There's not much to reconsider. There's no other way with so little time."

With that, Bog gave a solid knock to the top of my cranium, which jammed the helmet over my head, nearly taking off my ears. I didn't want to think about the carnage it was doing to my hair. If I didn't die and or get sucked into that mother of a black hole, I would at least need a thorough conditioning later.

My mind was set and I didn't have the time—or the need—to chat about it. I started my ascent up a ladder towards the only single door that led out of the docking bay. My strides were briefly slowed as I grabbed the tensile cable that hung looped on the wall; it was to be my lifeline.

The single metal door slid sideways, screeching and scraping across the floor. Of course it malfunctioned and got stuck less than halfway open. But Bog had expected as much and hefted his giant frame against it with enough force that I saw the ripple through the screen of my protective helmet.

Within a moment, the door was open just wide enough for me to squeeze through.

On the other side of the door was a small chamber, split in half by a glowing red energy barrier which quietly protected us all from being sucked into space. I stepped into the chamber and stopped just short of the barrier—and beyond it, open space. The port hub was just twenty metres away, Sparling having aligned *Orbital* with the hub.

The time to go was now.

I clipped the tensile cable to a hook in my suit, then attached the other end to a fastener on the wall. Without looking again to my comrades, I stepped as far back as I could, then took two quick strides forward and jumped with all the fury of heaven or hell and hoped for the best.

As I sailed through the barrier and into deep space, blackness pressed in on me from all around. Pinpricks of starlight hit my eyes and I listened to the sound of my heartbeat—*thump-thump, thump-thump*. The sound of my breath echoed in the confines of my helmet. If I hadn't been responsible for so many lives—not the least of which being my own—this would have been enjoyable. Peaceful, even.

I shook off the distractions of space and concentrated on the task at hand.

The port hub grew larger in my field of view. As it got closer, though, I realized that I hadn't thought through my plan very well. I hadn't made sure this cable had enough slack, for one thing. Or if I grabbed for the hub and missed, would I have so much slack that I sank right into the event horizon beyond? Worse yet, would I pull in *Orbital* along with me?

I tried to activate the propulsion pack on my suit to slow my descent, but it fizzled and wheezed, and I heard a *clunk* as it failed to start up. I should have fucking known.

Note to Brant Zenith: have Stairn cancel all orders on these shitty propulsion packs.

I had estimated that this spacewalk should last a mere five seconds, meaning that I should reach the hull of the port hub any second now…

Unfortunately, at three and a half seconds I reached the end of the tensile cable. The force of my movement caused it to pull tight and finally, as I should have guessed, break. My lifeline snapped, leaving me with a few metres of dangling cable behind me as I careened out of control, flailing wildly.

The remaining second and a half seemed to pass simultaneously in a heartbeat and with the slowness of eternity.

When I came into contact with the port hub, I was out of position and my hand failed to grasp hold of one of the outer rings around its hull. Damn!

I lurched my body hard, spinning sideways and hoping to correct my approach to give myself a second chance—a final chance. Readying myself as my body careened towards the second metal ring, I swiped my glove towards the ring again.

I missed it, of course. This time I didn't even touch the ring at all. I was royally fucked.

But sometimes luck is on one's side. A quarter of a second later, with the hub receding behind me, I looked back in the hopes of seeing *Orbital* one last time before I met my doom. To my extreme fortune, I noticed the remaining three metres or so of tensile cable following in my wake.

Miraculously, impossibly, I watched as the cable passed between the outer ring and the body of the port hub. I quickly realized that the cable wasn't following my drift exactly. My body passed on one side of the metallic ring jutting out of the port hub… and it looked to me that the cable was following on the other side of the ring.

Looking back at the cable dragging behind me, I recognized that I had yet another chance. As it drifted around the ring, forming a U-shape, my adrenaline surged. All I had to do was grab the other end of that cable to successfully create a loop for myself around the ring…!

But I only had a couple of seconds before my chance disappeared and the cable pulled away again.

Unfortunately, it was just outside my arm's reach, so I jolted my body forward, pushing my fingers as far as they would extend. With one final, desperate swipe, I snagged the end of the cable. My grip stayed true and I held on for dear life. I was securely in place.

I took a moment to settle myself. My heart pounded in my ears even louder than before and I felt the sting of sweat in my eyes as it cascaded down my forehead. I hoped I didn't get acne because of it.

I pulled myself towards the hub, and a moment later I impacted the hull in a spread-eagled position. I heard a series of small cracking sounds but couldn't tell what they signified. I imagined they were my bones, or perhaps my pearly white teeth.

"Captain!" Mara's voice crackled through the static in my helmet. "Are you alright?"

"Yeah," I replied, out of breath. "Tell Agent Stairn I should have worn the three-legged undergarments."

She laughed nervously and I felt the release of tension through the line, followed by dead silence. The suit's connection to *Orbital* had gone quiet.

"Tell Sparling to pull away to a safe distance, just in case I fail." The communication line in my helmet was definitely dead. Just my fucking luck. I did not want Orbital and her crew to perish if I did. I hoped they would use good judgment and do so even without hearing my order.

I looked over at my stationary ship and realized that they must not have heard me or they decided to allow loyalty to outweigh their own self interests. I was touched.

I sighed to myself and rededicated myself to the plan. I would find the panel that covered the hub's control. If I could reach it, I could determine whether those enemy fighters had somehow sabotaged the computer.

My theory was that these alien attackers, whoever they were, had disabled the hub's absorption generator, causing it to deactivate. Now it was running on reserve power—and when the reserve power ran out, we'd all be killed.

If this was true, all I needed to do was reactivate the generators.

Hand over hand, I used the small rivets and protrusions on the hull to make my way across the exterior plating. I knew approximately where I'd find the computer access, but it took me a few moments to get there and pry open the panel.

The controls were dark. No power at all. Shit! That was going to complicate things.

Instinctively, I ran my gloved hand across my faceplate to wipe the sweat from my eyes, and in the process I discovered the source of those cracking sounds earlier. The glass on my helmet lens was riddled with fissures.

I had no idea how long I had before the visor disintegrated.

Doing my best to ignore this latest calamity, I made my way across the hull, looking for another way to jury-rig the hub to direct reserve power to the computer controls. The wiring for the thrusters would be found in a different compartment, and if I could crosswire them right I could kickstart the computer.

I found the panel, but it had been riveted shut along the edges. I swore to myself when I failed to locate another, more accessible panel nearby. Either this hub didn't have one or it had been sealed over at some point and riveted into place.

I felt that I didn't have enough time to keep searching—and truthfully, I was having a bugger of a time grappling the edge of the hull and didn't wish to test my luck further.

So as a man of tact and subtlety, I did what came naturally; I began punching the side of the hub with all my might. My strikes were aimed at the centre and weakest spot on the covered panel. I continued hitting it even after I was sure I'd bruised my hand.

After a half-dozen punches, the hull began to dent. Ten punches later, it was beginning to shear from its rivets. Meanwhile I could see the lens of my visor fracturing more with each punch. It would be a race to see which gave out first.

To make things worse, my hand was probably broken by now. But my biggest worry was keeping myself attached to the hub as I continued my barrage.

Each strike felt like a pang of agony at the end of my arm. It took everything I had to force myself to keep punching. The mind and body, it seemed, really didn't like being superseded in this way.

At last, the panel wrenched free of the rivets and I slid my fingers through the gap. My hand hurt so bad, as though Bog had stomped on it a few times, but I ignored the pain as much as possible.

When the panel lifted free, I saw the wiring underneath. My memory was foggy, and at that moment I seemed to remember jack shit about electrical, but fortunately the hub had been designed for an idiot like me. The wires were colour-coded and labelled. I was a bit surprised once again by my luck as it seesawed like a pendulum between extremes.

I grabbed a handful of thruster wires and rubbed them up against the sharpened edge of the panel to peel back the protective coating. The sparks told me exactly which wires were live. I then followed the same procedure for the control screen's wires and moved the end of the wires closer together—

Zap!

I twisted my body around to see if the screen had lit up. Nothing so far.

I kept at it, again and again, pushing different live wires into each other, but I was running out of hope.

Only when I was down to my last option, when my nerves were frazzled from successive jolts, did I hit paydirt. The wires in my hands sizzled and snapped with electric current, and I looked over just in time to see the controls boot up. Fantastic!

As I made my way back to the screen, it flashed warning lights that even a geriatric dog with cataracts could have seen. The panel indicated there was less than a minute of reserve power left. Somehow knowing how long my life would last made me feel less tense.

Manipulating the computer system was a breeze. My finger blurred over the control, despite the broken bones in my hand. I was highly fortunate that I was able to use the touchscreen with gloves on. I kept an eye on the countdown flashing on the top right-hand corner of the screen, as though mocking my efforts. The numbers were a stark yellow.

Fifty seconds… forty-five seconds…

I ignored it as best I could and continued my efforts to reprogram the system. It wasn't until the countdown reached ten seconds that I really began to sweat. It was difficult to see through the torrential downpour in my eyes, and my ears were almost deaf to everything but my heartbeat.

"*Do you wish to initialize gravity generators?*" the screen asked.

I slammed the Y key. Y for yes!

Five seconds…

"*Are you certain you wish to initialize the gravity generators?*"

Holy fuck. Had this thing been programmed by *Orbital*'s creators?

Yes, God damnit! Y! Y!

Two seconds… one second…

Oh shit. Had I buggered it up?

At last, I saw a flash of dull blue light, and with it the final containment ring began to shimmer and disappear. The end of the glorious Captain Brant Zenith was at hand. Even I hadn't seen it coming.

CHAPTER SIX

Weapons at the Ready

I drifted ever so gently next to the port hub, awaiting my near instantaneous death. I forced my eyes to remain open; no way was I dying without appreciating my last glimpses of life.

My biggest regret at that moment was that no one would be left to celebrate my heroic actions. A man like me deserved a glorious send-off. But I realized quickly that no one here would get a funeral. It hurt me deeply to know that my crew would join me in my demise.

As for myself, I'd probably be forgotten within weeks anyway.

My heart slowed. *Thump… thump… thump…* I felt the vibrations in my hands and instinctively grabbed what I could, fighting the unbeatable gravity which would suck us to our doom.

It never happened.

Instead the port hub whirred to life and the containment ring brightened again, its blue aura shining into my retinas as beautifully as any desert oasis.

I looked down at the computer controls and saw that the screen read *"System fully operational. Reserve charges increasing to one percent… three percent…"*

I couldn't tell if the wetness in my eyes had been produced by tears or sweat, but it stung. I savoured the sensation as direct evidence that I was still alive.

My determination to treasure life lasted only seconds longer when I realized I still had a serious problem on my hands.

The first was that my visor was nearly covered in fissures. The cracks were dispersed as randomly as a spider's web and it was becoming difficult to see. I didn't imagine I had more than a couple of minutes before it failed entirely.

The thought of the other four protective rings had slipped my awareness. At least the final ring was up and running, keeping us safe. This meant I wouldn't instantly die on my way back to the safety of *Orbital*, but only so long as none of those other rings reactivated before I passed them. If the next ring activated before I passed it, I would be trapped between the two.

The screen told me that the next ring's power level had already increased to almost fifty percent. I vaguely recalled from a briefing years ago that once a ring was halfway charged, it would begin to divert energy to the next ring in the sequence, and on and on until all five rings were back to full operation.

Again I feared for *Orbital* too. They were waiting in place for my return, despite the imminent death looming just behind me.

I only had a few moments before the second ring began its gradual charge. I couldn't wait much longer.

I frantically placed my hands against the hull, feeling a bit like a rock climber. It took me a couple of seconds to position myself so I could push off and get back to the ship. Near as I could tell, *Orbital* was maintaining position a mere twenty metres past the outermost ring.

The ring was already at forty-eight percent. I had to go. Now.

I held onto the hub as tightly as possible, coiled my body, felt my muscles contract, and then pushed off with all my might. In that same instant, the hub's thrusters fired in reverse to maintain its position from my exerted force—but I was already sailing free through space again.

As I drifted by the next ring, I noticed a stream of energy leap from ring to ring, shooting like an electric spark. Shit! I hadn't been quick enough…The energy link was quicker than I was… I'd be too late…

I smacked my wristband communicator with the desperate hope that perhaps something in my suit could help me. The screen shimmered, then shut off. Fuck!

This pissed me off something fierce. Knowing I was doomed, I slammed the communicator into my chest. It was a primitive act, but sometimes I felt that way.

Without warning, my wristband lit up and I noticed the shine of the suit's jetpack. Could it be? Was there a chance?

Before I could think it through, my propulsion pack kicked in. The suit buzzed with energy and a moment later I was moving through space like a speeding bullet.

Not expecting the explosion of force, I inadvertently shot forward… but at a drastically incorrect angle. It took me a few seconds to right my course, but that action added time I didn't think I had.

My body skimmed past the next ring, only barely avoiding a deadly collision. I could almost feel its energy radiating up through my boots.

The immediate danger vanished before my eyes as I realized, even with my unexpected detour, that it would only take me a few seconds to make it to *Orbital* now. I had dodged yet another catastrophe. I didn't even want to think about how close I'd come to death.

Along my quick journey, I felt full to the brim with exhilaration and relaxation all at once, leading me to a state of hypnotic ecstasy. It was the type of moment I would cherish to my dying breath.

I plunged on course toward *Orbital*, the cracks in my visor getting longer by the moment. It was eerie, very eerie, seeing those fissures extend only centimetres in front of my nose. I only needed a couple of seconds more, but I wasn't certain I would make it.

Then it happened. I don't know if I heard or saw it first, nor did I have time to ponder the mystery. Two seconds before safety, my visor shattered, exploding into a million shards of splintered mayhem. I slammed my eyes closed in reaction.

None too soon, I felt my body crash into the small chamber just outside the docking bay. I didn't feel myself cross the barrier, but I must have, for *Orbital*'s protective shield went up around me, reinstating the atmospheric stabilizers and the life support.

I opened my eyes hesitantly and everything went bright red. For a moment I thought I had indeed died. I wasn't sure if my body existed anymore, but it almost felt like I was on my hands and knees.

Something grabbed at my shoulders. At that moment it felt like the cold, hard hands of death coming to embrace me. Strange, it felt almost tender.

All I could hear was the pounding of my heart; all I could see was red.

Before long, however, my other senses began to work again. The air smelled like oil and dust, my face soaked in sweat or blood, or God only knew what. And my mouth was dry, the taste of bile seeming to dominate my palate.

It would take me a couple more moments of disorientation to realize what had happened.

The red diminished and I saw that it wasn't blood but rather a energy barrier erected by my propulsion suit. Strange, I hadn't even known our suits had working energy barriers. It had undoubtedly saved my life.

And as for those cold, hard hands of death... they were large and rough and strong. They belonged to Bog. He hauled me back to my feet. My body ached under his powerful, vice-like grip. Nothing had ever felt so wonderful.

Note to Brant Zenith: erase that admission. Bog's embrace didn't feel wonderful. You have a reputation to maintain.

With a hiss of satisfaction, the helmet disassembled, leaving me free to breathe in the fresh-smelling but still stale *Orbital* air again. Glass from the visor had gotten tangled in my damp blonde hair.

I realized that the soles of my boots had been seared off, no doubt from the containment rings as I'd passed them. Only the suit's barriers had kept my feet protected. The cold steel surface of the docking bay floor under my feet felt oddly comfortable.

"Brant, are you all right?" Mara asked, cutting short my fresh appreciation of the cold floor.

"I'd like to think so. I need a mirror."

I had no idea what kind of injury the shattered visor had inflicted on my face, but my heart beat like a galley master's hammer during battle. I was petrified to see the damage, but I had to know.

Surprise registered on Mara's face as she led me quickly to a glossy piece of metal in the far corner of the bay. It was just reflective enough for me to see myself. I sighed hugely; there wasn't so much as a scratch on my face. My hair was a catastrophe, though—it was tangled and matted, and glass was embedded in it.

But that bothered me very little at the moment.

I looked up at Bog, who wore a giant grin. His cobalt skin resembled a textured bowling ball. I couldn't tell exactly what he was smiling at, but it was good to see him and Mara again. Hell, it was even a glorious feeling to see the ugly insides of *Orbital*.

The three of us stood in the docking bay a few moments longer, grinning at each other stupidly. I felt the tension lift off my shoulders as I saw the two closest people in my life share in my joy. They were happy to be alive, but I could tell that their delight was also due to seeing me alive and safe. I don't think I'll ever forget that feeling.

When our stupor finally slipped away, I broke the silence.

"Are we safely away from the containment rings?" I asked, almost forgetting about the danger still present. "Is everything okay? With the protective rings, I mean?"

"Yes, Captain," Mara said, reverting to using my rank. "Agents Sparling and Stairn moved us away as soon as you entered. They assured us that the fifth and fourth rings are fully functional. Number three is being charged as we speak." She paused for a long moment, looking perplexed and beautiful at the same time. "Bog, could you let them know that all is well down here?"

He nodded, a different type of smile touching his lips. It made him look like a chimp that had just stolen a banana from a zoo spectator. He left the bay quickly.

Now that we were alone, Mara looked at me intently. I think she was wanting to tell me something important, but for some reason my mind had turned back to the problem of how to attack my tangled and filthy hair.

"That was… amazing." She indicated the chamber from whence we had just come.

"I know," I said, only paying partial attention. But I agreed with her. I wasn't so good with humility sometimes.

"You could have been killed so many times."

I was still thinking about my hair, deciding that I'd use the strawberry-kiwi shampoo as my first line of defence when I got back to my quarters…

"Why did you risk your life like that?" she asked. "I almost… I mean, we almost lost you there."

I shrugged, my thoughts turning to the orange-mango conditioner; it smelled glorious and always left my hair with a lustrous shine to match my flawless teeth. "Who else was going to do it?"

Her face flashed red. Was she angry with me? I couldn't tell, but without so much as an adieu she turned and stormed out of the docking bay.

Having no idea what the hell had just happened, I followed dumbly, half a step behind her. I didn't know what angered her, but I was the captain of *Orbital*. This ship may be the ugliest and oldest girl at the prom, but if someone was going to risk his life for her, without regret or second thought, that someone would be me. It was a captain's duty to take care of the ship and crew.

I stumbled along, my body still in shock from the five or so near-death experiences I'd endured in the last half-hour. My right hand ached something fierce and it wasn't until that moment that I realized just how badly I must have damaged it. I couldn't wiggle my fingers, but at least my face had been left without a scratch.

Mara kept a quick pace as we moved into the corridor. She didn't look back at me once. I felt more than a little offended. After all, I had saved all our lives!

Seconds later, we walked through the doorway into the control hub. Unexpectedly, upon seeing my face, Sparling stepped quickly over to me and gave me a shy hug. Feeling embarrassed, she then went back to her station.

That was more like it!

I looked over at the only other member of my crew I hadn't yet seen since my amazing act of heroism. Stairn nodded very perfunctorily before going back to work. I didn't even get a smile from him.

"Captain, our scanners reveal five ships within thirty minutes of intercept of us and the space station." Stairn's eyes moved to the viewscreen, which whirred to life and showed the doomed station. "Orbital's systems are glitchy from battle and I cannot tell yet whose fleet they belong to, but if we are to overthrow our enemies, we must do it now. Our only other option is to flee."

"We can't flee," I said. "I will not flee."

Everyone stared at me, and I could see they were expecting the opportunity to voice their own opinions on the subject. I gave none; I was the captain, and this was my choice.

"Besides, why would God choose to abandon his most beautiful crew now?" I added, referring mostly to myself. "No, we must free the station from these hellish creatures. Bog and I will board the station ourselves. We will wreak our havoc and save the day, and hopefully a few damsels in distress in the process."

I flashed a perfectly charming grin upon my colleagues.

Stairn's face actually showed concern. "Captain, I would join you."

Apparently, my face betrayed my disapproval, as he didn't even give me a chance to reject his preposterous suggestion.

"You will almost assuredly need one more ally," he continued. "My services are required here and now. I will go with you."

I wasn't sure if I was more intrigued or offended at his self-confidence. In fact, I was sure of only three things. The first was that I didn't have the time or energy to argue with him. The second was that I sure as shit needed a stiff drink when this was all over. The third was my certainty that Stairn would meet his demise; he could count beans with the best of them, but he had absolutely no battle training and would serve merely as cannon fodder.

I thought I would be almost glad to see him removed from my ship, but instead I found myself unexpectedly protective of him. I wanted to argue and convince him to stay, but I just didn't have the moments to spare. I would have to appease myself by holding him back when the final moment came. This was going to be my fight, mine and Bog's.

"Fine, Stairn," I snapped. I didn't like having my authority questioned now that it mattered. "You will join Bog and myself as backup. Do you understand?"

"Perfectly, Captain."

His face remained stonelike, but for a split second I thought I saw something like mischief flash in his eyes.

I made my way back towards *Orbital*'s docking bay, followed by Bog and Stairn—and once more, Mara. From the corner of my eye, I saw her look up at me and I realized that I didn't really have a clue what was going through her mind. I hoped one day it would be easier to understand her. That was if I didn't get shot up and eaten by aliens.

As we suited up, Bog struggled to fit his giant frame into a custom-made black spacesuit. It was a curious sight to watch my friend slide his massive head, horns and all, into the helmet. There must have been some magic in that helmet for it to accommodate the odd protrusions.

Stairn, too, was soon fully immersed in the embrace of a suit, this one green.

Forlornly, I looked upon the fourth and final suit hanging on the rack. It was pink—not just a little bit pink, but hot freakin' pink! I choked down my outrage, trying to overlook Bog's almost uncontainable laughter; he knew that I would have no choice but to put on the pink helmet rather than the damaged blue one I had worn to the port hub.

My suit would be blue, but my helmet pink. Oh god.

Mara smiled with a certain satisfaction as I slipped the cotton-candy-coloured helmet over my head. Somehow this was all her fault.

"I told you five years ago after the first Alhalran mission that the pink suit would come back to haunt us," I muttered.

"Relax, Captain." She sealed the helmet to my spacesuit. "It fits perfectly. Besides, you look beautiful."

Her smile was almost unbearable, but I had to shrug it off. She had won this fight.

It took only minutes to finish our preparation. We then stepped into the small chamber and readied ourselves to exit. Once again, Sparling had positioned us to line up with one of the station's still functioning docking bays. We merely had to step off, tethered of course, and step over to the station.

"I sure as hell better not die with this thing on," I said under my breath. I didn't think anyone heard me.

We each picked up a propulsion weapon, the best we could find from *Orbital*'s arsenal of cheap and undesirable models. Bog was kind enough to have brought my propulsion gun. I recognized it by the gouge on the wooden stock. Despite that small imperfection, I couldn't seem to rid myself of the weapon. Over and over, it proved to work just well enough to save my bacon. I just hoped it wouldn't one day explode in my handsome face.

I would have preferred a more advanced form of weaponry—for example, electrical dispersion… or a drift pistol or spark gun. Even better, a wave weapon that used energy waves and which could deal out mutilating internal damage while leaving no more than bruises on the skin.

With disdain, I gripped my propulsion gun. It would have to do. I would have to rush headlong into battle shooting left-handed, too, considering that I could hardly move my right hand at all.

I looked over at Stairn, who was putting into his holster some kind of weapon that didn't look like standard-issue Militia junk. I couldn't quite make out what it was, but it damned well looked better than what I carried.

At least my gun still had one thing his didn't. I unscrewed the secret compartment at my pistol's handle and thought about lifting it to my mouth and taking a long swig of rum.

Unfortunately, I was blocked by that accursed pink helmet.

Before the three of us stepped onto the station, Mara decided that we needed to review our mission objectives. The first objective would be to gain a foothold on the station. After that, it would get complicated.

"Once you guys make it aboard, you'll have three areas of the station to target," Mara said, her staticky voice coming through the speaker in my helmet. "Our scanners show nineteen alien lifeforms aboard the station, none of which match any of the species in our database."

"Well, that sucks," Bog hissed. He already sounded winded. I couldn't tell if it was the result of his tight suit or his effort to ready himself for battle. "Only nineteen?"

Knowing Bog as I did, I could see through this act of bravado. He must have known there was a good chance we wouldn't all make it through this alive.

"Well, you can tell the story any way you'd like after the mission is complete," Mara said without a trace of annoyance. She was perceptive enough to know that we each dealt with stress in our own ways. "The first group you'll run into is stationed near the end of a long entry hallway. I'm uploading the building's digital blueprint so you can access it in your helmet's visor."

The specs suddenly appeared on my visor screen, showing the complex network of passageways and lifeforms inside the station. I was surprised that our helmets had this ability! I was even more astounded that our suits worked well enough to take advantage of it.

"Since when could our helmets do this?" I asked, incredulous. "This would have been nice to know before I jumped into space a half-hour ago. Wouldn't you agree?"

I would have punched the wall, but my right hand was still broken.

"Sorry, Captain," Mara said. "There was a malfunction in your blue helmet, and we just didn't have time to switch it out." I didn't say anything, and she took it as a cue to continue with the briefing. "Once you make it past the first group of aliens, you'll have three major objectives. The first will be to get to crew quarters. Many of the station's crew and attendants are being held there. The second objective will be to reach the armoury. This one is of extreme importance, because if the aliens detonate any of the explosives in that bay, things will get very unpleasant—very, very quickly. There are five aliens there at the moment, and if at all possible it would be wise to observe them to gain some idea of what they're up to."

"That may not be possible," Stairn said with unfaltering confidence.

Mara nodded. "Perhaps not. But we're getting signs of communications on an unusual frequency the aliens are using. Although we can't understand their language, hopefully listening in on them will give us some clues." She hesitated. "That frequency is being used everywhere except in the armoury."

"That would make perfect sense," Bog explained. "Some of the weapons stored there are highly unstable. They're probably worried using that frequency could set something off."

I made it a point to never doubt Bog's word. Even if I hadn't possessed a wealth of firsthand experience with accidentally blowing shit up myself, I still would have believed him.

"Okay," I said, my heart racing. It was good to feel alive again, even if I happened to be dead sober. "So there are aliens in the crew quarters and the armoury. You mentioned something about a third location?"

"That's right," Mara informed us. "It seems there are five more aliens at the station's intergalactic post."

Had I heard her correctly? "Seriously?"

"Yeah. They seem to be looking through the parcels. I bet they're looking for something in particular and haven't found it yet. I don't understand what could interest them so much."

It suddenly occurred to me that the aliens weren't the only ones with a parcel pickup at the Quazar station.

They freakin' better not be going after my parcel, I thought, suddenly looking forward to picking it up and making sure the contents were what had been promised to me.

"What makes the least amount of sense to me is why these aliens are still aboard the station at all," Stairn remarked in a steady voice.

I looked at him in confusion. What was he implying?

"It seems obvious," the logistics officer continued, "that the only reason the station still exists is through the brave actions of the captain…"

Note to Brant Zenith: give Agent Stairn a promotion for his ability to sum up the good work of his crewmates.

"…but if the captain had failed, which should have been expected…"

Note to Brant Zenith: assign Agent Stairn to latrine duty for all eternity plus a day.

"…then everything in this system, the station included, would have been pulled into the black hole. So why didn't the aliens evacuate?"

I had to admit this was a good point. Why were they holding hostages, rifling through the armoury, and raiding a post station with imminent death threatening them? And they were the ones who had created that very threat!

"Well, we don't have time to worry about it," I said. "Although if anyone should figure out the answer to this little mystery, please feel free to let the rest of us know."

With that, I gathered my composure. A moment later we three warriors burst out of *Orbital* and onto the space station's platform. Without a backward glance, I opened the outer hatch and stepped into a sizzling firefight.

CHAPTER SEVEN

The Galactic Post

We were welcomed into the space station like a blizzard in July. A blast erupted centimetres from my face, searing my eyes with bursts so intense that they could have tanned an albino at fifty paces. Only my godawful pink helmet's visor saved my retinas from instant obliteration.

I hoped the carbon residue left by the blast may have scuffed up the helmet, giving it a fiercer look. I did my best to envision myself as a heroic, charbroiled soldier hellbent on wreaking havoc rather than an underpaid, hardly appreciated captain whose decrepit gun could barely shoot the feathers off a turkey.

I led the tenuous charge into an antechamber to the side of the platform. From here, we hurried into a long hallway which would eventually branch in several different directions. Unfortunately, at the moment we were trapped on its far end, with nowhere to hide and precious little space to manoeuvre.

The hallway's tunnel-like shape seemed to have been designed specifically to accommodate Mackmians and their round bodies. Arched columns broke up the corridor at even intervals and the ceiling was about twice an average human's height. The only illumination came from glowing yellow light encasements, allowing us to see that our mysterious attackers were perhaps a few dozen paces away. It was impossible to get a good look at them.

The hallway looked like someone had dropped a plasma grenade in it. Black soot clung to the walls and clouds of smoke lingered in the air. Three Mackmian corpses lay nearby, their yellow blood pooling in corners. This really pissed me off. I vowed that the scumbags who'd done this would meet a very ugly end.

Another blast of weapons fire smashed into the ceiling just over my head and I dove for cover. Bog, all three hundred kilograms of him, hit the floor hard behind me. Even though our suits were pressurized, I could swear I heard him wheeze in dismay when he landed flat on his enormous torso.

Our first objective was complete. We had a foothold on the station. True, we were cowering behind cover, but it was a foothold nonetheless.

We took turns firing down the hallway. At times like these, I wished I had a better weapon. I almost salivated thinking about the Zigma Banisher gun hanging above my desk. That thing could probably have blown a hole straight through the aliens and out the other side of the station. I looked down at the propulsion gun with sadness, my finger following the gouge on the wood. If only…

Another explosion crashed into the wall behind us.

"I think our best course of action is to bust our way through," I said. "After that, there are three of us—and three points of interest on the station. We could split up and—"

"But should we really split our forces?" Bog asked.

"Actually, it seems tactically sound," Stairn shot back as another blast rocked the corridor. "It's best to take all three positions simultaneously."

Note to Brant Zenith: reduce Agent Stairn's latrine duty to only one year.

Something seemed out of place. How did Stairn know so much about military strategy?

"Okay," Bog finally decided, sounding conflicted over having to agree with Stairn. I imagine that must have hurt his pride.

Without any further discussion, I began assigning duties. "Bog, you'll take the armoury."

He nodded his agreement. We all knew that the security officer was the logical choice for handling weapons.

"Take some time to study the aliens there," I continued. "See if you can gain any clues as to whatever the hell they're doing. When you're satisfied that you've learned as much as you can, neutralize them. Then make sure no one else can access the armoury without your... approval. Contact me when this is complete."

"Absolutely." Bog had a devilish grin on his face which made him look like a mischievous demon. He was truly intimidating when he wanted to be.

"And try not to blow up the entire station while doing so."

"Sure," he replied, a little too casually for my liking.

My biggest problem at this point was how to convince Stairn that I should be the one to storm the post station. I paused for a moment to figure out the best rationale.

"I'll take the hostages in crew quarters," Stairn suggested, and it didn't sound like a request.

If I hadn't been so delighted by his choice, I may have argued with him more sternly.

"I'm not sure you can handle it alone, Agent Stairn."

"Captain, with the utmost of respect, I believe I am much more qualified to rescue the hostages than are you."

"Oh," I said icily, almost forgetting that I was glad he had volunteered for the assignment. "And what in the name of the devil's dirty diaper makes you think that?"

"Experience. Trust me, Captain. This objective is meant for me. I will not be deterred."

I could tell he wasn't going to argue about it any further. Besides, I had the opportunity to look gracious by letting him have his choice assignment.

Plus, that parcel of mine was calling my name.

"Okay, Stairn, you get the hostages," I conceded. "On one condition. Should you need assistance, don't hesitate to call for help."

He nodded in solemn agreement, but judging from the look on his face I felt suddenly very certain that he wasn't going to need any help.

We all knew what to do.

"What do you think our chances are?" Bog asked almost offhandedly.

Before I could answer, Stairn jumped in. "I have run a quick yet thorough calculation these past few moments. I would say the chance of individual success falls in the moderate range—forty-five to fifty-five percent per person, per objective. The chance of total success lies at twelve-point-five percent. Consequently, there is a very good chance at least one of us will not survive the ordeal."

Bog and I looked at each other, both having the exact same thought: *If someone dies, it's not going to be me.* We both turned to Stairn with the same assumption in mind. We remained silent, however.

"Do not worry comrades," Stairn said calmly, perhaps misunderstanding the look on our faces. "I will make sure neither of you are harmed."

I peered through the blackened haze just as a particularly large explosion erupted a little too close to my security officer for comfort. He dived for cover, barely missing out on having his torso torn in two.

"Son of a pregnant cow!" Bog wheezed.

He stood up gingerly, with some help from Stairn, and looked back at our unseen attackers. Bog had a distinct disadvantage; his enormous size sometimes made it very difficult to dodge weapons fire. But his Nova Martian genetics gave him the ability to absorb heat from weapons that would burn through other lifeforms.

Another blast struck just past my shoulder. I couldn't see the path of fire, only the origin point and the smoking crater in the wall behind me. I made sure to curse the Mackmian gods.

"Yeah, of course," Bog huffed through the continuous explosions. "They would have to be using spark guns!"

Spark guns were a sinister type that emitted a bright spark at the barrel's tip; the projectile then travelled instantaneously—and invisibly—only to explode upon contact. The guns were truly dangerous and often outlawed.

Luckily for us, though, our attackers had set their weapons to barbecue rather than nuclear meltdown. It was a matter of necessity, since they couldn't risk blowing holes in the hull.

Peeking my head around a massive arched column, usually light grey but now singed black, I saw how close to crispy I'd gotten. We were in a real bind. Our weapons sucked, but that wasn't new. What was new was the calibre of the enemy we'd engaged.

Looking through the black haze and blinding flashes of light, for the first time I saw the face of our enemy, if indeed it could be called a face. I had seen my share of unnatural-looking aliens in my time, but these creatures were rather awe-inspiring. They had a general humanoid shape but lacked any sort of enclosing spacesuit to hide their forms. What passed for bodies were lithe, composed of thick sinews, and the largest of these sinews trailed up their torsos. They reminded me of the Dwuvian species a little. They seemed to have two legs, at least, and their arms protruded from knotted shoulders. Truth be told, their colouring was the only easy way to distinguish one unnaturally tall alien from another; they stood a half-metre taller than myself.

I took aim, trying my best to expose as little of my pink helmet as possible. Strangely, I wondered if any of the creatures were laughing at my appearance. Either way, they would regret crossing me.

I squeezed the trigger and heard the typical click. Misfire.

Ah shit! In my excitement, I had forgotten that my weapon hated me.

The alien's head, or whatever was proper to call that sinewy thing with eyes, shifted out of my line of sight, thus saving his worthless ass.

Without warning, we were barraged by a jarring succession of blasts. I had to duck back to save my head from exploding like a water balloon. Just in time, too, as I could see the black marks left mere centimetres from my visor.

I looked over at Bog and Stairn. Bog was hugging the edge of the opposite side of the arch, awaiting a chance to get in a shot or two.

It occurred to me a moment later what was going on. The enemies were closing in as we ducked to avoid getting hit. But we were running out of time and space, and if they pinned us against the doors we would be nothing more than Telnian roast beef.

"Ah, screw it all to Balzak!" I shouted as I rolled out of position.

Incidentally, Balzak was a real planet. Its people served great mojitos and cabbage rolls. But I didn't have time to reminisce about my twelfth birthday right now.

I found myself directly in the centre of the hallway, exposed. A blast hit the floor directly behind me, almost searing my boots for the second time today. I wiggled my toes to make sure I could still feel them. I could.

I didn't have time to celebrate that discovery as I tucked and rolled heroically across the opposite side of the long hallway. Another blast struck the wall beside me and I retaliated with a well-aimed shot of my own. My gun let out its characteristic sighing whistle and struck one of the enemies in this torso, slamming him backward into a colleague. It was just the distraction I needed to make a brave dive behind the next archway.

Damn I was good!

I was only about a dozen paces from the closest enemy, and half that distance from my shipmates, when I looked past the column to ascertain what, if any, damage I may have caused to the alien troops. There was one more undefended archway ahead of me at this point, and for whatever reason I felt it was my duty to get there before the aliens.

I could see that the alien I'd shot down was regaining his feet. Blast it! The only consolation I took from this was that he appeared to be very shaky, almost drunk. He tried a couple of times to regain his balance but then stumbled and collapsed. He twitched but otherwise remained satisfyingly motionless.

I clutched my pistol and pointed it across the hallway. Now that I was armed with vim, vigour, and vitality—not to mention a great set of teeth—I took aim again.

That was a mistake. The rope-like alien fired back, striking the wall behind me and wrenching my arm violently enough to throw me off-target. My errant blast struck the bulbous light above us and exploded it on contact. The area containing the aliens was now shrouded in darkness.

Shit! Now my arm ached, the aliens were much harder to see, and I think a wedgy was forming in my rear compartment. I pushed the unpleasantness to the back of my mind and wracked my imagination for options. The good news was that we were no longer outnumbered. For once, my propulsion gun was actually good for something other than a rum flask.

Peering into the darkness, I realized that I no longer needed to give the fight quite so much effort; the bright yellow and red sparks from their weapons gave the aliens away. I decided I needed to get even closer.

A propulsion blast whistled by me and struck into the darkened corridor. It had come from Bog and obviously had some effect. I used the resulting break in the action to progress. I aimed at the same spot Bog had hit and fired indiscriminately, strafing for all I was worth.

I made it to the centre archway without sustaining any damage, and not a moment too soon. Once behind the next column, another spark blast cratered into the floor, tripping me up. I couldn't stop in time and crashed forward with about as much grace as a train accident.

Hearing a crunching sound, I was quite certain that I'd at least dented Mara's hot pink helmet. At least something positive had come from my fall.

My eyes welled up with tears as I felt a sharp pain in my neck. I pushed myself up, so disorientated and dazed that I didn't even realize the extreme pain in my right hand. The best position I could manage was a half-kneel against the inside of the arch, my mind reeling. I couldn't focus and my vision was blurry. Well, a bit blurrier than normal.

I could make out the murky edges of the creatures as they shifted location in the darkened corridor. I leaned back, trying to remain as hidden from their weapons as possible. I couldn't tell for sure, but the dark shapes seemed to be moving with greater efficiency.

My heart sank as I realized my imminent doom; they were coming towards me. I was a diminished threat now and they knew it.

With my head spinning like the water in a flushed toilet bowl, I grasped my propulsion gun and took aim as the creatures stepped into view. At that moment, there was no way either of us could miss. This would be my only chance, and the time was measured in milliseconds.

I squeezed the trigger...

Click. Misfire.

A grimace crossed the creature's face, and then his tentacled finger pulled tightly on the trigger of his weapon. I saw the spark slip out from the barrel, which was pointed directly at my flawless visage.

Without warning, a stream of light blue mist shot through the air and slammed into the creature. The alien was thrown back with such awesome force that even I was left rattled in its wake.

For a moment, I thought I had swallowed my own tongue, so powerful was the blast's shockwave. If I hadn't still worn that horrible pink helmet, the force may have blown the eyelids clean off my face.

I looked the big, twisted alien straight in his eyes. Or hers. God only knew at this point. Its face was a mess of complex sinews surrounding a set of fierce mandibles just behind the jaw. They strung around the creature's head to form what I could only call cheekbones, splitting on either side of its eye cavities.

I looked back in the direction of my team. Seconds later, a bright blue shield shimmered into view. The shield seemed to emanate from the wrist device attached to Agent Stairn. If I wasn't mistaken, it was a residual density shield that protected him from the powerful spark blasts hailing down on us from the lone survivor at the other end of the hallway.

In Stairn's other hand, he carried a wave pistol!

"Captain, are you seriously injured?" Stairn asked with the rigidity of a six-day-old diaper under the desert sun.

"I'll survive," I said, relief showing through the irritation in my voice. "Damn it, Stairn. When you said 'Be patient,' you freakin' failed to mention that you possessed density shields and wave guns. That would have been a damned fine thing to know about five minutes ago!"

Stairn didn't look back at me. He just held the blue glow of his density shield up a bit higher. As another spark blast sank into it, the three-metre-high shield shimmered. That blast normally would have been enough to scatter little pieces of Stairn throughout the station, but he wasn't even knocked off-balance.

I rose to my feet and felt two large hands grasp my shoulders to help me up. I looked over to see Bog, his face as awestruck as mine.

Stairn had by now closed the distance between the alien and himself, his shield absorbing spark blast after spark blast; some glowed green, others red, and several were even white... those were the most powerful blasts known to man. Yet the shield showed no outward sign of stress.

The sinewy alien kept firing, which was the only thing keeping it alive. As long as it kept up the attack, Stairn couldn't shift his shield away from his body long enough to take a shot with his immensely powerful wave gun.

At that moment, I saw Stairn do something I would never forget. He rapidly shifted the shield modulator on his left arm, causing the shield to shrink to about one metre in diameter. I couldn't understand why he would alter the shield, as it looked like instant and obvious suicide.

Indeed, the alien took advantage and fired a deadly hot white spark. Stairn couldn't possibly have seen the path of that blast, but he nonetheless pivoted his body, lifting his left arm to the level of his head and allowing the shield to catch the spark. The spark seemed to skim along the surface of the shield, and I felt the air burn from my position three or four paces away.

Stairn uncoiled his body, allowing his shielded arm to follow, and flung the diluted energy of the spark back at the alien in a fluid arc. Fear and surprise contorted the attacker's face as the white energy hit him like a supernova.

Its body evaporated into a gooey black mist.

Bog and I stared at Agent Stairn in surprise. Actually, surprise would be an understatement. I think I would have been less surprised by an avalanche suddenly cascading through the space station.

Stairn looked down at what was left of the aliens' bodies, apparently checking for signs of life. Satisfied, he turned around and came back toward us. He didn't show any sign of excitement, didn't even crack a smile.

Damn it, man, I thought. *You could at least strut a bit like a hero.*

He must have satisfied himself that we were on the surface intact. Stairn turned around, making his way to the junction at the end of the hallway. We had achieved our next objective.

True to his word, Stairn had kept us alive. Shit, it hurt to admit that.

"Captain, can you succeed at your next objective?" Stairn asked as we caught up to him.

I nodded, still feeling a little woozy. "Transmit an update to Mara when you complete your mission," I said.

Before saying anything, Bog leaned over one of the aliens and grabbed its tentacle-like hand. He peeled back what could have been called fingers and pulled free its spark pistol. It was strange to see the pistol's size alter when Bog picked it up. I had never seen a weapon shift to match its owner's dimensions.

"Today is going to be a good day," Bog stated with a broad, gleaming smile.

I could have laughed from the sheer joy of the moment, realizing that I could upgrade my own weaponry too. I grabbed the gun out of the hand of the first alien I had struck down. This one shrunk slightly to fit my hand. The weapon was a little larger than my propulsion gun and covered in symbols I couldn't decipher. But who cared what it said? All I had to do was point and squeeze the trigger.

At times like these, I really loved my life.

The three of us broke away and headed down our respective hallways. I happened to take the second hallway on the left, being reasonably familiar with the station's layout since I'd needed to make pickups in the past from this particular post station.

This hallway looked no different from the one I'd just left, except perhaps it was a bit narrower. It too had dark plumes of smoke drifting along the ceilings. Evidently the ventilation was also a casualty of the attacks. I followed the hallway for several minutes, hooking first right and then left. When it split, I knew well enough to follow the left branch.

During the walk, my mind spun. It took a good long while to finally feel my five senses return. So much had happened today, and I was realizing that the most striking event so far had been the actions of Agent Stairn. After six months of duty with the man, I had come to the conclusion that I knew absolutely nothing about him.

Note to Brant Zenith: take some time to learn more about Stairn.

I followed the hallway a bit further before veering off for the final time. I was now within several paces of the post station's large doors.

Suddenly I heard a series of voluminous crashes. Some sounded like an avalanche of rock and stone striking one another, while others had a soft, almost luxurious squish to them. I didn't hear any voices, but I could sense some sort of violent endeavour being performed.

I stepped closer to the double sliding doors of the post station. They showed signs of damage and didn't seem to close properly. My plan was simple: I would slip through the small gap with the skill of a ninja, then find a way to get near enough to the five alien customers I knew to be waiting within.

I pressed on my wristband communicator and tapped into the helmet's visor's controls.

Shit! My helmet's sensors were damaged and flashed red pixels across the screen. Nothing it displayed helped worth crap. I would have to rely on my considerable skills, not to mention my tawdry affair with lady luck. I hoped she'd continue to smile upon me.

The crashing and banging continued. At least my helmet's microphone still worked well enough.

Then I picked out a new sound, like ropes being pulled abrasively against one another. Based solely on their appearance, I could only conclude this was the sound of the aliens' language.

I slipped into the post station, expecting some carnage and chaos in the large elliptical chamber just beyond the doors. What I saw took me by surprise. Most of the high-ceilinged room was shrouded in dark shadow, although a series of diffuse lights shone from the sconces overhead. Much like our hallway battle, smoke clung to everything. It reminded me of Sunday night bingo at my grandma's sewing club.

Even in the relative absence of light, I got a sense of the catastrophe that had taken place here. The shelves, normally home to thousands of well-organized parcels and boxes of every shape, were in a shambles. The brilliantly shimmering security fields that typically protected the merchandise had waned. Within moments, I feared these energy shields would fail.

I was sure of only two things. Number one, using gin and tonic as mouthwash was an ineffective method of plaque control. Two, the next several minutes would prove very interesting.

I slipped further into the room, remaining deep in shadow and keeping myself hidden behind a row of support columns.

The room was so massive, almost like a stadium. It took me the better part of two minutes at my wary pace to approach the customer service desk and discover what was going on. When I was within a dozen paces or so, I halted my approach. I took in the scene, still standing deep within the shadows.

Behind the desk stood an oval-looking Mackmian in the button-up green leather vest and trousers standard to the Galactic Post. His girth stretched the threads of the uniform well past the point of decency.

But it wasn't his uniform I was most concerned about. The aliens had knocked down a large enough portion of the shield to gain entrance behind the service counter. At that moment, perhaps sensing help was on the way, the lone Mackmian had pulled a pistol on the nearest sinewy alien. He was too slow and the lean, agile alien caught his forearm before he could take aim.

The blast that erupted from the Mackmian's pistol inadvertently launched straight for me. I dove out of the way, hoping it hadn't seared off any of the parts I was most fond of.

With my good hand on the spark gun, and the other badly broken, I found myself unable to break my fall. Not for the first time today, I hit the ground hard—but thankfully not with my head this time. I did my best to roll a metre backwards and behind a column.

My fall must have made enough sound to give me away, because the three aliens harassing the Mackmian all looked sharply in my direction. Two of them turned their weapons on me and took careful steps in my direction. The column blocked my view of them, but I could hear their boots scuffing on the concrete floor.

My heartbeat thumped in my ears, but I rose to my feet, cursing lady luck for having betrayed me. I slipped into the darkest pool of shadow I could find and lowered myself to my right knee, waiting for the aliens to enter my line of sight. This time, with my weapon raised, I had the tactical advantage. All I had to do was sit back and wait for the next alien to cross my path.

Unexpectedly, an alien streaked into view a dozen or so metres from my far right. How had he seen me? I didn't have time to wonder. He fired a blue spark that shattered the column behind me as I leaped out of the way. Just in time, too, as the blast brought the column down in a heap of rubble.

Other blasts followed, and in the midst of the chaos I stood up and ran with my head down, racing towards the protection of another column in an equally dark section of the chamber.

What the hell? How had they found my hiding spot? Did they have thermal imaging? Even if they did, my suit was programmed to give off a heat signature that mimicked the ambient environment. Perhaps it was malfunctioning like every other thing I touched aboard *Orbital*...

I had to get to safer ground; the next round of weapons fire likely wouldn't miss. I was outnumbered, outflanked, and I'd lost the only real advantage I had: surprise.

Despite this, I felt oddly invincible with the spark weapon firmly in my hand. And yet this imagined invincibility did nothing to protect me from the telltale blue spark barrelling at me. I ducked, but not quite fast enough this time. The blast seared through the fabric of my suit just above my shoulder. It left the smallest of holes, but fortunately the worst of it was deflected into the wall behind me, which exploded in a flash of blue light.

I didn't have the comfort of time to think. I directed my fire at the spot where the spark had originated. *Begone!* I pulled the trigger.

With satisfaction, I watched my spark directly impact the dark form of my attacker. Streams of red energy shimmered across its torso, burning its skin. A tenth of a second later, the creature was launched backwards with so much force that it rattled my pearly white teeth.

I changed positions, not wishing to stay in any one place too long. That would be the quickest way to get myself killed. There were at least four other aliens in the room, and for some reason they could detect me even in the darkest shadows.

I stepped into the light, only offhandedly noticing now that the protective shields around the shelves of parcels had failed. I took aim at the next alien to scramble into view—and fired. The blast slammed into a tower of crates and produced an explosion of red light. The topmost crates began to teeter; a moment later, they came down like an avalanche, the force of which surprised even me.

The alien wasn't quick enough to avoid the cascading wave of carnage. I watched with some amusement as it was crushed by a giant wooden crate labelled "Smeltons Grand Piano, the only marble and granite piano you can trust." The impact made the queasiest squishing sound I'd ever heard.

That was two down and three to go.

I looked over at the Mackmian employee to check his status. Unfortunately, his prognosis was no better than mine. The third alien, whom I guessed was the ringleader judging from his boots—they were shinier; it's important to notice that type of thing—had wrapped his rope-like arms around the leather-vested Mackmian, holding his chubby neck in a chokehold. It wouldn't be long before my fat little friend met his chunky little maker.

I raised my weapon but knew it would do no good. If my aim was true, there would only be an abundance of Mackmian goo with some traces of black tendon scattered over the customer service desk.

Without warning, in what looked like the Mackmian's final seconds, the round fellow began to move, placing one stout foot after the other. He sped up his pace, carrying the sinewy alien on his back as though he weighed less than a feather. The Mackmian then jumped as high as I'd ever seen a Mackmian jump, which wasn't saying much, and twisted his body in midair so that he landed with the force reserved for gods and small nuclear weapons. I was certain the entire space station shook from the impact. The alien was nothing more than a leathery pile of sinew when the Mackmian stood up again after the ordeal.

I would have laughed aloud if out of the corner of my eye I hadn't seen two more sparks launch towards me. I evaded them, only barely missing death as they hurtled into the crates on the opposite side of the room. I hoped my parcel hadn't been among the casualties.

"Screw this," I muttered under my breath.

I held out my weapon and let go a blast that would have made God envious. In what may have been the proudest moment of my life, the spark didn't just hit one alien but both. It scorched the arm right off the first alien's body, then collided with his partner in crime. The alien's obliterated body shot into the air. Both aliens exploded from the energy they absorbed.

Before I could grasp the events of the past five seconds, the battle was over. Only the Mackmian and myself remained in the cavernous chamber, a reminder of how damned awesome I truly was.

I stepped toward the recent carnage and looked down at the floor to find myself standing in a puddle of oozing black tentacles from the Mackmian's attacker. The tentacles twitched like an epileptic donkey. I didn't envy the poor fellow; no creature should suffer such a fate.

But that was neither here nor there.

I grabbed the Mackmian's meaty hand and pulled him up with every ounce of strength I possessed. Soon I was able to help the fellow onto his feet. He merely turned and walked calmly back to his spot behind the customer service desk.

Stupefied, I watched as he returned to filing parcels as if nothing at all had just happened. He didn't so much as thank me. He didn't even acknowledge my presence! Didn't I deserve some recognition for my role in all this?

I approached just as the Mackmian turned his attention to a package of slim books and caught their titles: *The Zen of the Marauding Crusader* and *How to Catch a Shark with Your Bare Feet*. I waited for him to say something, but he continued to ignore me. I really didn't like to be ignored, especially by someone I'd just rescued.

I cleared my throat, then decided to remove my pink helmet. Standing in perhaps the only functioning light in the place, I thought that maybe if the Mackmian could see the cut of my heroic jib, he would give me my due attention. Releasing the seal, I pulled the helmet clear off, noticing for the first time that it had a giant gouge in it.

"Mara isn't going to like this," I said, wincing. "She's totally pissed at me as it is."

The Mackmian continued to ignore me. He had gone well beyond the boundaries of rudeness, veering dangerously toward ignorance. There was no excuse for that.

I cleared my throat for the second time. "Hello, Mackmian. Interesting day you're having."

It took him ten infuriating seconds to look up from what he was doing. Perhaps it was the impatience on my face, or maybe it was the spark weapon in my hand, but he suddenly became more interested.

"What can I do for you, valued customer?" he spoke with no emotion whatsoever. "Do you have a parcel to pick up?"

This really bothered the hell out of me, but I tried to remain calm. He'd had a rough day. The last thing he needed was another person giving him grief.

"Actually, I do, my good Mackmian," I said, trying my best to maintain an upbeat attitude. After all, I was having one of the best days of my life—that was, aside from breaking every bone in my hand, burning my shoulder, gaining a concussion, and possibly filling my underwear.

He picked up his digital clipboard. "Your name?"

"Captain Brant Zenith of the starship *Orbital*, Militia Space Fleet," I replied. "But you can simply call me Hero."

If he had any reaction to that, he didn't show it. After a minute of searching his clipboard, he informed me that my parcel was indeed ready to be picked up.

Elated, and almost forgetting my dislike of this man, I asked him to retrieve it.

He did so in the same slow manner as everything else he did, but I held my impatience in check. Mara would have been proud. Indeed, she probably would have been prouder of my patience than the fact that I had disintegrated six aliens and saved tens of thousands of lives in the last two hours.

I could easily attract women, but I would never understand them.

Not wanting to get sidetracked, I straightened as I noticed the Mackmian walking back towards me with a large shoebox-like parcel in hand.

"Ah, excellent work!" I said to my new best friend. Peering at the nametag on his vest, I finally took note of his name. "Fine fellow you are, Farnan."

I reached out to grab the parcel from his hands, but he yanked it out of reach.

"Identification please."

"What?" I asked, incredulous.

"Identification, sir."

"What the hell are you talking about?" I asked, feeling the weight of the proverbial last straw finally breaking.

"Customers do not receive packages without identification," Farnan replied calmly, if not a bit wheezily.

I was livid now. "What the hell do I need ID for at a time like this?"

"Those are the rules. We at the Galactic Post do not break the rules."

"And what the hell happens if I don't have my ID with me?" I asked, expecting his answer to piss me off but hoping for the best anyway.

I hadn't even thought to grab my digital ID card before leaving the ship. It was resting on the end table next to my bed. It wasn't the sort of thing one brought to a gunfight.

He didn't smile or show any other indication of his state of mind. "The Post will not allow parcels to be retrieved without verifying the customer's identity. There is no exception."

"So let me get this straight, Farnan. After saving your overabundant ass just a few minutes ago—" I pointed to the place where I had blasted an alien into a fine mist. "—right over there. See it? Yeah, you do. Indeed, after saving your station and, let's be honest, this entire star system… you still refuse me the one little thing I ask for? Even though it's mine to begin with?"

I couldn't see any way for him to refuse my request now.

"Parcels cannot be retrieved without ID."

At that moment, all my patience was used up. Slowly and dramatically, I returned my newly acquired spark weapon to its holster and raised my propulsion gun in its place; after all, there would be no point in absolutely disintegrating him.

I pressed the gun to his forehead, the barrel making an indentation in his slightly orange-tinted skin.

"Farnan, buddy," I stated with false charm. This Mackmian needed to realize with whom he was dealing. "I think you should take a moment—or even two, if you need it—to register the blunder you're about to make. Withholding this parcel is not in your best interest. Unless you want me to ventilate that bulbous skull of yours, I suggest you cough up my parcel and allow me to leave in peace. What do you think now?"

He didn't even flinch. I had to admire his tenacity.

"The Post will not relieve parcels without—"

That was the last push. With a slow and deliberate motion, I squeezed the trigger… and I continued to squeeze the trigger until the inevitable happened.

Click. Misfire.

"Identification please."

I felt exasperated beyond belief. "I don't have my motherfu—"

"If you don't have the necessary identification, a thumbprint scan will suffice just as well."

When I was finally able to stop cursing this Mackmian overlord, I slowly removed the glove from my left hand and lifted the thumb to his clipboard's scanner.

"You could have said that earlier," I said. "You know that, don't you?"

He didn't so much as shrug as the device read my thumbprint. It proved that I was who I said I was, for which I was thankful; I really wouldn't have wanted to use the spark gun as my next threat.

"Identification approved," Farnan stated emotionlessly. "Very well, customer."

He was about to hand me my parcel when he glanced down again at the digital clipboard. My hands were already outstretched to receive my prize when he pulled it away again at the last moment.

"There are shipping and handling fees incurred. How will you be paying?"

"With my boot up your fat ass!"

I have no idea what stopped me from jumping the counter and strangling him right then and there. But when I calmed down, I decided to ask how much I owed.

"That will be eight hundred Quazaran dollars. Or one thousand space quid."

"What?" I think my mouth was beginning to froth. "The parcel didn't even cost that much. Why the hell is it so much?"

Farnan checked his clipboard for that information. "The customer—you, I presume—requested extreme rush delivery. Therefore, the Post initiated the most direct line of delivery. The cost reflects the method of delivery. Nothing more, nothing less."

He went on to explain that "the most direct line of delivery" had involved shipping the parcel in its own state-of-the-art space pod, which flew many times the speed of light without breaks from the point of origin to the point of destination. What made this method so sophisticated, and so absurdly expensive, is that the pod was programmed to burn, drill, cut, or otherwise obliterate any obstacle in its way. This exact pod, the flight path record indicated, had found a way to penetrate a yellow sun.

Somehow that did seem to justify the price. I swallowed my anger and proceeded to pay—until I realized that I had left my money clip next to my ID in my bedroom.

"Son of a b—"

"The bill will be credited to your account," Farnan said. "Is there anything else I can help you with, loyal customer?"

I should have been content to leave with my parcel in hand, but I still didn't feel right about exiting without giving the Mackmian something to remember me by.

"Next time, remind me to beat the skinny back into you," I said.

I turned around and began walking through the partially destroyed chamber. I stepped through a shadowy section only to look down at the horrible pink helmet glowing brilliantly in the dark. "Son of a…!"

"Thank you for your business," I heard the Mackmian say behind me.

I ignored the taunt, placed my pink helmet under my arm, and proceeded out into the station.

CHAPTER EIGHT

Stonesend

After that frustrating stint with the Mackmian from hell, I completely forgot to gather information as to why the aliens had attacked the station in the first place. For all I knew it had simply been to beat some pretty back into Farnan—if it were true, I found it harder and harder to fault them for it.

"Mara, this is Zenith," I called into my intercom.

The speaker crackled, fizzled, wheezed, and possibly even belched before I was able to pick up the first trace of her voice.

"Say again, Mara?"

Again, the crackling... it was all I could do not to pull out my pistol and blast holes in the walls. Fortunately, Mara's voice finally came through.

"Come in, Captain."

"Yeah," I said in a surly voice. "I've finished up at the Post. How are Bog and Stairn doing so far?"

"I'm happy to hear it. Stairn and Bog returned to *Orbital* a few minutes ago. They were successful at meeting their objectives too."

"Good. I'm returning now. Have Bog join you. I want to see both of you at the docking bay."

As I strolled through the station's deserted corridors, I found myself in an odd and quickly changing mood. In one hand I carried the hot pink helmet of doom while in the other, broken hand, I gingerly held the parcel that I hoped would change my life forever.

That was if it contained what I prayed it contained. I'd never wanted a piece of jewellery so badly in my life.

I soon returned to the initial hallway where we'd met all that carnage a mere hour ago. I could still see Stairn's handiwork—the dead aliens curled up and obliterated on the floor. I stepped over the gooey black mess, feeling it squish underneath my feet when my last step didn't extend quite as far as it needed to. Shit!

In as masculine a manner as possible, I pirouetted up and over the last of the alien goo and made my way back to the platform from which I could step back aboard *Orbital*.

First, I slammed on the dented pink, glow-in-the-dark helmet, careful to avoid hair damage. As soon as the helmet touched my blue suit, I ran my finger across the edges to seal them together.

When the connection was made, I noticed a strange shimmering sight from the corner of my eye. The walls were beginning to glow and become ever so slightly transparent. Surprised, I looked down at my gloved hand. The image in my visor blurred and soon I found myself able to look through the glove and see the skin of the unmangled hand.

A moment later, I was seeing even deeper, down into the muscles. Then I perceived the skeletal outline of my hand. I closed my hand and watched the bones curl up into a ball. Cool! Somehow Mara's pink helmet had the ability to see in X-ray vision! Even in the year 2500, it was an unusual portable ability.

Next, I looked at my broken hand, giving the helmet a few seconds to readjust into X-ray mode. I winced at the image that soon appeared. Not only were the bones broken, but they were also misaligned. And my pinkie was a shattered mess.

I looked towards the entrance to *Orbital* and noticed the view go back to normal. It seemed the helmet only went into X-ray mode when I was studying something very intently.

I decided at that point to get back to *Orbital* and find out how the rest of my crew had fared. The doors hissed open, allowing me to enter the docking bay chamber unobstructed.

When I stepped inside, Mara was there to greet me. Her face was alight with a big smile. Her green eyes glowed like emerald jewels. Behind her was Bog, looking like a giant wraith covered in soot. Otherwise he looked unharmed.

My gaze drifted back to Mara. As I stepped closer, the visor shifted into X-ray mode. Before my very eyes, her clothing magically vanished and soon I could see her naked form. Her face wasn't the only part of her body to be blushing…

To my surprise, there was no underwear to be seen. Surprising and sexy! And being the gentleman of good taste I was, I stepped closer to get a better look. I didn't even notice at first that she was talking to me.

It had been a mistake to step closer, because as soon as I did my helmet went deeper than the skin and showed me her musculature. I stepped back a half pace and she returned to the sleek vision I was beginning to appreciate more and more.

With regret, I looked up at her face and realized that I had completely missed everything she'd been saying. I think she suspected I wasn't able to hear her for some reason, because she tried to remove my helmet.

I stepped back quickly, not yet ready to give up my new superpower. It felt like my day was finally taking a turn for the good.

Sensing my apprehension at having the helmet removed, Mara stepped away, giving me a brief glimpse of Bog without a uniform and undies. Holy shit! I was quick to turn my head to avert any further visuals. That was a close one! Bog was even more intimidating without clothing!

I removed the helmet for good measure. When I managed to come back to my senses, I noticed both Mara and Bog staring at me with some worry on their faces. I told them that everything was fine and then proceeded to the control hub.

We entered the control hub a few minutes later. Sparling and Stairn were already at their stations, engaged in their regular duties.

"Report," I said, still a little shaken. "What's happening?"

"Captain, sir." Sparling's young, tanned face looked surprisingly pale. She knew something I didn't, and that worried me. "Our sensors have detected several ships on direct intercept with us."

"How many ships?" Stairn had mentioned as much before we jumped aboard the station.

"Five, sir. They'll arrive within minutes."

"What else can you tell me about them?"

"They're shrouded, Captain, but our sensors and spatial attenuators can detect them on a microscopic level."

"Sparling, take a few deep breaths." I waited for her to do so. I needed her to regain her composure. "Tell me everything about those ships that you can. Do they belong to the same alien species that attacked us? Or are they more Mackmian garbage frigates?"

She shook her head. "Something is very strange. The ships are emitting a strong energy field that's distorting our sensors. Whatever they are, I cannot yet tell."

Suddenly, Stairn brought up an image of the *Tanslen*.

"Open a channel to the *Tanslen*," I said.

"It's open," Stairn replied.

Captain Ambden's symmetrically round face blurred into view. "Captain Zenith?"

"Captain Ambden..." I did my best to hide my growing anxiety. "It's been an interesting afternoon."

"That it has, Captain. Moon, stars, and planets our way."

Again, I had no idea what the hell he was referring to, but I let the odd greeting slide by without comment.

"Tell me, friend, do your scanners pick up anything unusual approaching?" I asked.

Ambden gave me a look of incomprehension. "Our scanners pick up nothing."

"Well then, here's the scoop. There appear to be five ships on their way towards us. Our scanners can see minimally through their shrouds, but we can't read anything beyond their existence at this point."

Ambden's giant wrinkly eyebrow lifted in an enormous arch. Thick, solid strands of brown hair protruded from each eyebrow. I think I even saw some hairs poking out of his forehead. I would need to have a chat with him about grooming when time allowed.

For now, that was going to have to wait.

"What's your suggestion, Captain?" he asked.

He must have known that his presence here in the system was unnecessary—indeed, unrecommended and against protocol. As soon as the battle had begun, Ambden's only task should have been to locate the wounded and fly them out of here, not returning unless instructed to do so.

"Captain, hold tight for now. Be ready to depart if I give you the signal." I relayed to the Mackmian. I tried to keep the urgency in my voice down to a controlled level.

Ambden responded with a nod. I gave Stairn the cue, and he temporarily shut down our communications link to the *Tanslen*.

I turned to Mara. "Have you relayed our situation to Militia High Command?"

She nodded in confirmation. "The high marshal was very distressed."

"Clearly the ships aren't ours," I mused aloud, more or less talking to myself. "We've only got three…"

I paced the cold metallic floor, beginning to miss the feel of shag carpeting beneath my feet. I hadn't expected a new enemy to come our way so soon.

"The way I see it, we have few options," I continued, my voice infused with natural confidence. "Those ships will be here momentarily, and I believe it's too late for us or the *Tanslen* to escape." I glanced at Sparling. "How fast are they travelling?"

"Three parsec-seconds, sir."

"That fast?" Mara said with some despair.

"Well then," I said. "That removes one option, doesn't it…"

In other words, we couldn't retreat. And even if we could, no way in a dog's dirty hell was I going to abandon the black hole I had so valiantly saved just a couple of hours ago. No, fleeing wasn't an option.

"A battle may be imminent," I concluded. "Which means we need to put ourselves in the best tactical position."

I looked at the main viewscreen and peered into the blackness of space. Even the stars nearest us did little to shed light on the situation.

I shook my pessimism away. This was no time for philosophy.

"Tactically speaking," I continued, "the best and perhaps only option at this point is to take a three-point precision stance."

My good hand clutched the handrail next to me. A few metres over, Mara was seated at her controls. Visions of the space station blurred across her screen.

"Captain, that would be a mistake," Stairn spoke up. "Multiple precision stances only work when all points or vessels have proficient weapons capability. I don't believe it's safe to assume Ambden's ship has any to speak of, and the space station absolutely does not."

I shook my head in disagreement. "That doesn't matter, Stairn. Our enemies don't know that. We need to seek the maximum advantage."

"But you're assuming they are, in fact, enemies," Mara stated. "We don't know that, either."

I dismissed Mara's take on the situation. She possessed no training in tactics. "Please, Mara, let the professionals handle this."

The look she gave me probably would have melted and then refrozen ice, but I hardly noticed.

"But isn't Mara correct?" Sparling cut in, meekly. I could see the look of uncertainty reflected in her eyes. She didn't normally contradict me. "We really don't know at this point if the ships are h–h–hostile."

I looked down at her and her voice faltered. She glanced away, afraid to continue.

"Bog, what is our battle status?" I asked despite not looking forward to the answer.

"I'd like to say there's good news and bad news." Bog paused. "But that would be a big fat lie. There's only bad news."

"But we have weapons, correct?"

"None that work properly."

"And what about the hull cannons?"

"Yes, that's one of two weapon possibilities."

"And the second?"

"The second is to get out and personally give their windshields a scrubbing." Bog's voice dripped with sarcasm. "*Orbital* is in rough shape."

"How rough?" I asked.

Stairn chose that moment to pull out his digital clipboard again. "Well, let's see…"

It quickly became evident that he was going to launch into a long and detailed list of the damage *Orbital* had sustained. When the hell had he found the time to put all this together?

Note to Brant Zenith: find out if Stairn has a twin aboard. His uncanny skill is really quite disconcerting.

"Portside hull at forty-eight percent, starboard side hull at fifty-two percent…"

At first, I listened intently to the report, but it quickly made me ill and I found myself zoning out.

"…men's latrine, third deck, at seventeen percent…"

I didn't know how a latrine could be at seventeen percent, but I wasn't in the mood to find out.

"…energy barriers are at three percent…"

Why had the men's latrine come earlier on his list than the energy barriers? I wanted to ask the question but managed to hold my tongue.

"…ballistic space torpedoes at negative seventy-five percent—"

"Wait," I interrupted. "How the hell can ballistic torpedoes be at negative seventy-five percent?"

Stairn pressed a button on his clipboard and pulled up the pertinent information. "Well, it would seem that a fire erupted in the weapons bay. One of the ballistic space torpedoes exploded, and now the torpedoes have been reduced to mere debris. It also appears that the torpedo generator has been damaged. There's no way to fix it."

"So let me get this straight," I said. "The battle caused the fire, which caused a torpedo to explode, which then caused the torpedo generator to sustain damage. Is that right?"

I thought I already knew the answer. I was wrong.

This time Stairn didn't even need to look at his clipboard. "Indeed, Captain, you are incorrect. It would seem that the battle had no direct impact on the weapons bay. It appears that someone or something left the bingo machine plugged into the same outlet as the generator."

"Oh, God," I muttered to myself, knowing full well what was coming next.

"This shorted out the circuits and started the fire," Stairn concluded. "A fire which spread to the ballistic torpedoes themselves. When that happened, the entire bay erupted. Everything inside was destroyed."

Note to Brant Zenith: we should probably relocate bingo to the medical bay...

"So, bottom line," I said. "What the hell is *Orbital*'s status?"

"The only thing holding *Orbital* together is rust, paint, and fate," Bog remarked wryly.

"Fate probably thinks it's crueller to leave *Orbital* intact," I murmured, looking around the more or less unscathed control hub. "I still think the three-point precision stance is our best tactical option."

"Captain, point stances will pin us in one spot," Stairn pointed out. He sounded so sure of himself. "It makes better sense to remain fluid and maintain proximity to the containment rings. Those should be our first and last concern."

I don't know if it was because I was sure of my tactics or if it was just to spite Stairn, but I found myself wanting to argue the point further.

"You're wrong, Stairn. Movement will only add an unknown factor into the mix—"

"Uh, Captain," Sparling interrupted.

"Just a moment—"

"Captain, your tactics are flawed," Stairn persisted with more intensity than before. "Remaining stationary would be a mistake. If we keep moving—"

"Stairn, you're a freakin' logistics officer. Tactically speaking, you're as useful as another pail of sand in the desert!"

Despite his earlier heroics, I was beginning to hate Stairn. He looked so tidy and pompous in his perfectly pressed uniform. I didn't even know when he'd had time to change.

Sparling tried to cut in again. "Captain—"

"Not now!" I snapped at her.

"Captain, I speak the truth," Stairn argued. "Anger will not help the situation—"

"Captain!" Sparling spoke one last time.

Spit flew from my mouth as I whirled around to face the pilot. "What?!"

"Those ships are now here," she whispered, activating the main viewscreen to show all five vessels now within firing range. They were unshrouded now and flying in a spearhead formation.

"Aww, for shit's sake!" I spat out, suddenly recognizing them. "Get Captain Ambden back on the line."

A moment later, the Mackmian's face displaced the image of the alien ships on the viewscreen. Ambden's face showed a high level of excitement.

"Galaxies align, and stars illuminate the heavens," the captain stated most joyously.

I hadn't a dog's clue what that was supposed to mean, but I too felt my previous tension dissipate. Indeed, now that we had both gotten a good look at the incoming ships, it was clear that these were not enemies.

They were allies from the Prime Star Force.

"Captain, the lead ship has opened a com link with us," Sparling reported.

"Put them through."

Orbital's viewscreen split in two. Ambden's face now occupied the left half of the screen. The face that appeared on the right side took me completely by surprise.

"Jonah Alexandre!" I had to take a quick breath to recover. "What the hell are you doing here?"

"I'm just here to say hello," said my old friend. "And to see if you need any help cleaning up this mess."

It was a rare occurrence that I ran into anyone from the Prime Star Force I could tolerate. This time, luck wasn't looking to kick me squarely in the front of the trousers.

"I see the high council has managed to pull their heads out of each other's asses long enough to promote you to captain," I said, genuinely pleased. "And of a Stellarcap-1, eh? All the way to the top of the fleet, my good man!"

Jonah was a gifted officer and brilliant tactician, but being promoted to a Stellarcap-1 was next level. Only the most decorated officers held that honour.

I quickly looked down at my armrest screen and brought forth some of the ship's technical specs that the Militia was entitled to. Its name was *Stonesend*, which I found curious. In Prime, a new ship was usually named for its primary sponsor—or at least, that's how it used to be. Embarrassingly, the first ship Jonah, Bog, and I had ever served on together had been called the *Ollyman*, named for a company that produced erectile dysfunction pills and haemorrhoid creams. Putting that on my resume had hurt the ego.

Thankfully, it was all in the past. And now it seemed Prime may have changed its policies. I wondered, could Jonah have selected it? It certainly wasn't the name of any company I'd ever heard of.

I looked at my friend closely, seeking to determine how the last seven years had treated him. He was still slightly stockier than average, but he was a handsome man with black hair, dark eyes, and pearly white teeth. He looked quite dashing in his Prime uniform. Even if it was the official uniform of hell, the navy blue and white pinned-up suitcoats were quite remarkable. The five metal clips denoting Jonah's rank were linked to the top of his coat's front. For some reason it occurred to me that those clips looked more like a stitched-up scar than a badge of authority. But who was I to criticize? Every time I stepped into my golden-tasselled uniform, I looked like I should be walking down the street with a trumpet in hand!

"I see you two know each other," Ambden remarked. "Small galaxies and smaller universe open to us all."

This time I could actually decipher the cryptic Mackmian expression.

"That we do, Captain Ambden," Jonah replied with modest enthusiasm. "Our reports show that the situation here has been temporarily stabilized. So I think a quick but formal sit down is called for, my fellow captains. Please choose a companion or two and relay your coordinates to my communications officer so we may energy-trance your way over here."

"I agree, Captain," I stated formally. "Be prepared to transport three from *Orbital*'s docking bay momentarily."

"Light and energy guides our way within this universe," said Ambden. "Please transport myself and my son Simbden aboard your ship when convenient."

As Jonah nodded his approval, his image blurred off the viewscreen.

I looked over at both Mara and Bog and requested that they join me aboard the *Stonesend*. Mara was the ship's ambassador, making her selection inevitable. But I wanted to bring Bog along for a couple of reasons, the first being that Jonah was still his friend as well. The second reason? He was my security officer, of course, and the jackasses employed by Prime were less likely to give me unnecessary grief if Bog was glowering over my shoulder like a demonic grizzly bear.

I led the way back to our increasingly popular docking bay. I left my spacesuit on since I didn't have the time to change into my typical captain's garb. Even if I'd had time, no way in hell was I going to let Jonah see me in that outfit.

Even though it was great to see my friend again, I wanted to make our stay as short as possible; my hand was beginning to ache something fierce, and I simply didn't want a long, lasting reminder about how spectacular Prime spaceships were.

As we entered the docking bay, I noticed that Bog, too, had remained dressed in his spacesuit while Mara wore her standard duty uniform. Technically we didn't need spacesuits anyway, since energy-trance transportation—usually just referred to as ETT—wouldn't expose us to the hostile conditions of space. The technology created an energy tunnel which linked to distant points of origin. The process required antimatter to be harnessed to expedite the transport of solid matter. While in the tunnel, the matter no longer existed in the universe, per se, and therefore wasn't subject to the laws of physics.

I had been trying to get *Orbital's* energy-trance device repaired and functioning again, but I'd been told to wait four to six weeks. And that was two years ago!

Such rapid transportation was an extremely technical and complicated affair, one that made me wish I could directly scratch my brain when I was done thinking about it. Honestly it scared the hell out of me, even though the sequence was nearly instantaneous. It wasn't exactly painful, but it felt sort of like being vacuumed down into a sink drain.

I swear it made me feel lighter, too; no one ever believed me, but it seemed like something on my person always ended up vanishing when I got to the other side. Like a sock or my underwear...

The last time I'd gone through the ETT, I had lost both legs of my vintage alligator skin parka pants. Do you have any idea how cold it gets on the fourth moon of Teln when you arrive on the ski hill with two and a half naked legs dangling out in the snow? I had been lucky to escape with my life!

I guess that was why I preferred black rift energy transporters, but that newer technology was hard to acquire and damned costly. It was typically used by people individually or in very small groups. I wish I had kept some black rift energy in reserve for emergency escapes.

I had Mara communicate directly with *Stonesend* so they could initiate the ETT sequence.

As the brilliant blue and red light shone, I perceived a hollow tube extended towards us from the Prime ship. We stood waiting for it to encapsulate us. Then I felt the peculiar shimmering sensation as the light absorbed me. It felt like a full body massage.

I slammed my eyes closed, anticipating the next disconcerting part of the process. When my eyes were open, I could actually see matter being picked apart within the tube, micron by micron—well, until my vision blurred as the eyes themselves were converted into an antimatter state.

A moment later, Mara, Bog, and I found ourselves in the bowels of the *Stonesend*. The giant room we landed in, large enough to house the entirety of *Orbital*, amazed me. The room was surrounded by at least twenty equidistant banks of equipment designed to facilitate the ETT effect, each one monitored by a security robot, a technician, and what looked to be a junior officer.

The large room looked fairly industrial, with metallic pillars and beams sectioning off the stations perfectly. The walls were a cold grey with little in the way of decoration.

My attention found its way onto one of the robots. It had a humanoid body, although its core had square-like dimensions and had been engraved with insignias which I couldn't decode. Its arms were piston-like extrusions with five digits from the metallic hands. The head was rectangular with a thin mouth and a visor that burned green; the colour, however, varied from one robot to the next, with others glowing blue, yellow, red, or deathly black. The colour seemed to presage what level of dismay you'd feel if you had a run-in with one of these creatures. If you saw it change to black, I think you could pretty well kiss your favourite body parts goodbye.

About a nanosecond after our arrival, one of the ETT platforms across from us whirred to life. A moment later, we found ourselves in the company of Captain Ambden and his son Simbden. I hadn't yet been given the opportunity to meet Simbden, but I knew he was in his mid-teens and had eight brothers and twelve sisters. Mackmians loved to breed, which is probably another reason I'd always liked their race so much.

I stepped forward to greet the Mackmians when one of the junior officers halted me with a haughty hand gesture. He was hardly an imposing figure. If he weighed more than a bowling ball, I would have been surprised. Even the thin black moustache planted directly in the centre of his pockmarked face annoyed me.

"Halt, visitors!" the officer said in a squeaky voice.

Bog took a step forward and the nearest robot's visor flashed red.

I must give Bog some credit here. Instead of mashing this imperious little fellow into mush, the Nova Martian looked to me for guidance in the matter. A big part of me wanted to see the officer reduced to paste—

—but Mara didn't give me a chance to voice an opinion. She reached up and placed a calming hand on Bog's shoulder. That was enough to end the confrontation before it began. I felt a bit disappointed. I'd wanted to see who would win between a single-minded killing machine and a robot. I'd probably find out eventually. If not today, then another day.

Bog stepped back and the robot's visor first turned yellow, then green.

"What brings you aboard the *Stonesend*?" asked the junior officer, seemingly unaware of how close he'd come to meeting an ugly demise.

Mara stepped forward and stopped beside me. "We were summoned by Captain Alexandre."

"I have no record of that. What are your names?"

Again, Mara took the initiative. She was really taking the fun out of going out.

"This is Captain Brant Zenith of the Militia spaceship *Orbital*," she said by way of introductions. "The man behind him is Lieutenant Bog, our chief of security. My name is Mara Olwen, and I'm our ship's ambassador."

The junior officer didn't even make eye contact. "Identification, if you would."

This was starting to give me a sense of déjà vu...

Mara smoothly pulled out our IDs, a stinging reminder that once again I had forgotten my own. Indeed, Bog was in the same situation, patting down the front of his uniform to find something that wasn't there.

I was glad at least Mara had thought ahead.

The junior officer took a few moments to scan our cards and then handed them back. He then walked up to a computer screen and began reading the information that appeared on it.

"Here it is," he said. "The captain has just cleared you. You're free to follow Security Robot 102 to the fourth deck's ambassadorial chamber."

Just as we were about to proceed, the officer raised his hand—right in Bog's face, close enough that my friend could have bitten it off. Or simply barbecued it if he'd breathed too heavily.

Mara reacted with lightning speed, pushing her way past me to stand between the horribly mismatched men.

"You must check your weapons with me here and now," said the little guy with a tenuous grip on life.

I half-suspected Bog might reach over Mara, palm the officer's greasy head, and throw him across the room. To my surprise, Bog merely stepped back a few paces.

This was becoming quite interesting. I wished I had brought popcorn.

"We aren't giving up our weapons," I stated flatly.

The officer looked backward to make sure Security Robot 102 was nearby. He cleared his throat. "You will give up your weapons or our security will remove them from you."

"They can try," I muttered.

"Remove your weapons or we will," the man said. There was a slight whistle between the gap in his teeth. "And then you'll be taken to the brig."

I stepped forward, making sure that the man knew who was in control of the situation. "I have to be honest with you, Junior. There is very little chance I'm leaving my weapon with you or your buddy here."

"First off, my name is not Junior," the man snarled back. "I'm Sci-Corporal Adamly. And second, you are guests of the *Stonesend*. You have no authority to make demands."

Mara leaned forward to whisper into my ear. "Brant, what are you doing?"

"Relax, I have this under control," I replied.

"That's exactly what I'm worried about."

I turned my attention back to the junior officer. "Junior, you're making this very tedious. Let us pass through and you can go back to doing whatever it is you think you do all day long when you're not whistling at visitors and staring at yourself in the reflective screens."

Mara sighed loudly.

"My name is Sci-Corporal Adamly!" the man answered, his voice dripping with vehemence. God, this was fun! "There's no chance of you going anywhere. Except the brig."

He stared directly at Mara this time, and I noticed her face flush. She was probably thinking about how best to punish me for this one.

Security Robot 102's visor seemed to have gotten stuck in a constant cycle between yellow and red. I almost felt sorry for the big bot.

"Buddy, there's really no reason to get hot under your scrawny collar," I said, striking the right balance between indifference and superiority.

Sci-Corporal Adamly started to shake with anger.

"You have no authority here, Militia man." With that, Adamly offered the least charming smile I'd ever seen.

One final push was all this situation needed. "Listen, Junior, why don't you run along and get Captain Alexandre down here? That way we can deal with someone worth talking to."

"Captain!" Mara hissed into my ear.

I did indeed have a purpose to my actions other than belittling this self-righteous junior officer. I knew for certain that if we left our weapons with Adamly, we would never see them again. That wouldn't have been so bad if I had brought along my propulsion gun, but in fact I carried the spark weapon I'd picked up on the space station. No way was I giving that up.

Another reason for my provocation was to assess Prime's reaction to even mild hostility. I didn't trust Prime, and we'd had few chances so far to test our latest treaty. I knew that if we were thrown in the brig, it would serve as a perfect test.

Meanwhile, Adamly had begun his final descent into frustration. His little frame swayed from side to side as he fidgeted with something under his uniform. A moment later, he pulled out a laser pistol and pointed it directly at Mara.

Shit! Well, that certainly hadn't been part of my plan.

"Whoa, Junior!" I raised my hands into the air. "There's no need for such hostilities now, is there?"

I brushed up against Mara and placed myself between her and the pistol. I could see that Adamly had his weapon set to maximum burn, meaning that if he fired the laser would burn through both of us, and probably even through the hull of the ship.

Perhaps I'd gone a little too far.

Note to Brant Zenith: junior Prime officers are touchier than I expected. Perhaps a little more tact is in order next time.

Adamly stepped forward and shifted the gun to aim right at my head. He got to within a foot, allowing me to see all the way down the barrel to the brightly lit actuator. This was a formidably well-crafted pistol. Not as flashy as the one that had nearly exploded in my face and robbed this portion of the galaxy from some seriously masculine beauty. But it was still a fine weapon.

"Your time aboard the *Stonesend* has been extended indefinitely, Militia man!" he sneered. I could tell he was battling with himself—to pull the trigger or not? I couldn't read which way he would go. Perhaps I had pushed too hard this time?

I smiled as handsomely as God had ever intended a human to smile. And if he did pull the trigger? Well, at least Mara was no longer in the line of fire.

"All of you get, down on your knees," Adamly yelled.

I noted that Security Robot 102's visor had gone black.

Following his orders would have been the wise decision, but I chose a different approach. My hands were already lifted to nearly the same height as the pistol and only inches away. Rookie move for Adamly to not adjust his position. With a snap of my left hand, I grabbed the pistol from his grasp before he could let loose a shot.

A half-second later, I had turned the pistol back on its owner.

At that moment, every security robot in the vicinity began to descend on us like a stampede. Their visors shone black. I knew that all the bots in the world wouldn't be able to save Adamly if I decided to squeeze the trigger. I could practically hear his heart fall as he realized it.

On the other hand, I had no idea what I was going to do next. I had meant to stir up a wee little bit of trouble, but somehow I'd gotten us in a really ugly position; indeed, Security Robot 102 had just converted one of his hands into a huge canon of a weapon. Intimidating arsenal. I recognized some of the red-coated electronic wiring and knew they weren't prone to misfire.

Bog had raised his weapon to Adamly's torso. I gave Bog credit for the choice. As long as one of us had Adamly in our sights, I figured we still had a chance.

"All Prime officers, stand down!"

The voice boomed from the loudspeakers in the ceiling. The entire room, crawling with beings both biological and robotic, seemed to freeze. The robots shifted into yellow mode and returned to their stations.

The next few tense seconds passed more slowly than a kidney stone through a Mackmian hippo.

"Stand down now," growled Captain Jonah Alexandre as he stalked into the room, descending a bank of steel stairs.

"Bog, I think you can lower your weapon now," I said through a tight-lipped smile.

Bog obeyed and holstered his weapon.

"These members of the Militia Space Fleet are our distinguished allies and guests," Jonah announced as he closed the last twenty metres between us. Before I could extend my hand to him, he continued. "If you don't mind, Captain, please return the weapon to Sci-Corporal Adamly and turn over your own weapons to me. Now."

Jonah's face was calm, but his tone carried enough authority to ensure my acquiescence and I found myself doing as I was told. No way would I make trouble personally with Jonah. Even if I'd wanted to, this was certainly not the time.

I deactivated Adamly's laser pistol, putting it in recharge mode. It would take ten minutes to reactivate. He snatched it back from me, a look of pure loathing on his face.

Next, we handed our weapons over to Jonah as ordered.

"Now, Captain," said Jonah, "you and your colleagues can accompany me to the ambassadorial chamber." Not waiting for an answer, he quickly stepped over to Ambden and Simbden, whom I'd forgotten about. "Please, Captain. Would you and your son follow me as well?"

The five of us weaved our way back to that steel staircase, robots staring at us all the way through their yellow visors.

Once we were up to the stairs, we left the room and entered an enormous corridor. Its design was similar to the corridors I remembered from the *Ollyman* except it reached approximately four metres in height and twice that in width. The corridors were pleasantly lit with a blue tinge and the walls showcased assorted screens and charts.

We followed this main corridor for about two minutes before veering down a secondary branch that varied in colour and size. Soon we stepped onto an elevator platform and began our ascent.

Jonah was silent, his face taut with concern, and I felt the need to break the silence.

"So, Jonah, what's it like being the second-best captain in the galaxy?"

He ignored me. I was beginning to feel like a schoolboy sitting in the principal's office.

When we arrived at the ambassadorial chamber, the door opened in a corkscrew fashion and I found myself face to face with a heavenly vision. The beautiful blonde seemed to have been personally sculpted by God. About twenty-five years ago, if I didn't miss my guess. And by her uniform, I judged her to be Jonah's second-in-command.

"My friends, welcome aboard the *Stonesend*," Jonah said as he positioned himself next to the ravishing beauty. "I'd like to introduce you to my first lieutenant, Marissa Monroe."

I stepped forward and extended my hand to hers. Instead of a hearty shake, I brought it to my mouth and let loose the kiss of the heavens upon it. I looked into her perfect blue eyes and felt sure she must be mesmerized by my presence.

The first five words out of her mouth would have swelled the heart of the devil himself.

"It is a pleasure, Captain," she said.

Monroe was a tall woman and stood nearly at eye level to me. Her long blonde hair was tied back, and her pale face had a beautiful cast of red.

After a moment, I heard Mara clear her throat with impatience. I regrettably stepped back and turned my attention to Jonah.

Before I could react, he gave me a strong embrace. Instantly I felt as though nothing had changed between us. We were once more just friends living out our dreams aboard a starship.

I saluted him. "Honour in all actions."

"God smiles upon the brave," he said, saluting in reply.

I completed the salutation: "And the devil takes the rest."

We'd spoken this exchange to each other thousands of times when we were growing up, but the others didn't know our history—well, except Bog of course. Monroe looked at us like we were on Cloobian space cocaine.

When the moment of male camaraderie was complete, I stepped aside and introduced Mara to Jonah.

"I'm pleased to meet you, Mara," he said. "I've heard plenty of great things about you. Perhaps most remarkable is that you've kept this rapscallion out of prison for so long."

Ambden took it upon himself to introduce his son. As I shook Simbden's hand gently, I noticed a couple of key features that really stood out. Simbden was a noteworthy five feet, eight inches. For a race that rarely measured five feet, unless you measured them sideways, this was a remarkable height.

"Captain Zenith, it is truly an honour to meet you." Simbden pumped my hand furiously, and I nearly cried from the sudden pain in my broken hand. Somehow, I endured. "I have studied all your adventures since your days on the *Ollyman*."

It was nice to finally have a fan. "Well, thank you, Simbden."

"Please, everyone take a seat," Jonah stated quickly.

It seemed we had a schedule to keep.

When everyone was appropriately seated around the room's central table, Jonah began speaking once more. "First off, I must congratulate all of you on your brave, decisive actions today. We have access to the Quazar station security feeds and witnessed firsthand many of the events which occurred on and around the station. Very well done." He nodded once in my direction. "You may not know just how important that victory will prove to be."

Jonah gestured to Monroe, who stood and activated the viewscreen situated at the end of the long room.

"This isn't the first time these specific aliens have found their way into the Quazar quadrant," she said.

"Really?" Mara asked.

"Yes, Ambassador." Monroe brought up an image of an alien spacecraft. It was different from the three we'd battled earlier but shared many of the same design elements. "This image was taken by the station's equipment three weeks ago. It would seem that their first foray into our quadrant went almost completely unnoticed. It's taken us some time to piece together this ship's voyage, since it did nothing to provoke any reaction. That is, until two days ago."

Monroe looked over to Jonah, who nodded his assent for her to continue with the next phase of the briefing.

"Two days ago, we found the ship again, this time laying tiny orbs of energy throughout this region of space. These orbs hardly emit any energy, don't show on our sensors, and are only about a hand's width in size. They almost escaped our notice until the *Malevolent* brushed up against one unintentionally, nearly obliterating the ship."

"What exactly are these orbs about?" I asked, genuinely intrigued.

"That's still under investigation," Jonah said, a bit more evasively than I would have liked. "What we can tell you is that these orbs contain more than enough energy to mimic a small red star. We don't know for what purpose they have been deployed. But if they're turned into weapons, I daresay we need to take concern of them."

"And now this attack," Monroe broke in. "Again, we don't know what to make of it."

Bog leaned forward, the chair under him seeming to groan at him with its creaking under his considerable weight. "What about the ship that laid those orbs?"

"It's vanished once more," Monroe said. "It remains a mystery."

"What is Prime's objective?" I asked.

"That, my friend, I cannot answer for now," Jonah said. "My current objective, though, is to escort you and Ambden back to Prime Station Alpha to review the situation with my superiors."

Bog seemed incredulous. "And leave the spoils to Prime?"

"Do not fear, Bog," Jonah assured him. "I promise that no salvaging will take place without the Militia's involvement. After our meeting, we will know better what is to become of this situation. Prime's only orders thus far have been to secure the region and begin deploying medical and engineering crews to ensure the safety of all who work nearby. Two medical transports have already been dispatched to care for the wounded aboard the station. And as far as the alien threat goes, whatever happens, they'll be met with overwhelming force. You have my word on that."

After a brief lull, Monroe turned the discussion back to the mysterious orbs of energy. Little was known about them. In fact, if the *Malevolent* hadn't bumped into one, it seemed no one would have been the wiser.

"What kind of damage did the *Malevolent* sustain?" Mara asked.

"There were no traces of an actual explosion," the first lieutenant explained. "But large portions of the ship simply vanished."

"An alien form of ETT?" I asked.

"No. I don't think so," Jonah said. "For all intents and purposes, the structure was left intact. But internal sections of the ship are gone. They don't exist."

Mara narrowed her eyes in confusion. "That doesn't make sense. How can parts of a ship cease to exist while the ship itself remains intact?"

"The crew has tried to explore the 'missing' sections," Monroe said. "Their exploratory implements stopped transmitting when they entered the void, only to resurface at random times, completely altered on a subatomic level. No one dared go so far as to send a living being into those sections."

I smiled to myself. "Someone should have tried sending Sci-Corporal Adamly."

Monroe ignored me and changed the subject. "I think this would be a good time to conclude our meeting, if there aren't any further questions." There were none. "All other concerns will be addressed when we get to Prime Station Alpha."

"I'll escort you personally back to the ETT bay," Jonah said as we stood up from our seats.

My friend led us out of the ambassadorial chamber and back down the secondary corridor that had brought us there. Monroe followed along with the Mackmians.

"Don't you trust me to find the bay by ourselves?" I asked, but even I couldn't keep a straight face. Jonah didn't react to the remark.

I looked over at Mara and saw that she had fallen into conversation with Ambden and Simbden about the crew capacity of garbage frigates. I felt no desire to join in on that.

"Brant, if you don't mind…" Jonah held me back a few paces as Monroe and Bog led the others onward towards the ETT bay. When we were outside of earshot, he spoke. "That scene you created with Adamly earlier could have been disastrous."

"Ah… well, you know…" I shrugged, unexpectedly feeling a little sheepish for some reason.

"Yeah, I do know. If I hadn't been expecting something like that to happen, I might have been picking up pieces of you, Mara, and Bog off the floor right now."

"That would have been a shame," I said sarcastically.

He smiled. "You're right. Losing a woman of Mara's quality would have been a catastrophe."

"What I meant is that it would have been a waste of manpower. Picking up pieces of Bog would have overrun Prime's budget for the year."

Jonah began to laugh. He handed me back the weapons, and I noticed that he'd activated a sophisticated disabler that would ensure that the weapons couldn't be used until we were back aboard *Orbital*. It was an old Prime tactic they'd taught us in the first year of the Academy.

We continued walking.

"Do me a favour," he said.

"Sure thing, buddy. What do you need?"

"When we get back down to the bay, keep your ego in check. Your anger, too. I don't want to clean up another disaster."

"I wouldn't trigger any sort of disaster—"

"You know you would. And it would mean a lot to me if you tried not to rub Adamly the wrong way again." I wanted to object, but he cut me short. "I know he comes off pompous, but it stems from his lack of confidence. I only tell you this because you and I have been friends so long. Adamly is a good officer. I've only recently transferred him to the ETT bay, and I did it to help build his confidence. Your actions today could have done a lot of harm. Don't start another fight—ever."

I could tell that he was extremely serious about this. I had to admire his protective stance when it came to the members of his crew. I touched my chin in thought. Would I have done the same?

"I promise that I won't rub Adamly the wrong way." I almost meant it. The man really did bother me on a level I hadn't expected.

"Good. Thank you."

Minutes later, we found ourselves back in the ETT bay, standing on the same platform where we had arrived only an hour earlier. Adamly stood at his station, his face bright red.

"Status, Corporal Adamly," Jonah said.

"ETT Module 102 working within optimal conditions." The junior officer's voice was still squeaky.

"Good." Jonah extended his hand to mine and bid me farewell. "In two days, my friend."

I winced as he squeezed my hand. It hurt like a bugger. "Until then."

I was about to make my way over to bid adieu to Monroe, but she was busy chatting with Bog. And not just chatting! The two were giggling about something! Well, Bog's giggling sounded more like a rock sifter struggling to grind through a boulder, but they seemed to be enjoying some type of moment together.

Seconds later, she was well on her way out of the bay. Damn.

When I looked at Bog, he gave me a mischievous smile in return. His eyes glowed an even brighter, even more excited red.

I turned to Adamly and gave him a pat on the shoulder. Just for a second, I noticed Security Robot 102's visor flash yellow.

"Keep up the good work, Corporal," I said, working hard to keep the sarcasm out of my voice.

Flanked by Mara and Bog, we waited for the ETT field to activate. Within moments we were surrounded once again by the creepy but wonderful universe of the subspace tunnel.

Once we'd arrived back in *Orbital*'s docking bay, I surveyed Mara and Bog to ensure they were okay. Bog was laughing hysterically and Mara was blushing. I looked down to see that the ETT had struck again; I was inconveniently naked from the waist down.

Aw, shit!

CHAPTER NINE

Falling Together

It took Mara but a moment to find me another pair of pants to wear. She left the docking bay, then returned with a pair of ultra-tight purple slacks.

"Here, wear these." She shoved them at my chest, doing her best not to look down. I found that rather disappointing.

"No." I cut her off with a defiant step backwards. "They're purple."

She nodded like I was stating the obvious. I guess I was.

"Purple," I said again. "You know, the colour of the fashionably confused."

"Oh God," she huffed in response, rolling her pretty green eyes to the ceiling.

"And if there's one thing Brant Zenith is not, it's confused. Brant Zenith knows what is fashionable."

"No. As a matter of fact, if there's one thing Brant Zenith is, it's a misogynistic, egocentric, arrogant child!"

Having been trained in the skills of observation, I was beginning to sense that she was angry with me. Bog, on the other hand, just did his best not to laugh in my face and incur any of her wrath for himself.

"That's four things, actually," I pointed out.

Mara ignored my correction. "Put the damn pants on and I won't hear any more immature dribble spill from your mouth!"

She said it with such intensity that I could only guess she meant what she said. I was forced to obey.

"I think I'll go alert Sparling to head for Prime Station Alpha," Bog said, heaving his giant frame with the sort of grace reserved for something between a ballerina and circus elephant.

My heart suddenly skipped a beat. "Maybe just hold on a moment, Bog."

He lifted a craggy, black eyebrow. His red tusks and horns shimmered with interest.

"There's something you should know about my last visit to Prime Station Alpha three years ago," I said.

I could feel the sweat form on my forehead. The day had finally arrived when I had to come clean about my infamous last moments there.

"What?" Mara asked.

Bog smiled. After all, he had been there when it happened. He still goaded me about it from time to time when we drank.

"Oh boy," I stammered. "How to say this…"

Mara sighed. "How about start with the truth?"

I ran my hands through my hair and took a deep breath. "Well, there's a slight chance I could be arrested the moment I walk my purple pants through the first entry portal."

Mara didn't show even a hint of surprise. "What does 'slight chance' mean, Brant?"

"I would say somewhere between absolute and definite," Bog chimed in.

I gave my friend a dark stare. "I don't think it's *that* certain. But I'd be lying if I didn't say there was a fifty-fifty chance."

Indeed, I knew it wasn't a certainty as I had in the past made an effort to thwart this impending arrest—at least, in my own

Brant Zenith kind of way. I'd slept with someone I had thought could help make the charge disappear.

I just wished I had stuck around long enough the next morning to find out whether she actually *had* cleared my record. Oh well.

Mara's face turned a darker shade of red. "Well, what kind of charges are we talking about?"

She sounded so angry—and I didn't miss the extra emphasis she put on the word we.

"Well, officially I was arrested three years ago on one count of atmospheric sedition."

"And three counts of verbally assaulting a Prime officer," Bog added unhelpfully.

"What the hell is atmospheric sedition, Brant?" Mara asked. "It sounds horrible."

"It's not as bad as it sounds… and it's a kind of a long story." I looked around, trying to find some graceful words to fill the void of my embarrassment. None came. "Initially I got a citation for loitering with an unacceptable odour upon my person."

As far as I could determine, atmospheric sedition was meant to describe any act of rebellion towards the establishment in regards to odours and air contaminants. Fuck, I hated Prime's pretentiousness.

"Odour upon your person," Bog blurted with a chuckle. "That's a smooth way of saying they busted your ass for stinking like a cesspool."

Mara didn't look convinced. "Really, Brant? That's very, very hard to believe. I know for a fact that you shower three times a day. What aren't you telling me?"

"Well, it's true. That one morning, I did stink. Before I could get to *Orbital* to shower and change, one of the station's junior security men halted me and began verbally abusing me in public."

"If I remember correctly, he called you unfit for public exposure and tried to escort you to a cleansing station," Bog said. "That's when you lost it and earned the citation."

"Yeah. There was no way I could go into a cleansing station. Just stepping on the putrid floor would have biodegraded my feet. And don't get me started on the miscreants who fall asleep in there. Do you have any idea what a slight graze by a Zentroid squidman does to one's nether regions? Not going to happen! So I told the security man, I think his name was Vetor, that I would burn in hell before I went in there—and if he so much as touched me, he would regret the day his mother had forgotten her birth control."

Bog nodded. "And that's when he received the two citations for verbal assault."

"Seriously, Brant?" Mara said, her face scrunching into a knot. "This is ludicrous, even for you! I left you alone on Prime's largest space station for two days, a station with about a thousand activities to keep you occupied, and all you could do was get arrested?" She seemed about as angry as I'd ever seen her. "Incidentally, you still haven't told me what you did to earn your atmospheric sedition charge."

"Well, I insulted Officer Vetor to the point that he decided to lay down the worst charge he could find. But… actually, no, I won't tell you what I was doing."

"I'm your ship's ambassador! If you get arrested upon our arrival, how will I be able to effectively do my job if you don't tell me the truth?"

I hesitated, having no desire to tell her the whole story. In truth, part of me was damned proud of what I'd done that day. I wish I could have shouted it from the rooftops. After all, my actions that day had saved thousands of lives.

This was not the time to get into that event.

"Don't worry, Mara," Bog said. "You probably wouldn't believe it anyway."

With a huff, she dismissed Bog and told him to report to the control hub and alert Sparling to set a course for Prime Station Alpha. Only when Bog was far from earshot did she return to the subject at hand: her concerns about my behaviour.

"Brant, I need to know why you do such crazy things whenever you get close to a Prime officer." Her voice was controlled, but I sensed her anger just below the surface. "For example, not thirty minutes ago you nearly provoked Adamly into a fatal fight."

"Me?" I asked incredulously. Perhaps the best way to avoid an argument was to play the cute, charming victim.

"Don't you dare start that act! You started a fight aboard an allied spacecraft in the midst of an army of security droids that were fully capable of ending all our lives. And let's not forget, you did it on a vessel commanded by a very close friend of yours. What were you thinking?"

"First off, they weren't droids. They were robots."

Mara then grabbed my suit by the collar and pulled me in close. Her gaze could have cut steel. "Push me further, Zenith. I dare you."

This time, I took some time to think up an appropriate answer. "It was a strategic move, Mara."

"Explain."

"First off, I wasn't about to lose my spark weapon to Adamly or one of his buddies."

Mara took a second and nodded, accepting my point. "And secondly?"

"Well, secondly is a bit more complicated."

She waited for me to explain. I looked into her flushed face and saw genuine concern there.

"It's been three years since I've been on a Prime vessel," I continued. "I needed to see their security protocols in action. Just in case."

"In case of what, Brant?" she asked, her voice softening a bit.

"What happens if our allegiance with Prime goes down the proverbial toilet?"

"My father knows well enough not to let that happen. Anyway, your actions today make it *more* likely that trouble will arise between our two organizations. You've jeopardized the treaty more than anything my father has ever done."

I knew that criticizing Mara's father would be the perfect way to receive a one-way ticket to Asskickingsville, so I chose my next words carefully.

"Mara, your father and I have very different opinions when it comes to the Militia's relationship with Prime. I doubt that's a secret to someone as perceptive as you." She ignored the compliment and bade me continue. "Prime is no good for the Militia. I think it's best to learn what we can from them in case the worst happens."

"I think what's worst for the Militia is an all-out war with Prime. You must agree with that."

"I don't know if that's true. But you're right. We don't have the advantage in either numbers or technology to win a war with them."

She shook her head sadly. "My father wants what's best for the Militia, and I can tell he's tired of the constant struggle to keep the Militia alive. It hasn't been easy…" Her voice trailed off and she took a deep breath. For a moment, I thought I could see her eyes become teary. "Brant, I need you to promise me something."

"What is it?"

"Promise me that you'll control your erratic behaviour when we get to Prime Station Alpha. Or the next time you meet anyone who decides to confront you. I need you to act like a captain."

Those words stung the ego like a kick to the biscuits. Not once had I received a thank-you from her for my actions in saving the ship or the Quazar system. But I caused one little squabble and all of a sudden I wasn't acting like a captain?

Unexpectedly, my temper flared.

"I don't know if it's escaped your attention, Ambassador, but I *am* a captain. A damned fine one at that."

"No. You're nothing but a child who holds a captain's rank." I was about to snap a really witty retort, but she beat me to the punch. "Brant, you're possibly the bravest man I've ever known.

I'm not questioning that. But I am *certain* that you're also the most foolish man I've ever known. That is a very dangerous combination. Too dangerous for a captain. Now promise me."

"I will promise no such thing."

She raised her hands in disgust.

"You offer me nothing in return for my sacrifice," I added. "Besides, my actions are what keep this crew alive sometimes. Have you thought of that?"

She must not have appreciated something I said, because she immediately turned on her heel and stormed out of the docking bay.

Shaking my head in confusion, I followed at a distance.

My journey back to the control hub was extended by a couple of absolutely necessary errands. The first stop was to my quarters. No way would I wear those pants any longer than I had to.

I also wanted to open the very important package I'd picked up at the Quazar station. It had been so long since I'd looked forward to something as much as this. Could it really be what I had been searching and dreaming of? I was minutes away from finding out.

I flipped on the light switch and to my surprise noticed Cerbot slouched in the corner. His rusty steel frame was haphazardly tilted at a seventy-degree angle, his head the only thing that kept his bulky frame pinned upright.

I slipped into a fresh pair of pants which was a massively frustrating ordeal with one mangled hand. When finally completed, I carefully removed the top half of my spacesuit, trying to avoid even more pain. I tossed it aside with the rest of the mismatched outfit I'd been wearing since the ETT mishap.

Curious, I then walked up to the little metal robot that couldn't, shouldn't, and probably wouldn't. I set the poor little guy aright and noted that he'd sustained some damage. And I immediately determined the cause: those globular acid bursts from the alien ships.

The holes in the robot's frames weren't substantial, perhaps the diameter of my thumb, but I could trace each hole from entry to exit. The acid had cut through him like a pin through fabric.

I rotated his body better to inspect him. There were three obvious perforations, all of which having just missed the vital circuitry. So why wasn't he still operational?

That's when I noticed the coup de grace: a nickel-sized opening at the top front portion of his head that extended down at a steep angle, coming out the bottom of the head on the other side. I had no idea how to fix the little guy, or even if it would be worth the trouble. The circuitry in his robotic cranium was too complicated for my foggy memory, but we didn't have an engineer on board. So I felt I had to at least give it a try.

The first strategy that came to my mind was the old reliable—banging my fist on the top of the head. After all, a similar technique had done a wonderful job keeping everyone alive back when I'd been rewiring the port hub to save the black hole's final containment ring. So why not now?

Bang!

I felt my teeth rattle with the impact. Then, without warning, one of Cerbot's four metal arms slapped outward in an automatic response and punched me in the groin.

I hunched over, consumed by a pain that could have dropped a rhino at fifty paces.

At first, I thought Cerbot's response had been self-protective and that he was back online, but after that shameful display of martial arts he remained as inactive as ever.

I was about to quit my inept attempts at robotics when I discovered the simple reboot switch just under the backside of Cerbot's head. Flipping it on, I heard a large crack followed by an odd popping sound in his metal cranium. There was a flash of flames somewhere within, followed by a cloud of ash-grey smoke erupting from the holes in his head.

I was forced to use the last of my personal CO_2 canister to put out the fire. By the time I had successfully extinguished the flames, dark grey smoke had filled my chambers.

When the smoke had diffused enough for me to find my way to the door, I stepped out into the corridor—just in time to get smacked in the face by a gust of icy wind. Pellets of sleet were only a moment behind it, and I swore directly to the Mackmian gods of fate.

Being ignored yet again, I took a left turn down the corridor and soon felt the cold dissipate. As usual, the ice had melted into the shag carpeting.

The second errand I needed to run brought me to the medical bay. The room was oval in shape with a high ceiling and reflective surfaces on the walls and tables. The air smelled like mothballs.

I hurried past the outdated lab equipment and headed for a shiny cabinet at the end of the room. Thankfully the medical bay hadn't been damaged during the battle, because the item I needed could have been compromised by those bursts of acids that had done in Cerbot.

I opened the cabinet and pulled out one of the dozen remaining bottles of EZ-Heal. I held it up for several glorious seconds, as though hearing a choir of angels chant down upon me from above. To a passerby, it would have looked like I was worshipping it.

The inscription on the bottle stated in bold letters that the liquid inside was only to be consumed in case of life-threatening emergencies. The alcohol content was rated at 143 percent. To others it was a poison, not to be trifled with. But to me it was a scientific miracle in a bottle.

I continued reading the instructions on the label. In the boldest of letters, it read, *"Take one capful every three to four hours to help stave off those irksome bouts of death during your space adventures."*

It had been quite an adventure just to acquire this supply of EZ-Heal a few years back, when it had become apparent that the ship wouldn't be able to attract a qualified medic. The efforts had largely been for nought, since Bog and I were the only ones who would touch the stuff. The rest of the crew felt it would do damage to the liver, brain, spleen, heart, and a litany of other highly overrated organs…

Well, all I can say is that I had turned out fine so far. Maybe one just needed a really high tolerance for alcohol. I'd barely felt any side effects, aside from my right hand once growing an inordinate amount of knuckle hair.

Nothing else I knew of worked half as quickly as EZ-Heal.

Anyway, it was worth the risk today. I needed my hand healed before we arrived at Prime Station Alpha. So I swigged a healthy portion, perhaps eight doses or so of the swirly, purple-pink liquid. I blanched at the flavour. Each time I drank the stuff, it tasted different. This time it tasted like Bog's socks smelled.

The pain in my hand subsided nearly immediately. I still could not move my fingers so I knew that the healing had not kicked in just yet. But feeling the release of pain was a blessing in of itself.

I put the bottle in my pocket and headed back to my quarters. I would need to hide it before Mara caught me drinking it again. The last time she'd caught me drinking EZ-Heal she'd threatened to tie a couple of my appendages together until they fell off. Or something like that. I couldn't remember which appendages she'd been referring to, and I didn't relish the prospect of finding out.

Fortunately, the smoke had cleared in my quarters well enough for me to find the unopened package. I tore open the paper wrapping, my heart racing. My skin was covered in sweat from anticipation.

My heart nearly stopped as I pulled the items out of the box. Fuck!

I had been expecting a Militon chain. I'd dreamed of possessing one ever since my childhood on Nova Martia, which had been filled with stories about how powerful they were.

A Militon chain was rare and known to grant its wearer many fantastic abilities. I'd heard that such a chain could cause a man to grow to three times his original size, or even shrink to the height of a thimble. The chain was reportedly able to absorb massive amounts of weapons fire and even harness then capture and store the resulting energy.

There were a lot of rumours about Militon chains, including one that said the wearer could dislocate time. I didn't know exactly what this entailed, but it had always sounded damned cool to me.

Whichever of the myriad of stories were true, I had seen one of the chains with my own eyes, and it had sparkled and shined. It was a piece of ornately crafted jewellery and I knew it would look great around my wrist or neck.

I shook my head in dismay. Instead of the mythical Militon chain, I found myself staring at a glossy boy band poster: the Sons of Sweetness, the biggest musical act in three solar systems. I wasn't sure which solar systems, but I truly didn't care.

It must have been a joke of some kind. I tossed that in the corner of the room.

The only other item in the box was a pair of dainty, flashy gloves. Silver with a purple hue. Size: ladies small.

Son of a bitch!

This parcel had been meant to bring about a substantive change to my life and everyone else aboard the ship—perhaps even a change to the Militia Space Fleet itself. I had worked so hard and sacrificed so much to attain them and instead all I had to show for my efforts was a blasted pair of a preteen girl's gloves. "Glitter Gloves," read the tag. "Make tonight the prettiest night of your life!" Well, I couldn't fault someone for wanting to try. But damn it!

They sparkled with light, and they were meant to stretch all the way up to the wearer's elbows.

Well, I was so pissed off that I nearly pulled the gloves apart with my bare hands. But I stopped myself and instead stuffed them in my pocket.

I stormed around the room for a few minutes, hoping to clear some of the frustration from my mind. I nearly died trying to pick up this blasted parcel. And to top it off, I'd had to put up with that stuffy Mackmian postal worker…

After a few long and infuriating moments, I thought to myself, *What the hell?* I pulled the gloves out of my pocket and decided to put them on. I don't know why I did it, to be honest. I guess I wasn't immune to wanting to have the prettiest night of my life.

The gloves surprised me. Even though they should barely have fit Mara's dainty little hands, once in place with my misaligned fingers they seemed to pull effortlessly over my large hands and muscular arms. And once they were secured in place, they did indeed begin to glitter and glow in a spectacular array. These Glitter Gloves sure lived up to their name!

Suddenly, I began to feel the real tell-tale effects of the EZ-Heal. Intoxication set in rapidly. One moment I was completely sober, and the next things began to get fuzzy. The walls started to blur, and it took me several tries to count how many hands I had. Twice I counted three, and twice I counted one. I just took the median and rounded it up to two.

I glanced down at my hands and noticed that the gloves were beginning to fade, the shimmering effect absorbing into my skin. Soon they vanished completely.

What the fuck? In my drunken stupor, I decided I must be imagining things.

I looked across the room to Cerbot—or at least, to where Cerbot was supposed to be. Somehow the little robot had managed to vanish again. What had happened to him?

Well, I no longer had the mental capacity to figure it out. The EZ-Heal was making me feel great. And kind of squishy.

"Captain, could you please return to the control hub?"

I thought it was Sparling's voice. Or it could have been God. I could no longer distinguish one from another.

"Damn," I mumbled, eyeing my bed with an eagerness that was growing even more quickly than my fingernails appeared to be. I looked down at my hands in shock and couldn't tell if it was my imagination or not, but the fingernails appeared to be about an inch long. Was this a direct effect of the EZ-Heal?

I punched my wristband communicator and responded with something that sounded like "I bwamma wayer."

I didn't know if Sparling understood me, but I really couldn't have cared less.

I took my sweet time getting back to the control hub. Along the way, I bumped into a few overly aggressive walls. Before I knew it, I tripped and landed directly on my face, nearly flossing my teeth with the shag carpeting.

When I finally made it to the control hub, I lifted my eyes long enough to determine that Mara was refusing to even look at me. Stairn had his head buried in his digital clipboard again. Bog appeared to be playing a video game that may have had something to do with cow-herding.

But as for Sparling, she looked right at me. Her face seemed particularly lovely, albeit blurry and getting blurrier with every minute.

"Kippen Ambn wints talka you preevitly," she said.

It took me an embarrassingly long two minutes to translate that.

"Ah," I said. "Sendin-it-true." I waved to the general direction of my office, hoping she'd know what that meant.

I meandered to my personal office, and my entry was ungraceful. I tripped again, only barely evading a headlong crash into the fish tank. I peeled myself up off the floor.

This conversation with Captain Ambden had better be short and require very little diction, otherwise all my years of brilliant service with the Mackmians, and especially Ambden himself, could fall apart.

I sat in my desk chair—hard. I had to shake some cobwebs out of my head before turning on the screen. When I did, Ambden's head seemed enormous and took up almost the entire monitor. My condition must have been playing weird tricks on me, as his large face kept getting redder and redder.

"Captain Zenith. Universes and Galaxies waver as times change."

Even sober, I wouldn't have been able to figure out what he was talking about. In my current state, I wasn't even going to try.

As the conversation proceeded, I had to work harder and harder to translate what I heard into what I thought he must be saying.

"I have a grand favour to ask of you, my friend," Ambden said, sounding a little uncertain of himself.

His round Mackmian face looked to be sweating, which I thought was fantastic; I'd thought the Mackmians were unable to sweat except on the balls of their feet. Strangely enough, they mimicked dogs in that way.

Yet another reason to love the Mackmians, I thought to myself.

"My son Simbden here would like to ask you something personal."

My head spun and the screen got even blurrier. Bright lights danced in my peripheral vision. I wasn't going to keep myself functioning this way for much longer, which meant I'd need to end this conversation quickly.

I closed my eyes one long moment and refocused.

When I reopened my eyes, the Mackmian staring back at me looked just like the captain's son. They did look a lot alike…

"Captain, once again it is a great honour!" the Mackmian exclaimed.

He looked a lot like Simbden, and I think it was Simbden's voice too. Weird.

"Thanks for that." I'm pretty certain I was looking in two very opposite directions by that point.

"It would also be the greatest of honours if you would allow me to join your crew when we arrive at Prime Station Alpha."

The Ambden mimicking Simbden paused for a long moment. His nose scrunched inwards, accentuating his four nostrils. I smiled inwardly, as EZ-Heal gave me a sense of smell to rival even the Mackmians. God, I loved EZ-Heal!

I wasn't aware he was awaiting an answer, so he spoke again.

"Captain, I can understand if you feel hesitant, but I can assure you that I will be very useful to you and *Orbital*. I'm a hard worker, and I specialize in engineering and electronics."

Ambden-that-was-Simbden suddenly looked again like Ambden. What was going on?

"So what do you think, Captain?" he asked. "Is there room aboard *Orbital* for one more? My son is very capable."

"Sounds good to me," I blubbered. As drunk as I was at that point, I would have graciously accepted an ear exam performed with a plunger.

"Excellent, my friend!" Ambden seemed very happy, but I couldn't quite grasp why. "With that, I will let you go back to your business. We'll meet in two days at Prime Station Alpha. Heavens bless the Zeniths!"

That last bit sounded very nice. I decided not to worry about the cloudy meniscus floating through my memory and realized that I probably had nothing to worry about.

Once more, I had handled my captain's duties splendidly. And with this latest victory under my belt, I decided to wander, stumble, and trip my way back to my quarters for some much-needed rest and relaxation.

A spark of unknown origin and complexity entered the circuits of the maintenance robot known as Cerbot. He awoke from a shutdown unlike any other he had experienced in his long, tedious life.

His ocular viewports searched the dark room in which he found himself. He corrected his orientation, as he'd been leaning against the wall at a thirty-three-degree angle.

He quickly remembered where he was: the captain's quarters. *Captain Zenith... Captain Zenith... Captain Zenith...*

The unbidden thought swirled around his rapidly rebooting mind. Something was different. His thoughts were no longer cold, stale, and specifically calculated. There was... something more.

Cerbot recognized his reflection in a mirror which stood centimetres away. He looked himself over and noted that the hole in the front of his cranium would need to be fixed. Indeed, he would require many repairs.

Other unbidden thoughts sprang to mind. A list. Suddenly his newly formed consciousness had a series of purposes—and with that list of purposes, Cerbot found a direction.

He rotated slowly and carefully, almost mathematically, inspected his chassis. He found a number of scrapes and holes, many of which were fresh.

But it was not upon the damage that his oval ocular viewports halted. He spotted the letters across the part of his body where his head met the solid cylindrical frame. He had never before thought about those letters.

"Cerbot," he said aloud. The sound of it did not satisfy him. "Cerbot."

He intonated the word several times over, experimenting with different frequencies and pitches. He settled upon one that eventually satisfied him. It was melodious albeit slightly tinny.

It was his voice.

But as Cerbot stared at the letters of his name, something didn't seem right.

"Cerbot... Cerbot... Cerbot..." He repeated it over and over, not changing tone, inflection, or frequency but diligently trying to figure out what was wrong.

Seconds passed which felt like millennia. Then there was a flash of acceptance, and his new awareness took hold.

It is decided, he thought to himself.

Rotating his domed head to face backwards, he rotated his corrugated arms to reach the offensive letters. He switched out his hand accessory and produced a pincher in its place. Then, with metal fingers extended, he extruded a very precise blast of acid that scoured off the dark lettering.

It only took two-point-one seconds to complete the task of spraying a new series of letters in dark paint. Once finished, he inspected his artwork. This was important. This was who he was now.

He read out the stylized letters with a sense of warm satisfaction. "Sirbot."

It felt meaningful. He was now on the right path to become what he was going to be. Sirbot had been born.

Captain Zenith... Captain Zenith... Captain Zenith...

His mind returned to this previous thought, and several times he repeated the name of the one he was determined to find. Sirbot would repay Captain Zenith for all that had occurred to him.

CHAPTER TEN

A Cold, Sharp Hello

I awoke with a cold, sharp metallic blade at my throat and an alarming case of cross-eye. I found myself no longer in my warm and cozy bed but sitting upright in my desk chair. It took a great deal of time for my eyes to reposition to dead centre—but when they did, I realized that I was now face-to-metal-face with Cerbot.

The robot, with one hand grasping the razor, caressed my throat while his second hand held a brush full of shaving cream. He quickly lathered me up. His chilly metal hands were remarkably gentle on my skin. But that did little to calm my nerves. To my great surprise, and chagrin, I realized that his last two hands contained a comb and, much worse, a pair of scissors.

In my current state feeling the aftereffects of EZ-Heal, I couldn't add two and two without an abacus, so it took me a few very terse seconds to realize that the little malfunctioning bot was indeed giving me a shave and a haircut.

I panicked and began to squirm. It did me no good, as Cerbot put down the comb and scissors, grabbed my offending hands, extended his arms to the needed length, and pinned my hands behind my back. I felt the cool inflexibility of his four metallic limbs on my body and smelled the residue of the globs of acid that had damaged him—and, come to think of it, even a hint of vanilla.

I struggled with all the ferocity of the gods, but to no avail. The little robot was immensely strong and I could do nothing to fight his grip.

I realized very quickly that trying to wriggle free when someone (or something) has a sharp blade to your throat is a very good way of locating the straight-lined path to death. Therefore, I kept still and quiet, but deep down in my soul I was whimpering like a pitiful little puppy.

Cerbot's hands moved with amazing speed. The blade whisked up and down my face with inhuman dexterity. I don't know if I was impressed or downright frantic at the flurry of quick strokes. Every few seconds he wiped off the excess shaving cream on the opposite arm, from which dangled a clean white towel.

What the hell was going on here?

In several tense moments—for me anyway; Cerbot kept humming some strange tune I couldn't distinguish—he completed the shave. My hands remained pinned as he put down his shaving equipment and went back to work on my hair.

That's when I really began to freak out. Before I let his scissors touch my hair again, I frantically shook my head, doing my damnedest to break free of his grip. I couldn't feel any cuts on my face, so I couldn't discern the quality of job he'd done, but I couldn't imagine myself loving even my own offspring, if I had any, more than I loved my hair. I couldn't let Cerbot mutilate something that God himself had blessed the universe with. It would be a blasphemy.

In my desire to escape, I spotted something odd. Cerbot's identification marker had changed. It now read Sirbot. What the hell? How had that happened… and what did it even mean?

I kept struggling for all I was worth.

For a few hopeful moments, my efforts seemed to work. The newly christened Sirbot wasn't able to make any progress and couldn't snip a single strand of my golden locks.

I think he began to get frustrated, if robots could become so, because he put down the scissors. From between his fingers, he produced an electric spark arc that glowed blue. In fact, there were two arcs, about six centimetres apart.

To my dismay, he brought those sparks closer to my head. Sweat poured down my head, and it smelled just like EZ-Heal.

His hand stretched past my face, and I felt the sharp burn of those sparks touching the back of my neck. The last thing I remember was letting out a sigh as Sirbot once again plucked up his small black comb and shiny scissors.

Knock, knock, knock.

I heard the knocking sound once more, perhaps a minute later. I was lying facedown in my pillow, my body flat and spread-eagled. I was pretty certain an ocean of drool was dribbling down my chin.

"Is it who?" I mumbled through dry lips and an even drier mouth.

"Captain, it's me, Mara. Could you let me in please?"

I shook my befuddled head and rubbed my eyes with the palms of my hands. "Okeed. I'll be dare."

I crawled out of bed, fighting with some offending blankets wrapped every which way around my body. So ferocious were their grip that in my gallant quest for freedom I felt my legs get pinned in place. I landed unceremoniously on the floor, my face hitting the carpet.

That was the third time in two days I'd hit the floor. It seemed to hurt less than the first times. I felt that my body was becoming adapted to it.

I stood up and hobbled to the door, having to use every ounce of my memory and mental stamina just to remember where it was.

I ran my hand on the door sensor to trigger it, and it opened with a whir. Of course, true to form for *Orbital*, the door froze halfway open. I put my back to the wall and pushed with all the hungover force I could muster.

When the door was fully open, Mara stood in front of me with a digital clipboard in hand.

Double shit! I quickly placed my hands in front of my favourite appendages, for the sake of propriety.

"Can I come in please?" she asked sweetly.

"Um… sure." I didn't look her in the eye.

She stepped into the room and I noticed the look of satisfaction on her face. "Brant, I'm impressed!"

"You are?"

"Yeah. Your room is spotless. Besides the bed, of course. I guess you were just getting some much-deserved sleep."

She gave me a warm hug. I didn't know how to process that, but it was better than the typical threats she directed at me, so I hugged her back. She felt warm and smelled sweet, like lilacs. This was highly distracting as she exhibited two of my favourite things at once: female beauty and the heavenly smell of lilacs.

We stood like that for a few long moments, and I began to wonder what exactly I'd done while under the effects of EZ-Heal to warrant such a welcome from the normally frosty ambassador.

I looked around my chambers and did, in fact, realize that it was perfectly clean. I couldn't account for that, for the last thing I remembered was Sirbot…

I quickly let Mara go and rushed over to the mirror, remembering the assault.

"Brant, is everything okay?"

With visions of scissors and snipped hair floating in my memory, I ignored every word coming out of Mara's mouth.

My appearance in the mirror was nothing short of shocking. I ran my fingers down my perfectly smooth face. Not a nick, scratch, or dry spot was to be found. In fact, not even an errant hair extended its unwelcome presence.

Satisfied, I allowed my gaze to creep up to my hair. It was one thing to shave someone perfectly. Shaving was easy. But cutting hair was an artform. That malfunctioning little robot had been messing with a work meant to be spoken of in the same breath as the masterpieces of DaVinci or Michelangelo.

But when I looked up at what I feared would be the worst nightmare of my life, instead I merely felt astonished.

My hair was flawless! It was superb, even for me.

In my thirty-five years of life, I couldn't think of a happier and more relieved moment. My blonde hair was perfectly combed back, at just the right length. The sides were meticulously trimmed, verging on the immaculate.

I took the handheld mirror and searched every corner of my scalp. Not a single hair was out of place, even after I'd slept on it. It was a glorious moment.

Sirbot, you little metallic god!

Elated, I ran over to Mara and kissed her hard on the lips. I don't know what came over me. I think the kiss lasted for several seconds—and they were quite nice seconds actually. But when realization of my actions took hold of my still foggy brain, I thought of the impending physical pain she would inflict on me.

To my great and overwhelming surprise, she didn't pull away.

Knock, knock, knock.

Feeling embarrassed, Mara did at last push gently away. What the flying shit had made me so popular all of a sudden?

"Enter," I hollered.

This time, the door opened, all the way this time, revealing my favourite pain in the ass—Agent Stairn. He stepped into my chambers as if he owned the joint.

"Captain, I have new lists for you," he reported.

And indeed, in his hand was another of his infamous digital clipboards. However, Mara was still within arm's reach, and I could still taste her kiss upon my lips—

"I've come to give you the final report on *Orbital*'s status. Inert systems at seventy-two percent, bingo machine at zero percent, laundry chutes at fifty-six percent..."

As the list went on, I looked over at Mara and her typically flushed face. Catching her eye, I detected a sparkle I hadn't seen in quite some time. In fact, I couldn't even remember when I'd last seen it.

"Okay, Stairn. Good work." I grabbed the digital clipboard from him. "I'll take it from here. You may return to your duties."

To his credit, Stairn merely nodded and turned to leave.

"I swear, I think that guy believes he owns the place," I said once he was gone. "What do you have in your hands, Mara?"

She looked down, remembering that she was indeed carrying her own clipboard. "Oh, these are Stairn's and Bog's mission summaries for your perusal."

"Oh, good."

I suddenly realized that I was sober once more, which meant we were probably rounding on twenty-four hours since I'd taken the EZ-Heal. I tested my once-broken hand and noticed that it worked perfectly. I looked down at my fingernails and vaguely remembered Sirbot clipping them too. I think I was falling in love. Ah, Sirbot...

"Brant, could I talk to you for a moment?" Mara sounded a little nervous, which was very unlike her.

"Sure," I said, winking at the handsome reflection in the mirror.

Her voice seemed shaky at first, and it took her a couple of timid moments to get her words together.

"Could I talk to you about what has been happening here between us?" Mara stepped closer. Her normal imposing glare seemed to melt.

I reached for the digital clipboard and took it from her hands. She let it go without argument, hardly noticing.

"Yeah." I made eye contact. "I already know what you're going to say."

I think she was holding her breath. "You do?"

"I'm no idiot. Despite what you may think."

"Brant, I don't think you're an idiot."

"No, sorry, not an idiot. Rather, a child holding a captain's rank." Score one for the Zenith!

"I'm sorry I said that, Brant." Mara stepped a bit closer. "I was angry for what you did on board Jonah's ship."

"Oh, I see." I turned on the digital clipboard in order to give my next comments an air of casualness. "You want me to make the promise, right?"

"What?" Mara asked, confused.

"I told you once already that I won't promise to kiss Prime's ass, no matter how angry you get. So if that's what you want to discuss, you better be able to hold your breath for a very long time."

God, I was getting tired of arguing with her all the time.

She shook her head in distaste, then took a deep breath. It seemed to take some effort to control her rising anger. "That's not at all what I came to talk about—"

"No, Mara. I understand. I really do. Sometimes I take risks that seem... um... cavalier. Or..."

"Foolish?"

"Not the word I was looking for." I looked into her emerald-green eyes. "It's just the way I operate. I won't do something I believe is wrong. Standing down to Prime is at the top of my list of things that are wrong."

She nodded and I could tell there was something more she wanted to tell me.

I continued speaking anyway. "I know I like to live a fast and scary life, but that's what *Orbital* needs right now. Hell, that's what the Militia needs."

Mara shook her head in confusion. "I don't agree. The Militia needs stability. The Militia needs to be able to grow."

"The Militia needs to improve," I said sarcastically.

"Exactly!" Mara spoke with a degree of intensity that took me aback. "That's one of the things I wanted to talk to you about. Well, not the main thing, but now's as good a time as any, I suppose."

"Go on."

"Well, I think you stated it very well. The Militia needs improvement." She ran her fingers through her strawberry-blonde hair. "You and I can't easily effect change with the Militia as far from home base as we are, but we can improve and fix *Orbital*."

"How in god's name do we do that?" I blurted out, letting years of frustration get the better of me. "We have the budget of a travelling one-man puppet show!"

"I have some ideas about that. The first is that our arrival at Prime Station Alpha will be monumental."

I hoped not. "How so?"

"Well, Prime doesn't want our upcoming mission. I figure they passed it on to us, and we can use that to our advantage."

"You're not making sense." I shook my head. "Prime has sent five of their most powerful ships to the Quazar black hole to seal the area. I would say we stand a very good chance of—"

"That's not what I meant. Our new mission is awaiting us at Prime Station Alpha. Remember?"

Then it hit me. High Marshal Olwen had told us about the mission just before all hell broke loose with the Mackmians. The

Mondorians needed help with a problem that had something to do with their sun. It was… disappearing? Was I remembering that correctly?

"Ah, shit. I totally forgot about that. But this new business with the alien threat has to take precedence. Your father needs to see that."

"I don't know if it will be that simple, Brant. We may not be able to back out of it."

"To hell we can't!" Once again, my temper took control of me. "We can't pass up on investigating the most important event in the past ten years just to help a planet full of backwater—"

"I wouldn't call them a backwater, and we don't know that—"

"Never mind," I muttered. "So what do you suggest we do?"

Mara seemed surprised that I would ask for her advice, but she quickly recovered. "I think we have to continue onward to Prime Station Alpha. Once there, we use the opportunity to our best advantage. For example, we can ensure that *Orbital* gets some necessary repairs. It's really taken a beating."

"I know. Have you heard what happened to the bingo machine?"

Mara chuckled at that. "That's one thing I've always admired about you, Brant. Your ability to make the best of bad situations. You always make me laugh."

I shrugged at the compliment. Besides, I hadn't been joking. The loss of the bingo machine had stung me to my very soul.

My thoughts turned to ship repairs.

"We need to focus on our weapon systems. I mean, we can't be rushing into space battles with nothing more than a proverbial water pistol. Truthfully, I'm pretty damned surprised we didn't die at least ten times out there by the Quazar black hole."

"Yeah, that was pretty exciting, wasn't it?" she said. "I was captivated by your command abilities throughout the battle."

She stepped closer. I could tell she was trying to initiate something, but I didn't know what. She hadn't been so warm to me in years.

I looked into her perfect emerald eyes. "Sometimes I surprise even myself."

Her face scrunched. She seemed to be battling within herself to understand something I'd said. "Brant, sometimes you really confuse me."

"I'm a complicated guy."

I raised my arms wide, producing a smile that would have made angels weep. She punched me lightly in the chest and then laughed.

But the smile slowly slid from her face, and I sensed Mara was about to surprise me with something completely different.

"So, Captain Zenith, where do we go from here?"

She moved so close now that our chests were touching. I could smell the sweetness of her perfume and the fragrance of her conditioner. Lilacs again.

"Well, like you said, we have to wait until Prime Station Alpha," I said. "After our repairs are complete, time will only tell."

"That's not what I meant. Where do you and I go?"

I wasn't sure what she was even talking about. Why in hell did I have such trouble understanding half of what Mara said to me?

Before I had a chance to answer, we were interrupted by the familiar crackling of *Orbital*'s intercom.

It was Sparling's young voice. "Ambassador Mara, you are needed at the control hub."

Mara looked into my eyes with some frustration and disappointment. I knew not why.

"Agent, can it wait for a few minutes?" she asked.

"I don't think so, Ambassador," Sparling replied. "It's your father on long-range communications. He seems to be quite insistent on speaking with you."

"Okay. I'm on my way."

Mara sighed and lowered her head onto my chest for the briefest of seconds. I could feel her radiant hair upon my face and the smell was heavenly.

She stepped away but then paused a moment before leaving. "Oh. Incidentally, have you seen my parasol lately?"

"Huh?"

"The purple one. You know, the one with large white flowers on it?" When I didn't comprehend what she was referring to, she huffed in disappointment. "Brant. It's the one you bought me years ago, just before our first mission together. You remember, don't you?"

"Oh, yeah, *that* parasol," I lied, although it did sound familiar somehow. "Sorry, I haven't seen it in a very long time."

"If you see it lying around, please let me know."

"Will do."

And with that, she walked out, her quick steps taking her out of my chambers and back to the control hub.

Whew. I didn't know what she had wanted from me just moments ago, but I sensed that I had dodged a well-aimed bullet. I scratched at my more-than-perfect hair.

Then, looking down, I realized that I was still holding the digital clipboard with the mission summaries from Stairn and Bog. I debated which to read first and decided to bite the bullet and begin with Stairn's.

Orbital Mission, Objective Log

Space Date: 14th Hour of Day 120 of Solar Cycle 2500
Location: Quazar Space Station
Agent Lazarus Stairn, Logistics Officer

- Entry to Quazar Space Station through main portals A1–A2 successful.
- Captain Brant Zenith, Security Officer Bog, and I within entryway A1–A2 found ourselves under serious attack by four alien lifeforms. (See pages 48–49 of Objective Log for full descriptions of alien lifeforms, which herein will be noted as Alien Aggressors.)

I felt myself cringe at the fact there were at least forty-nine pages to this report. When the shit had he found time to put the report together? I'd never know.

I continued, thanking the cruel mistress of fate that he had at least condensed it into point form.

- Zenith makes illogical and dangerous move down hallway to attack Alien Aggressors 1 through 4. He took four steps into the open, following no trained pattern. His moves surprised all, including Alien Aggressors. Zenith is successful in eliminating two Aggressors. His first attack was fired from a range of three metres from first Alien Aggressor…

I skipped past the fight re-enactment, doing my best to ignore his less than flattering comments about me.

- After my fellow crewmembers and I parted company, I journeyed alone down corridor C2 for approximately 33 seconds before I was the victim of another spark blast. This one was blue, aimed from approximately 16 metres away and directed at an angle approximately 19 degrees horizontal. It crashed overhead, approximately 1 metre above.

The explosion burned blue and encompassed an area approximately 3 cubic metres. I rolled out of the way and delivered an attack upon the next Aggressor. My aim was approximately 14 degrees from horizontal and I found that my attack was successful, and the Aggressor perished without another chance to continue the attack. The Aggressor's body split at about mid-waist. The top portion slumped at an angle approximately 65 degrees from horizontal. The bottom portion slumped in a mirror angle to the first.

- I continued forth down corridor C2. No more Aggressors were to be seen until I reached my target room—crew quarters, which was so named CQ1–5.
- Rounding the final corner, I was besieged by another attack. This time the spark blast came from 6 metres away with an approximate angle of 17 degrees from horizontal…

Despite having woken up a mere thirty minutes ago, I found myself yawning. I don't know why it surprised me that Agent Stairn was able to take such an exciting series of events and transform them into a literary sedative. I ground my teeth, bore the brunt of it, and continued for another twenty pages.

When I finally got past the space battle, having ascertained that none of the residents of the station had been killed during our time on board, I realized that Stairn had proceeded to provide very detailed reports of each resident. It seemed he had interviewed no less than sixty-two people.

I only paid attention to the highlights:

Space Station Resident #27: Alandanon Skainian

- The Alien Aggressor repeatedly used a small handheld device to fire a glowing blue beam upon each inhabitant. Resident #27 states that the beam warmed the core of her body and cured her Qwernian shake flu.

I couldn't determine the relevance of the Qwernian shake flu part, but this resident was the only one to mention the glowing beam to such an extent:

- Glowing blue beam took approximately 16 seconds to encapsulate entire Mackmian body.

I found it pretty incredible that the Alien Aggressor's glowing beam could tackle a mature Mackmian woman so quickly. But I was straying from Agent Stairn's report…

- Resident #27 found the opportunity to glance upon the device used by the Aggressor and reasoned with some certainty that it was a polarized quid-ray, or something remarkably similar. I can only deduce that the Aggressors were learning about the species upon the station. I have acquired a sample of the Aggressor's quid-ray device.

I read through the pages as quickly as possible. Even though I had every intention of carefully studying the report, I found my mind drifting and my eyes skimming.
I did my best and soldiered on.

Space Station Resident #53: Traken Maldin

- While working on the universal array in the confines of Decks 1 through 4, Sections A1–2, Resident #53 was discovered by Alien Aggressor I previously labelled #7. Aggressor #7 assaulted Resident #53 by means of minimal spark blast to abdomen area, approximately 3 centimetres below naval. I estimate the spark blast was approximately 6% full power, leaving burn marks on Resident #53.
- Aggressor #7 then forced a computer override using Resident #53's genetic code. Resident #53 realized that Aggressor #7 was conducting a vast survey of the region, including the Dilane system, and even the Prime Star Force's core: the Mazoid system.
- Resident #53 was able to subtly corrupt the data within Aggressor #7's field of view, providing misinformation. Resident #53, more so than any other, deserves credit for services rendered.

I continued scanning his report, but the most useful details were within the previous passages.

After a horrifying two hours, I managed to finish Stairn's report. Happy to be finished, I closed it down and opened Bog's report.

Bog's Report

Space Date: Awe, crap, I don't know. Ask Stairn later.
Location: is the Quazar station.

Well, two of those slimy looking tall black skinned bastard aliens jumped me in the hallway. I couldn't tell which one. I was close enough to jam the spark weapon into one of their bodies and blow it into oblivion. The other backed away, and I fired again, barbequing its ass too.

I managed to make it into the weapons bay and did my best not to explode anything that would kill us all. Two bastard aliens hid behind the most volatile kegs. I snuck around their backsides and after an ugly firefight, I eliminated both aliens.

The Mackmians on duty were very pleased with my performance. One female Mackmian found a way to show her appreciation. It was kind of disturbing and does not need to be mentioned again.

All Mackmians from the weapons bay are alive. The station's weapons were partially modified. The Mackmian report states it better than I could. All is well now.

End Report

I would have to clean up the mess I'd made when a few remnants of EZ-Heal shot out of my nose while reading Bog's report. The report didn't follow Militia standards, but damn had it been entertaining.

I decided to ignore the Mackmian report on the modifications and instead began my own report. It wasn't as detailed and horribly boring as Stairn's, but it did a good job competing with Bog's report for pure entertainment. I did my best to skip over the fact that I really didn't know why the Alien Aggressors had attacked the Galactic Post. But overall I gave my report a solid A+.

Since we were now only hours from Prime Station Alpha, I decided to do what any good captain should do when given the opportunity. I slept.

CHAPTER ELEVEN

Prime Station Alpha

*O**rbital* completed its journey to Prime Station Alpha several short hours later. Like a haemorrhoid on Prime Star Force's ass, I knew for certain our visit was one they wouldn't forget either. That made me smile.

As *Orbital* approached the titanic station, I noticed that it hadn't changed much in the years since I had last visited. The core of the station was so unlike the Quazar station that it was hardly worth mentioning the two in the same thought. The size of Prime Station Alpha was unmatched in the known, and perhaps unknown, universe. Prime Station Alpha was that fleet's pinnacle facility, the heart in the horribly corrupt monster that was Prime. Every time an unwary alien nation sought introduction to our quadrant of space, Prime seemed to find its way to the forefront of inductors—and those negotiations always took place at Prime Station Alpha. Why not? The station was revolutionary, state of the art… and a bane to my existence.

Unfortunately, even I had to admit that the station was formidable, which bothered me to no end. The exterior core looked like a massive cylinder stretching for several kilometres from head to toe. Its black and grey metallic surface shimmered against the backdrop of stars, interrupted occasionally by the yellow glow of lights dotting it.

From the centre of the cylinder branched sixteen evenly spaced spokes that protruded at ninety-degree angles. It was along the flanks of these spokes that the station received ships, and I could only guess that it could accommodate a thousand of the largest vessels in all the galaxies—not to mention an untold number of smaller ships in its docking bays; I had heard numbers ranging between two and three thousand.

Prime Station Alpha dominated the region of space between here and forever. I could smell the burning of my enamel as my teeth grinded together.

The seething that I felt about Prime Station Alpha was in direct correlation to the opposite feelings engendered by Militia Space Fleet's base of operations. Instead of a superstation of menace and doom, we occupied a Mackmian moon that had previously been the site of an intergalactic refuse dump… the one used by the Mackmians before they'd harnessed the Quazar black hole some five years ago.

I tried my best to look on the bright side for a change. Sure, the Militia's station was small, antiquated, cramped, horribly decorated, abysmally furnished, underpowered, poorly built, situated somewhere between nowhere and never mind, and smelled like a pair of Mackmian undies in the summer…

Was I working towards some sort of point?

Fortunately, my train of thought was disrupted by the sight of the *Tanslen* already attached to one of the station's docking arms. *Orbital*, to my embarrassment, was small enough that it would fit in one of the interior bays. I knew that our repairs would benefit from being moored inside, but it was a blow to my ego nonetheless. Grind, grind went my pearly white teeth.

I watched on the screen as *Orbital* found its way into the belly of the corrupt beast. The walls of the bay were racked with repair equipment. Prime technicians were already waiting for us in pressurized suits—and as soon as the ship stopped, they got to work clamping equipment onto the hull. I didn't like them touching my ship, but Mara was right: we needed the repairs.

Still, I wondered, not for the first time, why in God's black hole of an ass *Orbital* needed someone in Mara's position. Sure, she was intelligent and a gifted speaker, and she knew one or two languages short of a million even without synaptic translators, but we were too small to require an ambassador. A ship like ours, with the most skeletal of skeleton crews, only needed a captain to lead it. Me. I was as gifted with my voice as I was with my hands. In fact, I found it rather insulting that High Marshal Olwen didn't think I could handle speaking for the Militia. I suspected he only wanted an excuse for his daughter to learn and experience space from the best.

I looked over to Mara and read in her eyes two possibilities. The first and least probable was that she was hoping to heavens above that I would behave myself. The second and most likely was that she was admiring my new haircut.

"Brant, I need you to do your best to keep calm when we board," she said, staring me right in the eyes.

"Sure," I replied with as little enthusiasm as I could muster.

She placed one of her hands on each side of my perfectly shaved face, something I would have found sexy were it not for the next words out of her mouth: "I'm not playing with you here, Zenith. This is an important day for *Orbital*. An important day for the Militia, in fact. Do not ruin our opportunity with your reckless behaviour."

I really wanted to shrug her off, but she held me in place.

"I know that I can't make you promise anything," she added. "But Brant, for my sake and the sake of your anatomy, at least try to keep your ego on the downlow."

She stepped away and I shrugged off the low blow as best I could. That one had hurt.

"Captain, I must insist that you wear your Militia uniform when you go over." Mara raised her left eyebrow, all in a huff. "This is an official function, after all."

It would have been easier to heed her warning about my ego if she hadn't also insisted on me walking aboard that station dressed as a member of a marching band. I looked down at the bulky, uncomfortable uniform with its vibrant gold tassels crisscrossing the green fabric. It made me want to heave.

I also felt conflicted about being told to behave myself when the truth is that I had saved everyone's life aboard the station the last time we'd been here. Sure, I'd gotten arrested for the deed, but that didn't change the facts.

Almost no one besides me would ever know this truth.

Like a tidal wave of sewage crashing in upon hapless sunbathers, advertisements trumpeting the achievements of Pierre Mordeau, high marshal of the Prime Space Force, spilled onto every screen in our control hub. His overweight face beamed all the bullshit the peoples of Prime ate up without validation.

"Can you shut that shit off?" I blurted out.

Hearing Mordeau's voice talk about yet another magna fuel tax and how it was going to keep the galaxy running smoothly really irked me. I'm not sure how a tax that burdened every living being in this region of space would help those same people live more cost-efficient lives. He just wanted control and that's what it was all about. In fact, Mordeau was the antithesis of the idea of true space exploration and colonization. He was dangerously ignorant, lazy, and dim-witted. How had he been elected yet again?!

I heard the crunching sound of metal on metal, the cue telling us that *Orbital* had been connected to the station via a docking tube. The time for diplomacy had come.

I led the crew down to the docking bay, doing my best to avoid any reflections that might serve to remind me of our attire. Mara didn't suffer from the same affliction; she seemed oblivious to just how ridiculous we looked. If she weren't so radiant, I would say that her uniform was the biggest eyesore of all, with the extra shoulder tassels ambassadors wore to denote their position. If she had just kept her Orbiter level uniform, she would only have looked as ungodly as the rest of us.

When we got to the docking bay, I decided that only Mara and myself would venture onto the station for now. Stairn and Sparling would coordinate the repair efforts and Bog would oversee security during the operation.

Mara stood next to me in the small exit chamber as we waited to hear the hissing of the pressure seals. A fresh gust of wind blew into our faces, and I sensed that my hair looked fantastic at that moment.

We walked quickly up the docking arm where our typically broken exterior door magically opened properly.

We made our ways into the core of the space station. No sooner had we set foot on the wide entry corridor than we were met by two Prime officers.

My heart chose to skip a beat. I hoped I wouldn't be flagged down for my past "crimes." I would admit that atmospheric sedition did sound pretty badass when said aloud, but it was embarrassing to know that I had been busted for stinking so bad.

During the intervening time, of course, I had done my best to expunge my record by seducing a midranking security engineer to dissolve the criminal record in Prime's memory banks. I'd treated her like royalty for a night… and then hadn't been able to find the time to stick around in the morning. I hoped she had at least liked the note I had written on a napkin before leaving. I couldn't remember what I'd said, but I'm sure I had said it with the usual Zenith charm.

I just hoped my all-too-brief paramour had executed her part of the plan. I hadn't been able to check with her beforehand. To be honest, I couldn't even remember how to get in touch with her!

I looked around and quickly noticed a half-dozen heavily armed drones hovering near the ceiling. Prime maintained a high level of security. If ever a firefight were to break out, I knew for certain we would be riddled with more holes than the socks on a Telnian cow herder.

I could feel sweat form on the base of my back as the two Prime officers just ahead stepped into our path. I noticed that they were sub-lieutenants.

"Identifications, if you please," said the taller officer. He sounded polite and I could see from his insignia that he held the rank of sub-lieutenant second class. A rank he would have received after two years of service if he had been an average officer. He looked all-business.

I looked over to gauge Mara's mood. On the surface she seemed perfectly composed, but I knew her well enough to detect a hint of concern, perhaps even fear.

As the moments ticked by, I noticed the light reflecting off the scanning monitors the two men were using to identify us. Was something wrong?

"Captain Zenith, when were you last aboard Prime Station Alpha?" the taller officer asked. Did I detect a hint of tension in his voice?

I dared not lie this early in our game. "Three years."

He nodded his acceptance. I couldn't tell whether it was because of his uncertainty of the timing of my previous visit, or whether my answer matched his records. If it matched his records, I may indeed be in some trouble.

"Good," he said. "Our records confirm this."

Uh-oh. Trying not to get worked up, I decided to hold out a little longer before beginning to panic.

"What was the reason for your last visit, Captain?" the man asked.

"Mostly pleasure. Booze and women," I stated bluntly. The easiest way to disguise a lie was with the truth.

I heard Mara gasp, but she refrained from looking at me. Her green eyes were colder than ice.

"Well, there are some conflicting files in front of me," the sub-lieutenant said. "You wouldn't know anything about this, would you, Captain Zenith?"

I shook my head, sounding as innocent as I could. "I have no idea what you're referring to."

"Fair enough," he said indifferently. "Well, what can you tell me about atmospheric sedition?"

Aw, shit! "I don't even know what that means."

"That's okay. I'll put in a word for my superior to explain it to you personally."

I was sweating profusely now. The air smelled more sickly than sweet, and the tall ceiling somehow seemed lower and more claustrophobic than it had only moments ago.

It occurred to me that perhaps I had left too quickly three years ago when I'd spent that mutually beneficial romp with the security engineer. Perhaps when she'd asked if she could see me again, I shouldn't have answered with "Okay, bye." Obviously she either hadn't done the job at all, or she hadn't done it well enough.

A minute passed in silence, the only sound coming from the shorter sub-lieutenant's screen and his increasingly condescending sneers. From the portion of the screen visible to me, I realized he was analyzing *Orbital*. And he wasn't admiring it.

Well, I wasn't admiring him either. He was short and forgettable, with a receding hairline and dark stubble. He also looked vaguely familiar, but I couldn't place why or where. And I found it hard not to sneer right back at him.

"Just what are we supposed to do with this?" the shorter officer murmured to himself in reference to something that had appeared on his screen. Something about *Orbital*, no doubt.

I tried my best to hold back my temper, if only to keep Mara from later murdering me in my sleep—or even worse, shaving my head.

My impatience with these sub-lieutenants was growing thin and I wondered if pulling my spark pistol might not be such a bad idea after all. But a dozen more security drones were already approaching—and the moment I pulled my weapon, all hell would break loose.

If Mara hadn't been standing near me, I may still have tried. And yet I wouldn't risk her life so cavalierly. Maybe it was something she had said about what had happened on Jonah's ship, or it could have been the sinking sense of déjà vu I felt, but I decided to keep my anger in check a little while longer.

"Surely Ambassador Olwen can continue on with her duties aboard your station," I said, trying to make the best of the devolving situation.

The tall, polite one spoke indifferently yet without contempt. "Not since she came aboard with you, Captain."

Perhaps some name-dropping would help. "But she and I have a meeting with High Marshal Mordeau in less than an hour."

"I'll send word that this meeting will be postponed. Or perhaps cancelled."

Damn it. Trying to get past this guy was like trying to soften steel. I'd had a feeling I might get held up at security, but I hadn't expected Mara to get pulled in with me.

We waited tensely, knowing that the sub-lieutenants had notified their superiors about us. I was certain we were about to be arrested.

Within a few minutes, an even taller security officer squeezed his way past the drones surrounding us. I couldn't see a name on his uniform, but I could tell he must be one of the highest-ranking officers aboard Prime Station Alpha. His rank indicated that he was a full lieutenant. The title itself was a bit misleading. To achieve this position, he would have already donned the mantle of captain, the only distinction being that he didn't have a ship directly under his own command.

It shouldn't have surprised me that we were assigned such a prominent escort, given that we had been on our way to meet with the most powerful individual in the most powerful fleet in this part of the galaxy.

"Captain Zenith and Ambassador Olwen, please forgive my tardiness," the full lieutenant began. "I had an unavoidable delay."

He lifted the digital sensor pad mounted to his forearm and pressed a series of controls. In response, all but one security drone cleared out. The original two officers looked up in startlement, but they held their tongues.

"Now, what have I missed?" asked their superior.

His eyes bored into the short officer who had only moments ago been insulting *Orbital*. The short sub-lieutenant handed him a digital document pad; the lieutenant's eyes alighted with fire when he read the report. I didn't know what this meant.

When he was done reading the report, the lieutenant turned back to us. In the process, I noticed that he had a wave gun in his holster. His movements gave me the sense that he knew how to handle himself.

"Could I see your ID cards, please?" he asked.

Mara handed the lieutenant our IDs and he scanned them through the sensor pad.

"Very good, Captain Zenith and Ambassador Olwen. I am very glad to have made your acquaintance. If you would."

He gave me a long look I couldn't quite decipher, then lifted his arm to indicate the direction he wanted us to go. We followed him past the shellshocked sub-lieutenants.

The taller sub-lieutenant took a step forward. "But, sir—"

The lieutenant superior gave him a look that could have cut the man in two. At that point, the tall officer chose to remain silent. If only his shorter colleague had shared his wisdom.

"I've found Telnian space kennels that were worthier of salvage than that barge," muttered the short man. He gave himself a self-congratulatory chuckle, seeming to believe we were already out of hearing range.

Well, I heard the remark anyway. I wasn't sure if Mara or the lieutenant had been able to, and it didn't matter. My temper finally snapped…

…and so did the clasp holding my spark pistol in its holster.

Before I could fully turn to face the pair of security underlings, I felt Mara's hand grasp mine. She was trying to soothe me, but of course it didn't have a chance of working.

To my surprise, the lieutenant stepped smoothly between me and the officer who I'd been about to set straight.

"Silence!" the lieutenant snapped in the most menacing voice I'd ever heard.

The short officer cowered, his face reddening in embarrassment.

The lieutenant grabbed the man's ID card and scanned it. "Well, now… your name's Hubert Adamly?"

Well, I thought to myself. *That's a weird coincidence!*

What were the chances of two Adamlys pissing me off in exactly the same way no more than two days apart?

I didn't have time to ponder this as the ranking officer began in on Hubert again.

"It looks like you have a few very difficult days ahead of you." The lieutenant stepped in so close that he could have counted the greasy little hairs on Hubert's head, should he have wanted to.

The squat man began shaking in panic. There must have been a ten-centimetre height difference between the two men.

"You don't know, do you?" the lieutenant glowered. The man shook his head. "Ah, well, you're in for treat."

I was beginning to enjoy the show.

"It seems to me that you have a choice between three options," the lieutenant continued. "Hubert, do you want to know what those choices are?"

Hubert stood motionless.

"Here's the problem for you, Hubert." He said the name with a measure of disgust. "You see, you have intentionally insulted delegates of our esteemed allies, the Militia Space Fleet."

"Twice," I stated without thinking.

Mara looked at me with mild exasperation.

"Yes, thank you, Captain." The lieutenant snapped his fingers. "That's true. You have insulted the captain and the ambassador twice. Be thankful that I don't multiply the offence by two."

The lieutenant paused for a moment, seeming to get lost in his own thoughts. I think he was enjoying himself almost as much as I was.

"Now where was I? Right. Three options." He put his hand on the now-cringing Hubert's shoulder. "The first and possibly most expedient is a court martial. But court martials can be challenged, and even beaten. Rarely, but they can be. No, Hubert, I think you may want to hear the other two options before you choose door number one."

I almost began clapping. I couldn't think of a time in my life when I had so thoroughly enjoyed my time aboard a Prime vessel.

"Yeah, Hubert, I think you'll find some real satisfaction in this next option," the lieutenant continued. "Option two is that you spend one month and a day cleaning the drains and sanitation ports of Prime Station Alpha without a breathing apparatus."

"A month and a day?" Hubert stammered.

"For each offence. But option three, Hubert! That's where the fun begins."

The lieutenant was playing Hubert like a Stradivarius on opening night. Indeed, Hubert didn't look like he wanted to know about option three, but I certainly looked forward to hearing it—and Mara seemed nearly as intrigued as I was.

"Option three…" The lieutenant paused for effect, and I could almost hear the drumroll in the background. "…has you sporting the new rank of second level private, D-class, of Station Milnor near the Embedian asteroid field."

Hubert didn't understand this punishment so well, and I had to admit that other than the magnificent demotion it didn't live up to my high expectations.

"Doesn't sound so bad, Hubert? Well, second level private, D-class, is five steps below the required rank you'll need if you ever want to man a Prime ship. It ranks just between robotic janitor and a doorstop. But the silver lining here is location, location, location. Station Milnor is about eight trillion parsecs away from anything that even resembles civilization, and the station is only about ten percent bigger than a shoebox. But don't worry about feeling overly cramped, as you'll be totally alone for your entire five years of service."

Hubert turned green with that.

"Now, now, Hubert, it's not all bad. I have to accompany our esteemed allies here to their meeting with High Marshal Mordeau. You've heard of the high marshal, haven't you? Well, the good news is that you get a solid hour to decide which fate you want. Now, don't decide to leave your post, because if I return and you deprive me of the presence of your smiling face, I will be forced to choose your punishment for you."

With that, the lieutenant led us down the corridor and away from Hubert, who was certainly having a worse day than I was.

After a few minutes of navigating the large, winding corridor, Mara interrupted the silence. "Do you normally let the accused decide their own punishment?" she asked, a bit taken aback by poor Hubert's fate. I could tell by her voice that she was still worried about my criminal record.

The lieutenant chuckled. "No. The court martial threat is real, but probably overkill. I simply made up the other two options. I'll probably find some other tasks to punish him with."

I laughed hard enough to dislodge a kidney stone. I paused for a moment and faced the officer. "What is your name, Lieutenant?"

"Samuel Benson, Captain."

"Nice to meet you, Lieutenant." I wasn't yet ready to like a Prime officer, but I couldn't find my ready supply of distaste when talking to him.

"Please, Captain, I would prefer if you called me Samuel when not in presence of other officers."

"Then likewise. Call me Brant. As you know, this is Mara, daughter of High Marshal Olwen."

Benson shook Mara's hand warmly.

I studied Benson as we made our way towards our destination. He was perhaps a centimetre or two taller than me and his shortly cropped black hair revealed a near perfect hairline. He was handsome, if in a rugged way. His wiry frame made him look taller than he was.

As we walked, he passed me a digital pad. "This is quite an interesting read, Captain."

I knew he was referring to my arrest.

"However, our upcoming meeting is far more important to both our organizations than this messy legal business," he added. "One day, when we both have fewer pressing matters at hand, I'd very much like discussing the matter with you."

I breathed a sigh of relief.

We soon came to an adjacent and even larger thoroughfare; this one was twelve paces across. The well-lit corridor teemed with a variety of races. The vast diversity of Prime was part of what made her so formidable, and Prime Station Alpha was perhaps the greatest testament to that. The luminous place was alive with activity, from the bleating of Telnian dogsheep to the dry rumble of unbridled muletens. I could make out a dozen spoken languages, in every imaginable octave and frequency.

Apart from the station's denizens, the curved glass walls all around me revealed the glimmering majesty of space; opposite them were screens showing station maps, emergency exits, and charts of neighbouring regions of space. The state-of-the-art design made me angry. Why did our own headquarters have to look like a squashed shoebox that had fallen out of a dumpster?

Along the way, Mara was asking the lieutenant a few questions about the station itself. His answers were friendly albeit elusive. He occasionally needed to remind us that he was unable to divulge too much, what with being the head of security and all.

It was a pleasant enough walk. Pretty much the only feature marring the corridor, in my estimation, were the constant digital advertisements showing off the high marshal in one pose or another.

Once more I did my best to ignore that man's bullshit. I had a feeling I'd be floating in it soon enough.

Moments later, my eyes and ears were captivated by a couple of friendly faces. Captain Ambden and his son Simbden stood not five paces in front of us, exiting from their very own docking arm. I hoped they'd had a cleaner entry aboard the station than we'd had. Both wore bright and energetic smiles. Ambden's looked like something out of a cartoon, with his massive, squat proportions.

God bless the Mackmians; they always made me smile.

Ambden had chosen to wear his customary uniform, only slightly stained with some sort of gravy. In contrast, Simbden was dressed in a simple black and grey pantsuit I'd seen many times in the general Mackmian population.

"Captain Zenith!" Ambden held out his broad and jiggly arms, drawing all sorts of attention from onlookers, not the least of which was the tall and skinny man he nearly close-lined with his flabby arms. "Destinations unite for gods and planets!"

He stepped closer and gave me the biggest and quite honestly squishiest hug I'd ever received. He seemed genuinely ecstatic to see me. I wasn't sure why, but I couldn't help but think I was forgetting something.

"You don't know how glad I am to see you again, my friend." The Mackmian captain let me go and stepped aside, allowing me to take in the sight of his son.

Simbden spoke next with youthful jubilance. "My captain, sir. Once again allow me to thank you for letting me join *Orbital*'s crew. Honours above me."

Oh shit! The fog of my drunken stupor suddenly dissipated enough to allow me to remember the agreement with Ambden. I tried to think of all possible ways of refusing the boy now. None of them seemed promising.

"Simbden," I said shaking his hand and trying to buy time. "Mechanical and electrical engineer Simbden… you are indeed welcome aboard *Orbital*. But I'm afraid you'll have to wait some time before you join the crew."

Simbden's face dropped in despair. It would have been comical if it wasn't so tragic.

"You see, *Orbital* is in need of major repairs and will be in Prime's docking bay for some time."

I looked over at Benson and he nodded in return.

"Preliminary reports estimate four days," Benson confirmed.

My heart nearly sank into my colon. Shit. Four days aboard Prime Station Alpha!

"I wouldn't feel right introducing you to *Orbital* under such circumstances," I said. "You understand, don't you?"

Simbden picked up his gear and stepped past me with a giant smile on his face. "Don't worry, my captain, sir. I've been studying *Orbital* for some time now. Well, in truth a very long time… since you began working with my father. I promise you that I'll be a great help to the Prime staff. I feel it is my honour to help out with this. Thank you."

With no other warning, Simbden took off and made his way through the crowd like a gazelle on speed—in the direction of *Orbital*, by the looks of it.

"Does he know where he's going?" Benson asked, trying his best to track the energetic and agile young Mackmian through the throngs of people.

Ambden watched his son disappear off into the distance. "Don't worry. All paths lead to the heavens."

Damn it, Ambden, make some freakin' sense!

"I'm just joking, Captain. Young Simbden there knows Prime Station Alpha like a Mackmian souerd."

Well, that sounded like a good thing as far as I could tell.

"He has a fascination with learning." Ambden scratched his chubby face. "He loves technology above all else. Before he could waddle, he could already recite every room in Prime Station Alpha without ever having set foot on her. I accidentally left out a few copies of *Space Architectural Digest* during his weaning years…"

Benson signalled to an adjacent corridor and another security officer rushed quickly to his side. The lieutenant said something quickly and the junior officer nodded.

"Captain Ambden, sir, Corporal Lockley here will escort you to your chambers," said Benson.

"Of course, Lieutenant." He then nodded to each of us. "Captain, Ambassador."

Before Ambden stepped past me, he leaned in and whispered some heartfelt and intense words: "Captain, he's my firstborn. Keep him safe."

As he stepped away, I felt the complexity and uselessness of his next words coming before they left his oversized lips.

"Glorious paths and space abundant to us all!"

Benson smiled at that and continued to lead the way towards our impending meeting.

"Captain, you invited Simbden to join our crew?" Mara asked, falling into step beside me.

I couldn't tell if she was upset, and to be honest I wasn't sure how to feel about it myself. But I couldn't admit that it had been the effects of EZ-Heal and not my intention to recruit the young Mackmian. I needed to think of something to smooth things over with Mara.

I said the first thing that came to mind. "Well, yes. As we discussed, *Orbital* needs improvement. The ship's falling apart one strand of shag carpeting at a time. What more could we need than a mechanical engineer?"

"Very clever," she said. "Don't you think he's a bit young? I mean, how old is he?"

He was fifteen, but I didn't want to tell her that. Besides, Mackmians matured quicker than humans. "I didn't ask, but I hear he's supposed to be quite good."

"Why didn't you talk to me first?" She seemed genuinely disappointed to have been left out of the loop. She was making this very difficult.

"I didn't have the time, Mara. Ambden was pressing me on it, and in the moment his son seemed like a good addition to the crew. He's young, and that's a good thing. He can learn and serve many good years with us."

That sounded pretty respectable.

"Can you please let me know when next you plan on such a big change to *Orbital*?" she asked. "That would mean a great deal to me."

Our journey lasted several minutes longer. There were still throngs of people scurrying about, some of which seemed unusual.

Speaking of which, I suddenly noticed a group of Mafian Tenlords. The seedy organization, prominent in the underworld of the circus circuit, had always fascinated the hell out of me. We passed a long stream of the tiny, waist-height Mafians, each of them pulling along cages of the strangest creatures the galaxy had ever known.

I leaned over and whispered in Mara's ear as a Jernsi Jekyl shrieked by, its five and a half eyes blinking at me. "You see, Ambassador? I am behaving myself well thus far."

She thought about that for a moment. "Lacking the chance to misbehave is not the same as behaving yourself."

I shrugged. Semantics!

Our walk through the station took us from the larger corridor to one that was less frequently traversed but more richly decorated. I recognized this as a linkage between the core corridors and the command sector. We went up a flight of stairs where Benson scanned us past three progressively more intimidating checkpoints, the last of which required a pat down which made me feel like having a cigarette afterward.

Finally, we reached a corridor edged by a handrail overlooking another corridor below. I was busy peering down when I heard Benson trying to get our attention.

"Captain, Ambassador, we have arrived at the Grand Council Room of the Universe."

The name was cheesy and pompous, of course, but so too was Prime.

A pair of extremely large doors towered over us, framed within a grand arch. Upon one of the doors was the giant insignia of Prime Star Force, chiselled out of gold. The emblem was comprised of a scale holding a constellation on one side and books on the other. Every time I saw the insignia, I hated Prime more.

The other door showcased an elaborate carving of the great Battle of Zen, one of Prime's crowning moments from more than two hundred years ago. They still clung to it, as though every officer alive today had played a part in the victory. It seemed self-righteous to derive glory from a battle very few alive had even witnessed.

The doors swung open after Benson used the sensor pad on his forearm to gain entry. As we passed through the entrance, I looked up and noted a sea of red-light indicators, signalling the presence of micro-armaments aimed in our direction, ready to obliterate us should we take a wrong step.

I swallowed my anger, pride, and the acid reflux of EZ-Heal in an effort to keep calm. I doubted this meeting would prove to be a highlight of my life.

Mara led the way, followed by me.

However much I loathed the prospect of this meeting, I wasn't expecting the reception awaiting us. Only two steps in, we were both stopped short by the bright flash of a wave pistol about six paces ahead of us. Someone was firing right at us!

The blast spun out of the pistol with such speed that it created a tornado of air and humidity in its wake. Quickly and without thought, I grabbed Mara by both shoulders and threw her out of the way. She landed on her side with a thud and slid across the floor.

The wave blast crashed directly into my chest, like a boulder plopping into a calm body of water. It launched me backward with such extreme force that I didn't even register Benson's face as I blew past him and back out into the corridor. Before I knew it, I sailed over the protective handrail and found myself careening towards the lower level.

My landing was softened by something that gurgled—specifically, a giant purple and green squid-lizard known as a Queel. I felt fortunate that the poor beast had broken my fall, although I doubted the Queel felt the same way about me.

I felt its long tentacles droop over my shoulder and reached for it, only to discover a stream of efflorescent beige slime trickling down my uniform and into my pants. Not liking what was taking place below the belt, I quickly stood up and ran my hand down my pants, scooping out a disturbingly gooey ball of slime. I tried to fling it onto the floor, but it wouldn't easily detach from my outstretched fingers.

It wasn't all bad, for I found the strong smell not at all repugnant. In fact, it smelled like flowers in bloom.

My chest ached from where the blast had hit me, but I didn't feel seriously injured—at least not physically. The procession of Mafian Tenlords, the same we'd encountered earlier, had huddled around me to launch a verbal assault at me in a language I didn't understand. They were short but plentiful and they blocked my exit, gesticulating madly. All I could make out from their speech was the suggestion to remove my head or various other body parts… I didn't like the message or their tone of voice.

As I pulled my spark weapon free of its holster, I noticed that their voices lowered in volume and anger. They seemed to conclude it would be a good idea to step out of my way.

I stepped over and past them, approaching a set of stairs that led back to the upper corridor and the entrance to the vaunted Grand Council Room of the Universe. I took the stairs two at a time.

The enormous doors to the council room opened wide before me and I saw Benson quickly approach, stretching his hands ahead of him in a soothing manner. I looked past him to see that Mara was uninjured.

And beyond her was the accursed Prime officer who'd shot me, the offending wave pistol still in his hand.

"Peace, Captain." Benson bodily blocked my way, preventing me from taking a clear shot at my attacker. No doubt he could see the murderous intent in my eyes.

The lieutenant pressed down on my arm, causing me to lower the weapon. I was growing impatient by his attempts to divert me from my purpose and was about to press the weapon into his own chest when Mara jumped in.

"Brant, are you okay?" she rasped.

When I didn't answer and she saw my determination to inflict violence, she also stepped into my path.

"Captain, there's no need for violence," Benson pleaded. "Please, put your weapon down. I think it was an accident."

I looked past Benson and saw that the offending officer was no longer holding the wave pistol.

But it wasn't just any Prime officer, I soon realized; it only took me a moment to recognize the face I hated most in the universe—the one belonging to none other than Pierre Mordeau, the high marshal of Prime Star Force.

Again, my first instinct was to raise my pistol and blast his ass back into yesterday.

"Please, Captain..." Benson was doing his best to stop me. "It was merely an accident."

Mara was now close enough that I could feel her breath on my neck. "Brant, don't do this. Remember what we talked about. Do you remember how badly we need those repairs?"

I could barely acknowledge her. My mind stormed with thoughts of retribution.

She placed her hand overtop my weapon. "Don't do this!"

I couldn't understand how she could have shrugged off the offence so easily, since the blast could have just as easily hit her as it did me. Just thinking of the possibility of her getting hurt was pushing me over the edge.

"Brant, do this for me."

I looked directly into her eyes long enough to slow my heart rate, allowing me to take control of myself again.

I inhaled one of the deepest, darkest breaths I'd ever drawn, doing my best to exhale my rage. It was perhaps the longest minute of my life.

When I'd finally cooled down enough to fight the urge to commit manslaughter, I began walking further into the chamber. Benson remained by my side and guided me towards the giant table that dominated the meeting room.

I glanced up at the high ceiling and observed the ornate decorations, large and intimidating like everything else aboard the station. However, I was in no mood to appreciate the décor. Instead I concentrated on the long table and the other people already seated around it, waiting for me and Mara to take our seats.

In fact, there were seven others in the chamber, all but one of whom I'd had the opportunity to meet before. Standing at an average height was High Marshal Mayer Olwen, Mara's father. His wispy grey hair and thick spectacles would have rendered him recognizable a parsec away. He stood on the near side of the table; evidently, this side was reserved for the Militia's representatives.

Across the table, on the side reserved for Prime, sat Jonah and his lovely first lieutenant, Marissa Monroe. Next to her was a slim woman with a rank insignia I wasn't familiar with.

"Captain Zenith, this is Commander Genwin Marsdale," Benson said by way of introduction. "She's Prime's High Intelligence Officer."

I was surprised when Marsdale offered me her hand. I was unaware that anyone in the Prime's upper ranks had any tact. After shaking hands with both me and Mara, she leaned back and picked up the digital pad that sat on the polished surface of the table.

Marsdale looked very keen indeed for an intelligence officer, from the smart alignment of her uniform to her perfectly combed dark hair, tied just above her shoulders. She had an aquiline nose, pointed ever so slightly upward.

As I took my seat, she didn't speak a word. She didn't have to.

To her right was the very man who'd just attempted to kill me, a man I'd been waiting three years to cross paths with again.

"Captain, of course you know High Marshal Mordeau," Benson said carefully, still trying to keep the peace. The expression on his face was almost apologetic.

Mordeau looked up with self-assumed pride, and stupidity, in his dull brown eyes. This was the esteemed first officer of the most powerful fleet in the known universe, the so-called Holder of Universal Order, and undisputedly the most powerful being in the galaxy. And I was as impressed today as I was when I had first met him fifteen years ago.

Which was to say that I was more impressed with the Queel goo trickling down my nether regions.

I took a long look at the man towards whom I'd harboured a great deal resentment, hatred, and anger much of my adult life. Mordeau was grossly overweight, more closely resembling a roll of jumbo toilet paper than a man. His chunky face barely contained his sagging jowls and a field of acne dominated his nose. His hair had receded so far that it had been fully vanquished; taking up the void of hair was a patch of dry, scratchy skin afflicted with psoriasis.

It was good to see that he looked as horrible as I felt he deserved.

Even so, he was adorned in Prime's highest-ranking uniform, similar to Jonah's but with a few extra insignias across his chest.

And there was the offending wave pistol, resting idly on the table in front of him. I quickly calculated that I would be able to draw my own weapon and blow him into an exploding wad of corpulent goo before he even managed to touch the gun. He wouldn't even know what had hit him. But could I beat the security drones gazing down at us? They reminded me of the ones that guarded Inferno's gambling den on Omicron One.

I thought of Mara. Swallowing my pride, my chest still aching from the attack, I chose to keep my mouth shut.

Mordeau spoke first. "Zenith, I see you're looking gooey."

He laughed, which sounded like a wheezing elephant. He seemed to enjoy the thought that he'd nearly annihilated a visiting official.

How the hell had he been elected to high marshal again? The thought flashed through my mind once more.

When no one returned so much of chuckle at his pathetic joke, he fell silent again.

As I was about to respond, I felt Mara's hand subtly grasp my wrist. Unfortunately, my will to return his verbal volley got the better of me.

"I'm glad to see you've taken my advice, Mordeau, and invested in weapons training," I mused. "I don't care what anyone says about you, your aim is not as shitty as I remember."

I felt genuinely conflicted between trying to appease Mara and avenging myself upon this fat scourge of the universe.

At first, he laughed. Then he seemed to realize I had insulted him, and the sound trailed off.

"Please, if you would take a seat," Marsdale invited smoothly. "It is indeed an honour to have with us the leaders of the Militia Space Fleet. You are all welcome. Shall we begin?"

With these few sentences, the tension in the room subsided enough to allow the meeting to commence.

"I would first like to apologize for the incident of misunderstanding which just took place," Marsdale continued, turning to me. "Please accept the repairs to *Orbital* as a gift from Prime Star Force."

Before I could respond, Mara stepped in. "Thank you very much, Commander Marsdale. We are indeed honoured and grateful. And we know that it was just a mishap. No major damage was inflicted. Apology accepted."

I looked over at Mara, feeling betrayed. She returned my expression of anger with a mixture of emotions I couldn't decipher. Accepting the gift of repairs felt like selling out, although I took some consolation in knowing that I could always find a way to show Mordeau exactly where we stood at some later point.

"I heard that you've had the opportunity to study the incidents at Quazar station two days past," Mara added.

Marsdale nodded. "Yes, we find the actions of *Orbital* and her crew to be extremely commendable. Most courageous."

I nodded to the woman with a small smile. It was nice to finally be given some credit where it was due. Mordeau, however, seemed to give no such credit; he hummed to himself, having picked up his gun and begun spinning it absently on the tabletop.

"The new alien race appearing in the Quazar system took everyone by surprise," Benson said. "Captain, your actions probably saved a great number of lives. As it stands, due to your actions, fewer beings aboard the station were harmed. Other than the aliens, of course."

"I've named them the Quazarns!" shouted Mordeau, sounding extremely proud of himself.

"Very clever."

"Thanks, Zenith," said Mordeau, mistaking my sarcasm for a genuine compliment.

"Bozo," I muttered darkly, just quiet enough that the esteemed high marshal couldn't hear it.

Benson, who obviously had better hearing, let out a quick and uncomfortable spark of laughter. He stifled it before drawing more attention to himself.

Mara looked over at me with some annoyance, but then seemed to remember that thus far I hadn't yet killed anyone. She let my comment go without reprimand.

"Commander Marsdale," Mara began, shifting her attention back to the briefing. "We were told about the aliens… er, Quazarns… releasing what has been referred to as energy orbs. What more can you tell us about them?"

When she mentioned the Quazarns' name, Mordeau bowed his chunky head in pride.

"Yes, the energy orbs," said Marsdale. "They are indeed very interesting. Everything we've learned so far is…" She paused, searching for the right words. "…inconclusive."

Marsdale's hands went to work on a panel of controls built into the dark tabletop. Instantly, a three-dimensional hologram sprung to life, displaying one of the orbs. The lighting in the room darkened, giving us a better look at the hologram, which rotated slowly.

"These orbs have led to a great deal of debate," Marsdale said. "They're no larger than a man's head yet contain the power of a small sun. Our technicians have at last had the chance to capture one of these orbs, bringing it to a remote station in the Edelan system. That way, should disaster occur, there won't be any widespread effects."

"But what are they used for?" Mara asked.

"That part is still not entirely known to us. We've determined this much, though: the orb seems to have built-in amplitude resonators which mimic the properties of dark energy, which as you all know have been incorporated into dark rift transport. The difference between dark rift transport and the energy orbs is that the orbs are thousands of times more powerful. And perhaps even more worrisome is the fact that the orbs seem to mimic dark energy in a way no one has ever seen. Our scientists haven't dreamed of an energy capture device of this magnitude."

She paused, taking some time to think through what next to say. This was obviously a difficult decision for her, as I could tell she didn't want to reveal too much in front of High Marshal Mordeau. But she was bound by our treaty to disclose anything we needed to know.

"So what's the lowdown here?" I asked, cutting to the chase. "I mean, what do you expect to happen? And how long before we should expect it?"

The high intelligence officer's dark hair shifted as she furrowed her forehead in concern. A strand of hair caressed the side of her cheek. She still couldn't quite decide what to say.

"So far we've considered four possibilities," Benson cut in. "The first is that the energy orbs act as a giant relay. With enough of them scattered throughout the galaxies, they could form a web."

"But to what purpose?" I asked.

"That we have not yet learned."

"It's a weapon, of course," Mordeau cried out with certainty.

"What makes you believe that so strongly, High Marshal?" Mara asked.

"Because I know."

His answer struck me as very curt, and Mara obviously wasn't satisfied by it. Indeed, she pushed for more.

"Energy fields this large often emit misleading status reports." Mara pointed to the relevant sections of the holographic display. "The technology seems to mimic Mackmian portals, as well as

Telnian gravity fields. Is there a specific piece of technology that leads you to believe this is a weapon?"

The high marshal simply shrugged. "But it has to be a weapon."

"Yes, but what makes you believe that?" Mara asked again, getting frustrated now.

"Because what else could it be, silly girl? Why else would these energy sources have been scattered across our territory?"

Only Mara's stern grip on my wrist held me back from reaching across the table and throttling him. Even she was barely controlling herself from not murdering the pompous ass.

"It's true that it may very well be a weapon," Benson said soothingly. "However, there are clues that this 'web' could be related to communications. That's the second possibility."

"It sounds very much to me like you doubt that," Mara replied, and much more shortly than before.

"Unfortunately, yes. My gut tells me that a race of humanoids wouldn't go so far out of their way to set up a proverbial telephone line, not using such an extremely powerful technology."

"So what's possibility number three?" I asked.

"A weapon, dammit," Mordeau stated with absolute certainty.

I looked at his scrunched-up pug of a face and almost felt sorry for him. How the hell in Jupiter's three nipples had this man ever kept such a powerful position?

"Well..." Benson sighed. "Yes, the third option is that it could, in fact, be a weapon."

With that, the high marshal seemed to beam with pride. I very nearly envied his ability to be so certain of anything. Worry that he might be wrong never seemed to enter his mind.

"And the fourth possibility?" Mara asked, her eyes avoiding Mordeau entirely.

"A means of transportation." Surprisingly, this came from High Marshal Olwen. Up until this point, Militia's high marshal had been silent, and I'd been thankful for it. His wavering mental capacity worried me when it came to high-stakes negotiations.

To this fourth possibility, I noticed that the gathered Prime officers nodded in confirmation.

"I take it transportation is the most likely explanation," Mara said.

"Yes," Benson confirmed.

But it was High Marshall Olwen who launched into the explanation. "It's very clear to me. The orbs' energy patterns are too strong to be used for anything else. The orbs are far enough apart that travel between them, at the fastest conventional rate of speed, would be in the order of weeks. But the amount of power in the orbs could facilitate transportation in a matter of seconds, like dark rift transport. Which would leave this quadrant of space very, very vulnerable."

"So, as I said, a weapon." Mordeau slammed his hand down on the table. "We must take action!"

"That is exactly right, High Marshal," said Marsdale. She turned to Olwen. "Have you spent a great deal of time studying such energy sources? Because your analysis is spot on."

I could see the light in Olwen's eye flicker and then vanish. Once more he registered confusion and perhaps boredom. He looked over at Mara, and she understood perfectly that the brilliant man who had started the Militia so many years ago was losing his ability to follow along. I hoped the Prime officers didn't pick up on it too quickly.

"Yes," Mara said, stepping in. "My father's career has encompassed a wide variety of missions and explorations that have produced an almost unheard-of quantity of information." She hesitated. "So what can we at the Militia do? How can we help Prime Star Force?"

Mordeau looked across the table at her with cold curiosity. "What does the Militia have to do with anything? The orbs belong to Prime, as they all fall within our territory."

"And the Quazar incident?" I asked. My heart raced as I began to intuit where this was going. "The Quazar system is in our territory."

"I would say it's neutral," Marsdale remarked.

I frowned at her. "Only the outer regions. The black hole itself is clearly in our space."

"So what, Zenith?" Mordeau asked. "What's your point?"

"The Quazar incident is our concern, not Prime's. We were there when it all went down. And the Mackmians are our clients, not Prime's."

"And yet Prime ships currently hold the station down." Mordeau broke into a smile, as if to imply there was nothing more to say on the matter.

I absolutely believed there was a great deal more to say. "That means nothing to me, Mordeau."

"Are you going to start a battle with us to reclaim Quazar?" Mordeau asked. "I welcome a war."

Before I could respond, Marsdale stood up and cut us both short. "There's no reason for any altercation between our formidable fleets. We are allies. There will be no war under *any* circumstances."

Mordeau looked up at his intelligence officer with a look of cold defiance, but he backed down.

It was becoming very clear to me how Prime continued to grow in strength with an asshat like High Marshal Mordeau leading the way. The simple truth was that he only led when the decisions were unimportant. He was a figurehead.

"We have no intentions apart from continuing our kinship and camaraderie with Prime," Mara assured everyone.

In the meantime, it seemed that High Marshall Olwen had come back from his momentary lapse.

"The Militia will not interfere with Prime in this matter," Olwen declared.

I looked over at him with disbelief and disgust, then trusted that Mara would step in and help with her father.

"But Father," she began, "we should put forth our efforts to aid—"

"No. When it comes to the Mackmians, we will give Prime room to breathe. We have priorities elsewhere."

It was spoken so definitively that I could see little room to present an argument. I found myself hoping that this was the mentally encumbered version of the old man, and that in a moment the real High Marshal Olwen would arise and fix this mess.

God, I missed the old Mayer Olwen.

"High Marshal, we must take part in this mission," I said with as much force as I could muster, hoping to snap him out of whatever spell he had fallen under.

"No, Brant," Olwen said. "Those are my orders. When our prior commitments are completed, we will return to help in the Quazar system. This is final."

"Ha!" Mordeau laughed in triumph. "Zenith, it seems *he* knows his place."

And with that, my hand went straight for my spark pistol. I was shocked when Mara was quick enough to stop me before I could pull it above the table. Things were heating up...

"You have the guarantee of Prime Star Force that your assistance will continue to be welcome should you gain the resources needed to commit to the project," Marsdale stated with what sounded like genuine consolation. "We will keep you up to date through High Marshal Mayer Olwen. The Militia will not be left out of the loop."

My eyes still burned with an icy death, pointed directly at Mordeau.

"Now, Zenith, I think it's time to talk about the spoils," Mordeau said, stoking the fire his intelligence officer had been trying to quench. I could tell he was enjoying his victory.

"What are you talking about?" I asked.

"The spark pistols you took from the Quazarns will belong to us, since you've forfeited your right to them."

"What?!" I spit out in disbelief.

"Zenith, those weapons belong to Prime. You won't need them anyway. As far as I've just heard, you're leaving. Now put the gun down before you accidentally hurt someone."

I snapped, and nothing could hold me back. The room erupted in a flurry of action as I leaped to my feet, blind to everything but my own fury.

"Go to hell!" I raged between clenched teeth. "And if you need directions, I have a map written here on the bottom of my boot!"

I even went so far as to show him the bottom of my boot. At that moment, I remembered exactly why it was so important that *Orbital* have an ambassador.

Mordeau got to his feet as well, utter disgust written over his slack features. "How dare you, Zenith!" Saliva spewed from his blubberous lips. "I'm a high marshal and you're the captain of a flying toilet! You will do as you're told, or I'll have you taken to the brig for the rest of your days."

My finger inched its way towards the trigger. I was seconds away from firing—

"Brant, you will obey," Owen ordered with a sigh. "It's best to leave this to Prime. Your weapon is inconsequential at the moment. You will do as I order."

It was a direct command from my superior, my colleague, and my good friend. The one man I had sworn to follow. Looking into his eyes was a brutal experience, seeing the light in his grey eyes flicker back and forth from cognizance to bewilderment. I wasn't sure if it would hurt more or less to know for sure which version of the man had given me that dreadful order.

With those words from Olwen, I was utterly betrayed.

This was it for me. Everything fell apart. Never had I ever felt so defeated, so demoralized.

I closed my eyes a long moment, hoping I could undo the events of this meeting. Or at least wait until Olwen came to his senses.

My knuckles were whiter than snow when I lifted the pistol and, with all the effort I could dredge up, placed it on the grey metal table. I did my best to ignore the sight of Benson training his weapon in my direction. He was just doing his duty.

With a sharp metallic click, the pistol left my grasp.

"Lieutenant Benson, get this man out of my sight and don't let me see him again," High Marshal Mordeau said angrily.

I was oblivious to everything going on around me, except for Benson's loud sigh as he began to escort me out.

Before I stepped out of the room, I spoke one last time. "This isn't over, Pierre. Our paths will meet again—and soon."

"And it will end exactly the same way, Zenith."

His voice sounded like a nail being hammered into a coffin; I did my best to decide whether that coffin was mine or his.

The only thing I was certain of at this point was that this meeting would require retribution, or my name wasn't Brant Zenith.

CHAPTER TWELVE

Two Steps Forward

As I left the council room and wandered downstairs, I found myself surrounded by the horde of Mafian Tenlords and their underlings. Their procession, made up of all types of animals and walking plants, paraded by like a thundering rain shower. And they all seemed to be very pissed off. It felt to me as though all of God's creatures were in an uproar by my very presence. I guess I had that effect on people.

I felt so dispirited, so beaten and lifeless, that I hardly made much of an effort to defend myself from the accusations they threw at me as I passed. The large corridor with its tall ceilings and domed glass seemed to be set ablaze with angry circus performers dead set on exacting revenge on me for having fallen earlier on one of their precious creatures.

In the midst of the conflagration, I noted a singular Tenlord who looked like he may have been their leader. He was about average height for a Mafian, which meant he rose no taller than my waist. His head, the largest part of his body, was grey and covered with spiky black hair common to members of his species; it reminded me of the plume of a Roman centurion. Indeed, the longer the mullet displayed, the higher the individual's rank.

They were typically very interesting humanoids to deal with, unless they were pissed at you for squishing one of their prized Queels.

To make matters worse, I could only understand about one in every three words shouted at me. For the past fifty or so years, Prime Star Force had employed a type of synaptic enzyme translator which could be taken via inhaler. It was a remarkable technology that only took moments to absorb into the body and worked for years.

The only downfall of the synaptic enzymes was that they could be damaged by the overconsumption of alcohol. So it wasn't hard to see why my enzyme translators weren't up to par.

The Mafians' gesticulations were becoming extreme—they verged on the hilarious, as their favourite gesture of anger seemed to involve running each of their hands down the sides of their ears and then throwing their hands out in a violent gunning motion. It was quite amusing, but I didn't think they would appreciate my laughter.

I began to pick out the same two words over and over again: "shiasti rastin." I didn't know what *shiasti* meant, but I was pretty certain that *rastin* referred to a devil.

I looked past the Mafian Tenlords and saw the Queel I had been so intimately acquainted with about an hour ago. As it slithered closer, I noticed that only one or two of its twelve slime-encrusted tentacles seemed to have been harmed. I really couldn't tell what the Tenlords were making such a big stink about.

"Shiasti rastin, miva tella youva ontera dettaer."

This time, the leading Tenlord spoke slowly enough for me to pick out the individual words.

"Mivian youvian annestaer saestraian," I replied. It either meant that I was truly sorry for my actions, or perhaps it meant that I wanted to sleep with his younger sister.

Instantly the Tenlords erupted in a roar of anger and a new swarm of rapid gesticulations. If they had been armed with their weapon of choice, the rapscallion deboner, I'm sure I would have found myself walking around without any bones in my body.

I had to conclude I had indeed said something about wanting to sleep with the fellow's sister.

"Skavian da shiasti rastin!" shouted the enraged mob. Angry fists rose in the air all around me as they chanted.

I didn't much like the sound of this! The word *skavian* meant "to skin."

To my great relief, the doors to the Grand Council Room of the Universe reopened and Benson stepped through alone. He made his way towards us and greeted me with a solemn nod. Then he cracked a grin at my predicament.

"Captain Zenith, I see you've found some new friends." Benson stepped over a couple of their heads, and I noticed that the Mafians simply ignored him. "It's a good thing that Prime disarms all non-official fleet visitors."

"Yeah, it seems I'm a popular guy of late," I said sarcastically.

At that moment the Mafian leader pulled forth an instrument that resembled an ice cream scooper. He brandished it menacingly, poking its rounded metal "blades" into my chest.

Benson seemed either intrigued or amused, I couldn't tell which. "Wow, Captain Zenith, you must really have angered Melnian here. He's now holding the Blades of the Acrofted. It's a traditional and very rare weapon that they use only when their honour is wounded."

I guess the Blades of the Acrofted had looked too much like a kitchen implement to be stripped away by security.

"Really?" I asked, genuinely curious. It wasn't my first time in this type of position, although it was the first time it had happened in the presence of a Mafian Tenlord. "I wounded his honour?"

"Yeah, or perhaps—"

"Perhaps?"

I was tempted to put my hand on the little Mafian's head and push him away, but he seemed quite adamant. And he did seem quite skilled in the use of these so-called blades.

"Perhaps it is not his honour that is wounded," Benson mused. "Sometimes this reaction occurs when his pocketbook is wounded. They take their profits just as seriously as their honour. Sometimes it's simply that you've caught him during his yearly attrocian period."

"Attrocian period? What's that?"

"Unfortunately for you, Captain, it's the time of the year when their backsides erupt into a very itchy and painful rash. I've heard it's quite excruciating for them, and it takes but the smallest offence to set off a very serious incident."

"Oh great," I muttered to myself in despair.

"Hold on a second." Benson tapped on the shoulder of the little Mafian with the eye-catching mullet. When the lieutenant spoke, his words were quick and upbeat but with an undertone of seriousness.

Melnian the Mafian Tenlord, armed with the Blades of the Acrofted and standing within striking range of my heart, then answered in return.

"Queel Toulantin ainta promantian lanffa skeeteraboslom. Shiasti rastin hastae morane indabout Queel Toulantin hasenta greementaen."

Benson nodded in understanding. I could tell he was trying to conceal a smile but failing to do so.

"So?" I asked incredulously.

"Well, the good news, Captain, is that you have indeed not injured his honour but rather his pocketbook. Such as it is, money will be sufficient to repair the injury."

"What do I owe him for? It's not like I stole his purse."

"No, but you crushed his prized Queel, Toulantin. Now he believes the gods will not bless him with a profitable circus, because

Toulantin will not be able to stage his 'acts of the impossible' at the next performance."

"What? I only broke him in a couple of places."

Benson failed to stifle his laugh, which angered Melnian and his circus from hell all the more. Once more Melnian poked me in the chest with his two-pronged salad extractor.

I looked around the corridor and realized we essentially had the entire passage sectioned off to accommodate our show. No wonder the Mafian Tenlords made such a profit; they could elicit a huge crowd without so much as a rehearsal.

"Santien shiasti rastin hastae promantian youvian skeeterboslom," Benson stated calmly. "Combienian troublom Queel Toulantin?"

"What did you say?" I cut in before Melnian the Menacing could fillet me.

"I told him that you're willing to pay the price for the damage done to the Queel, and I asked him how much he requires for reparations."

Melnian's response was quick, concise, and very strict sounding. Again, I caught the words "shiasti rastin" and was beginning to grow paranoid about them.

Benson nodded his understanding and Melnian lowered his weapon a bit. But it still hung close enough to skewer me should he chose to do so.

"Captain, it would appear that Melnian here has set the price," said Benson. "And I doubt we could dissuade him with anything less."

"So how much?" I asked.

The stalled crowd was beginning to grow agitated from our long blockage of the corridor.

"Apparently he wants two hundred Mafian rubblelinas," Benson informed me.

"Which is…?"

"Approximately ten thousand space quids."

I almost wept. It was a very, very large sum, verging on the astronomical.

If only I'd had my spark weapon in hand, I'm sure I could have thought of a much cheaper way to settle this argument. But I choked down an internal sob, grieving the pistol I'd had to leave behind in the council room.

"What? Ten thousand quids... is he nuts?" I groaned, trying not to draw any further attention. I didn't like to let others know how destitute I truly was.

Benson hung his head. "I'm afraid he is, Captain. But I'm sure—"

"I couldn't sell *Orbital* herself for ten thousand space quids. Actually, I probably couldn't sell *Orbital* for a box of matches and a tube of toothpaste."

The lieutenant laughed again, setting off another chain reaction that led to anxious shouting from our new adversaries.

"Sorry, Captain. I'll soothe them once more." Benson began talking to the Mafians again, in a very peaceable fashion.

My mind spun. Even if I served aboard *Orbital* for ten years, I would only just barely be able to afford such an exorbitant fee.

"Lieutenant, ask Melnian if there is perhaps another method of payment he would accept."

"But Captain, you should know—"

"Please, Benson, just ask."

"Yes, sir."

Benson once more spoke to Melnian, and soon their conversation settled down from its peak of high passion to a pervading sense of calm. They looked in my direction from time to time and I could only guess what kind of negotiations they were engaged in.

By the end of the conversation, it almost seemed to me that Melnian and Benson had become the best of friends.

"Well, it would seem that there is, in fact, another method of payment you will be able to produce," Benson explained. He then paused, struggling over whether to continue. "But…"

"But what?"

"Well, Melnian mentioned something about a very traditional, very solemn, and very unbreakable pact of marriage to his younger sister." Benson was beaming red by this point.

Aw, shit! Once again, I had found myself under threat of a shotgun marriage. How did I keep doing this to myself?

First things first. If Melnian's sister looked anything like he did, absolutely not. If she was sweet and nice and had hair nearly as substantial as Melnian's, maybe there was a chance…

What the hell was I thinking? No way could I ever marry a Mafian. Their short, sharp teeth alone would mean the death of me.

"Okay, Benson, tell him I'll pay the money. But make sure he knows that I'm flattered and honoured by his offer of his sister." I scratched my chin nervously. "I'll just need to find a way to scavenge the funds. I really don't want to end up running away from another convoy of Mafians… they are very persistent, not to mention eager to show their distaste when you blow them off repeatedly over the course of eight months…"

"Captain, please hear me out. It's not as bad as it sounds, for I have the authority to pay your debt."

"But why would you do that?" I asked, taken aback.

"Well, if I remember correctly, you didn't launch yourself through the Grand Council Room of the Universe, out the doors, and across the corridor to land upon that Queel on your own. If memory serves, it was my high marshal who instigated the situation you find yourself in."

"Yeah, that's true," I said, realizing that none of this was actually my fault. I had completely forgotten! Usually in a situation like this, it very much *was* my fault. "I'm glad to take you up on your offer, Benson. But are you sure you won't suffer personally for making it? Your high marshal hates no one more than me, and god knows it's mutual."

"I'm certain. The scene back there wasn't Prime's finest hour." Benson spoke solemnly and with a degree of shame. "Commander Marsdale will approve of my judgment, I'm certain of it."

"In that case, thank you, Lieutenant." I refrained from shaking his hand, out of respect for the fact that our negotiations with the Mafian Tenlords wasn't yet complete.

"I will tell Melnian of your unfortunate but unavoidable refusal of the marriage," Benson said. "I'll simply tell him you're already spoken for, which is the easiest way. Just do your best not to be seen with too many different women from now on." He sighed. "I'll also tell him that he should expect payment by this evening."

"Perfect."

I felt a little better considering everything that had happened to me lately.

As my eyes turned back to the arched entrance to the Grand Council Room of the Big Asshole, I wondered suddenly what was being discussed inside. Whatever it was, it seemed to be taking a long time considering that the Militia had done such a thorough job of castrating itself.

Benson began talking once more in the strangely rolling tongue of the Mafians. With surprise, I heard those words again: "shiasti rastin."

"What are you talking with them about?" I asked nervously.

"Melnian here wants to know where you want Toulantin the Queel sent."

For a moment I thought I had misheard him. "What?"

"Yeah. It seems you haven't specifically paid for reparations but rather an outright purchase of the poor, oozy creature."

Strangely, this wasn't the first time something like this had happened to me, either. A very similar situation had led to Sirbot coming aboard.

"Can you simply thank him for the offer but let him know that it would be best for Toulantin to stay with him?"

"I'll see what I can do, Captain, but they may not allow such an agreement. They are an oddly honour-bound race."

The scene had quickly deescalated, and the Mafian Tenlords were now orchestrating their procession of extreme oddities back into a single-file line. The crowd of commuters, too, had become much less tense as traffic began to move.

Before Melnian left, however, he had one final incomprehensible verbal exchange with Benson. It only lasted a few moments.

"You are in luck, Captain," Benson said as Melnian and the others prepared to move on. "Melnian will allow you to release the Queel, although he has extended permission for you to reclaim the Queel anytime from here on out, should you so choose."

"Thanks again, Lieutenant, but I don't think I will. Are we concluded?"

"Seems so."

With our business concluded, Melnian then nodded and led his cast and crew down the corridor.

Benson and I walked away in the opposite direction. He was leading me back towards *Orbital*.

After a minute or two of burning curiosity, I needed to know the truth.

"*Rastin* means devil, right?" I asked.

"Demon actually."

"So what does *shiasti* mean?"

"*Shiasti rastin* means, literally, demon hair." He said this with a smile on his face.

"Demon hair?" I asked in disbelief, having no idea why they would call me such a thing. As I raised my hands to my normally glorious hair, I felt something that startled me to within a millisecond of having a heart attack.

I stepped forward so I could see my reflection in the overhead metalloid arches. When I saw it, I nearly dropped my chin into my colon. My hair was standing straight out in all directions. I looked like a dandelion ready to shed its seeds.

I pressed down on my hair, but it sprung up again just as quickly. I ignored the laughter all around me. All that mattered now was fixing the problem.

Unfortunately, nothing seemed to work.

It was at this moment, when all hope seemed lost, that I felt a tendril of goo slide down my wrist. In desperation, I threw the efflorescent Queel slime into my hair, concluding that it could not make the situation any worse. I ran the goo through my hair like a journeyman barber…

Kablam!

To my utter shock and amazement, not only did the slime flatten my hair into its normal glorious state, but it gave it a healthy shine. I hadn't felt so good since Sirbot had done his handiwork the other day.

I wasted no time and asked Benson to hurry back to the Mafians so I could have the Queel sent to *Orbital*. He left my side to do as I asked.

I wandered back towards *Orbital*, not sure what else to do with my time. The journey only took me a few minutes, and as I rounded the final corner into the pressurized tube that led to the ship herself, I noticed a rush of unfamiliar technicians clothed in dark uniforms. Although each varied in size, ethnicity, and even species, they all had one commonality: a total lack of humour and air of belligerence. I could hear rumblings of "blasted Mackmian" and "bossy little bastard" and quickly realized they were referring to Simbden.

Upon boarding the ship, it quickly became apparent that long swaths of hallway panelling had been removed, revealing electrical wiring, fissure junctions, digital box indicators, and a slew of other apparatuses I didn't fully recognize or know the purpose of.

For a few minutes I wandered the leprous-looking hallways. It was kind of surreal seeing the missing panels of shag carpeting.

I wasn't quite sure which looked worse. The first room I came to was the vacant chamber opposite the cooking station. I heard a clash of metal and an oddly tinny metallic voice that wasn't speaking English.

I poked my head into the poorly lit room and was brought up short by a translucent glow. There was Sirbot, the confusing robot and terrific beautician, hard at work. His four arms were a blur, each acting independently of the other three. I was most intrigued by the third arm—or at least, the one I so labelled. He was using it to reshape a cylindrical piece of carbon alloy. One end was pinned beneath a metallic clamp that extended from the floor. I thought the cylinder had previously been used as a housing for fuel.

Sirbot seemed either indifferent to or unaware of my presence.

Suddenly, the robot looked up at me with the strangest expression—if I could call it an expression. What I saw in his mechanical glowing eyes was a look of cognizance I hadn't ever seen in a robot. If I hadn't known better, I might have concluded that the bot had developed some form of sentience. And although his digital mouth didn't form any expression whatsoever, I could swear Sirbot was laughing. There was a certain twinkle in his electric blue eyes.

"Proshay, Kaptain," Sirbot said with a raspy voice. He lifted the second metallic clamp of a hand to his forehead and saluted.

He then went back to work. I shook my head, bewildered.

Perhaps this whole episode should have worried me more, but before I could enquire further I heard a loud crash in the distance and a series of angry voices. I left Sirbot to his own adventures in order to investigate the commotion.

It took me only a moment to follow the source and locate my new engineer up in the control hub. Simbden was hanging upside-down, suspended by a pair of booster boots which were expelling a small but expanding cone of grey exhaust. Upside-down as he was, it seemed to me that he was as comfortable as a Telnian cow pasturing on a range full of burble berries and twine.

He was fixing two fissure junctions on opposite sides of a control station, his face barely recognizable behind the welding goggles plastered to his now charcoal-coloured face. He was humming to himself some Mackmian song, stopping only long enough to yell at a Prime technician who seemed too afraid to argue with him.

His self-assured and commanding presence was so dissimilar to the one I'd previously observed of him that it took me aback. I was sure going to need to learn more of my newest recruit.

"Simbden?"

He couldn't hear me over the noise and clamour.

"Now listen, Primey," the young Mackmian was saying to the technician. "We need to connect that fissure control junction to the panel's main readout module. When that's complete, we can hardwire the systems directly to the overall relay junctions. That will correctly link the two. Do you get it?"

I stepped forward and tried again to get Simbden's attention, and in the process I noticed my captain's chair. Something looked different about it.

"Can we rewire the control module on the captain's chair to instantly bring me a Martian Breeze every time my mouth shows signs of dryness?" I asked facetiously.

When Simbden turned to me, there was surprise in his eyes, visible even through the thick reflective goggles. He activated his thruster boots and spun himself right-side-up. His expression showed a mixture of curiosity, annoyance, and unbridled eagerness... and perhaps a little bit of suppressed flatulence?

"My captain, it's good to see you!" he said with enthusiasm. "Already ahead of you, sir. I have fifteen variations of beverages at your disposal."

He motioned me closer to the captain's chair. When I peered down at the command module on the armrest, I could see that he wasn't joking in the slightest.

He activated some of the features to show me further what he had done.

"You see, with just the slightest of touches, you can access every brand of Galagian root beer, or Callibian sodas, or Mackmian pine juices… but that's not all. If you just slide your finger across this bar, you'll see that you can instantly call forth the dispenser."

I looked over to the bar he was referring to and saw that the newly designed captain's chair had a mammoth-sized cup which could hold enough liquid to rehydrate a Mackmian rugby team.

"Wow," I said, not sure if I was more affected by the intuitiveness of his work or the fact that my drink dispenser had taken precedence over a whole slew of other repairs. I liked his work ethic and ability to put Brant Zenith first, so he wasn't going to receive any admonishment.

Well, not from me. If Mara or Stairn found out, they probably wouldn't be so lenient.

"Good work, Agent Simbden," I said. His young face beamed with pride. "What's going on with all the disgruntled Prime officers?"

He disengaged his zero-gravity boots completely, and a moment later they made contact with the floor. He lifted his goggles, leaving a definite figure-eight shape of soot and debris around his eyes.

"Oh, the Primeys? They seem to think they know something no one else does. Within five minutes of watching them work, I knew that I needed to step in, or you'd be here forever and a birthday waiting for the repairs to get done."

I think he sensed my scepticism.

"Don't worry, my captain. I promise you that I know this ship better than anyone else, and your repairs will be finished quickly. I've collected the least incompetent of the bunch and they've been almost useful thus far. I'm sure the major repairs will be finished within two days."

I lifted an eyebrow in surprise. "Oh?"

"In fact, it's a shame that we don't have a full week with Prime's repair equipment. With a few more helping hands, I'm sure I could fix your ship to the point that its own creator wouldn't know it was broken."

"I don't think it was created," I said under my breath. "Rather it was summoned from hell."

But Simbden was already back to his duties of soldering some wires. He hardly noticed as the blue and yellow sparks nearly singed his soot-encrusted face.

I looked around the control hub at the mess of components lying about. And there was my deep blue spacesuit hanging precariously over the railing. My propulsion gun rested on another ledge. I grabbed it and holstered the blasted weapon.

I turned back to speak once more with my new engineer.

"Simbden," I said, swaying out of the way to avoid the offending sparks, "what's the deal with Sirbot?"

"Ah, yes. The little repair robot. He's malfunctioning severely." A ripple of annoyance crossed his features. "I was going to take a look, but he doesn't seem to want me anywhere near him. It's odd. He shouldn't be able to resist repairs, but he continues to do so. But anyway, *Orbital* is my first concern." He paused a moment. "But I think there's something very strange about him."

"What do you mean?"

"Well, he's not programmed to speak other languages, for example. But he is definitely doing that. And each time I get close, he brings up his carbon residue pinchers and releases sparks at me. Don't worry, Captain. I'll fix him yet."

"No, please don't."

"Captain?"

Thinking quickly, I decided that he didn't need to know about the possibility of Sirbot having stumbled into sentience—and more importantly, gaining the godlike ability to cut my hair like a pro.

"I want to see where this odd behaviour leads," I said. "The space fight versus the Quazarns—" I really hated calling them that "—really messed up his circuitry and I want to learn more about it. Don't alter him."

"Yes, sir."

I nodded, he nodded, and I nodded once again for good measure.

With that, I decided to leave the heavy work to the professionals. I had another obligation to attend to—and afterward, I was going to need some alcoholic entertainment to keep me occupied for a few hours.

CHAPTER THIRTEEN

Insignificance

"How did you find me?" asked the large, rotund robot standing behind the counter. Its mechanized voice was deep and hollow, rumbling like a bowling ball drifting down a metal gutter channel.

I didn't respond immediately. Instead I scanned the periphery, having found myself standing in a poorly lit corridor known for housing the seedier side of Prime Station Alpha's commercial sector. I suspected the authorities knew about its existence, but I doubted they wished to turn on the lights, causing the rats to scatter.

This corridor was narrower than those on the upper levels and the dim yellow overhead lights shone just brightly enough to allow pedestrians to see their way from one seedy shop to another. The air seemed dryer and staler than the upper main corridors.

I stood at the entryway of one of the shops. Well, perhaps entryway was being too generous; the entrance was completely blocked by the proprietor's bartering robot, which looked like an enormous metallic panda bear. The stuffed animal type of bear children slept with at night. I wondered what would possess someone to create a robot with this particular look.

His smooth face had a narrow, visor-like channel where his eyes should have been; the rest of his face was a plane of flat metal. The visor glowed red, giving me the notion that he was not to be trusted.

"I looked," I said, answering the robot's question.

Peering into the dingy store behind him, I saw the barrels of several weapons, all currently aimed in my direction.

I sighed to myself. It all too often came down to this.

"Not good enough, human." Its robotic voice grated even more deeply. "Speak now or forever hold your peace."

Actually, I held my piece in my hand, tucked carefully behind my back. I had taken the opportunity back on *Orbital* to grab my untrustworthy propulsion gun; it didn't work well, but at least it never abandoned me. Sneaking it past security had been a minor adventure, but as usual I'd managed to find a way. A team of robots had been working clean-up around *Orbital* during the repair process, carrying out a dumpster of mechanical clutter every day; I had used that dumpster to smuggle the gun past security.

I looked the bear of a robot in the visor. "I found your location written down somewhere."

"Where was it written?"

"Inside a toilet stall." I half-expected to be annihilated on the spot.

It was hard to read the bear-bot's expression, since it possessed no discernible features and most of its body was obscured in shadow.

Suddenly, the oddest thing happened. A grumble erupted from deep within its circuitry. At first, I thought perhaps it was arming a bomb with my name on it, but instead it turned out to be… a chuckle. Its big burly frame trembled from the laughter, which sounded like it had originated from inside a steel volcano.

The weapons inside the store, the ones pointed at me, disappeared, melting back into the darkness.

"What would you like, human?" the bear-bot asked, decidedly more friendly.

"I require two doses of black rift energy," I explained. I had used up my last charge and hated not having at least one extra in case of unforeseen circumstances.

For what I had planned, violence and retribution, I was going to need the black rift energy. The problem was cost. Being a relatively new and difficult technology to produce, it was massively expensive. It was also illegal on Prime Station Alpha, unless you were granted a permit. Which of course I hadn't been.

"Fifteen hundred space quids," the robot said.

I activated my wristband communicator and pulled up my credit information. I only had 1,006 space quids, and most of that was locked away in a century-old savings account. I'd known I would have to invest early if I had any chance of retiring in two hundred years.

"Would you take ninety-seven quids?" I asked not-so-hopefully.

The bear-bot's visor briefly flashed red. It then began laughing, and the rumble of mirth carried on for two seconds longer than the last time.

That's when I recognized what—or rather, who—I was dealing with.

The robot spotted the change in my expression. "What?"

"You're sentient," I said, getting straight to the point.

This was no *it*. His visor burned crimson, reminding me of a lava lamp.

"Very astute, human," he replied after a slight whirring sound. "Captain Zenith of the Militia Space Fleet Ship *Orbital*."

"Very right. Do you have a name?"

"Mal."

"Mal..." I pondered the single syllable a moment longer. Ha! "Mal... as in malfunction?" I hoped I was right and not just being an insulting prick.

"Very good again."

I decided to push my luck. "For how long have you been sentient, if you don't mind my asking?"

"Perhaps I do not know you well enough to mention."

"Perhaps not," I agreed.

This struck me as the perfect opportunity to gain a better understanding of what had happened to Sirbot. I was certain he had been touched by the spark of sentience, somehow, and it seemed possible that the same thing had happened to this robotic shopkeeper.

"Ninety-seven space quids is a laughable offer," Mal said.

I wasn't certain why he didn't tell me to piss off right there on the spot. "You should see the rest of my bank account."

He chuckled again. The bear-bot liked jokes. "I already have."

Not only did he possess an exceptionally rare sentience, but he seemed to possess the ability to hack or link into secured files. I tucked that information into my sometimes-not-inebriated mind for safekeeping.

"You must know that your offer is far too low," he said.

I merely nodded in agreement. "Perhaps a trade?"

"That is something I would entertain." His robotic voice rang less tinny and somehow sounded more human. "Whatever could you offer?"

I looked around the corridor and watched as the various humanoid-ish creatures shuffled behind me, oblivious to my dialogue with the robot. Their footwear scuffed along the metallic floor.

"I could offer my services," I suggested with a measure of hope. I had skills... or so I liked to believe.

"Hara, hara, hara!" Mal laughed, apparently not believing me. "I doubt that you have any services I would value at the moment, Captain Zenith."

Ouch! That hurt the ego. What was this galaxy coming to that I had to convince a metallic barrel with a voice of my value?

"Well, I am a pretty good dancer," I said sarcastically.

"That is subjective and not a skill I require at this moment." Mal paused. "Our conversation has been more noteworthy than is typical, but I have other matters to attend to. Now, if you don't mind…"

He lifted a massive, riveted paw the size of my torso and pointed it in the direction from whence I'd come.

"Hold on." Feeling desperate for the black rift energy, I raised my propulsion gun. The dent in the wooden stock still showed. "What about this?"

"Threat or trade?" he asked. The cylindrical cannons from the darkness behind him flared up again. "The first is stupid and the second offers me nothing I am interested in."

With my hand raised and my weapon pointed point-blank at Mal's face, I had to make a decision. I couldn't trade the propulsion gun. It was integral to my plans of vengeance and whatnot.

I slowly lowered the gun. "Neither. I'm offering a trade of skill."

"Gunslinger, huh? Interesting. That could be useful one day, I suppose."

"Great!" I replied, my elation getting the better of me. I wasn't thinking clearly. Offering my services as a gunslinger to a robot I'd just met probably wasn't the soundest idea I'd ever had.

"But that day is not today, Captain Brant Zenith." With that, Mal stomped on my plans like a hippopotamus on a snail. "That will be all for now. Good day, Militia man."

I slowly tucked the propulsion gun back into its holster. Fuck! I was so frustrated that I thought my ears would fall off from all the fuming going on between them.

I slammed my right hand into the wall beside Mal—the very same hand whose broken bones had only just been restored—and suddenly the strangest thing happened. For a second, my hand shimmered silver. I was certain it had to be the aftereffects of having taken too much EZ-Heal.

I shook my head and began to walk away.

"Stop!" Mal bellowed after me. He raised his massive mitt of a hand. "Come back."

I stood in place, not knowing what to make of this. My hand went back to my propulsion gun, tucked away alongside my grotesque yellow, white, and green uniform.

"Perhaps a trade is not impossible, Captain," Mal said once I'd returned to the shopfront.

"Am I missing something?" I asked, not sure where his sudden interest arose from. Perhaps it had been my temper?

"You most certainly are."

"What the hell does that mean?"

"It means that you are welcome to this." Mal lifted his metallic mitt and opened it. From within, I detected the dark glow of black rift energy. A single sliver. The mysterious substance had the fascinating ability to both absorb and give off light at the same time.

It was right there for the taking. I just had to reach out and grab it.

My hand stopped just millimetres from the sliver of black rift energy. My fingers shook from excitement.

"What do you wish in return?" I asked sceptically, perhaps even fearfully.

"A favour to be granted in the future."

"I don't know what that means."

"You aren't meant to," he responded. "But it will not be for murder."

It was a strange proposition. But I wanted the black rift energy so badly that I was ready to do almost anything for it.

"Before I agree to anything," I began, lifting my right hand, "did you see anything unusual from me a few seconds ago?"

I hoped he might have some insight into the shimmering effect I'd just detected on my hand. Or perhaps it had been nothing but my imagination.

"I saw…" Mal's visor turned green, which I took to mean he was in deep thought. "I saw something of value."

I stood in silence, waiting for more. Nothing came.

"That's all?" I asked. "Perhaps a little more information?"

Mal shook his wrecking ball of a head. "When next I call upon you, I will explain further."

He dropped the sliver of black rift energy into my wristband communicator, which quickly absorbed it.

Before raising his hand again, he politely and firmly bid me adieu. But before I left, he offered one final cryptic comment: "Two years and a few days."

I walked quickly through the corridors of Prime Station Alpha, my hands shaking despite my best efforts to steady my mind. I compulsively patted my side and my pockets, doublechecking to make sure I had the weapon, the remote control to return the weapon to me, and some EZ-Putty I had received for free with the last batch of EZ-Heal. It worked at sticking almost as well as the medicative miracle did at healing.

Now that I had the tools, retribution was at hand.

I sidestepped several Oceaniz settlers arduously pulling their large carryon luggage through the station. I barely paid attention as a small tower of luggage tipped over, spewing their contents all over the floor—clothing, souvenirs, knickknacks, and even small plant life. Most passersby were of the kind variety and helped the settlers pick up their belongings and give them a chance to freely be on their way. However, there were also a few opportunists who took advantage and began hauling off whatever they could get their grubby hands, paws, or tentacles on.

I pushed past the spectacle and stepped through an unobtrusive maintenance door. It was the same one I had used three years ago on my way to earning that atmospheric sedition charge. The little corridor beyond was as forgettable as I remembered.

I soon found I was almost losing myself in a vast miasma of circuitry and wiring. After an hour of searching, bumping into miscellaneous control panels and relay boards shining like fireflies in the dark, I at last discovered the secondary service tunnel I needed—and then continued on, taking several more rights before a series of three lefts.

Shaking my head in frustration, I snuck past a long row of computer banks and came to an access panel built into the wall. The only light shone from a screen up and over my shoulder; like all the other screens, it would light up when the motion sensor was tripped. So far, nothing.

I knelt down and swept off nearly an inch of dust that had settled over a fresh air intake duct. I recognized the corners where screws fastened it to the wall. Shit, I had forgotten to bring the correct driver to remove the screws!

Suddenly, a memory flashed to mind.

Reaching below the panel and perhaps a metre to the right, I came to a gap in the base moulding. I dug my finger and thumb into the opening and pulled out a small metallic disc that flashed green from the reflection of the computer display screen above my head.

Ha! It was still exactly where I'd left it.

I made quick work of opening the intake cover and made my way through the ductwork. I had to activate my wristband communicator, which served as my lone source of light in the darkness.

In only a few minutes, I would be able to exact my revenge. And it was a long time coming, not only for the recent events in the council room.

Inside a poorly lit, unmanned interior section of the station, I pulled myself out of the ductwork. I found myself once more in a narrow central corridor that ran mostly vertical from the lower decks to the upper decks. Full of conduits, piping and all sorts of mechanical noises I cared not a damn for I made my way through. It was an access shaft for workers of the station to quickly travel to and from different levels. It was still dimly lit and completely empty of life. Using the light of my wristband communicator I found the metal ladder I was looking for. It was fastened against a wall that appeared to rise up into the depths of darkness of the station above me.

I climbed six levels on that ladder before managing to locate the duct where I needed to renter. Hopping off the ladder and onto a small platform, I opened the panel and squeezed myself into that duct.

I travelled within those narrow confines for several minutes. It was arduous and required me stop several times to catch my breath. But it was worth it. I carefully freed the duct's panel and let it drop free with a minor creak of resentment.

I paused for several minutes, which felt like forever. I feared that someone nearby would hear me. But when I didn't encounter any sign that I'd been detected, I stepped through into a dark and dusty space between two walls, a narrow horizontal service corridor filled with the kind of central heating and cooling shafts that ran throughout the station. It was dusty between the two walls and I struggled to stifle the sneeze always at the tip of my nose. Still, I soldiered on.

More importantly, beyond one of these walls was High Marshal Mordeau's private office.

It was a tight squeeze through the service corridor, my tassels brushing up against my cheek due to the walls pressing in on both sides. I took a few more steps and stopped, lifting my fingers to my temples as though to stir a memory. Somewhere nearby was an opening that would lead to Mordeau's office. On the other side, it was cleverly disguised as a piece of decorative wainscotting, a false front.

Having forgotten exactly how many steps to take, I got onto my knees and made my way along, pushing on each and every panel as it presented itself.

It wasn't until I reached the very last panel that I noticed a crack of light piercing the dark passage. This was the one.

I peered through the miniscule slant of light, but it was only wide enough to confirm that the room beyond the walls was indeed Mordeau's office.

After crouching there for several minutes, hearing no sound from the office, I pushed the false panel open. It creaked, and to my ears it sounded like a battle horn. I realized that I was probably being too sensitive.

I slipped into the well-lit office, remembering that this wasn't Mordeau's office but rather the one belonging to his executive assistant.

The assistant wasn't at her desk. I thanked the Mackmian gods of fate for that little bit of luck.

Standing up, I walked towards the door to Mordeau's inner sanctum. The door was cracked open, and I stepped through, shutting it behind me. The unoccupied office was set to dusk mode, but just enough light shone from the sculpted wall sconces to confirm that the high marshal wasn't present.

It was impossible not to be flooded with memories of the last time I'd visited this office, on that fateful evening three years ago. During that visit, I had come to learn something which to this day still made my blood run cold. Mordeau, I'd discovered, had ordered his engineers to install a self-destruct button in his office.

The man wasn't just a pretentious, pompous asshole; he was a full-fledged sociopath!

One day the shit would hit the fan and the high marshal wouldn't think twice about killing his own people. But I was determined not to let it get that far—not on my watch.

After I left Prime, I hadn't had any real allies high up to take this info to... and I hadn't wanted Mordeau get wind of my cognizance of this information...

So I'd conspired to sneak into his office and do a little rewiring, a little jury-rigging, a little tinkering here and there to redirect the explosive charge from the station's reactor. Ever since, if Mordeau ever had an inkling to press that big red button, the results would be far less cataclysmic; a small explosion would rupture the septic pipe which I knew ran between the deck plates above Mordeau's desk and dump sewage over him.

It seemed a small price to pay to save everyone's lives. When the shit hit the fan, it would also hit the high marshal's all too corpulent skull.

Well, there had been one other small price to pay, of course—my pride. After being forced to dig around in that septic drain for an hour or two, to lay the explosives, I hadn't exactly come out smelling like a rose.

Hence, my subsequent citation. Atmospheric sedition my ass.

Shaking my head at the unpleasant memories, my feet shuffled over the plush carpet towards the high marshal's desk. On the way, my knee bumped into something I couldn't see and hadn't expected, and I froze in place.

Looking down, I realized my mistake. Mordeau was present, after all. There he was, in all his glory, laying on the floor and staring up at me with open eyes. He wore a mostly white tanktop and colourful boxer shorts. His top didn't cover the immense gut spilling out of it.

Holy fuck! I nearly jumped out of my uniform—hell, out of my skin. Out of my soul! I reached for my propulsion gun and raised it in defence.

The high marshal didn't so much as blink in reaction to my presence. For several long moments, I stared down into those godforsaken piggish eyes. He remained motionless.

He snorted again and rolled over, mumbling something incomprehensible to himself.

I exhaled a sigh of relief. He slept with his eyes open! And he must have rolled onto the floor from the couch. Talk about a sound sleeper.

I did indeed wish great harm upon this man, but I didn't wish to be found responsible for that great harm. I was smarter than that.

I wasted no time linking the remote to my pistol. A blue switch on the side of the remote blinked twice, confirming that the link was operational.

Next, I reached under and affixed the weapon to the underside of the desk, using a wad of EZ-Putty, and positioned it just right so that barrel aimed right where Mordeau's nether regions would be. I was very careful to keep it out of view, somewhere he would never see it unless he got down on his hands and knees and physically crawled under the desk. I placed it carefully so it was well out of the way, and he wouldn't have occasion to kick it loose by mistake.

Luckily for me, the desk was as opulent as the rest of the man's taste. It was exceptionally large and there were several deep nooks and crannies that served as perfect candidates.

Once it was done, I stepped back and admired my handiwork. When the time was right—and it would be just about perfect in a few days or weeks from now, at a moment when I was back aboard *Orbital* but still in the vicinity of the station—I would pick up this remote, flip that blinking blue switch, and cause the gun to fire straight at Mordeau's gonads.

Then the gun would vanish into thin air, black-rifting back to safety in my quarters aboard *Orbital*, leaving no evidence of how the affair had been carried out.

It would be the perfect crime.

I should have just left then and there, but I couldn't help lingering and reaching for that godawful red button at the corner of the desktop: the self-destruct button that had started this whole affair in the first place. Its red light glowed dimly, protected by a clear cover.

Closing my eyes for a moment, I imagined Mordeau pressing it one day in desperation, only for hot shit to come raining down on him like the righteous judgment of a vengeful god.

Excellent! At least that atmospheric sedition charge hadn't been earned in vain.

At last, I backed slowly away from the desk, stepping over the sleeping island of blubber and resisting the urge to kick him.

"Zenith…" the high marshal whispered urgently.

I froze in place. None of this would work if he woke up and saw me. Fuck!

"Zenith…why are you here…?" His voice sounded extremely disturbed.

Not sure what else to do, I reached out to cover the man's face. What the hell was he doing here anyway? According to his personal schedule, he was supposed to be in conference for several more hours.

"Zenith… don't do it!"

With that, the man rolled over and let out a long, piggish snort.

I breathed a sigh of relief and thanked heavens that my heart hadn't given out. Luckily, he was still asleep. Damn could the man sleep!

I quickly made my way out of the office and back to the safety of the dark service corridor pressed between the walls. I shimmed my way back along the same route, and minutes later I was many levels below, on my way to meet Bog for a well-deserved drink.

"Whaddya like?" the bartender called to us, his voice nearer that of sandpaper than silk.

I put up two fingers and pointed at the wonderful cocktails Bog and I were already indulging in.

We sat in an obscure drinking den off the beaten path. This watering hole was a tribute to Earth's big band era and the musicians were pumping out lively music. The literal big band was made up of a few aliens native to this corner of the Gambit Galaxy, many of whom made a regularly sized human look like a toddler in comparison.

I found myself finally able to relax and enjoy a few hours away from the issues of *Orbital* and the tensions between the Militia and Prime. Bog sat next to me sipping lava brew, the massive stone mug releasing a plume of orange steam. I feared some of it would bubble over and melt the table.

It made sense, though. Bog required heat to survive. Every night on *Orbital* he fell asleep in a radiant chamber that heated the air to several hundred degrees Celsius. It resembled an oven more than a bedroom, but it worked for him.

Through the dim and smoky air, the bartender soon brought forth another Martian Breeze for me and another lava brew for Bog. The place had an intimate feel and I could smell the burning embers of exotic trees, rugged perfumes, and even the whimsical mist lifting off the vines crawling up the room's structural pillars.

"This is more like it," I said softly. "Just like the old days, my friend."

Bog remained silent, his red eyes aglow. His horns shimmered red, too, which to me was a dead giveaway that something was bothering him.

"I'm not complaining..." he finally rumbled. It sounded like boulders rolling downhill.

"But..."

"But...?" His red eyes smouldered, literally. "You know I don't complain."

"Not too much anyway."

He flashed the smallest of grins, barely moving the rough lips beyond his front tusks.

"But what are we stumbling into?" he asked once the grin had subsided.

"Well, I don't know about you, but I'm hoping to stumble into someone curvy before the night's out."

"I'm being serious."

"Me too."

"God damn it, Zenith," he exploded, and a little bit of Nova Martian saliva flew out of his mouth.

I moved my head just in time to avoid being scalded. The projectile hit a metal chair behind me and collapsed one of its legs. The Mackmian sitting on it didn't seem so happy when his rotund body hit the floor. He looked about ready to start a fight, but then he saw the size of my security officer and quickly backed off. A nearby server ran to get him a replacement seat.

"We barely made it through our last series of mishaps," Bog said. "I'm all for a rough-and-tumble outing, but things are getting hairy out there."

"Mackmian gods of shitcicles, you sound just like Mara!"

"Good. Maybe you should listen to her more." He hesitated. "And while you're at it, maybe you should retire your womanizing with her. I'm tired of watching the two of you dance around each other."

"What the hell are you talking about?" I nearly choked down the straw the bartender had stuck into my Martian Breeze. "Mara can't stand being near me ninety-nine percent of the time. And the last one percent, I think she'd rather I fall out of an airlock than get in her way."

"You're so blind it hurts. But I suppose I'm not interested in that right now."

"Well, what the good Mackmian shit are you interested in then?"

"Back on *Orbital*, during the opening minutes of the battle in the Quazar system, you sent me to contain the fires down below. I must admit there were some real dodgy moments." He stared into his lava brew, which released an unpleasant sulfuric smell. "The fires were not the issue. But you know how I feel about the cold. And in case you hadn't noticed, space is one giant, endless ocean of cold."

"I know, buddy."

"I'm not sure you really do." He looked me right in the eyes. "You know that I'll follow you into any hellhole you should stumble into. That will never change. I would not abandon you and truth be told I love the excitement of it. But—"

"I know," I said solemnly. "I know. I really do. I myself had a pretty dicey moment when I was working on the final protective ring around the black hole. For a moment, I felt certain that my number was up. I'm still not really sure how I survived."

Bog's eyes flared. "I think about it all the time, you know."

"Think about what?"

"The endlessness of everything. Space. We've spent the past two decades travelling all over the known universe, and the sheer immenseness of it is overwhelming."

"I find it beautiful," I said. "Sometimes it seems like the most beautiful thing in existence. The wonders, the vastness, the completeness of it all…"

I paused, staring into my Martian Breeze, stirring the icy beverage with a piece of fruit the bartender had served alongside it. It looked like a carrot and tasted like kiwi. The condensation on the side of the glass trickled down the narrow stem towards the table.

"But sometimes it also scares me," I said. "It can be so heartless that I don't know how to hold on to anything that makes me feel… secure…"

"Well, I think about it too." Bog lifted his hand to indicate to the bartender that he wanted another drink. "Even after all this time, travelling as far and wide as we have… hell, we've served together in two different galaxies, millions of lightyears apart. We've been further out and spent longer away than almost anyone else. And I still look at space in awe."

His voice was deep, but I could sense the small rise in pitch. He was deep within himself. I realized that I was hearing from the innermost part of him. We were rarely so sincere with each other; it was almost surreal, but I wouldn't have missed this for all the Martian Breezes in the galaxy.

"The sheer size of the universe is impossible to comprehend, isn't it?" he continued. "I can't get my mind to accept it…"

I thought about what he was saying very carefully, and in this rare moment of shared humility I allowed myself to acknowledge a truth I had never admitted out loud, and rarely even admitted to myself.

"I find it harder to accept just how small and insignificant I am in this universe," I said in a quiet voice.

And I meant it. In this vast universe, I was pitifully unimportant, especially since I usually held myself in such high regard. Just like the Militia's small sliver of space, our existence was all too underwhelming in a universe as vast as this.

"How many years past do you think we are?" Bog asked, lifting a stony eyebrow.

I frowned, not understanding the question. "Come again?"

"When do you think we'll leave behind all these bullshit shenanigans? When do we find the path we promised ourselves as children? When do we find our truer purpose?"

I found the question strange coming from someone who had been through so many so-called bullshit shenanigans with me. I once saw my massive brother punch out a concrete support column on an abandoned building to see how long he could hold it up.

"I wouldn't know," I remarked offhandedly. I wondered if he remembered something of our childhood that I had forgotten.

He nodded in understanding, and I was thankful when he let the subject drop.

My friend gulped down the last of his lava brew in one swig. When it was empty, he dropped the stone mug into his mouth and crunched it down too.

I didn't envy what his toilet would go through in the morning.

It was near midnight when I stumbled back towards the temporary quarters Benson had assigned to me on the station while the repairs continued aboard *Orbital*. Only a little buzzed from the Martian Breezes, I stood outside the doorway, waiting for it to open.

When the door opened, I grabbed the digital document pads sitting on the desk—they were from Stairn—and began to read. Normally reading Stairn's reports was like wearing underwear made of barbed wire, but somehow I didn't hate doing it tonight.

It didn't take long before I began reconsidering that opinion. After reading for an hour, my head was becoming foggy.

I was thankfully interrupted when the door chime activated. My wristband screen lit up and I saw an image of Mara standing outside my door. I don't know if I was more surprised that my wristband's digital screen was working or that Mara had come to see me well past midnight.

I walked to the bathroom and ran my hands under the water and through my hair. To make sure I looked top-notch, I grabbed some Queel goo. The final product satisfied even my discerning eyes.

I walked to the door, wondering why I cared so much about how I looked to her.

"Mr. Zenith," Mara said when the door opened. I'd never heard her call me that before. She wobbled a little, so maybe she'd had a few drinks herself? "Are you going to invite me in?"

I looked down and noticed that in one hand she held a bottle of Earth alcohol. Jamaican rum, by the looks of it. Earth beverages weren't cheap this far out.

My excitement must have shown, as she danced her way into my room. She activated her own wristband communicator and caused the lights in my room to dim. Some soft Nova Martian music began to play.

What the hell was going on here?

And what was she wearing? The form-fitting blue nightgown clung to her body. It most certainly wasn't Militia-issued attire. Not unless the Militia had started shopping at the sexier side of the lingerie boutiques...

"Mara, what are you doing?" I asked, befuddled. I couldn't shake the feeling of déjà vu.

"I'm here to enjoy this bottle with you. I know you like to drink, and I thought you'd like some company." She lifted the bottle and a pair of glasses, and in the process dropped the bottle.

Being the gifted athlete I am, I caught it in one quick swoop.

Mara began swaying to the music, her strawberry-blonde hair dancing around her shoulders. "Brant, I'm excited!"

She spun up to me and pulled me close. She smelled very nice and very hard to ignore. To prevent myself from feeling overeager, I gracefully created some distance for the holy spirit between us.

"Why are you excited, Mara?"

I stepped back and looked into her green eyes. It was difficult not to stare. Her nightgown began to open, revealing the lacy undergarments beneath. She was breathtakingly beautiful, but I knew my boundaries.

However, those boundaries didn't prevent my eyes from straying a little off-course.

"Mara, have you been drinking?"

"Maybe..."

"Okay. Tell me about what you're excited about."

"Oh, I am excited..."

"I've heard. But why?" I asked patiently.

"Tomorrow we'll receive a final briefing about our upcoming mission to Mondo 4. And the day after that, we leave."

She poured us glasses of rum and handed me one, nearly spilling half of the liquid onto the floor.

"A lot of good that does us," I remarked.

She hiccupped. "Why do you say that?"

"Because Prime will only steal the mission away from us, just like they did with what happened in the Quazar system."

"Oh Brant," Mara said, spinning gleefully. "You don't trust me, do you?"

"You know I do."

"So don't get so angry."

"That's impossible." Venom dripped from my voice. "Prime steals from us at every opportunity. You were there. You heard High Marshal Assface."

"You left before the meeting was done," she said, taking a sip of rum. Her face was flushed and she was beginning to slur her words. She was typically the most articulate person I'd ever met.

Not tonight, it would seem.

"And what changed after I left?" I asked.

"I informed Benson and Marsdale that we aren't to be shipwrecked upon the events at Quazar."

"Oh, and how did that go?"

"Well, I would say." She paused and smiled. "We have a signed declaration now that the *Perigee*, one of our sister ships, commanded by our very own Captain Sia Lews, will run point on the Quazar mission."

My mouth fell open in disbelief. "What?"

She quickly showed me her wristband communicator, bringing up the document in question. "See? Here!"

I browsed the file on the screen. "But it says that Prime will be assigned to the mission for the near future. Until they deem the system to no longer be in peril… well, that's horseshit. As I've always said, this should be a Militia matter."

"Brant…" Mara was having to concentrate hard to push through her alcohol-fuelled haze. "We're a space fleet of just three ships." She held up a finger for each ship and counted them with the other hand to make sure she'd gotten it right. "Even our sliver of space in this galaxy is quite large for our small group. So what more do you want right now? At least *Perigee* will be involved from this point on. And when we're finished with the Mondorians, we'll return to Quazar."

Upon thinking about it further, I realized she was right. What more could I expect? Sure, I hated Prime and everything they stood for, but they *were* better equipped to deal with this crisis. We were pitiful in number. Truth be told, we needed Prime's help.

It took me a few moments to sift through my resulting emotions. Sure, I was pissed because of High Marshal Douchebag launching me out of the council room. But I had exacted my revenge. He wouldn't expect the upcoming attack, which would come when the moment was right. All I had to do was bide my time and keep that remote close.

So I raised a glass in a toast. "To *Orbital* and her crew. May we make a difference."

Her smile radiated like a beacon as she clinked her glass with mine. "Yes. A difference we will make."

She took a large sip of rum and put the glass down. I caught a glimpse of something shiny in her other hand.

"What is that?" I asked.

"Oh this!" She raised her closed hand.

As her fingers opened, I saw what she was carrying.

"A piece of jewellery?" I asked confused, not understanding what I was seeing.

"It's better than that!" she said with an elation I did not understand. "It's our new insignia badge!" She stepped in close to me. "Now everyone will know which space fleet you serve with."

Mara pinned the golden, half-golf-ball-shaped insignia on my jacket. Its lettering denoting our fleet and ship name.

"Wonderful." Like the scowl on my face and terrible tassels on my shoulders weren't evidence enough that I served for the Militia.

Mara mistook my sarcasm for honesty and smiled. "I'm glad you like it. I gave one to each of the crew already. She hiccupped once more.

She spun to the music playing in the background. "Dance with me."

"In a bit."

I tried to fight the urge to treat her like every other woman I had ever pursued. I honestly wanted to peel her out of her clothes, as scantily clad as she was, and use some non-Militia-sanctioned tactics on her. But… I couldn't.

Could I?

Her eyes must have read my intentions because she leaned in and pressed her lips onto mine. I tried to find a reason not to kiss her back and the only thing I could think of was that it felt wrong. She was my colleague and subordinate. And she was drunk.

I gently pushed her back and she pouted a little bit.

"What gives, Zenith?" she asked, giving me a look that could have melted the ice on Pluto. "You don't want to have fun with me?"

"Oh, for sure, Mara." I made sure to maintain a healthy distance between us. "But I was just wondering, what are you most looking forward to during our mission to Mondo 4?"

Anything to get her sidetracked. Why was she coming on to me so brazenly? We'd never had anything but friction between us over the past five years! I must have missed a board meeting or something.

"Brant, you are such a wonderful listener!" she exclaimed. "I'm so happy to be able to help the Mondorians. And who knows? With some luck, maybe we can bring the Mondorians into the Militia. It's been a dream for me to do so. I also dream about learning from their biologists. You know how much I love growing things. I'm told they have the most exquisite plants…"

I did remember her love of plants. We had an entire hydroponics bay with an array of vegetation that she tended daily.

"Where was I?" she asked after sipping more rum.

"Mondo 4 plants and stuff."

"Oh yeah." She pushed me on the shoulder. "You're great listener! Anywho, I've heard there's a tree that has leaves so broad that each one can cover ten square metres in shadow."

She extended her arms in excitement—and with that, her gown opened completely. Her figure caught my greedy eyes. I reached out to caress her but quickly pulled back.

Damn, that had been close. She was a few beverages past sober and it felt wrong to give her my attention like this. Plus, I suspected she would literally murder me if she discovered tomorrow morning that I had taken advantage of the situation.

No thanks. I preferred to live.

At that moment, the door chimed once more.

"Thank the Mackmian gods," I murmured. I didn't have much willpower left.

"Come in," Mara exclaimed into the rum bottle instead of her wristband communicator.

When I tapped on my communicator, Stairn's face looked back up at me. At that point, I would have let in the four horsemen of the apocalypse to save my soul from Mara.

Stairn stepped into my chambers and noticed Mara.

"Captain, I didn't know you had company. I can come back in approximately seven hours and forty-nine minutes. I wish to talk to you before our meeting with the Prime officials."

"Agent Stairn," Mara began, "don't you think Brant is a great listener?"

To his credit, Stairn didn't say anything; he just raised an eyebrow. His dark hair was immaculately combed back and he looked like he had just finished a five-hour meditation session; his moral compass was pointed due north and it took me a moment to remember that I hadn't done anything wrong. Yet.

"Come in, Stairn," I said, looking at Mara as she poured herself another one. What's more, she was filling my glass as well.

Mara tossed the nearly empty bottle of Jamaican rum on the floor and pointed to the door.

"I'm going back to my quarters," she said. "Brant, you know where to find me."

She bumped into the doorframe, paused, and then realized that she'd spilled a third of her drink over her half-naked body.

And just like that, she was gone, leaving me alone with the logistics officer.

"Sorry to interrupt, Captain," Stairn said, but I'm not so sure he was sorry.

"No, Stairn, your timing was perfect."

His eyebrow arched again.

"Never mind," I added.

"Indeed." He handed me some more digital pads. "These are the reports from the Prime technicians working on *Orbital*." He handed me three other pads. "And these are the star charts and information briefings pertaining to the Mondo 4 mission."

I grabbed them from him and walked back to the desk where the earlier pads had been left in a stack. I put down the ones in my hand, picked up the others, and handed them back to Stairn.

"I signed the inventories and made notes on missing items," I said. "We can discuss it further with Prime tomorrow. After all, they did state that we were entitled to rearmament. The next two pads are about the battle in the Quazar system. I've reviewed the reports, made notes as they occurred to me, and signed off. They are yours to file. The final two pads contain recommendations about minor upgrades I'd like to see made to *Orbital*. Nothing serious, just repairing little quirks here and there."

For the first time in almost six months, I saw his expression change.

"I don't know what to say," he said, bewildered. "What has changed, Captain?"

I knew what he meant. I hadn't looked through six document pads in one evening since Stairn had taken over as logistics officer. I hadn't even realized *Orbital* had six working pads aboard the entire time I'd been captain.

"It seems like there's a huge amount of shit destined to come our way in the next several days," I said. "I just thought it best to clear up some homework before it arrives. Who knows… it may just come in handy to know what's on these pads."

He nodded solemnly. He prepared to turn and leave when I stopped him.

"Agent Stairn, do you mind if I ask you a question?"

"I think you just have."

I ignored that little quip. "I couldn't help but notice a certain skillset you demonstrated back on the Quazar station. Can you explain that? Your file mentions nothing of previous training."

He took his sweet time answering me. I tapped the edge of a pad, growing increasingly impatient. As the seconds ticked on, I began to regret asking.

"There is a great deal you do not know about me, Captain. One day, perhaps, I will be willing to share more. For now, I believe it is best the way it is."

I nodded in disappointment, and he turned to leave.

"Stairn," I said, stopping him again. "I know why Sparling is aboard *Orbital*. I know why Mara is with us. I definitely know why Bog's here. I might even know why Sirbot is here. For that matter, I may have finally figured out why I stay aboard. But maybe you can answer me this: why are you on my ship?"

He stepped back towards me, letting the sliding doors closed behind him.

"I mean, from what I saw on that station and how you conducted yourself, I would think *Orbital* would be your last choice."

I could see he was calculating his answer once more, but fortunately this time it didn't take him so long to spit it out.

"I am searching for something," he said cryptically. "I have not found it yet."

That didn't clear anything up, but I could tell he wasn't going to elaborate.

With a nod, he left my quarters.

I punched on my wristband communicator and waited for it to whistle back at me. "Mara, are you there?"

The only answer I received was the sound of snoring.

"Thank the Mackmian gods," I whispered to myself.

With that, I went to sleep.

"Dirt dry." That was what Captain Zenith's last evaluation report had stated about Agent Lazarus Stairn. Stairn couldn't have cared less. As long as he maintained his position aboard *Orbital* and with the Militia itself, he didn't care what the unpredictable, often lazy, and always egotistical Captain Zenith thought of him.

Lazarus Stairn was an agent by choice. He could have fulfilled the necessary documentation to become a full member of the Militia weeks ago. He had just passed his six-month optional evaluation and was now entitled an official rank and assignment aboard *Orbital*. Had he forgone the evaluation, he could have maintained agent status, but he had desired the challenge—and to his surprise, he'd even sought out the captain's opinion. The fact that the captain had thought him dry didn't matter; the fact that the captain found him exemplary at his work *did* matter.

He simply didn't fully understand why it mattered to him.

He was extremely overqualified to be a lowly logistics officer in the Militia. Truth be told, he was extremely overqualified to be in the Militia at all. Few had his range and years of experience.

But his long search had swayed him in unforeseen directions and demanded unexpected duties from him. He wouldn't allow himself to be deterred simply because the Militia Space Fleet was hardly a speck on any interstellar chart.

His mentors wouldn't have foreseen his choice of such lowly duties. They would have understood, but nevertheless they would have found it humorous. Lazarus Stairn did not find it to be humorous, as "dirt dry" as he was, but he could understand when other people's perception differed.

The lure of immense power and knowledge drove Lazarus Stairn. He had heard rumours long since forgotten. Distant voices on the solar winds had described it. The Universal, it was called. He felt it beckon him.

For the last thirty years, this search had swayed his every action. The moments, the scant seconds, when he'd felt its presence had been the moments in his life most worth living for. Three times in forty years, he had directly touched the Universal… and each time it left him with a gaping hole in his soul. If joining the Militia, and consequently *Orbital*, was a necessary step, he would endure it—if only to grasp hold of it once again. For that, anything was bearable.

Besides, the *Orbital* wasn't a complete loss. The crew was made up of intelligent and compassionate people. In a vast galaxy full of the most unimaginable darkness and the souls it devoured, it was a pleasant diversion to spend time with such individuals.

Captain Zenith irked him, although he would never say so. Brash and arrogant, self-indulgent and cocky, the captain showed signs of extreme brilliance Stairn couldn't ignore. The captain's career seemed to be spiralling into the sinkhole of nowhere, and on several prominent occasions Stairn had been tempted to lure the captain away from all this and instead take up with him on his search for the Universal.

But those moments were fleeting and Stairn was grateful each and every time he decided against such an action. The captain epitomized uncertainty through recklessness and indifference, despite his brilliance and cunning foresight.

No. Stairn couldn't risk so many years of patient training on such a person.

Besides, *Orbital*'s circumstances were in a state of rapid change. The sedentary life he'd enjoyed here, the one that had granted so much time to process and explore, was slipping away like sand through an hourglass. He anticipated having to leave *Orbital* before too long. He didn't relish such an act of betrayal, but time would soon tell where his search led.

Where the Universal led.

CHAPTER FOURTEEN

Meeting

Approximately six hours and forty-nine minutes later, I was walking through the station's large central corridor, on my way to find some breakfast, when my attention was stolen by something flashy that beeped on my wristband communicator.

I looked down and saw that the screen was displaying a digital map of this portion of the station. That was weirder than usual and I shook my wrist to try to work out the glitch.

It didn't work.

Looking closer, I saw that my present location was indicated on the map by a blue dot. There also appeared to be a red dot blinking nearby. Surely it had to mean something!

I decided to treat this as something other than a glitch. So I did the only logical thing and began walking towards the location of that confounded blinking red dot.

I was still in the large, populated central corridor when I reached the point in question. I looked down at the screen and saw the red dot continuing to blink. Then I carefully turned in a circle, trying to determine what I was supposed to be looking for…

There! Just to my right, I spotted a flickering yellow light between two stone arches.

When I came closer to investigate, I discovered a narrow opening normally covered by a decorative panel. Prime Station Alpha continued to surprise me with its hidden passages. This passage was just wide enough for me to slip through when I turned sideways and sucked in my stomach.

The concrete walls pressed in on me as I shuffled further into the darkness, certain that parts of my terrible uniform must be taking abuse from the mortar that infrequently bulged from between stones in the wall.

It turned out to be fortunate that I hadn't eaten breakfast yet. If I'd been only one or two kilograms heavier, I suspected I could have gotten wedged in here for the rest of eternity.

That yellow light flickered again, showing me where the passage ended in a tiny nook before a steel-studded door. Peering down at my wristband communicator and its map, I confirmed that which my eyes had seen. I had just enough space to pry open the door and step through...

...into a small rectangular room built from cement blocks. The chamber was illuminated by a single yellow bulb suspended overhead by a metallic beam.

And there was someone with me, an individual looming in the shadows at the far end of the chamber.

"Captain Zenith, can you see me?" he asked.

I thought the voice sounded familiar, but I couldn't quite make out the man's face. He appeared to be shorter and heavier than me.

When he stepped forward into the beam of light, I finally figured out who he was—and I was not pleased.

"Hubert, what the hell do you want?" I said to the disgraced security officer who'd only yesterday had his life turned upside-down on account of ridiculing *Orbital* in front of his superior.

I wasn't certain if Hubert Adamly intended to do me harm for the misfortune that had befallen him, so my hand went to my propulsion gun... only to remember that I had been forced to sacrifice it. My retribution against Mordeau had been more than important enough to sacrifice my only working weapon.

Studying Hubert, I raised my hands in a defensive position.

"Captain Zenith, good," he said with a slight whistle in his voice. "I have a message for you."

He stepped forward, his hand raised in front of him. I couldn't see what he carried and wondered if I might have underestimated the man's desire to end me. Any number of explosives or poisons could have fit in the palm of his chubby little hand.

When he opened his palm, I saw that he held a digital storage device. He placed it between his index finger and thumb and activated a glowing yellow button.

The device projected images onto the cement wall. The scene was dark—space, I surmised—and I detected a red dwarf star off in the distance. In the corner of the video feed was a timestamp which revealed that the footage had been taken two weeks ago.

Hubert ran his fingers along a slider on the micro-projector and the video fast-forwarded. The stars moved, but nothing else about the image looked familiar to me. I'd seen too many random stars and planets to recognize any of them by sight alone.

"What are you showing me?" I asked.

No sooner were the words out of my mouth than I began to recognize what I was looking at.

"It's the Mondorian solar system," I gasped, my breath stuck in my throat.

I leaned in closer, trying to determine who might have recorded this video footage. The Militia didn't have any satellites near the Mondo system, and the Mondorians certainly didn't possess any of their own far enough out to record such a distant perspective. In fact, when the Militia had engaged the Mondorians in talks about joining the fleet, they had asked us to respect their privacy and even remove the few satellites we'd already installed in the area. Which the Militia had done.

"Where is this taken from, Hubert?"

He scratched his lower chin. "Well, we have a satellite array on the edge of Prime space. One of those satellites was able to pick up the events you're about to witness."

"You mean you were spying on Militia space," I said. "This is a breach of the accords!"

"I'm not showing you this to start a galactic incident. Although we both know how well the Militia would fare if one were to occur."

I appraised him and observed the heavy bags under his eyes. His dark stubble was longer than it had been when we'd first met and his uniform was unkempt. He appeared to have been through the wringer.

"You would be surprised what the Militia is capable of, Hubert."

"I suppose I would be," he said. "In fact, I'm surprised *Orbital* is still flying at all. It should have been decommissioned centuries ago. I'll never understand why it hasn't gotten pulled into some gravity well and disintegrated by now."

I felt a strong urge to the throttle the man—and if it had been even a week ago, I probably would have. Instead I did my best to contain myself.

"Hubert, I'll ask one more time: why are you showing this to me?"

"I have my orders."

"From whom?"

"I've been told not to say. I'm only supposed to share the information with you, so that's what I'm doing."

He wasn't here by choice, of that I was satisfied. "Well then, get to it and quit wasting my time."

The video sped up. Soon after, I saw a flash of grey light in the corner of the image.

"Hold it a moment," I said. "Play that back."

Hubert did as I asked. I stepped closer to the concrete wall, trying to get a better look. If I was understanding the video correctly, a sphere of grey void energy had suddenly spawned out of nowhere. It shouldn't have been possible.

As the video continued, the sphere of void energy grew larger, eventually encroaching on a nearby planet. Not just any planet, but the blue-green world of Mondo 4. And the void sphere continued its expansion until it filled nearly the entire system. It got so big that the video feed had to zoom back to capture what was happening.

"You have to be shitting me," I murmured. As the video feed zoomed out to its widest possible angle, it revealed the presence of a Prime ship. "You have a vessel of your own in the Mondo system?"

Hubert ignored the tone of my voice. "Keep watching, Captain."

I did as I was told and watched as the Prime ship backed away from the grey void.

"The ship's name is the *Dawnstar*." Hubert pressed a button on the projection device and the image froze in place. A list of names appeared. "This is the crew manifest aboard the *Dawnstar* at the time of the incident."

I used my finger to scan through the list of names, studying them carefully. Some of them I recognized from my years in Prime. However, most were unfamiliar.

"I want to speak with this crew," I said angrily.

"That isn't possible."

"Why the hell not?"

"Because we don't know where the *Dawnstar* is right now."

I had pissed off a great number of people in my time. And in all that time, I had developed a certain skill for being able to figure out when people were lying to me.

Hubert was not lying.

I began to pace in circles around the sub-lieutenant. I could tell it annoyed him, but I didn't much care how he felt at the moment.

I stepped up to the crew manifest once more, determined to get to the bottom of this mystery. "Something's off."

"What is it?"

"At the time of the recording, this crew manifest was up to date. Correct?"

"I believe so," Hubert said. "The satellite confirms that the *Dawnstar* uploaded the manifest just after it left the system."

"Did it upload any information about the void sphere itself?"

Hubert brought up a series of digital readouts, but the information I was looking for wasn't there. I couldn't tell if someone at Prime was playing games, perhaps trying to withhold this vital data, but so far Hubert seemed honest.

"Okay," I conceded after a while. "Is there a log of visitors aboard the *Dawnstar* at the time of the recording?"

He brought forth the information I'd requested, and I perused the list of about a dozen names.

"And do you have a passengers log from before the *Dawnstar* arrived in the Mondo system?"

He nodded and brought up the list. It read exactly the same.

"Give me two logs previous," I continued.

When he did so, I saw that this list had been logged a day before the last one.

And then it struck me: there was an extra name this time around.

"Look," I said, pointing at the name that hadn't been present in the previous two logs. "This person was missing from the passengers' log after the incident. What could account for that?"

Hubert looked closely. "Andelson."

"Maybe this Andelson person has some useful information about what happened."

"I don't know," the other man said tersely. "And to be honest, I don't care to be here any longer."

"I don't care what you want, Hubert. Whoever sent you wanted me to know this information. So it's your duty to help me."

"That may be true, Captain, but I must be going. I've shared with you all the information I can."

With that, he handed me the small data storage device. I took it, then quickly exited the tiny room and returned through the narrow passage.

As I walked away, one question nagged at me: who had given Hubert the order to tell me about this? And the more I thought about it, I realized I had a good idea of who it must have been.

I headed to Bog's quarters to run my suspicions by my closest friend, but there was no response when I knocked on the door. Then I remembered that he and I were both supposed to be attending another meeting with Prime shortly, so it was possible Bog had already made his way there.

But Stairn hadn't been invited to that meeting, so I figured he might be available for a last-minute visit. And if I made the Prime officers wait, all the better.

When I knocked on Stairn's door, he answered. When I showed the data storage device to him, he began to study the information it contained. I relayed all the details of my conversation with Hubert, which the logistics officer took in stride.

Stairn studied the projection while sitting on the edge of his desk. He was dressed sharply in his Militia uniform, and for some reason it looked a hell of a lot better on him than me. I couldn't account for that. The gold tassels seemed almost groomed, and his new ID tag glistened and reflected the lights around us.

"Do you think we can trust Hubert?" Stairn asked. "This could be a lure to throw us off. There's still so much we don't know about what's happening in the Mondo system."

"I thought of that. But Hubert wasn't lying to me. If he was, he's a supremely gifted actor."

"It would help to know who gave Hubert this information. He doesn't seem to be clever enough to have made the decision on his own."

I nodded. "In fact, I have a pretty good idea who gave him the order."

Stairn raised his eyebrow in interest.

"I think it was Benson," I said.

"Why would he do so? He's supposed to be meeting with you in a few minutes. He could have told you himself…" He trailed off, still putting the pieces together. "Unless he didn't want the other people at the meeting to know…"

"Right." I paused. "And I suppose if it wasn't Benson, it could have been Marsdale. She would obviously have had access to all this intelligence."

Stairn stood up from the desk. "We need to speak to this Andelson person."

"I agree. But how?"

The man's eyes lost focus for a moment, as though he were going deep into his own memory. "I seem to remember something about that name. Someone called Andelson came up on a series of petty charges on Lariss II."

"Lariss II? That's not even in this galaxy. It's in the Milky Way. If this is true, Andelson must really get around."

"Yes, I remember now. I once tracked him down to Lariss II, but after that the trail went cold. I wasn't able to catch him."

I looked at Stairn, only partially surprised that he had been in a business of tracking people down. As important as our current dilemma was, I was eager to hear about Stairn's past life. There was more to him than met the eye.

"Tracking people down was a pastime of yours, Stairn?"

"In a roundabout sort of way, Captain."

"What does that mean?"

He remained silent as he looked back at the projections on the wall.

"Another thing you probably don't feel like explaining to me, Stairn?"

"It's not important right now. What's important is that I never caught up to Andelson."

I shook my head in disappointment, wishing Stairn had opened up to me. But it seemed he wouldn't be sharing anything further about his mysterious past. I forced myself to think about the problem at hand.

"And you never heard from Andelson again?"

"No," he replied. "I suspect that he changed names after that, but of course I can't prove it. I may have only missed him by a matter of hours…"

"Were you able to gather any clues about where he might have gone?" I wasn't too hopeful. It could be tough to track down people on backwater planets and moons.

"No…" Stairn put a finger to his lips, looking thoughtful. "But this passenger manifest from the *Dawnstar* certainly helps. In addition to Andelson, there's another name I can't account for. Someone named Manz Dee."

"Holy fuck!" I shouted, a memory snapping into place when I heard him say the name aloud.

Suddenly, all the pieces fell into place.

I hurried towards the meeting with Prime, Stairn trailing in my wake. I had asked him to join us. Normally, I wouldn't have bothered due to his rank and the fact that for six months Stairn had felt like a wet diaper… and yet he had proved himself surprisingly knowledgeable of late.

When we approached the doors to the meeting room—not the Grand Council Room of the Universe again, thankfully—we found Bog and Mara standing just outside the door.

Unable to contain my excitement, I shared with them everything that had transpired in the last hour.

"No shit!" Bog yelped, inadvertently dumping his steaming hot mug of Nova Martian coffee all over his hand. He didn't seem to even register the heat, though. He simply placed his hand into the massive maw he called his mouth and slurped the spilled coffee. "Are you telling me the Dirge was on board the *Dawnstar*?"

"Yeah," I affirmed, lowering my voice by instinct I suppose. "He may have some idea of what's going on in the Mondo system."

Stairn spoke softly, his voice barely louder than a whisper. "Who is this Dirge?"

"He's a rogue, an unknown," I explained. "He sometimes goes by the name Manz Dee. But whatever his real name, he has the very bad habit of being in places just before shit goes down."

"And you know this man?" Stairn asked.

"I haven't met him personally, as far as I know. I only know of him from the rumours that circulate. His reputation is… splotchy."

Mara sighed. "So, this Dirge. Does anyone know what he looks like or where we could find him?"

Before I could answer, the doors to the meeting room opened.

I didn't step inside right away. Instead I studied Mara for a few moments, observing that she seemed no worse for wear after the previous night's drinking. I wondered how she had managed to pull that off.

I also observed that she had something dangling from within the confines of her uniform.

"Mara, what is that?" I asked.

"Oh, this?" She reached into her uniform and pulled out a propulsion gun that looked a lot like mine. It even had the same gouge at the base of the stock. "This is yours, isn't it?"

What the fuck? How the hell had she gotten that? I had left it in the high marshal's private office. I remembered very clearly placing it just so…

I took hold of it and looked more carefully. Yes, it was mine.

"Where did you get it?" I asked, perplexed and deeply annoyed.

Very quickly my annoyance shifted to fear. What if someone had found it in Mordeau's office and delivered it to Mara? Was it possible this was part of some sort of sting operation to track down the true owner and uncover who had placed it there?

I scanned the corridor around us, but nothing seemed out of place. No security robots or personnel.

"I found it in my quarters," she said, not noticing my stress levels spike into the ceiling. "My wristband communicator tells me it was teleported to my location last night via black rift energy. But my communicator can't tell me where it came from. Must have happened sometime after I went to sleep."

I checked the weapon and confirmed that it hadn't been fired since I'd left it attached to Mordeau's desk. I ran a hand across my forehead where fine beads of sweat had formed.

I took Mara's hand, surprising her. Surprising me, she didn't pull back. I lifted it up and searched her wristband for an answer to the mystery.

"Oh, for shit's sake," I exhaled angrily.

It immediately became clear that there had been a horrible mistake—or rather, a perfectly predictable malfunction. That gun had been programmed to black-rift back to me only after blasting Pierre Mordeau's gonads to smithereens. That was supposed to happen in days or weeks from now, when it was convenient for me to do so from a distance.

Somehow the remote had malfunctioned and sent the pistol away far too early—and to Mara's quarters, of all places.

"Do you know why it showed up in my quarters?" she asked.

"It's not important."

All I could think of was that the remote had spent too long inside *Orbital* and been ruined by association. It didn't make sense but nothing aboard *Orbital* ever had. In my head, I ran through all the troubles I had endured to get inside High Marshal Dickhead's office. It had all been for nothing.

I had limited time to berate my luck, as we were soon being escorted into the meeting.

Upon entering, I saw that High Marshal Olwen was already seated at the polished metal and glass table. I hoped he hadn't accidentally sold the Militia for a burrito.

In his prime, Olwen had been brilliant, honest, and brave—the most outstanding commanding officer I'd ever served with. But these past years had exacted a terrible toll on his mind... and it was becoming more and more evident every time he joined us for an official function. Although there were still flashes of brilliance, they were interrupted by long periods of foggy confusion.

Mara and I needed to deal with this, but I just didn't know how to go about it. Someone had to step in to run Militia the way it needed to be run. But until this week, there hadn't been anything worthwhile for us to deal with, nothing to draw attention to our high marshal.

I just hoped he wouldn't be too much of a problem today. God, I missed the old Olwen.

Around the table was gathered Olwen and none other than Samuel Benson. Within a few minutes, we were watching the same recorded video Hubert had only just shown me; the image was distorted and kept falling in and out of focus.

Worst of all, I had to pretend I was seeing it for the first time. Although at least the audio was new.

"Mondo was debou—" a voice reported on the feed, followed by several seconds of crackling static. "—orrible grey void... time short. Please send hel—"

And that was it.

"That message was sent two weeks ago," explained Benson. "The transmission wasn't received until three days ago, just before the Quazar incident."

"Why haven't we seen it before now?" I asked.

"Because we're still trying to understand what's happened. It seems that we sent a ship, the *Dawnstar*, to investigate the disturbance in the Mondo system. That ship was inexplicably lost after sending this transmission."

I looked over at Benson, once again wondering if he had been the one to give Hubert the order to brief me on the situation early. If so, what had he hoped to gain?

As I watched, Benson operated a set of controls built into the table. "Just a moment. We're receiving a communication feed with Mondo 4..."

Seconds later, the table's holographic emitter lit up and a stark white Mondorian appeared in front of us. I recognized him as Izaak Kaazi, one of his people's most preeminent scientists. His eyes were wide with any number of emotions. He looked excited, relieved, and perhaps even scared at the same time.

"Izaak, it's good to see you," Mara opened warmly.

I knew she and Izaak had a professional history, and that she liked him a great deal. In her ambassadorial role for the Militia, Mara had led the fleet's talks with Mondo 4. As far as I recalled, Izaak had been involved in those negotiations.

"Mara," Izaak said with a sigh of relief. I couldn't quite tell whether it was because he was happy to see her personally or if it was because he was just grateful to finally reach someone— anyone. "It's so very good to see you again." He stiffened when he saw Olwen standing just behind Mara. "High Marshal! I'm really hoping for some help. I've been trying to send a transmission outside our system for two weeks, but I didn't think our messages were getting through."

"It seems they're coming through now," Mara said. "We're at Prime Station Alpha at the moment, conferring with our friends here—"

"Thank our Divinity!" Izaak shouted. "Is there anything you think you can do for us?"

"Izaak, we've only been able to receive a few jumbled messages and images so far," she continued. "All we can make out is some kind of spherical grey void in your system. I'm sorry that we haven't been able to fully figure it out. Tell us what's going on. Has something happened to your sun?"

The Mondorian's face fell as he steadied himself, leaning against a wall next to him. His skin was so very pale. I'd seen fresh snowfall less white than he looked at the moment.

"Yes. Our sun has been partially absorbed by a mysterious grey void," Izaak explained. "For a while there, we lost the ability to transmit or receive any messages."

"Survivors?" Stairn demanded, cutting to the chase. After all, we'd already heard reports about something anomalous pertaining to their sun.

Izaak nodded. "Oh, yes. It was the strangest thing... the light faded, sort of like a solar eclipse, but everything else remained... remained constant..." The Mondorian was visibly agitated. "Here, I'll try to resend the observations we've made so far. I pray that they make it to you."

"Yes, we're receiving them now," Stairn stated, his fingers working on a tabletop panel.

I stepped up next to Mara. "Doctor Kaazi, my name is Brant Zenith, captain of the *Orbital*. Can you quickly summarize your situation?"

"I would be all too eager, Captain. The void I described has come and gone twice since its first appearance two weeks ago. And if my calculations are correct, there remain only hours, maybe less, before the current window closes. After that, we won't be able to communicate again for several days." He paused to wipe blue droplets of sweat from his forehead. "As you know by now, two weeks ago a strange grey void swallowed our primary sun, Mondo, leaving us only with light from our secondary and tertiary stars. Then the void seemed to swallow our planet as well. I can't explain it. The inhabitants of Mondo 4 should be dead by now..."

My heart raced with excitement. Losing our opportunity to assist with the Quazar situation had stung like someone pouring vinegar on a wound. But this was turning out to be much more than a consolation prize. Whatever was going on around Mondo 4, it was very serious.

If my memory served, the Mondo system contained three suns, seventeen planets, thirty-seven moons, and at least six hundred million lives.

Ironically, I hadn't felt so elated since my discovery of EZ-Heal.

"Captain," Izaak continued, "with each cycle, the length of time it takes for the void to release us gets longer. It may not be long before our world is completely and forever lost."

I tried to remain calm, but I had never encountered anything like this in all my fifteen years of adventuring. For the first time in a very long while, I was actually glad to be sober.

"Doctor Kaazi, we will leave here shortly," I assured him. "However, it will take about ten days to reach you. We will review your data en route."

"I'm grateful, Captain, and appreciate any aid you can render." The Mondorian scientist hesitated. "I would love to ask for you to make even greater haste, but I'm not sure it would do any good. If we disappear into the void, you may not be able to help or communicate with us. I just don't know."

"We'll do our best to get there as soon as we can," Mara added, sounding heartfelt. "Please hold on."

With that, the image blurred and then vanished entirely.

We tried for several minutes to recover the signal, but to no avail. The meeting room fell into a deep and prolonged silence as we all reflected on what we'd just heard.

"I believe the grey void has enveloped the planet once again," Stairn stated. "Even more quickly than the doctor expected, it would seem."

"It appears so," I admitted glumly.

I had to take a few moments to compose myself. Olwen, of course, wasn't yet privy to the details I had learned from Hubert. But if I was right about Benson, then he was the one behind it.

Still, I had to be careful.

"The *Dawnstar*, it seems, had some interesting passengers aboard," I explained.

"What do you mean, interesting passengers?" Mara asked.

I looked over at her and then her father. Olwen's face was angled down and the light in his eyes appeared partially extinguished. I could tell that my friend and mentor wasn't really with us at the moment.

I briefly explained recent events. I felt I had no choice but to tell them everything I'd learned about Andelson, Manz Dee, and consequently the Dirge. I couldn't see any way around it.

"Andelson's name was on the *Dawnstar*'s passenger manifest," I said. "At least, it was. Two days later, there was no sign of him. While talking it through with Agent Stairn, it struck me that perhaps Andelson was an alias for a man named Manz Dee."

"And what does that mean exactly?" Mara asked. She was showing great patience as I did my best to get to the point without leaving anything out. At least, without leaving out anything relevant.

"I've heard some shady shit about Manz Dee… from people who've dealt with him…" I trailed off, uncertain where to go with it. "I've also known him by another alias. The Dirge."

"Oh!" Mara exhaled. "I've heard of him."

This took me by surprise. I hadn't realized that Mara had any contact with the sorts of unsavoury characters I did. The Dirge sure wasn't a common name in polite society.

Stairn gave Mara a pointed look. "What do you know of him?"

"He is a forebearer of doom," she replied.

"That's a dramatic way of putting it," Bog said with a smirk.

"It's what I heard from some travellers I dealt with a few months ago," Mara said. "I purchased some hard-to-find hydroponic equipment off them and they had some interesting stories to share. They assured that wherever that name is spoken, terrible things have happened. Or will happen. Why else would he be named after a song sung at a funeral?"

Stairn canted his head. "Valid point."

"Nevertheless, doom or no, I think our best chance to help will be to find the Dirge and discover what he knows," I chimed in again. "Unfortunately, there's only one place I know to begin looking for him: Roustabout's. And it's two days in the wrong direction."

Roustabout's was perhaps the slickest, raciest, and most dangerous neutral space bar in the universe. I'd wiled away plenty of hours there over the years and I had a contact or two. It was also the site of the galaxy's best duelling dens.

Even more, it was only place I'd heard the Dirge could be found to frequent. At least, that's where he supposedly made all his deals.

"Is it really worth going so far out of the way?" Mara asked quietly. "Just to look for a man who may not even be able to help us?"

"I think so. The *Dawnstar* disappeared near the Mondo system, the Dirge seems to have been aboard her, and there's been no word from the ship since." I looked over at Benson to confirm this. He nodded in affirmation. "Trust me. If anyone has leads on the Dirge, we'll find them at Roustabout's."

No one argued this point, which bolstered my street cred a little.

"I agree, Captain," Stairn offered after a moment, surprising me. He almost never agreed with me. "But I do suggest that if it takes more than three days to find the Dirge, we should consider changing tactics."

Before replying, I noticed Mara take Benson aside and whisper something into his ear. I could only guess that she was trying to further persuade him of the importance of our mission to find the Dirge.

Olwen stood nearby, too, but he barely seemed to be paying attention. I sighed again, unhappy to see him suffering so.

Stairn gave me a hard look. Had I been silent a little too long?

"Anyway, Captain, like I said… we must locate the Dirge within three days," Stairn said. "Not only that, but I contend that we must reach the Mondo system in thirteen days, maximum. And I don't think we should go in blind."

Lt. Benson looked forward catching my attention.

"I'll recommend to Prime's high council that we send the *Doomsday* to the Mondo system immediately, to ensure that help has the potential to arrive as soon as possible. That way we can relay to you any developments in the system," Benson said, stepping away from Mara. "With your approval, of course, Captain."

I inclined my head towards him, not bothered this time that Prime was sticking their noses in our business. On the one hand, my preference was always for Prime to stay the hell away from me. But I had to admit, logically, that they could be helpful in this instance. We were severely shorthanded. Plus, I had never met the *Doomsday*'s fabled commander, Captain Maximillian Flint. I wondered what he was like in person.

I shivered with excitement and fear, my mixture of emotions potent. It had been so long since we'd been responsible for such an important mission. I didn't even mind that it would mean taking a few weeks off from alcohol and womanizing.

CHAPTER FIFTEEN

Rotations

Kaboom! *Orbital*'s cargo bay erupted in a ball of fire and the intensity of the explosion could be heard and felt even on the safer side of the heavily shielded security door.

Simbden looked sheepishly through the portal where Mara and I stood. A group of repair drones lay on the bay floor, melted from the extreme heat of the inferno. I had to squint through my fingers just to see them. It felt like looking at the sun from the equator on Mercury.

"I don't understand it, my captain," Simbden said, his voice shaky. "Everything in the cargo bay was working perfectly an hour ago."

The Mackmian engineer handed me a digital document pad with a complete list of all the upgrades that had been completed so far. Aided by the station's crews and robot drones, the repairs had been coming along wonderfully.

Or so I thought.

I browsed the list and found it to be thorough. I was also a bit annoyed to see that the list, which seemed to have been compiled by Mara, was organized into three categories: Essentials, Non-Essentials, and Zenith Indulgences.

"Really, Mara?" I said. "You have a category named Zenith Indulgences? I hardly think this is the time to bring up that damned bingo machine."

Mara raised her eyebrow diplomatically. "Humour, Captain. Besides, Simbden was the only one who saw this exact list."

"Uh, actually…" Simbden suddenly looked a bit embarrassed. "Well, I sent it out to all the technicians…"

"Oh, fuck." I sighed, realizing that dozens, maybe hundreds, of Prime personnel had seen Mara's little joke.

I was becoming rather restless and impatient. It had been three days since our repairs began and we were still waiting on the weapon systems, armour plating, shielding, guidance computers, and a whole list of other very important systems to come back online. Each time I was told we were nearing completion, something went wrong and set us back.

"First it was the weapons bay," I said, walking away from the cargo bay. From the shouts behind me, it seemed the blaze was at least dying down. I looked down at the pad in my hands and read the report. "Prime's advanced weapons systems, all tested at one hundred percent. Two hours later, the whole network shorted out, nearly melting half of *Orbital* in the process. How do you explain this, Simbden?"

"I can't, my captain." The engineer fell into step beside me and Mara. "What's worse is that we've tried two more times since, in two different array matrices, and both times we've gotten the same result."

If Mackmians could sweat, I'm sure Simbden would be a salty pool right now.

"The only good news I can offer you regarding the weapons, my captain, is that *Orbital*'s original systems are operating at the same efficiency they were before the battle at Quazar. We restocked the ballistic space torpedoes and got those up and running again."

I ran my hands through my hair and grimaced. I didn't know if that was a point in our favour. We really, really needed better weapons than what we'd had in our arsenal during that firefight. And now we had a deadline eating away at us. If these improvements didn't stick and soon, we would be forced to disembark with pretty much all the same deficiencies as before. And I had no idea when we'd have the chance to enjoy such first-rate facilities again, never mind get them free of charge.

"Not enough. I need better news," I said curtly.

I felt bad the moment the words left my mouth. I knew it really wasn't his fault. I had watched him work closely the first days of repairs, and every Prime technician had marvelled at how competent he was, despite their initial loathing of him.

He hadn't just been competent. He'd been formidable, working with speed and tenacity.

Besides, I knew *Orbital*. The ship just had a way of breaking down. No matter what was done to her, somehow, someway, it always reverted back to the same terrible state it had been in five years ago. My crew and I were fortunate it hadn't yet killed us all.

"Sorry, Simbden." I put a hand on his shoulder to demonstrate my loyalty. "I'm only mad because deadlines are biting my ass right now."

He perked up at that. "Well, my captain, do you remember the state of *Orbital*'s hull when we first arrived at Prime Station Alpha?"

"Of course. I've seen underwear from a Telnian cow herder with fewer holes in it."

"I don't think he wants to hear too much about that particular story, Brant," Mara remarked sarcastically.

I looked over at her with annoyance, still peeved about the list she had helped share with the entire station.

"Go on, Simbden," I said.

"We began the fusion of a radical new metallic polymer to patch those holes. The process is quick. We analyzed *Orbital*'s hull and then synthesized the polymer. We started on the vital areas first. Just as before, the repairs were going very well." Suddenly he looked very, very embarrassed. "And then they simply fell off. We thought we chose the wrong ratio of elements in the polymer. That was the only answer that made sense. So we tried again, even more carefully this time, but the patches still didn't take. I took the whole evening to think about it. I've completed dozens of polymer repairs on my father's ship and never had any bad results!"

Just before we walked out of view of the cargo bay, I heard the doors open. I turned in time to see a few still-functioning repair drones at work sweeping up the remains of their melted robotic brothers.

"I hesitated to try again after our recent failures," Simbden continued. "But this morning, without trying anything new, the holes were all substantially repaired. I can only surmise that the polymers can take up to twelve hours to set. Maybe it's like blood cells, clotting the holes in the ship's hull. Well, anyway, the ship's hull is now at a hundred percent. Even the holes in the control hub are rectified."

"That is a significant achievement," I admitted. "Thank you, Simbden."

"You're welcome, my captain. But I don't know if I can take the credit. I don't even know what we finally did right. It's almost as if…"

"As if what?" Mara prompted.

"No. It's a silly thought."

But I gave him a look that encouraged him to go on. Lord knows, I may have said some silly things in my career.

"Well, my captain, I was thinking that everything we do seems to get undone," Simbden said. "It almost feels like someone, or something, is unravelling our accomplishments. I'm beginning to get the sense that someone doesn't want *Orbital* to be fixed."

The air hung heavy as the three of us pondered any number of dark scenarios. Personally, I couldn't believe anyone else out there would think *Orbital* important enough to sabotage. Normally, the Militia's miniscule budget and bad decisions were sabotage enough.

"Keep up the hard work, Simbden," I said, snapping out of it. "We only have two days and three hours before departure. And we *do* depart, no matter what shape we're in. I'd rather it be with some working weapons, a guidance system, and perhaps even an engine."

Mara and I left Simbden to go on with his work and made our way up to the control hub. When we entered, technicians were still hurriedly working on every console. I was nearly blinded by all the sparks from repair guns.

I detoured away from the chaos and headed towards my office, and this time I kept an eye out to make sure I didn't trip over Sirbot. Indeed, I found the office empty of lifeforms, artificial or otherwise.

"What the hell!" I shouted, stopping in the middle of the room.

Mara, who had followed me in, froze in place. "What is it?"

"My Zigma Banisher is gone."

I was pissed. The Banisher was one of my favourite weapons.

"Maybe you misplaced it," Mara said, trying to calm me.

"No, I haven't taken it out of this room in months."

"Well, maybe one of the technicians knows where it went."

"I doubt those Prime dinks would fess up to it." I felt so frustrated and insulted. "Damn *Orbital!* If this ship had working cameras, maybe I could track it down."

"Brant, take a breath and calm down." She paused for a moment, an idea coming to her. "Maybe Benson could help."

"Perhaps."

At that moment, I saw Bog come into the control hub through the half-open door. I waved him into my office.

Bog's face turned darker several shades of obsidian when he saw the expression etched on my face. "You look pissed!"

"There seems to have been some sort of security breach."

"What sort of security breach?" he asked, all-business.

"I'm missing my Zigma Banisher."

Bog seemed surprise. "You too?"

"Me too? What the hell are you talking about?"

"Well, first Shoe lost her parasol—"

"I didn't lose it!" Mara retorted. "It just vanished. It must have been taken. It was where I always keep it—in the corner of my quarters, overhanging my bed. Brant, you should know. You saw it the night before the mission…"

She trailed off, suddenly becoming very self-conscious. I had no idea what the hell she meant, though, since I hadn't been to her quarters since the last time she had summoned me for accidentally shooting a hole through her favourite collection of ancient photographs.

I started to protest. "I haven't been—"

"Anyway, I don't want to talk about it," she said with a huff. "All that matters is that the parasol is missing. I don't know who took it or when exactly."

Bog sighed. "And I'm missing something too."

I looked up at his large obsidian face in surprise. Were his horns actually glowing red? He seemed hesitant to tell us what the matter was.

"C'mon, Bog," I said. "Just spit it out. We're all professionals here."

He scratched at his round chin with a big, stony hand. "It's not important."

"Just tell us what was taken."

"I'd rather not, if you don't mind."

"Well, now I'm minding. Bog, don't make me turn this into an order. This could be important to the mission and *Orbital*'s safety."

His horns were definitely glowing, getting redder by the moment. He looked almost like a teapot getting ready to whistle.

"Fine, screw it! I'm missing Mr. Wiggles."

He left it at that, thinking we must have had even the foggiest notion of what he meant.

But then it hit me. "You mean your lucky underwear?"

He didn't deny it. If anything, his horns turned even redder. I couldn't stifle a chuckle, which only seemed to set him off further.

"Mr. Wiggles?" Mara asked innocently enough, an eyebrow raised.

"Yes! It's gone! And it's tragic. Do you have any idea how many years Mr. Wiggles and I have been together?"

"I'm very, very afraid to ask," I said, trying and failing to contain my sarcasm. "Anyone else missing anything of varying importance?" I chose my words carefully so as not to offend anyone. They both shook their heads. "Good. Now, let's look at this with a clear view. We have a parasol stolen a certain number of days ago, my Zigma Banisher, and Bog's lucky underwear. What does it mean?"

"Who the fuck knows?" Bog said vehemently, smoke erupting from his mouth. "But when I catch the SOB who stole my gitch, he'll wish he never met me."

"What if he needed it more than you do?" I asked.

"No one could need it more than me."

And that's the way he left it.

At that moment, I spied Stairn and Sparling entering the control hub. And sure enough, there was Simbden, right behind them.

I decided at that point to take advantage of the fact that the entire crew had found themselves in one place. Plus, I needed to do something to take my mind off the missing Banisher. I bade them to follow me into my office.

I cleared my throat as they crowded in.

"I would be lying if I didn't admit some anxiety over our upcoming mission," I said, sounding uncharacteristically captain-like. We were getting close to launch and were probably all feeling the same anxiety. "Our weapons are still limited, the engines aren't dependable, and our sensory equipment is sketchy at best…"

Well, it might not be awe-inspiring, but I wanted the crew to know the truth. They needed to know what we were facing.

"What's worse is that the toilet seats are always cold, and the shag carpeting makes my feet itch," I added, having remembered that humour could help in such moments. My crew chuckled in response. "But the important part is that we do have a mission. A *real* mission. It's the opportunity we've been waiting for since that fiasco on Alhalran."

I walked around my desk, looking each crewmember in the eyes. Against all odds, I found myself doing something I hadn't done in public in a very long time; I spoke from the heart.

"I know *Orbital* isn't the finest ship in the universe. But right now, she's our home, our protector, and our charge. Millions—no, hundreds of millions—may perish without our help. I see on each of your faces something I haven't felt in years. I see inspiration and eagerness. I feel courage and strength in having you here with me. For that, I thank you."

The room turned electric with positive energy. I couldn't remember sharing such a satisfying moment with them in all the time we'd been together. This mission would be different than anything we'd done before. One way or another, we would prove our worth.

This I vowed to myself.

CHAPTER SIXTEEN

Roustabout's

I was really looking forward to the upcoming night! Unfortunately, it started off somewhat badly—with yet another verbal berating from our ship's ambassador.

"Brant!" Mara called out, trying to keep up with my rapid pace through *Orbital*'s corridor. I had just changed into my favourite bar clothes…I mean undercover outfit, ready for our mission to Roustabout's to find the Dirge. I had never looked better, if I do say so myself. "Zenith! We need to talk about the mission."

I stopped dead in my tracks, allowing her to catch up. "Go ahead."

"We need a better game plan if we're actually going to track down the Dirge," Mara said, catching her breath.

Ever since departing Prime Station Alpha two days ago, I had been thinking quite intently about our impending stopover at Roustabout's. According to rumours, the Dirge was immensely tall, as much as three hundred centimetres in height. It was possible he had black hair and brown eyes, or blonde hair and green eyes, or maybe grey hair and hazel eyes. Or no hair and black eyes. Or black hair and no eyes? The rumours were essentially useless.

That said, every report agreed that the Dirge was indeed a man—a man with two arms and two legs. Oh, and he also wore a Militon chain, the same type of superpowered item I had been trying to acquire for myself. The chains were elusive and rare, nearly impossible to find or acquire.

As I've already explained, the chain bestowed any number of enviable powers on its wearer: the ability to change in size, absorb weapons fire, and even dislocate time—whatever that meant. Some extreme stories claimed it contained the power of a thousand suns and when used as a weapon could saw a moon in half.

I wanted one of these chains more than almost anything. But I had to admit that the prospect of owning one also scared me a bit. It was sometimes said that only the most dangerous and demented creatures wore Militon chains.

I had seen a Militon chain once, and it had looked like a simple bracelet. The one I saw had been silver and shimmered ever so slightly when worn around the wrist. I'd almost mistaken it for normal jewellery except that it glowed a radiant silver.

"Brant, even if you can find the Dirge, how on earth do you expect us to capture him?" Mara demanded, pulling me back to the present moment. "After all, he must be at least clever enough to have escaped from the *Dawnstar*, a Prime ship, possibly one of the most fortified and heavily guarded type of ship in the known universe…"

I had no idea how I was going to manage it, truth be told. I just knew I was going to try.

"Wait a minute," I snapped. "What do you mean 'us'?"

But as I recounted her question in my mind, a searing detail caught my attention.

"You seriously think I'm not joining you on this mission?" she asked, incredulous.

"Of course, Mara. This isn't a typical ambassadorial mission, now is it?"

"Every mission involving you is potentially an ambassadorial mission."

I had to admit that stung.

"No," I said, leaving it at that.

"No? No, what?" she replied curtly. "No, you don't always need an ambassador to clean up your mess? Or no, you think you can force me to stay behind? Because if I remember your last few diplomatic missions, it seems to me that a certain ambassador had to bail you out of trouble on more than one occasion."

I could tell I was quickly losing the argument—and losing my desire to keep fighting.

That's when the perfect idea struck me.

"Fine, Ambassador," I said. "You win."

She stepped back a pace, not having expected me to give in so easily.

I sighed. "You want in? You're in."

With that, I picked up my pace and speed-walked back to the control room. Mara hurried behind me, trying to catch up.

"Brant, I don't under—"

When I entered the control room, I gestured expansively. "Actually, the entire crew is going to be part of the mission," I finished, loudly and jovially.

There was a nervous chuckle from Sparling, a grimace from Stairr, a blank look of confusion from Simbden, and a deep grumble of joy from Bog.

I looked for a moment to the main viewscreen, which showed a live view of the neutral space station known as Docentric, of which Roustabout's occupied about one-tenth. Being neutral meant Docentric didn't favour any specific fleet, nor did it refuse any type of customer. It hired its own security force, made up largely of robots, which interpreted galactic law in its own way. Like all neutral stations, Docentric placed a premium on personal freedom, and with that came more than average amounts of adventure, danger, and just plain weirdness.

Truthfully, I had only intended to slip aboard Docentric with Stairn, as coolly and quietly as we could; after seeing his earlier performance with the aliens aboard the Quazar station, I figured it was time to start testing his true abilities. Normally I would have chosen Bog, but I required stealth and subtlety on this mission and Bog didn't exhibit either of those traits in great abundance.

Mara's hands were on her hips. "Explain yourself, Brant."

"Well, I was thinking about what you said. Roustabout's is huge. Bringing the whole crew will only help us… we'll have more eyes on the lookout for the Dirge, right?"

"Yes," she said slowly. "Actually, that's exactly right."

"But your safety is my concern," I continued. "That's why you will be accompanied by Bog here."

Bog let out another deep rumble, decidedly less joyful this time.

Mara's gaze was steady and I couldn't guess what she was thinking. "Agreed. When do we leave?"

Crap. I had half-expected her to back out.

"In a few short hours," I said. "Everyone, get ready for Mission: Roustabout's."

Sparling looked uncomfortable. "Um, Captain… sir?"

"Yes, Sparling."

"Well, sir…"

"Make it quick, Sparling."

"Someone should stay aboard *Orbital*. It would be better… better to be ready… for a quick escape."

"Good thinking, Agent. You're right. Congratulations. The job is yours."

I didn't catch her muttered response, as I was already on my way out of the control rub, en route to my quarters.

As I rounded the corner and stepped through the half-open door, my foot suddenly slid out from underneath me, and I damn near impaled my groin on the low table near the doorway.

"What the shit?!" I blurted to myself in disgust.

A tendril of slimy goo was trailing from the bottom of my boot.

Oh yeah, I thought. *My new Queel, Toulantin.*

I sighed, hoping to God that the Queel hadn't decided to redecorate my bed with its efflorescent slime. But even my vivid imagination and a bottle of EZ-Heal wouldn't have prepared me for what I was about to witness.

In the middle of my horrible little room, Toulantin and Sirbot were engaged in a perplexing battle of limbs—squid lizard versus metallic robot. Each had four or more limbs and all I could do was watch and avoid a whirling frenzy of ooze and sparks.

As I got a handle on the situation, I started to understand what was going on. Toulantin was trying to slime down a corner of the room to serve as his living space while Sirbot frantically tried to keep the same corner clean and pristine. It would have been comical if it didn't require me to dodge out of the way.

"This is getting ridiculous," I murmured to myself. And with that, I grabbed my best shoes and got the hell out of my chambers.

It took me several short minutes to push through the Docentric's busy main corridor and locate the sprawling, well-lit entryway to Roustabout's, one of the most dangerous and exciting bars in existence. Beings of all races, species, and types of circuitry were lining up outside the club, although the queue moved quickly.

The plan was for me to enter first—alone. I wanted to scope out the club before the rest of the crew got involved. It was important for me to understand exactly what I was getting them into.

When it came my turn to step inside, the first thing I noticed was the smell: the pungent combination of alcohol, acidic cocktails, gaseous inhalations, and the sweat of thousands of ruffians visiting from hundreds of planets. It made one's hair stand on end.

The place was enormous. Even if every cubic metre hadn't been contaminated with the fog of multicoloured smoke, I wouldn't have been able to see the ceiling; I knew for certain that Roustabout's had fifteen circular floors of drinking, smoking, and debauchery, although I'd only personally explored about a dozen of them.

Hazy neon, radon, and solar lighting filtered down from the far reaches above me. It made me dizzy to remember that the floors hovered over top each other instead of being anchored in place, and they didn't even hover concentrically. Nor did they stay in the same place for more than an hour at a time before spinning like a wagon wheel. All that movement made getting drunk at Roustabout's a hazardous prospect.

"Zenith to crew," I said into my wristband communicator. I had to speak loudly, as the bar was noisier than a neutron bomb. "I'm inside. The club is busier than expected. I'm heading up to floors twelve and beyond. Let me know when you arrive, and then stick to your assigned floors. Stairn, I'll meet you at the prearranged spot. Everyone, be careful."

In short order, the crew's acknowledgements came through.

Simbden: "Aye-aye, my captain."

Sparling: "Loud and clear, Captain."

Stairn: "Yes, sir."

A second later I heard Bog's voice chime in: "Sure."

I heard the reverberations of loud music from my friend's audio feed. Then I realized why—there they were, sitting at the end of the bar just ahead of me. How the hell had he and Mara managed to get in first? The pair looked as though they'd been there for at least twenty minutes.

Bog wore a massive grin as he raised his glass in a toast, his red eyes glowing through the light haze of smoke that drifted through the first floor.

Fuck, I thought to myself. *Give them an inch and they bugger the plan...*

I figured he was just retaliating at me for having changed the parameters of the mission at the last minute, dumping Mara on him. I had known, of course, that my friend would have wanted to make this a night not soon forgotten. Mara's presence—indeed, the presence of the entire crew—changed things.

"Sorry, Brant," Mara murmured when I approached. "He insisted on coming early."

I simply nodded. "Well, Bog, you know what you have to do."

And with that, I wandered past them and deeper into the club.

I truly enjoyed my meanderings through Roustabout's. It was noisy, full of beautiful women, and there was plenty of alcohol. I couldn't contain the huge, schoolgirl-like smile that spread across my face. I felt alive!

My first task was to scan my ID card through the club's central computer. It read my info and instantly set up an account to charge any drinks I ordered. Ordering never took long; the hovering robodrone waiters found customers in seconds and returned with drinks only moments later.

Manoeuvring through Roustabout's could be tricky, and tonight was no exception. I had to navigate around robodrones, tentacles, tails, and enlarged feet. As I ducked under the trunk-like limbs of an Asserkian farmer, I suddenly came face to face with someone I hadn't seen in several years. My heart skipped a beat.

Andrana. Even her name warmed a man's blood. Her great big green eyes sprung open as she recognized me. She was a Sandarian swimsuit model with many, many curves and she knew exactly how to draw a man in.

Literally. With her four lithe arms, she dragged me into the middle of an immense dance floor. I had half-expected a slap, so this was certainly a nice surprise.

Our dance quickly got very steamy as she writhed and contoured her body around mine, keeping to the hypnotic beat of the music.

"So, Brantly," Andrana purred into my ear, her many hands scouring my body for anything she may have forgotten after all this time, "where have you been?"

Typically, I would have gladly taken in all of the attention Andrana could offer me. But I had an important mission to attend to. So I spun her around to open up some space between us, but that only thwarted her for a couple of seconds.

This could be trickier than I'd thought.

"Well, Andrana, my duty calls me to many places. But my mind always finds its way back to you. I often think of that glorious night we shared back on Mebdin II. Do you remember?"

Her flushed face scrunched in anger and her voluminous auburn hair suddenly seemed redder than it ever had.

"I've never been to Mebdin II!"

With a huff, she pushed me back, probably hoping I would chase after her to continue our dance. I did not. By the grace of the Mackmian gods of fate I was able to give her the old tally ho. I needed to stay focused on my mission and couldn't be distracted.

I felt it a particularly smooth move: the moment her hands broke contact, I ducked off the dance floor. Roustabout's had so many patrons bumping around that it was easy to slip away. And if time permitted later, who knew? I could stumble onto her and demand to know why she'd left just as we were beginning to catch up. It was an old trick I'd learned years ago—and it rarely failed.

I heard Stairn's voice in my earpiece. "Agent Stairn, checking into Roustabout's..."

About twenty seconds later, Simbden checked in. I wished them both luck with their upcoming duties.

My eyes darted everywhere throughout the lower levels of the club, often with bright red and green strobe lights blinding me and the fragrance of a thousand perfumes clouding my senses. I made out all the regulars: Mackmian miners from the closest asteroid belt, a mob of Ilsian scientists, and even a dancing choir of Pygmy Ransals.

On the tenth floor, I encountered the Aniscen sanctuary dwellers. They were relatively harmless, at least to anyone who didn't have red hair. It was a very long story and not worth getting into, but I knew this could spell serious trouble for Mara if she came up this far. I even brought up my communicator and tried to warn her, but all I got for my efforts was a burst of static. I had feared our communications might not work at the bar's higher levels, and it seemed I had been right.

My next objective was to finish my third Martian Breeze. After that, it was to rendezvous with an old informant of mine who I'd made contact with before arriving on the station. His name was Rankid, and he had gotten a job as a bartender up on the twelfth floor. If anyone would have an idea of where to find the Dirge, I figured it would be Rankid.

He was a Malufian lowlander and had three long necks attached to three heads. Each neck was the length of his two arms. Not all Malufians looked the same, of course, and Rankid was unique; he also had four noses. The fourth nose made him really popular with the ladies; they rested on his middle head, one above the other. I just had to look for the group of screaming women and I'd know he was near.

I approached the bar where he'd told me he usually worked.

"Barkeep," I called when I spotted him; he hadn't yet seen me. "I would like one Martian Breeze and your whereabouts the last week of the first month of Space Date 2498."

One of the three-headed bartender's faces dropped in horror at the mention of that date, and for a moment I thought he was going to toss the three glasses of Telnian grass fire he had just finished pouring and run for the nearest exit—which in this case would have been right off the balcony and into the unassuming masses below.

Luckily, he recognized me quickly and his whole body rippled in relaxation. It was quite fascinating to behold.

"Captain Zee!" He shooed away a nearby pack of Salian hunters and several other very disappointed women blocking my way to him. "Last I heard, you were shovelling shit out of a Mackmian freighter."

I winced at the analogy and had to correct him on it, even though it wasn't far from the truth. I ran a hand through my hair, trying not to get it entangled in some of Roustabout's hovering drones.

"Well, let's just say my future is looking up," I said.

"That's what you said five years ago," Rankid said sarcastically from his smartest noggin.

The long necks redirected his two duller heads to other tasks as they went about the business of collecting orders from paying customers.

"Sorry, Zee," he went on, the middle head continuing to give me his full attention. "I forgot how touchy you can be."

He handed me a Martian Breeze, no doubt hoping it would smooth over my rougher edges. It took a couple of strong sips, but I did relax.

I leaned in close to his intelligent head and spoke with a quiet voice. "I'm looking for a man."

He smiled, showing off his pearly white teeth. "Last time, back on Prime Station Alpha, you said the same thing. Except it was a woman you were after."

I couldn't help myself from laughing on that. "This is different. Important."

"How important are we talking?"

My face must have darkened a shade or two. "Well, Rankid, given the choice between successfully completing the current mission or stuffing a stellar grenade up Mordeau's ass, I may actually choose the mission."

"That important, huh?" He paused to think a moment. "What's his name? What's he look like?"

"As for his name…" I leaned in closer. "…he's known as the Dirge. I was hoping you would be able to tell me what he looks like."

At that moment, all three of Rankid's faces dropped in surprise. It took him a moment to recover.

"Ah, him." He paused, clearing all three of his throats in a manner reminiscent of acapella. "I would be lying if I told you the Dirge hasn't been very popular of late. Not a day goes by that I don't hear about the man."

"I see. Well, you should have lots of information you can share with me."

He shook his head. "This time, Zee, I want nothing to do with the matter."

I stared at him a moment, gauging him, looking for an opening. His eyes on his largest and dumbest head were trying to avoid contact. But his middle head was the trouble one for Rankid; the twitch on its forehead was a dead giveaway.

Before the middle head could look away, I had my answer.

"What'll it be—blackmail, bribery, or threats?" I asked, flexing my fingers in a lightly threatening manner. "You know you'll feel better telling me."

"It's been some time since you've resorted to blackmail. Last time was threats and bribery, no?"

I nodded my head. I had hoped I could buy his information, but I would resort to worse—if I had to.

"For the Dirge..." he whispered. "Zee, it's just too dangerous."

"You have no idea," I said. "I'll owe you a solid favour. You know very well that few people in this galaxy can offer you the same service for so little. This won't fall back on you. I promise."

"It sounds reassuring." Rankid seemed to be appraising me. "Okay, I give in. There's a man I know who can confirm his whereabouts. For certain. Trust me, Zee. He *knows*."

That sounded promising. "Okay. Where is this man?"

"He's in the bar now, in fact. And no more than one hundred metres from you."

My heart began to beat with an excitement long forgotten. At least I wouldn't need to track the man down.

At that exact moment, the whole bar erupted into chaos as a powerful blue glow shot up from the lower levels like a spotlight, blinding everyone around me for a few moments. When my sight returned, I stepped over to the balcony and peered over the polished steel railing.

Whatever that spectacular explosion had been, the floor several levels down was covered in the smoky aftermath. I couldn't tell what had happened, but it had been big and disruptive enough to cause everyone to stop drinking, dancing, and carousing.

My heart sank as I thought about the other members of my crew. I brought up my wristband communicator. "Mara, come in. It's Brant. Is everything okay?"

I heard some crackling from the communicator just as Stairn came around the corner. After my meeting with Rankid, the plan had been to meet up with Stairn. I guess I'd lost track of time… it seemed to happen to me often in a bar.

In any other situation, I would have laughed at his flowery embarrassment of a shirt and tight blue leather pants. His outfit was louder than almost everything else in the club.

But the present moment was too serious for that.

My ears burned with static, then suddenly I heard Mara's voice pushing through it: "Brant… yes, all's good."

The beating of my heart relaxed a hair, but I still didn't like this. I needed to know what was going on.

I nodded at Stairn to join me by the bar, where Rankid's middle head was craning over the railing to take in the spectacle below. I could tell by his reaction that it wasn't as exciting for him as it was for me.

"Rankid, this is Agent Stairn," I said by way of introduction. "Now, tell us more."

"You know our rules, Zee. The information is for you alone. Take it or leave it."

I looked at Stairn, and he instantly knew to step away. "I'll check on Mara and Bog," the logistics officer said. "I didn't like what I heard down there."

Stairn stepped away, his hand going for his weapon and unbuckling the first of two clasps.

"Be careful, Stairn," I called after him. "Call if you need help."

As I watched, Stairn positioned both hands on the rail and then vaulted himself up and over the balcony rails and onto whatever floor below he was fated to land upon.

I had to admit, that was damned cool!

I shook my head and went back to work. "This informant, Rankid. Where is he?"

"Well, Zee, that's the tricky part."

"What does that mean?" I didn't like guessing games. "You told me he was nearby. So where?"

"Two minutes ago, I could have pointed him out to you. But now I can't see him. That blue explosion sent everyone scurrying."

I looked around to confirm that everyone was, indeed, moving about in a mad rush to get away from the explosion.

"Then give me a reliable description and point me in the right direction," I snapped.

He pointed to a crowd of partygoers standing amidst the blue haze where the commotion was getting louder. It was adjacent to the dingily lit entrance to a VIP area: Smelters Drinking Den.

"That way, Zee," said Rankid. "He has shoulder-length grey hair and short white stubble. He's pale and a fair bit past his prime. Earlier he was in a heated discussion with a group of those big brutes."

Oh shit. My heart skipped a beat when I saw the brutes Rankid was pointing at. They were Brunken, an enormous and immensely dense race of violent monsters.

I gave Rankid a surly look as I walked away. "If I get nothing from this man, the deal is off!" I said as a goodbye.

I jumped onto a transport pad that would whisk me to the lower level.

The Brunken were always around three metres tall and powerfully built, almost as large as Bog. They had grey skin and bulging muscles. Quick to anger and difficult to appease. My last and only previous confrontation with one had been on the moon of Distarius. The only way to conclude the argument I'd been having with the Brunken in question had been to drop a very large boulder on his head.

The entryway to Smelters was crowded, with bar patrons scurrying in every direction. I navigated through the onrush of bodies and made my way inside.

Just as I stepped foot in Smelters, I had to dodge a purple wave blast that suddenly rippled in my direction. After ducking, I pulled forth my weapon and breathed deeply. I looked in the direction of where the blast originated. It appeared to be a smoky mess of a room. I noticed several other obscured but brilliant flashes of light and heard the accompanied sounds of commotion. There was surely a battle brewing ahead.

Armed and ready, I stepped into the fray, hoping that the Dirge was going to be worth all this effort.

If I were a little more conventional, I would have feared having to run headlong into a firefight like this. I had no idea who I was looking for, not really, or why the customers here were shooting at each other.

But I wasn't conventional. In fact, as much as I liked to complain, I rather enjoyed the excitement.

To my relief, it quickly became clear that the Brunken had only been crowding the entrance. They didn't seem to be holding Rankid's informant or barring my entrance. I managed to skirt past them easily enough and stepped deeper into the smoky chamber.

Quickly, however, I found myself ducking out of the way of yet another blast, this one yellow. I couldn't even tell where it had originated.

I broke into a sprint and dove behind a smouldering bartop, and in the process I managed to avoid getting hit by yet another blast, although I felt it singe the backside of my pants. I looked down to see a small tendril of smoke billow up.

Fuck! My whole outfit was shot straight to hell!

That's the moment when I caught a glimpse of Rankid's informant. He was just as he'd been described—a little old man with wispy white hair and grey stubble across his face. He was cowering behind another section of that very same bar. So far, he looked unharmed, but just as singed as I was.

I looked over the bar, trying to spot our assailants. I caught a glimpse of one through the smoky hazy—and unless I was mistaken, I recognized the species.

"No wonder their shots are so accurate," I muttered. "They're Shaydren."

"That they are, young man," said the informant. He hopped over to my side of the bar, wheezing a bit from the exertion. "Now tell me: what kind of man runs headfirst into a situation like this? Are you stupid or crazy?"

"Depends on which day you catch me, old man."

He laughed in response. "My name is Caesar Roman." He held out a weathered, wrinkly old hand to me and I quickly shook it. He had a noticeably firm grip, more so than I had anticipated.

Caesar Roman was human, or at least close enough that I couldn't determine otherwise. His long, dark shirt was burned through in a couple of places, which made me feel slightly better about myself.

But my thoughts were laser-focused on the Shaydren who were shooting at us. They were dangerous. Actually, they were beyond dangerous. In the seediest corners of the darkest sides of forgotten moons, I'd knocked heads with people who told stories of the Shaydren—very disturbing stories indeed. They were tales of entire species completely and unexplainably vanishing. Creepier yet, whole solar systems were said to disappear. All due to these mysterious Shaydren, a lean and sinewy race with narrow shoulders and waists. Their grey skin gave off the impression of withering parchment, and their piercing white eyes were the stuff of nightmares.

I didn't know if I could believe the tales, but the ones who whispered them hadn't seemed like the types to shiver from any old gust of wind.

These Shaydren were well armed with what I could only assume were electrical dispersion weapons. There looked to be about four of them, each armed with a short-barrelled rifle unleashing deadly blasts of black and yellow lightning.

I normally didn't feel fear once adrenaline kicked in, but I had to breathe very deeply at this point to calm my nerves. My hands trembled from the surge of fear. This was very much not good. I would rather have faced that rampant horde of Brunken beasts back at the entryway than be facing off against a group of Shaydren.

"Are you armed, old man?" I asked between deep breaths.

"Only with my charm."

I think I may have laughed, but the next blast of weapons fire drowned it out. I was beginning to think every story I'd heard about the Shaydren must be true, since they seemed to know exactly where to aim even though I was out of their direct line of sight.

I looked up at the ceiling where the ventilation fan was sparking. If the fan kept running, maybe it would clear out the smoke. That might give us a fighting chance of getting out alive.

Another blast exploded through the protective bartop. Shards of electrified steel tore free from it and nearly impaled us. I took one of the shards through my right earlobe; it stung like a bitch and started to drip blood down my shirt. Fuck again! Now my shirt was screwed beyond repair!

Fortunately, Caesar fared better, but the shock of the explosion so close to home had knocked some extra panic into both of us.

I grabbed the old man and hauled him as quickly as possible across the floor. I was only granted two or three seconds before another electric dispersion seared a hole between my legs, sending us flying onto Smelters' dance floor, recessed a half-metre below the rest of the bar.

Our landing was fortunate, as we happened to end up under the steel cage that had previously been surrounded by the overhead lights. My groin was smoking, and I frantically patted out the tendrils in a blind panic. Once the heat had dissipated, I checked my nether regions to make sure I still had a reason for living. To my joy, they seemed to have been only grazed.

Another electrical blast caught the metal frame above me and refracted away into the smoky regions from where I'd been only moments ago. I thought I heard an angry growl of pain behind me somewhere, but I didn't have time to think about it; the Shaydren were still skulking in front of me.

I peered through the steel tubes around me and fired off a shot from my propulsion gun.

Click. Misfire!

For a brief moment, a clear view opened in front of me and I made out a Shaydren attacker. I pulled the trigger again and let loose a blast.

Unexpectedly, my weapon's blast shattered onto a sheet of angled glass. What I'd thought was the alien had turned out to be a blasted mirror's reflection!

With only a moment's notice to calculate the trajectory of the real enemy, I rolled onto my back and pulled the trigger twice, catching the Shaydren warrior by surprise.

In response, he disappeared. He didn't jump, didn't dive out of the way, didn't even explode. He just disappeared and so did the projectile I'd fired at him.

I didn't have much time to nurse my feelings of confusion, as my eye caught sight of a maintenance robodrone as it flew towards the ventilation fan on the ceiling and began repairs. Moments later, the fan came to life. I silently thanked my favourite Mackmian

God of fate. So powerful was the fan that it took only seconds to clear the room of haze.

Once cleared, I felt the torn shards of my shirt rise with the windy uplift of the fan. Quickly, the room seemed to brighten. It looked like a completely different space than it had only moments ago. And I certainly couldn't see any sign of the Shaydren warriors who had been blasting bolts of lightning at us like an angry storm cloud.

"What the hell?" I asked, looking over at Caesar. He didn't look quite as surprised as I did.

I looked harder, expecting another round of lightning to come at me, but there was nothing. No sign of Shaydren anywhere.

I didn't know what was worse—being swarmed by unseen fire or waiting to be surprised at any moment from a formidable enemy.

The question was moot, since at that moment I swore I could feel the floor tremble beneath my feet. Lying on my side, I was ill prepared for the giant pair of hands that grabbed me by the waist and neck, hoisting me vertically.

I was heaved out of the cage that held me and discovered the Brunken squad staring at me. The same squad I had passed at the entrance. My arms flailed at my sides, and I tried to keep them still. I was ready for anything.

The huge Brunken lord—I could see his ranking insignia, showing the Three Mountains of Brash, the official sign of the Brunken monarchy—stepped close to me as his comrade held me with a death grip. He was taller than the average Brunken, probably more than three metres in height. His left arm smouldered, and I noticed the remnant of yellow acid still burning on it. He must have been hit by the Shaydren, too.

His large eyes and gargantuan grey face regarded me with disdain. He was pissed!

"You da dead man!" He spewed forth savagery, some of which came from the half-eaten lunch still floating around his widely spaced teeth. "Attack Borkrieg? Borkrieg squish you now."

Borkrieg! Oh fuck!

My mind went back just over a week to the last time the *Orbital* crew had played a game of corralling. Out of all the ships we'd identified, several had been Brunken—the ships I myself had bet on.

And those ships had been commanded by none other than the infamous Borkrieg, hero of his people. What were the chances of actually running into him?

The other Brunken who held me then handed me over to Borkrieg. Borkrieg grabbed me like a strand of half-cooked spaghetti and roared some sort of curse into my face. My eyelids nearly fell off.

He squeezed my body as though wringing out a wet towel, and the pain became unbearable. Because he gripped me not around the waist like his cohort had, but around the arms, I was only partially able to move my hands. My right arm burned from the friction and the pressure he exerted on my chest was excruciating. I would soon fall unconscious, both from pain and lack of oxygen.

My head wobbled like a toy on a spring, and I felt my eyes begin to close. Seconds away from passing out, I lifted my nearly dead arm and fired what could have proved to be my final shot. It was not well aimed and didn't strike Borkrieg in his heavily armoured torso.

Instead my propulsion blast struck him in the foot.

With a grumbled yell, Borkrieg dropped me like a soiled diaper. His foot smouldered and my legs gave out upon landing. The emanating smell reminded me of wet, burning dog fur.

Borkrieg pulled out a cannon he called a hand pistol and aimed it at me. Luck smiled down on me once more; at just that moment, a posse of security robodrones flew in, their huge array of weapons all locking onto us. In all languages at once, the heavily armed drones demanded our immediate surrender.

Borkrieg looked down at me with hatred and then up at the drones with annoyance. Three very long moments elapsed as he decided what to do.

Slowly he lowered his cannon, pointing it at my feet.

"All altercations must be settled in preapproved duelling dens," one of the robodrones stated, its ultimatum careening out of the angry-sounding speaker. "Transport will begin immediately."

Without a further thought, all five of us were transported via ETT through walls and floors into the duelling den.

Lazarus Stairn's fall from the upper balcony of Roustabout's sped him past the next several levels before he landed without so much as a thud in another bar, smoke still billowing all around him from the explosion. The descent had been formidable, to say the least.

The scene where he landed was only barely short of catastrophic.

The aforementioned explosion, he ascertained, had been caused by a Protection Bot 1102, from a series of warrior robots whose forms were large and blocky. These were double the height of an average human, built in the twenty-fourth century, and possessed of an extremely limited intelligence. But what they lacked in smarts, they made up for in firepower and physical resilience.

Unfortunately for everyone on this floor of Roustabout's, all three Protection Bots were connected via wireless command linkages in their processing cores. So if one of them went haywire, the other two were quick to follow suit.

Which seemed to be exactly what had happened, although Stairn had no way of knowing what had set the first one off.

Stairn ducked past a crumpled metal barstool as it whistled by his head and crashed into a pane of mirrored glass behind the nearby bar, scattering all the patrons who had been either too stubborn or intoxicated to leave after the initial blast only moments ago.

He took a good look at his immediate surroundings and quickly determined the best course of action. The Protection Bots were spread out over the mangled bar in triangulated positions.

The nearest one dodged Stairn's well-aimed bipolar wave gun discharge. Barely. In doing so, the bot contorted its large cubic frame in an awkward position. Stairn ran straight at the creature, leaped over it, and narrowly avoided its huge steel arm which swung towards him like an axe. Stairn rolled and lifted his pistol again, firing a wave blast that landed directly under the bot's chin. Its head glowed red hot with the energy and smoke erupted from its eye sockets.

Moments later, the bot's head exploded like a hand grenade… a blast that would have killed Stairn had he not ducked behind the being's own body just in time.

Of course, the attack didn't go unnoticed by the other two Protection Bots. Like a mechanical stampede, they broke into sprints, jumping over or stomping through anything in their path. Any table not previously destroyed got squashed under the force of their metallic feet. Some became inadvertent projectiles, speeding unpredictably through the bar.

Even Stairn, with his innumerable abilities, hesitated in the face of this display of stampeding death raining down through the usually noisy and glittering club. This entire level of the bar had now been deserted, thank heavens, and he found himself alone—and hopelessly outmatched in size and strength.

The floor shuddered beneath his feet and he reacted instinctually, aiming himself at the next closest Protection Bot. He rolled again to avoid the bot's foot stomp and kick at him. But knowing the most glaring weaknesses of this series of bots, Stairn could turn the situation to his advantage; all he had to do was keep moving and keep himself directly beneath them as much as possible. Luckily for Stairn, he could comfortably run beneath and between the legs of these enormous machines.

As nimble as he was, though, he had to admit that he was winded. He grunted as he attempted to jump clear of the steel boot swinging at him hard and fast. He couldn't move fast enough, and the boot made contact, skidding him across the floor. He caught most of the kick's force with his arms and spun, using all his skill to land on his hands and feet in a crouch.

He had no time to catch his breath. The other bot was already on him! Its steel foot missed by millimetres, delivering a devastating crunch to the floor and sending a hail of shiny metallic tiles into the air. He rolled further away.

Stairn found himself on his back behind the two bots. Weapon raised, he finally found the opportunity he had been looking for. He pulled the trigger at the bot in his immediate sights. The wave blast struck true, searing through the bot's thick, heavily cabled neck. Its head sheared right off.

But he couldn't congratulate himself, as the hundred-kilogram head dropped like an anchor, nearly crushing him beneath it. He rolled out of the way again, missing the crash of sparking, tentacle-like wires burning so close to his face.

The final bot stopped in its tracks and twitched. The programming that linked the three together was unreliable and Stairn surmised that its computerized brain couldn't endure the shock of the lost connection now that it found itself alone.

Its body began to glow a bright yellow, and it took Stairn a moment to realize just how unstable it was. Heat was radiating from its core; another explosion was imminent.

Stairn looked around and realized he had nowhere to go, nowhere that would provide any protection; he calculated that the blast radius would be much too large to escape. He even feared the explosion might be large enough to harm those sheltering on the adjacent floors.

Thinking quickly, Agent Stairn flipped the dials on his wave pistol, rapidly loosened the lineal wire connections, and reset the weapon. He sprinted towards the bot, launching himself just high enough to latch on to its chassis. This was a painful manoeuvre, as he seared his hands. But he ignored the pain as best he could for the two seconds it took to push the wave pistol into a nook in the bot's torso and jump away for all he was worth.

He managed to roll no further than two metres before the Protection Bot exploded in a catastrophic kaboom. A horrific ball of shimmering energy burned through the air, glowing yellow and orange.

However, milliseconds before this inferno of death could reach Stairn, the bipolar wave gun imploded, sending out an even faster shockwave of shimmering black rift energy which absorbed all but the faint tinge of fire.

In under a moment, the danger was over.

Stairn walked away unharmed, more or less. His eyebrows were well-singed.

The duelling den was located a safe distance away and below the rest of Roustabout's, somewhere down in the bowels of the station.

So quickly had events unfolded that my mind was befuddled. I now found myself sitting in a small glass cubicle beside Caesar. In another glass cubicle across the narrow hallway, three Brunken warlords stared menacingly at us; their cubicle looked like it might explode under the pressure of confining the enormous men and the huge weapons they carried. Their ugly, grey-skinned faces were contorted and mashed up against the glass, making them appear both funnier and more intimidating at the same time.

The size of the cubicle allowed my fears to subside a bit. These warlords could hardly move, and they would have no chance to raise their weapons. But I also knew, from experience, that these cubicles could contain an exploding sun and not so much as crack from the pressure.

These were the waiting rooms of the duelling den. I looked down the length of cubicles on my side of the enclosure and noticed we weren't the only specimens paired off. There looked to be at least three other groups awaiting their chance to settle scores. The huge vault door at the end of the narrow hall would allow us entry to conclude our dispute, each in turn.

Our cubicle had a communication device connecting us directly to the Brunken. Its purpose was to allow combatants to negotiate, and perhaps forego their intended violence.

After the confrontation, Roustabout's would charge the winner the price of disposing of the dead, while the loser's account would be saddled with the expense of using the duelling den in the first place. If the dead didn't have the necessary funds, the winner would have to cover both charges. I had always found that somewhat irksome. Many people chose to conduct their killing away from the station, knowing they couldn't afford the price of their eventual victory.

I pressed the button to open communications and tried my best to soothe the savage beasts. It did me not a lick of good; even with my waning synaptic translator enzymes, my Brunken tongue was too rusty.

Borkrieg's voice sounded deep and harsh. I think he wished a type of disease to befall my mother, one I wouldn't wish upon even my worst enemy. I knew at that point that the duel was inevitable.

To my relief, though, it seemed only Borkrieg himself wanted to kill me. I think it was a source of pride, or perhaps privilege.

Having no choice but to stare at the giant warlords across the way, I began to grow uneasy. Maybe it was the sinister "You will die horribly, you bug" expression writ upon each of their grotesque faces, or maybe it was my nerves catching up to me after the turbulent past hour.

The minutes ticked by slowly as I heard the sound of weapons blasts behind the huge door just ahead. At times I felt the floor quiver from particularly large explosions. Violence in the duelling den was a foregone conclusion.

A robodrone suddenly zipped down the narrow hall and opened the door to our cubicle. It pinned our hands to our bodies with some sort of field beam and led us into the duelling den.

Moments later, the Brunken were led to the opposite side of the narrow arena. It was approximately the length of a lawn bowling field and featured bleachers along both lengths.

Following a bit of guidance from the Brunken warlord and myself—that is, that we intended to fight alone—Caesar and the other two Brunken were escorted behind the shielded viewing area.

As was typical, the stands were packed with anxious spectators and gamblers; perhaps a thousand were in attendance. The dens were among the most exciting forms of entertainment in the Gambit galaxy.

Although I'd previously tested my skills in the dens, I didn't feel too optimistic about this outing. In earlier contests, the chances had been stacked in my favour. I was more than a decent shot and agile enough to win against most of the drunken rapscallions with which I had contended. But even if Borkrieg was a lousy shot, he would have to aim almost directly at the roof to completely miss me with the missiles his hand cannon could produce. My only way to win would be to fire fast and hit him before he could get off a shot.

Unfortunately, I was armed with Militia equipment. My propulsion gun could kill, but it lacked wallop. Worse yet was that the gun's projectiles slowed with each use until it could be recharged—and I hadn't taken the opportunity to fully charge it during our voyage from Prime Station Alpha to Roustabout's.

Note to Brant Zenith: from now on, weapons must be charged before the grooming equipment.

With the potentially slower projectile, the Brunken warlord, although less agile and quick-footed, might just be able to sidestep my shot. I simply wasn't sure.

Another disadvantage was that Borkrieg was armoured like a tank. I'd taken a long look at him and his goons during our wait in the cubicles, noting that each wore a heavy metal shell covered by an energy-absorbing fabric. Other than his limbs, neck, and head, Borkrieg had almost no unarmoured targets. Shooting his limbs would offer me little chance at victory and I was afraid that *Orbital* itself lacked the firepower to puncture his diamond-hard head.

I was screwed.

The cheers erupting from the zealous fans snapped me out of my reverie. Now was not the time to give up on myself.

As the Brunken warlord and I faced off, each of us looking in opposite directions, waiting for the green light to engage and give us the go-ahead to turn and shoot, I decided on my strategy. I didn't fear that he would turn and fire before the green light; should that happen, a protective shield would block the incoming shots and the security robodrones would mow him down with the hammer of hell. I had seen it happen on occasion. It was better to be too late than too early.

I watched one of the viewscreens which housed the giant traffic lights of red, yellow, and green. They were visible from everywhere in the duelling den. Only the red shone as hoarse screams and laughter filled the small arena. From where I stood on the concrete floor, all I smelled was popcorn, sweat, and death. Not too appetizing, although I wasn't in a position to critique it.

Above the arena, robodrones projected images of the matchup's odds. I winced. At the moment, the odds favoured the Brunken a hundred twenty-five to one.

I pointed to the nearest bookie. Recognizing the gesture, and using a small handheld gambling device, he commenced a wireless link that shone in my direction. I saw the link light up on my wristband communicator and quickly typed out my intentions—to place a bet for one thousand and six space quids on my victory. As soon as I sent the funds, he acknowledged the bet.

All around the duelling den the yellow lights flared to life telling me that the moment had almost arrived. My heart thumped like a mallet in my chest, and for some reason I thought of Mara and hoped she would be safe should I fall. I knew these moments could be my last.

The green light bore down on me like a tidal wave, and I instantly dropped to my right knee, still facing the rear wall. In the quickest movement of my life, I spun to find Borkrieg already aiming his cannon, ready to fire. I dove onto my stomach just in time to feel the ballistic cruise missile he launched rustle my already singed hair.

The energy shield behind me absorbed the explosion—and much of the sound. It looked like a stone crashing onto the serene surface of a pond; it rippled through the shield's energy and spread to the outer edges of the arena.

None of the blast touched me.

Surprise registered on Borkrieg's scarred and horrible-looking grey face. He knew he had lost his chance. I took aim and fired on my enemy, my only shot at survival.

Begone!

Despite the low energy level, my propulsion gun fired, its slim projectile striking with amazing force just below the Brunken warlord's chin. It burned through Borkrieg's neck and severed his spine. A wisp of smoke erupted from the wound, and he fell to the ground in a huge lump, dead.

Cheers and boos erupted, my account was credited the amount of my bet, and my informant and I were transported to the atrium of the duelling den. Borkrieg's dead body was transferred there as well, along with his two kin.

I didn't even have two seconds to take a breather and enjoy my victory. No sooner had we made it to the atrium than the remainder of Borkrieg's crew stormed in, descending on me like a biblical flood as I stood over the warlord's smoking body. They must have come to interrogate me about their dead captain.

"Speak plain, pissant!" yelled a brutish Brunken lieutenant not present at the duel. He raised yet another hand cannon at my head. "What happened to da captain?"

This was not what I needed at the moment. My synaptic translators worked like crap and now I was forced to stare down another massive barrel of doom. I closed my eyes and hoped for the best.

When I opened them again, I looked up into the lieutenant's crater-shaped black eyes and said, "I killed your Captain Borkrieg." Sweat trickled down my forehead in waves. "He challenged me to a fight, and he lost. I had no choice. I killed him. That's all there is to say."

The lieutenant's eyes widened in final understanding and his face shifted into an unreadable expression. He looked at the two Brunken who had witnessed the event. They nodded and he twitched violently, the weapon's barrel jerking enough to dent the skin on my forehead. I saw the weapon's actuator light up briefly, damn near giving me a heart attack.

Without warning, he lowered the hand cannon, leaned down, and wrapped his arms around me and squeezed. I thought I was done for, but he let go peaceably.

"Good! Me now Captain Kiln! Kiln hate Borkrieg. You, Captain Kiln's good friend!" He smiled awkwardly, patted me on the head, and strolled away, taking the rest of his crew with him.

CHAPTER SEVENTEEN

Cause and Effect

Without delay, I grabbed Caesar Roman's oddly firm forearm to get him moving and we hightailed it out of Roustabout's. I really didn't want to wait for the Brunken to change their minds. I also had to worry about angry gamblers who had bet against me wishing retaliation. It wasn't unheard of.

It didn't take long for me to wind through masses of partygoers, drinkers, and fighters. My eyes felt like they were attached to springs as I searched every angle for even the slightest hint of the Shaydren.

My immediate goal was to get Caesar to the safety of *Orbital* so I could extract vital information about the Dirge. I grabbed hold of Caesar's old, weathered arm and pulled him along as quickly as I could.

Roustabout's wasn't your typical watering hole. In the past hour, from the looks of it, there had been at least one more major, station-shaking explosion, a particularly ugly firefight, and whatever the hell else had happened on the levels down below. Even with all of that going on, the denizens of the club were hopping around like jack rabbits on methamphetamine.

It wasn't so glamorous to me. The high-pitched sounds, the lights bouncing off the walls, and the repugnant smells nearly gave me an epileptic seizure.

"*Orbital* crew," I spoke into my communicator. "Home base, now."

I didn't detect any of the usual static on the line, so I assumed they had all heard me.

Moments later, I heard the familiar voices of my crew.

"Bog and I are already aboard, Captain," Mara stated excitedly.

Relief settled over me. Until that moment, I had been growing more and more lead-footed at the thought that Mara might have been harmed in all the chaos.

"Agent Stairn here. Reporting in from *Orbital*. I also await your return."

And finally, only a minute or so before Caesar and I reached the ship, I heard Simbden's voice: "On board, my captain!"

"Good! I'll see you all in the cargo bay in about thirty seconds."

As we rounded the final corner to the docking port, my heart sank. Standing in the middle of the doorway was another giant Brunken warlord. He, she, or it was blocking nearly the entire portal opening. His white leather lab coat seemed oddly out of place compared to his colleagues a few minutes ago.

I was in no mood for this. I broke into a headlong sprint towards the giant Brunken, beyond which lay freedom from this wild night. I pushed Caesar to the left of the Brunken as I dove to the right in an effort to slip by him.

The brute slammed into me, lifting me up and pinning me to the wall. I grunted, noting with satisfaction that at least Caesar had managed to get by. The Brunken had my torso firmly in his palm and he seemed intent on keeping me there.

I looked down into his grey face and dark eyes but didn't see malice or aggression. I didn't understand the soft look he gave me…

Another thing that surprised me was the Brunken's smell. Was that the faint odour of disinfectant? Curious.

My breath was beginning to falter. It felt like trying to breathe with a Mackmian elephant sitting on my chest. I could feel my face turn blue.

Without warning, I felt myself crash to the floor. I looked up to see the huge Brunken's eyes roll back into the back of his head. He became motionless and even began snoring.

Caesar must have done something very clever to make the Brunken collapse into unconsciousness like this. But I didn't know what he'd done and it didn't matter. I was struck by the realization that he must be formidable if he knew how to debilitate a Brunken so quickly.

Caesar gave me a hand to get to my feet and then followed me into the portal towards safety.

As we hurried along, I called over my shoulder, "We need to talk!"

"Surely it can wait—I need to get out of here," Caesar replied, surprising me by keeping up to my pace.

I couldn't argue with that. "Agreed. Join me for a ride on my ship. We can take you away from here."

He grunted in agreement.

It took us a couple of tense minutes to navigate my way to *Orbital*'s cargo bay. The alcohol I'd consumed at Roustabout's was beginning to wear off and I felt a throbbing headache take hold. It had been a long day and I was in sore need of some rest.

But that would have to wait.

We found the rest of the crew waiting in the cargo bay—well, everyone except Sparling, who to my knowledge was still manning the control hub. I didn't know what had happened to everyone, but Stairn was covered in hydraulic fluid and scorch marks. Mara and Bog looked unharmed and relieved to see me.

As for Simbden, his face was glowing for some reason. He looked like he had just visited heaven.

"Bog, escort our new guest to Quarters 2B. Mara, Stairn, Simbden... follow me." I brought my wristband communicator up to my mouth. "Agent Sparling, ready us for departure. Make haste."

Our march up to the control hub was quick, and when we arrived we were just in time to watch our escape from Docentric on the viewscreen. But even once we were underway, my breath was heavy and my heart continued to race. I dreaded whatever new enemy might be lurking around the next corner. First those mysterious attackers in the Quazar system... then the Brunken, followed by the Shaydren... it was enough to give me indigestion.

What the hell had I gotten us into?

"Well, that sucked some serious ass!" Bog exclaimed with a scowl when he returned from bringing Caesar to his berth.

Over the next hour, Bog filled me in on a few parts of the mission I had been blessedly oblivious to. Shortly after seeing Bog and Mara in Roustabout's, apparently a pair of robodrones had flagged down Bog because the random DNA verification scan he'd undergone upon entry had confused him with a Pygmy Dwarble who was wanted in twenty-three solar systems for a counterfeit jewellery scam. Bog had been none too pleased with the poking and prodding the robodrones had initiated—in some very unpleasant places.

I just rolled my eyes, only half-listening to the minute-long barrage of swears which Bog's story devolved into near the end.

"Can we halt the fucking swearing for just a god-damned minute?" I blurted, cutting him short. "We have some serious problems here and I would greatly appreciate suggestions. First things first: I'm told this Caesar fellow I brought on board knows about the Dirge's identity and where we can find him."

"It should be simple enough to get the information out of him." Bog cracked his knuckles for effect.

"Hopefully it's as easy as all that. When I first spotted him, Caesar was in the middle of being nearly mowed down by a Shaydren gang."

Mara took a sharp intake of breath. Even Bog's face paled a shade.

"Yeah, exactly my point." I turned to the ship's pilot. "Sparling, keep a close eye on our course and make sure we're not being followed."

"Yes, sir."

I turned back to the others. "When we've gained a safe distance from Docentric, we'll need to have a very important talk with our new friend Caesar Roman."

Stairn frowned. "Captain, from everything I've heard of the Dirge, I would expect some difficulty tracking him down, even if this new informant of yours knows where to find him. The Dirge wouldn't have managed to escape the *Dawnstar* if he didn't know how to cover his tracks."

"I agree," Bog said. "All the more reason to make it very clear to Caesar that we expect no surprises."

"But if he knows the Dirge, why would he even bother helping us?" Mara asked.

I had to admit, I'd been thinking the same thing. The truth was, we didn't know anything about Caesar, except that he didn't get on well with the Shaydren. Of course, no one did.

"I didn't have the chance to learn much about the man before all sorts of hell broke loose," I retorted. "But I agree he might be difficult to work with."

Mara sighed. "How can we even trust what he has to say?"

"I don't know," I said. "But I did save his life. Hopefully that will count for something."

"Only time will tell," she remarked.

I knew that we were potentially sitting ducks in case the Shaydren wished to attack. I didn't have much of a plan to evade this race of space ninjas, but there was security in numbers. Or so

I hoped. So the best I could come up with was to get Sparling to pick up our pace and join in on the flow of other traffic leaving the station.

Indeed, dozens of ships were currently streaming away from Docentric from a wide variety of angles. They were heading out just as dozens more were coming in. Docentric nearly rivalled Prime Station Alpha for its level of traffic.

Our passage into the busy lane of departing ships was smooth as Sparling found a nice opening between several Mackmian super frigates.

I smiled as confidently as I could to the crew. The Roustabout's operation may not have been flawless, but I couldn't have hoped for a better result.

As the minutes passed, I gripped the armrest of my chair, white-knuckled. Gradually, though, as I awaited an attack from any and all corners, I loosened my hold.

And as the minutes dragged into hours, I even allowed myself to relax. A little.

When I finally felt confident that the immediate danger had passed, I decided to go have a talk with our new informant. Bog accompanied me down to Quarters 2B, where we came to a standstill in front of the closed door.

When I knocked, the door rattled, threatening to fall right out of the frame. The crooked door had dropped on its side, creating an opening wide enough for the occupant of the room to come and go as he wished.

Fuck! This had been our most secure sleeping chamber, the only one I had thought would serve as a detention cell when the need arose.

Note to Brant Zenith: just retire. The spatial attenuators don't work, the weapons don't work, the atmospheric stabilizers are sketchy, the bingo machine is destroyed, and none of the doors open properly...

It didn't surprise me that Caesar Roman was no longer here. Fortunately, Bog had slapped a tracker on the old man's clothes earlier. So he couldn't have gotten far.

I punched on my wristband communicator and tried bringing up the signal from the tracker. Nothing! I swore a vile oath at the Mackmian gods of fate.

"Mine is shit too," Bog remarked, staring at his own wristband.

As he stepped closer to me, though, both of our wristband screens blipped in unison. This caught us both by surprise. But at least we were getting a signal now.

We pushed on, realizing that the only way to keep the signal strong was to push our wrists so close together that it looked like we were walking through the ship arm in arm. I shook off the subtle embarrassment.

A cold blast of wind smacked us in the faces as we rounded a corner and entered a part of the ship where the atmospheric stabilizers happened to be malfunctioning again. It was damned annoying, but we pushed through without comment, ignoring *Orbital*'s ways.

The signal led us right to the doors of the docking bay—and that's where we caught him. I could tell that he was trying to use *Orbital*'s ETT. I'm not certain where he thought he would send himself, but I suppose it was fortunate on this occasion that the ETT was yet another thing aboard our ship that didn't work.

"Give me one good reason not to blast your old wrinkly ass right off your old wrinkly body, Caesar," I shouted as we walked into the bay.

Caesar reacted by freezing in place right in the middle of the cavernous chamber. He held up his hands peaceably. It occurred to me that perhaps instead he had been seeking to steal our lone escape shuttle. I hadn't manned it personally in over a year and I wondered if it even turned on.

"Captain Zenith, there's no need for such aggression," he said in a steady voice.

"You're right." I kept my weapon trained on him. "Although you weren't saying the same thing back when I was helping to prevent you from being annihilated by a squad of Shaydren."

Bog and I closed in on him from opposite directions. We had him cornered.

"Captain, I appreciate all the help you've provided me thus far." Caesar sounded so smooth, so eloquent, which only irritated me more. "But you're better off without me. Trust me on that one."

"I don't think so," I snapped. "I don't trust too many people, especially ones who are beating off lines of very dangerous beings hell-bent on killing them. Truthfully, there is only one place I would trust you right now."

Dragging the old man as easily as he would have carried a pitcher of malt liquor, Bog removed the informant back out into the corridor. It was almost comical to see the three-metre-tall Nova Martian haul the other away.

Unfortunately, we couldn't take him back to Quarters 2B, not with the door hanging wide open. But it occurred to me there *was* one other really secure place I could take him. I smiled at the thought.

Bog seemed to have had the same idea, because he was already headed off towards the lavatory. The one whose door had a nasty habit of trapping members of the crew inside at the least opportune moments.

"Where are you putting me?" Caesar asked as Bog opened the door and threw him inside.

The Nova Martian smiled. "Look around. What do you see?"

"A toilet, a mirror, and a sink." The answer dawned on him. "You must be joking. You can't keep me in a bathroom. And it stinks!"

"Well, technically we're only throwing you inside," I said. "The malfunctioning door will do the rest. You'll stay put for a while—that is, until I can figure what the hell I'm going to do with you."

And with that, Caesar Roman, the man I had risked my life for more than once already today, found himself trapped in a lavatory.

I looked down at the newest and youngest member of *Orbital*'s crew. Simbden was a contradiction of Mackmian qualities. Like so many of his fine race, he was the essence of hard work and dedication. The nearly endless hours he'd put in on Prime Station Alpha trying to fix *Orbital* were a testament to that. He hadn't even allowed himself time to relax and explore the station, taking not a moment's enjoyment outside his nightly sleep or feeding routine.

Simbden was much less round than his brethren Mackmians. He verged on being labelled slim, which I knew for certain wasn't considered an attractive quality among his people. Of course, I couldn't have cared less. He surprised me with his youthful dedication to our cause and I respected him greatly for that. After many setbacks, Simbden still maintained heart and spirit in his work. I greatly commended him for this dedication.

For this reason more than any other, I had offered him the night at Roustabout's to experience life and enjoy himself. And it seemed he had, in fact, enjoyed himself a great deal in those few hours.

"My captain, I am forever in your debt for allowing me to join you at Roustabout's," he stated enthusiastically. "Stars and fortune shine upon you."

We were walking along one of *Orbital*'s corridors, the floor characteristically covered in shag carpet and bracketed by walls of a colour that could only be described as psychedelic puke. Our destination: the kitchen.

"So I take it you enjoyed your time, Simbden." I was trying to pry some juicy details out of him. I'd had more than my share of excitement at the club, but not the kind of excitement I had hoped for Simbden to find.

I was eager to hear of the young man's adventures.

His face glowed brightly. "It was... well, it was very informative."

"What's her name?" I asked. I could tell when a guy had met a special girl.

He hesitated, briefly surprised by my comment. "Her name is Sandrine."

"And you were able to navigate around her machinery?" I asked wryly.

He turned a shade I had never seen a Mackmian turn before. I hadn't even known the Mackmians had a blue tinge to their skin. It was very amusing.

"My captain?" he faltered. "I merely fixed her sifter."

"Oh, I bet you did." I gave him a light slap on the shoulder. He was so embarrassed that I half-expected him to run away right then and there. But he didn't and I couldn't contain my smile.

At that moment, Bog and Mara rounded the corner. They were engaged in a heated discussion.

"...doesn't matter what he did," Mara was saying with vehemence. "It would be inhumane to do so!"

"We risked our lives for that old bag of bones," Bog replied. "And if he can only thank us for our efforts by trying to ditch us, then I say good riddance."

I almost expected to see Bog literally erupt, so intense was his anger. I had to agree with him.

"Oh, and I take it you're inclined to agree with your security officer?" Mara asked me sharply, as if the entire situation was my fault. "Really? The lavatory?"

"Have you looked around *Orbital* lately, Mara?" I asked. "It's not like we have many amenities available to us. I tried to put him in secure quarters, but you know how that turned out."

Bog shrugged. "And the bars on the old detention cell, two decks below, have all rusted away. What choice did we have?"

"So you chose the lavatory of doom?" She sounded so exasperated.

"We can either put him there or staple him to the outside of the hull," Bog said.

This caused Simbden to frown in concern. "No, we should not do that."

"Thank you, Simbden," Mara replied. "You boys could learn something from the young man."

Simbden nodded. "If we puncture *Orbital*'s hull, we risk losing vital atmospheric pressure fluid. I haven't figured out how the hull keeps reopening from damage that seems to be decades old."

The Mackmian didn't even seem to have an opinion on Bog's suggestion to staple Roman Caesar to something—anything.

"Okay, we can discuss this a little bit later when we all cool down," I said, trying to deescalate the scene.

Breaking Mara's gaze and regaining several degrees of body heat in the process, I looked over at Simbden and once again brought up his unknown adventures with the so-called Sandrine.

I thanked my favourite Mackmian god of fate that Mara relaxed a bit at this change of subject.

"Simbden here was telling me about a girl named Sandrine he met on Roustabout's last night," I explained. "He told me he gave her sifter a once-over."

Bog smiled, all ears. "Oh, yes! Do tell—"

"C'mon, guys, leave the poor man alone," Mara interrupted. "Simbden, you don't have to put up with this."

"No, Miss Olwen. I don't mind so much."

"So Simbden, what was her sifter really like?" Bog asked, cutting right to the chase.

Mara had obviously heard enough. "If any of you want to actually talk like officers, you can find me in the control hub."

And as she left, I reflected on the fact that it was just as well that she went.

Over lunch, Bog and I discussed with Simbden the finer points of diplomatic exchanges with members of the fairer sex. It took some time for us to pry the small details from him, but it turned out that the young Mackmian wouldn't tell us the best parts due to "honour."

"My captain, can I ask you a question?" Simbden asked, growing more serious.

"Fire away."

"How do you protect yourself?" He began tapping on his nose. I could see the four nostrils flare with the motion.

The question took me off-guard. Before I could answer, Bog stood up and strolled away, his laughter growing.

Simbden went on. "I mean, these sorts of encounters could really cause me some serious problems, couldn't they?"

"Well, I'm no doctor, but I would say that it's best to keep yourself on guard. You never know how things can end up."

I'm not sure he really understood my meaning. I just wanted him to know that protection was important, since I didn't think a bottle of EZ-Heal could stave off any irksome bouts of fatherhood. And I knew for certain that Mackmians would never avoid those types of responsibilities, should they happen.

"But my captain, I didn't breathe through my outer nostrils the entire time I was aboard the station. The smell was too powerful for me to take."

I laughed at my folly. He had been talking about his nose and I had been talking about his... well, let's say it wasn't on his head. I had almost forgotten just how immensely sensitive a Mackmian's sense of smell could be if he used all of his nostrils.

"Well, just take your time to breathe normally now that you're in the clear air," I said.

"Thank you, my captain."

With that, I left Simbden and headed towards my next order of duty—one which was to be found in my bed.

After I'd gotten some sleep, Bog and I returned to the lavatory. Caesar Roman had been given enough time to stew in there, I felt. So we opened the door and allowed in some fresh air.

"Walk with me," I said to him—and it wasn't a suggestion.

Bog nudged him forward, taking the rear of our procession as we walked through the corridor.

I didn't give the man time to speak before I began. Considering all the recent conflicts from which I'd barely escaped with my life, I wasn't in the mood to give him much leeway.

"There are some people who are counting on us to find the Dirge," I explained. "You know where he is, and you will lead us to him."

I led Caesar to *Orbital*'s dimly lit, low-ceilinged conference room, a shoebox-sized space less than a dozen paces in length and decorated in art deco. And shag carpeting, of course. Ten stiff-backed chairs were strewn about an oval table.

Overall, I wasn't sure it was much better than the improvised jail cell we'd just freed him from. But it was all we had.

Above the oval table, perhaps the only thing I liked about the room was the domed glass ceiling allowing the sight of the space beyond.

"Sit." I pointed to the seat furthest from the room's only doorway.

Bog kept his weapon levelled at Caesar, who got the point immediately and planted himself down in the chair.

"What do you want with the Dirge?" he asked, studying me. His wrinkled face scrunched up a little more.

"He has some information about a situation in the Mondo system. I need that information."

Someone less observant may not have noticed the hint of distrust flash across the old man's face. I would have to feel him out.

Caesar rubbed his stubbly chin. "What situation are you referring to?" he asked hesitantly.

"Listen, buddy," Bog said. "You're not here to ask all the goddamned questions. How about an answer or two first?"

"Or what? Will you lock me in another bathroom?"

Bog pointed to the nearby domed ceiling menacingly, beyond which lay the cold reaches of space itself. "There are worse places to be."

The threat backfired, as Caesar suddenly clamped up.

"Caesar, you asked me what kind of man I was when I jumped into Roustabout's den to save you," I said. He nodded. "Well, I'm the kind of man who takes things like this very personally. I can promise you that."

I stepped around the table and sat on the seat nearest his.

"I don't have the time to waste finding him," I continued. "If we don't catch up with him in the next couple of days, we will be forced to move on. And if you aren't willing to help, I'll drop you off at the nearest station and you'll no longer have to deal with me or *Orbital*."

"But the nearest station is Hazenist," he exclaimed. "That's near the Shaydren border!"

"Yes. I'm not an evil man and feel absolutely no desire to retaliate against you. But that doesn't mean I won't let others do it for their own reasons."

He gave me a dark look. "The two are one and the same, Captain Zenith."

"Then we understand each other."

Caesar remained silent for several long and tiresome moments. My patience was wearing thin. I had half a mind to jettison his elderly ass out a portal and go on without him.

"Captain, if you meet the Dirge and he gives you what you're looking for... how can I know you won't harm him?"

"How well do you know him?" I asked, pensively. "You seem very concerned for his well-being."

"That is a long story. But I can tell you that he and I have worked together for a very long time. I won't lead you to him if he's going to be harmed."

"I can promise you that I have no interest in harming him."

"I simply don't believe you."

"Listen," I said. "I have a mission that's very important to me. I don't care about the Dirge except to ask him a few questions."

"Questions about what?"

Bog growled, losing his patience. "That's none of your business."

I silenced my friend with a look. "Caesar, you have two choices: tell us where to find him or run the risk that I hand you over to Bog and walk away. Choose wisely."

I doubted if Caesar was fully convinced of my threat, but I hoped he didn't think he had much of a choice in the matter.

He thought about it and then gave me his answer. "I have one condition."

"What's that?" I asked.

"When the time comes, you will drop me off at Saladan Prime."

That was not an unreasonable request. It was only a day's travel from Mondo 4 and located in neutral space.

I nodded. "It's a deal. You find the Dirge and I drop you off on Saladan Prime."

I held out my hand to seal the deal. I still believed in honour, even if so many in this deep, dark galaxy did not.

We shook hands.

"You will be pleasantly surprised, Captain Zenith, that the Dirge is holed up in a small settlement on one of the moons of Merk," Caesar said. "It's the fourth planet in the Ashenon system."

"Yes, I know where that is. It's almost directly on our way to Mondo 4." I hesitated, still not trusting the old informant. It seemed a little too convenient. "I hope it's only coincidence and not a ploy, Caesar."

"Stick to Militia space and it should be smooth sailing," he promised.

"One can hope."

Suddenly, an explosion rocked the deck, shaking the conference room. The overhead lights exploded, raining down glass on us.

"Fuck!" I yelled, immediately charging towards the door. "Bog, get Caesar back to his cell, then join me in the control hub."

Bog grunted in acknowledgement, but I was already halfway out the door and running through the corridor.

When I got into the control hub, circuits were exploding in panels that I hadn't even realized were there. I looked to the viewscreen and saw the crimson-gold arc of incoming enemy fire sizzling across our hull. *Orbital* shuddered all around me and I was having trouble reaching the captain's chair.

"Where the hell are those blasts coming from?" I yelled at the crew, all of them at once. I didn't care who answered, but I needed an answer quickly.

Before anyone could respond, fire erupted from the ceiling near the dome and the air became black with smoke. I knew there would be no immediate help coming from Simbden; with all this damage, his hands would be tied just keeping us from exploding.

Ahead of me, Sparling had been thrown to the ground and was trying to get back to her feet. As I watched, she clawed her way back to the pilot's station, opened a panel on the side of the console I hadn't noticed before, and pulled a yellow lever.

A moment later, the exhaust fans along the ceiling near the dome kicked in, venting the thick black smoke.

"Nice work," I said.

"Thank you, sir," she replied. "I've been learning a few new tricks from Simbden."

"Well, keep it up." Speaking of the engineer, I toggled the communications panel on the armrest of my chair. "Simbden!"

I half-expected to hear back nothing but static. To my surprise, though, the Mackmian's voice came through loud and clear.

"Yes, my captain."

From the noise in the background, I could tell he was under a barrage of trouble down in the engine room.

"What's the chance that our engines won't blow up and kill us all?" I asked, not looking forward to the answer.

"If we don't get hit too many more times, I think I can put out the fires and repair the worst of the damage."

And at exactly that moment, a sleek fighter shimmered into view right in front of *Orbital* and rained down a torrent of crimson laser fire. The Shaydren! The information coming through on the screens told me it was tearing holes in *Orbital*'s hull.

Our engines went dead.

"Thrusters?" I asked, my heart feeling sick.

"Online and operational," said Stairn. "But we cannot outrun a Shaydren fighter with thrusters, Captain."

"Thank you, Stairn."

I wasn't blaming him, but I was sure losing hope. We were just fighting too many uphill battles in too short a period of time. I looked down at my armrest screen and saw that *Orbital* was jettisoning gas from the port hull. That couldn't be good.

"Two more fighters," Bog reported between clenched tusks.

I turned to stare at him, wondering at what point during all this chaos he had managed to return from belowdecks. I seemed to have lost track of a few moments there in the heat of the battle.

But I didn't have time to dwell on that. My gaze returned to the viewscreen, where I watched as the two new fighters swooped in and began a boarding sequence. They circled in on *Orbital*, their concentric rings narrowing and their speed diminishing as they prepared to dock with us.

Bog grabbed the controls for the hull propulsion cannons and began to inflict hell on one of the black fighters. His aim was true enough to sear off a piece of its long wing and send it spinning.

"Die, you dirty bastard!"

But his glory was short-lived, as the Shaydren fighter quickly enacted a move I'd never seen before in all my experience in space. The sheared-off wing began to slowly regrow. The skin of the ship was ensconced in a blue electrical arc which almost acted as a mother's embrace. It would only take a few minutes for it to be fully functional again.

The other two ships circled like vultures, boring silvery holes in our hull cannons to ensure we wouldn't be able to fire again. We were literally cannon fodder, unable to move and unable to fight back. I listened intently to the groaning of the hull as it shook under the stress of enemy bombardment.

We were doomed. I searched my brain for options, but none came. We were too far from a port or anything we could use for cover, and Militia backup was days away. Even the nearest Prime ship was nowhere close enough to be of help.

I looked over at Bog and Stairn and pulled free my propulsion gun, expecting us to be boarded any minute.

At least I didn't have to worry about Caesar Roman, who to my knowledge must be safely secured once again in the lavatory. No need to worry about his escape; all I needed to worry about was being captured and executed by these accursed Shaydren.

I launched up from the captain's chair, waving for Stairn and Bog to follow me. Without a word, we brandished our weapons and exited the rear of the control hub.

Bog made his way to the rear of the ship where the first of three portals were found.

Stairn and I made our way to the core of the ship. We traversed the main corridor to where it split in opposite directions.

I left Stairn at the first portal, then continued down the corridor towards the second.

Those would be the most obvious points of entry for the intruders.

My hands were shaking in expectation as I slowed down in front of it. I'd been hoping to never see a Shaydren again, never mind so soon.

I propped myself into a little nook in the corridor that offered a good angle of the portal, then did my best to slow my breathing and relax my nerves. As I waited for the first surge of combatants to come crashing through an exploding door, I found myself in utter shock.

"Drop weapon," said a slimy-sounding voice from directly beside me.

My shock deepened as I felt the business end of a pistol touch the side of my head. How had the intruders got on board so fast, and without coming through the portals?

However they'd gotten aboard, I had to believe they were after Caesar Roman. I just didn't believe that the firefight in Smelters had been a coincidence. I strongly suspected that they were after Caesar—and their appearance here and now confirmed my suspicions. I recognized that it was only a matter of time before they dragged him away, leaving us to meet our deaths.

Or perhaps they'd do us a favour and destroy us on the spot.

I lowered my right hand, holding the gun loosely. The intruder was on my right side, and I wouldn't have much chance of reacting fast enough. I'd have to spin, bring up my arm in a tight angle, and fire before he managed to paste my brains all over the shag carpeting...

The deck trembled under my feet and suddenly the portal burst open in front of me. Nothing could have prepared me for the sight that met my eyes: charging through the portal were a trio of Brunken warlords!

What the hell were they doing here?

Swarming in like a herd of oversized Telnian cows, they had to duck under the ceiling support arches as they lifted their hand cannons to drill a hole through the Shaydren holding me captive. Their missiles hit it with the force of an avalanche, launching it back ten metres. I almost felt bad for it as its body exploded like a snowball.

When I focused on the Brunken, I realized that I recognized two of them. Leading the pack was Captain Kiln. Behind him was one of the warlords I'd encountered in the Smelters VIP lounge; I didn't know his name, but he was just as big and ugly as the others.

The third Brunken, I noticed, wore a white leather lab coat. Strange attire for a Brunken... wait a moment, he was the one who had pinned me up against the wall as we'd been trying to escape Docentric!

"Friend of Kiln," said the alien captain. "Kiln help you out too."

Kiln gave me a lopsided, toothy smile. I almost felt like petting him like a puppy, but I kept my hands to myself.

"Kiln, Brunken, destroy Shaydren," Kiln added with pride.

I didn't know for certain if their speech pattern always sounded so adolescent. It could have been that my malfunctioning synaptic translator enzymes were too far gone.

Looking through the open portal, I saw two Brunken ships flanking the Shaydren fighters. It seemed the Shaydren, as phenomenal and mystical as they were, hadn't seen the Brunken coming and had been caught unprepared.

As I watched, the Shaydren took off and flew as fast as they could in the opposite direction of us... leaving us alone with a boatload of our new warlord friends.

The Brunken had saved my life. Had saved all our lives. Had saved *Orbital* itself.

And now I had a new, very large problem on my hands.

CHAPTER EIGHTEEN

A Healthy Admission

I could add up every exciting, noteworthy moment in the last five years of my life and they wouldn't nearly have matched those I had been through in the past couple of weeks. Since the Alhalran mission years ago, my life had been an unending stint of boring and meaningless duties heavily seasoned with drinking, cheap women, and irresponsible gambling. Somehow my life had taken an abrupt turn, leaving me bruised, battered, broken, terrified, embarrassed, and overworked.

And yet I wouldn't have traded any of this for all the money in the universe! This was why I had become an officer in the first place.

I had to admit that standing amidst this trio of Brunken warlords, though, did make me feel very small. Despite having grown up with the towering Bog, it was a wholly different feeling when you knew the massive beings near you could unexpectedly inflict pain at any moment.

I found myself clueless as to how to deal with them. It was clear enough that Captain Kiln, my new bestest friend in this galaxy, didn't mean me any serious harm. But I just didn't know enough about them to be certain. Mostly, I didn't know how creatures as habitually stupid as they were reputed to be could even pilot their ships, let alone build them.

But the proof in front of me was undeniable. My crew would have been reduced to nothing but squishy vapour right now without their help. I guess I didn't know everything there was to know in the universe.

Captain Kiln suddenly started to speak in fluent Brunken, a language that reminded me of the sounds a wildebeest might produce while making love to a cactus. I signalled to him with my hand politely to wait a moment and he nodded his understanding. Or at least I hoped so.

I slowly raised my wristband communicator to my lips and spoke calmly, trying not to cause any disruption.

"Zenith to Bog and Stairn, what is your status?"

The communicator crackled in rebuke, but I was fortunate enough to get two responses.

"Bog here. No enemies on board. Kinda sucks. All is quiet. And you?"

"Stairn here too, Captain. My entry portal is vacant. Is everything okay at your end?"

I looked into the warlords' eyes, hoping they wouldn't grow suspicious. Truthfully, they looked bored. As a boarding party trained for battle, they seemed ill-equipped to handle peaceable situations. That was fine with me.

"Well, I can't quite define 'okay,' but I'm alive. I just have a little situation brewing here." My voice wasn't much louder than a whisper so as to not stir up any trouble. "No danger yet, Stairn, but I need you to head to the control hub and help Agent Sparling with tactics. You'll understand when you get there."

Stairn responded quickly. "Yes, Captain. I'll keep you posted."

"And Bog, I need you to wrangle up our esteemed guest and bring him to me at the portside portal. Make it quick."

"Will do."

The next few minutes, as I waited for Bog to return with Caesar, felt long and tense. Although this situation was a far cry from the last time I'd stared down the barrel of a Brunken cannon, it wasn't easy to shake the angst that came from being around them. So far, they were content to wait with me in silence.

When finally Bog and Caesar rounded the corner, my security officer raised his weapon in front of him. Before devastation rained down on us, I lifted my hands and stepped between everyone. I didn't know what the Brunken were up to, but they had saved us, and I knew better than to provoke a fight in such tight quarters.

"Whoa!" I exclaimed, looking directly into my Nova Martian friend's eyes. "Bog, lower your weapon."

I was beginning to wonder why every situation in my life seemed to escalate to battle, war, and then imminent death so quickly. But I didn't have enough time to find an answer to this.

He tried to protest, but my intense eyes alone told him to can it.

"They saved me from the Shaydren," I continued. "They stopped the attack."

His eyes remained suspicious. But he was paid to be suspicious, so I couldn't hold it against him.

"That is indeed correct, Captain," Stairn spoke through the communicator. I guessed that he was back up in the control hub, watching us on the viewscreen. "No signs of the Shaydren vessels. Only the Brunken. They're holding steady next to us."

"Good. Thank you, Stairn. Let me know if anything changes."

Bog reluctantly lowered his weapon, which greatly helped to diffuse the situation.

A moment later, Captain Kiln gave the signal for his two mates to do the same.

I was surrounded by the massive Brunken on my left and a slightly larger Bog on my right. I felt incredibly small at that moment.

When everyone seemed sufficiently relaxed, or a lot less poised for obliteration, I decided to bring our new informant into the mix. I looked past Bog, directly into Caesar's old, wrinkled, and stubbled face.

"What the hell do you make of this?" I asked Caesar, not sure whether he would be helpful. However, I had a hunch that he was the right person to sort this out. Judging from how capably he'd carried himself at Roustabout's, I figured he was up to the challenge.

"Why do you think I would know anything, Captain?" Caesar asked, his voice steady. He was smart enough to have distanced himself from the centre of the would-be carnage.

"How about we drop the act?" I said. "I think you know a great deal about the Brunken, and it seems to me that you would benefit greatly by helping us out."

"You are mistaken, Captain Zenith. I don't believe I can help you."

I looked into his eyes. It's not often that I can say with absolute certainty that a man is lying, but the spark of defiance in his gaze set me off like a stick of explosives. I damned near drew my weapon and kneecapped him right then and there.

"I know you're lying," I whispered vehemently, tired of having to put up with his self-serving attitude. "Help me out with this one and, as I've already promised, you'll be released—as soon as we find the Dirge. It does you no good if a firefight starts here and now, or if the Brunken decide to take us all prisoner. You're only days away from being free, Caesar. Can the Brunken offer you the same deal?"

My words must have made some sort of impact because he thought about it and quickly responded. "I have one condition."

"State it."

"I will no longer be kept in that disgusting lavatory! The rest of the voyage, I'll be treated like any member of your crew. I will not be treated like a prisoner."

He was pissed. I guess I had failed to realize just how personally he would take it.

One thing I realized, though, was that I was losing valuable time. I could feel Captain Kiln's mood grow darker with each passing second.

"Deal," I said, having no choice but to give in. "But you will not be allowed to wander alone. I've already seen what happens when you take it upon yourself to leave your quarters. You owe me a new door, by the way."

"I apologize for that, Captain. But the door wasn't my doing. Your crazy little robot did that when he entered. You cannot blame me for not wanting to spend my time with that psycho robot, can you?"

Really? Sirbot had done it? I couldn't process all the crap that was rolling downhill at me.

"So help me out here," I said. "I don't want a ship full of pissed off Brunken. I want to thank them, get ourselves repaired, and get the hell on our way. Agreed?"

"Agreed. Do you mind if I take the lead then?"

I nodded my approval. I was grateful, actually.

"Captain Kiln, I am friend of Zenith," said Caesar as he turned to our new guests. "Friend of yours. I was there when the terrible Borkrieg was slain." I had to swallow down my annoyance for Caesar clinging onto my earlier victory. My pride did not need the massaging at that moment.

He offered a quick nod to the Brunken captain. This seemed to work, since Kiln put his weapon away and tapped Caesar's head with two meaty fingers.

Caesar grimaced with pain, silently so, and resumed speaking. If you could call it speaking. "Friend Kiln, I thank you for your service." He paused for effect, or simply because the Brunken weren't quick thinkers. "Your service today, right here."

"Ask him what his intentions are," I whispered.

"Friend Kiln, what will you do now?"

Kiln looked back at his two shipmates, each of them having to crouch to fit under the crisscrossing arches in *Orbital*'s hallway. It really was the worst spot in the corridor for so many large beings to be congregating. They all looked uncomfortable and I felt bad for them.

"Friend Zenith needs help," Kiln finally said. "Kiln help Zenith."

My synaptic translators only worked intermittently, but that part was clear as day.

"Friend Kiln," I said, mimicking Caesar's pattern of speech. "What do you mean? How do you wish to help me?"

The Brunken tapped me on the shoulder and spoke happily. "Kiln help Zenith on his ship. Kiln stay with Zenith for some time."

I looked over at Caesar, my eyes beseeching him for help.

He quickly spoke up. "Friend Zenith thanks you greatly!"

"What the hell are you doing?" I asked through the side of my mouth, trying not to betray the smile I had glued onto my face to disguise my fear and anxiety. "I only wish for us to fix up *Orbital* and get the hell on our way, not invite the whole damn fleet of Brunken onboard!"

"Captain, please, you will cause a scene," Caesar whispered back.

The expression on Kiln's face shifted and told me everything. Confusion and suspicion were growing in those bleak, grey irises once more.

Caesar turned back to the Brunken captain. "Friend Kiln, we would be greatly thankful for help in the future. But Zenith cannot spare time to wait for repairs just now. Can we meet in the future to accept your offer of help?"

It took Kiln a few extra seconds to process this, after which he looked disappointed and possibly insulted. I feared the worst.

Before responding, Kiln looked over at his compatriots and nodded. One of them then turned and strolled back through the portal towards his own ship. It was the one in the white lab coat.

We waited awkwardly for a few seconds, until that Brunken returned, carrying enormous trunks beneath each arm, as well as two canvas bags of nearly equal size. I estimated that each one weighed more than I did.

I looked over at Kiln quizzically. "Friend Kiln, what is happening?"

"Friend Daisee will stay with Zenith. Friend Zenith will be great mates with Daisee." Before I could object, Kiln spoke one more time. "Kiln's ship stay with Zenith's. Zenith is Kiln's friend."

With that, Kiln left alongside the third Brunken, leaving me in the black-blood-spattered corridor with the so-called Daisee and a dead Shaydren soldier. All I could do was swear to myself.

Bog, whose presence I had very nearly forgotten about, smiled at this latest development. No doubt he was enjoying my discomfort.

"What the hell was that!" I exclaimed at Caesar as we walked away from the portal. "How did I end up taking one of them aboard?"

I was so exasperated by the whole situation that I was beginning to sweat in places I wished not to.

Caesar held up his hand to counter my objection. "Captain, all you said was that we shouldn't invite the whole damned fleet of Brunken aboard. Well, now we only have one. And we are free to handle repairs and be on our way."

"One Brunken is more than enough," I whispered darkly, keeping my voice low enough that Daisee wouldn't catch on. "What in God's green earth am I going to do with it?"

"Her."

"What?"

"She's a her. Her name is Daisee. You heard Kiln."

Bog's smile grew wider. I ignored him.

"But she's bald and as big as a shuttlecraft," I protested.

"That's the way it is with the Brunken." Caesar shrugged. "The men have hair, the women do not. And sometimes the women are as big as the men."

Caesar must have been able to tell this didn't exactly please me. Anyway, her gender didn't matter a damn to me.

We escorted Daisee towards her chambers, located across the hall from my own. The only reason was to ensure that I could keep my eye on her.

"Daisee thanks Zenith," she stated, touching my back as she followed behind us. I didn't think anything of the physical contact.

"Why, Daisee?" I asked.

She looked at me, perplexed by the question. I really needed to upgrade my synaptic translator enzymes when I got the chance.

To fill the gap in conversation, Caesar took it upon himself to speak on my behalf. I caught bits of Daisee's side of the chat, including the phrases "slave of damned Captain Borkrieg" and "relieved that he is dead." It seemed pretty evident what she meant.

I managed to piece together Daisee's woeful tale. She had been handed over to Borkrieg when she was just a teen, hardly older than a child, and been forced to serve aboard his ship. For three years, from adolescence to adulthood—Brunken apparently grew up very, very quickly—she had grown to despise the captain.

Since I'd killed him, she seemed to feel indebted to me.

As the dialogue between her and Caesar continued, however, her tone seemed to get cooler. I could practically feel the temperature drop.

Eventually she stopped walking, still holding the four million or so kilograms of baggage on her as if they were nothing more than a stack of throw pillows.

"Captain, she is deeply offended by your reluctance to allow her on board," Caesar explained.

"Well, it's not like I plan to throw her off the ship. But how can she last long, since I'm barely able to understand her? Besides, what skills does she have?"

Caesar smiled. "It's funny you should ask, Captain. Daisee here is a fully trained medic."

"A doctor?" Bog wondered aloud.

I felt just as surprised. "You're kidding me."

With that, I turned to the Brunken, who was looking at me as though I had just run over her favourite dog.

"She is indeed," said Caesar. "Brunken are very much against dishonesty. So when she tells me that she is extremely gifted, I must conclude that she isn't just praising herself. She's probably a phenomenal healer."

As I studied her more closely, I was lucky that she didn't seem to recognize the disbelief written on my face. How could a creature so large, so simple, and seemingly so ungainly be a doctor? It didn't seem possible.

But I couldn't deny her the right to board the ship, at least not without a much better reason than my fear that she may get hungry one night and decide to eat me as a snack. Nonetheless, I vowed to myself not to let her lay her healing hands on me.

"Daisee, welcome to *Orbital*," I said, speaking slowly.

Apparently she understood the message. Her shining grey face beamed like a sun and she dropped her bag at my feet. She hugged me tightly and again I detected the particular scent of disinfectant that seemed to follow this particular Brunken around.

As good as it felt to make her wishes come true, I really could have done without the slap on the ass she gave me when we started moving again.

We led her to her quarters, where I instructed Caesar to take her inside and show her around.

When Bog and I were alone in the corridor, my friend began to chuckle.

"So the doc has a crush on the captain," he rumbled. "That's so sweet!"

"You know, I have a lavatory with your name on it," I snapped. He backed off.

My thoughts couldn't help but return to the perplexing series of events that had transpired over the last few days. I had an untrustworthy informant, a new engineer barely old enough to have lost his baby teeth, a robot more intent on breaking things and styling hair than serving his programmed function, and now a giant warlord of a medic. All of this in the earliest stages of *Orbital*'s most important mission in years.

I came out of my reverie as the doors to Daisee's quarters opened. Caesar stepped out alone. It seemed she needed some time to rest, which suited me just fine.

"How can she possibly be a medic?" I asked Caesar as the three of us walked down the corridor. He seemed to know so much more about Brunken than I did. "Or more generally, how do the Brunken manage to survive in space considering how simple-minded they are? I doubt one of them could tie their shoes without help."

"The Brunken aren't a typical species," the informant said. "Now, Captain, about these new quarters you promised me..."

"This way."

I led him down the hallway further and he and Bog followed.

"What do you know about innate traits?" he asked cryptically.

I frowned at him. "You mean, like a baby's ability from birth to breathe or suck on its mom's teat?"

"Exactly, Captain. Well, the Brunken are, as you say, total simpletons in a general sense. But they have some very specific innate skills. Each Brunken seems to have two or three skills that transcend their natural simple-mindedness."

"Yes, but the ability to design a spaceship isn't nearly the same as innately knowing how to breastfeed," I pointed out.

"You would think so, Captain, but the Brunken are unusual. Somehow, members of their species are born with the ability to easily master highly specific, and highly useful, skills—such as engineering spaceships, understanding the planetary sciences, or mastering the practice of medicine." He paused for effect. "It wouldn't surprise me if Daisee is very gifted. Only time will tell."

"So even through the Brunken are dumber than Telnian dung heaps, they can solve quantum theories, design interstellar megaships, and cure diseases?"

Caesar shook his head. "Heavens, no. Well, not individually. You don't expect a red blood cell to fight off infections, or a white blood cell to carry oxygen. But when the right Brunken is assigned the right duty, as a whole they become extremely proficient. However, like I said, each Brunken has only two or three innate abilities. So Daisee may be extremely gifted in medicine—and, for all I know, glassblowing. Beyond each individual's two or three very specific talents, they are like children."

I thought about that for a while. It didn't seem possible, but very strange things seemed to constantly occur all around me. I was in no place to disbelieve. Although I did wonder how Caesar had come to know so much about the Brunken. One day I would need to ask him.

"I do believe I will be keeping my distance from our new medic," I concluded.

"Well, I don't know about that," Bog said with a tone of curiosity, giving our informant a none-too-subtle shove into his new chambers.

We were at the doors directly adjacent to Bog's chambers. It seemed logical to place Caesar next to the ship's security officer.

"Enjoy," I said, then turned my heel to walk away.

I left the two men and headed back to my own quarters. It had been an extremely long day and night and I needed nothing more than a hot shower, a couple of Martian Breezes, and a long hibernating sleep.

But while walking past the infirmary, my thoughts wandering, something far less desirable happened. Without warning, I felt myself being lifted by two enormous grey hands that wrapped themselves around my waist.

I didn't have enough time to let out even a grunt of surprise as Daisee lifted me into the medical bay and planted me firmly on a diagnostics bunk. I guess she wasn't as tired as I had presumed. I also couldn't help but notice that she'd found our medical bay.

I was taken aback by her size. Even though the medical bay had a tall ceiling, she still had to scrunch down to fit under parts of it.

"What the hell?!" I said, not having expected such an assault. "Daisee, what the shit are you doing?"

She palmed my face with her enormous mitt, cutting off my protest. Although I could only see through a slit between her meat-stick fingers, I figured out that she was holding something very slimy and worm-shaped...

What happened next will haunt me to the end of my days. I felt an odd sensation as a tiny, very thin worm wriggled its way into my right ear canal and, I could only guess, dissolved inside my head. My eyes jumped open, and my entire brain lit up like an explosion! I could suddenly see vivid flashes of aroma, hear rays of colour, and taste wrinkly textures of knowledge. My senses were tangled up and bewildered. The sensation was neither painful nor pleasant, but it was intense.

She let go of my face and body, but it took me minutes, hours, or days—I couldn't tell which—to recover my mind well enough to start moving on my own again.

"What the fuck!" I screamed.

"Captain, cured," Daisee stated.

I was pissed right off. "Cured of what, you giant oaf?"

She grabbed my right ear between her massive finger and thumb and began to twist. I screamed in pain, but she didn't stop—and it occurred to me that she wouldn't stop until I did something. But what?

I quickly realized that I had just called her an oaf. "Daisee, I'm sorry."

She let go of my ear and smiled, seemingly proud of something. "Good, Captain."

Okay, so I understood the reason for the ear twist. But I sure didn't understand the reason for the worm she had put in my brain. Feeling very freaked out, I sat on a nearby examination bench and put a hand to my stinging ear.

"Daisee?"

"Yes?" she asked in her deep, guttural voice.

"What did you do to me?"

"I gave you talk!"

"I already had talk."

"Not good. Now you talk good."

And like a flash it hit me that we were communicating in flawless Brunken. The worm must have altered my brain in some way to better understand her. I wondered if it would work for other languages as well, although I would hate to need one for every language in the universe. My brain would pack up and vacate through my other ear if that were the case.

When she was satisfied that I had calmed down, she grabbed me by the waist and proceeded to lift and contort my body in all manner of humiliating ways. I felt like a wet towel being wrung out.

I was careful how I phrased my next question.

"Daisee, what are you doing to me?" I asked in fluent Brunken. It didn't quite seem so guttural and stupid to me now. Simple yes; stupid, not so much.

"Daisee gives captain physical."

I tried to push her hands away, which was like trying to carry a boulder up a hill. "I don't need a physical," I insisted.

She ignored that and began to remove my clothing.

Now I was getting worried. There truly was nothing I could do to stop her. She was so freakishly strong that I doubted two of me could have contained her.

As I stood there in nothing but my silk boxer briefs, hoping against the worst, Mara walked through the door.

"Captain, you shouldn't have!" Mara said mockingly.

"Thanks a lot. But trust me, I didn't." I tried not to grind my pearly white teeth. "How are repairs coming along? Are the Brunken ships still maintaining their distance?"

"Repairs are slow, Captain. Simbden has partially restored the engines, but other systems are interconnected and keep fighting with him. Still, he seems confident enough. Yes, the Brunken are nearby, thank the stars."

Mara turned to the Brunken. "Daisee, my name is Mara Olwen. It's nice to meet you."

She offered Daisee her hand, and to my surprise Daisee was very pleased to return the handshake. Mara, true to form, began introducing and welcoming the large warlord. I was taken completely by surprise at Mara's warmness, even eagerness, to welcome our new visitor.

It was just so disconcerting to have been saddled with this particular new crewmember—against my will, to make it worse. I doubted Daisee would be staying too long aboard *Orbital*. But for the time being, I couldn't press the matter. The only reason we were still alive was because the Brunken had saved us from the Shaydren.

"Brant, did you hear that?" Mara asked suddenly, snapping my mind back into focus. I shook my head. "The poor girl. She was a slave on board her ship!"

"Yes, Mara, I heard all about it." I sighed. "Could you maybe continue your discussion with our new doc after I'm done being stripped and God knows what else?"

Daisee gently nudged me to lay belly-down on the examination bench. I struggled against her, which turned out to be a colossal mistake. With both hands wrapped around my waist, she lifted and stuffed me onto the bench. I felt the cartilage in my nose shift as she pressed my handsome face into the old, cracked leather. The bench smelled like sweat socks worn by a hippo.

"Mara, can you please leave now?" I asked, my voice muffled.

When I tried to squirm, I felt an even a greater push into the bench. But Mara must have left, because I heard her footsteps get quieter as she walked out of the infirmary.

The next thirty minutes were mentally scarring. My extremities and innermost cavities were thoroughly checked, prodded, and examined for any and all abnormalities. Whatever Daisee felt she needed to do to deem me healthy, she did. I learned very quickly to remain submissive. When I cooperated, her touch was as tender as a basket full of kittens gracefully lapping milk. When I fought back, she became as aggressive as a cheetah pouncing on a gazelle.

Eventually my way-too-personal physical came to an end.

"Good, Captain," she said simply.

Daisee gave me my clothes and handed me a pink lollypop for my troubles. I walked out of the medical bay feeling sore and somehow cheapened. Putting the pink lollypop in my mouth, wondering where she had gotten it, I headed back to my quarters for some rest.

CHAPTER NINETEEN

Lures

"I've called each of you here because I don't have a god-damned clue what to think about any of this," I said from the head of our tiny, dingy conference room. The entire crew, except Daisee, were positioned around the table with me. It had been twelve hours since the Brunken had stormed aboard and saved our pretty hides.

"To what are you referring, Captain?" Stairn asked mildly.

"Well, I don't know. How about the fact that we're floating through the cosmos, having endured yet another attack? The area around Docentric is supposed to be a safe region for us, yet we've barely survived the trip. Which brings me to another major concern: the Brunken megaship. What do we do about them?"

"I say we do nothing and be thankful for their company," Mara said.

"I typically wouldn't agree, Shoe," Bog said, "but we're in no condition to refuse help. Not when we could face another Shaydren attack at any time. And who knows what's waiting for us on Mondo 4?"

Stairn nodded his agreement as well.

"Okay, I think we hope the Brunken stick around for a little while longer," I said. "Simbden, how are the repairs coming along?"

His slim Mackmian face scrunched in concern. "Engines are at eighty percent, and the weapons are only at twenty-five percent, my captain. Atmospheric stabilizers, except for those persistent weather anomalies, have also been restored. I would say I need another sixteen hours to complete the work."

I noticed that the haggard expression on Simbden's face made him look ten years older. I could tell he hadn't slept in the past two days, and it was wearing him down. I would have to order him to his bed before this meeting ended.

"Good work, Simbden." When I nodded to him in approval, his tired face lit up with enthusiasm. "Now, Bog brought up a good point regarding the Shaydren."

The atmosphere in the room darkened a shade. Twice I had managed to get the better of that dangerous, seedy species. I didn't want to test them a third time.

"We've never been even a faint concern of the Shaydren, near as I can tell," I said. "Now all of a sudden, they've attacked us. It's not a coincidence. We need to press Caesar to help. I sense that he's the key."

"What are you suggesting, Captain?" Mara asked.

"Nothing. I don't know what to do with the man. I don't trust him. Even though he's pointed us in the direction of the Dirge, I feel as though he hasn't fully cooperated. But we don't have any choice. We need to find out what the Dirge knows about what happened in the Mondo system."

Agent Stairn surprised me by strongly agreeing. "I agree with the captain. We must learn more about the Dirge. We must press him for answers."

Bog smiled a broad, tusk-filled grin. "Now that's what I'm talking about." That was probably the first time Bog had ever sparked up with something Stairn had said.

I looked at Bog with an eyebrow raised. I knew exactly what he had in mind, but he wouldn't act against Caesar without my express order.

"Everyone, back to your duties," I said, concluding the meeting.

The crew stood up and began departing the dreary, low-ceilinged room. But before they had all left, I pulled Bog and Simbden aside.

"Simbden, you're doing an amazing job," I said. His face beamed. "But now I need you to tackle a very special project."

He was quick to agree. "Name it, my captain."

"I need you to go to Room 6B."

"But those are my quarters…"

"Exactly. I need you to go inside. And when you get to your bed, I need you to lift the covers, lay down, and sleep for a while."

His face fell in anguish. "But, my captain, you said I was doing a good job. Why are you sending me to my quarters?"

"You're exhausted. I'll take the engines at eighty percent for now. We're about a day away from our meeting with the Dirge, and in ten hours I need you back on duty to finish the weapons repairs. You can't work when you're nearly falling over from exhaustion."

He lifted his head and nodded in acceptance.

As it turned out, Caesar's quarters were directly on the way to Simbden's, so the engineer found himself trailing Bog and me for the remainder of our walk.

When we got to Caesar's door, Bog swiped his armband communicator, which brought up the manual security code to get inside.

"Simbden," I said. "Before you retire, could you ask Agent Stairn and Ambassador Mara to join us?"

He nodded in response and began walking away.

We stepped into the room to find Caesar, none too pleased to be disturbed without a knock on the door first.

"Captain, I thought you agreed that I was to be treated like a guest aboard *Orbital*," he said. "Is this how you treat all of your guests?"

"Perhaps you're right. I will knock in the future. That is, if you grace us with the information we've come for."

"What do you need?" he asked.

Looking around, I realized with annoyance that even his quarters were bigger than mine. What the hell? But at least they were equally as ugly.

Shaking off my annoyance, I took a seat beside him, blocking his exit. For whatever reason, I kept getting the urge to do so.

"We're only about a day from Merk in the Ashenon system," I said. "I need more information about the Dirge before we arrive. What are we getting into? Where exactly is he?"

Caesar appeared to be struggling with a dilemma. I assumed it was with the fact that he would have to give up his friend. I personally couldn't have cared less about the Dirge, as long as he helped us with the crisis in the Mondo system.

"Merk is a dangerous place," said Caesar. "It will not be easy to reach the Dirge."

At that moment the door opened and Mara and Stairn joined our little conversation. They also hadn't knocked.

"I am prepared for danger," I told him. "Because of the Dirge's reputation, I expect this won't be easy. Just tell me what you know. Then, as soon I come face to face with the Dirge, you're free to go."

He took a moment to consider that proposition—again.

Caesar eventually nodded. "The Dirge's base of operations is called Obsidian. It's on an asteroid orbiting Merk's largest moon, Vega. To get to Obsidian, you'll have to pass through three layers of security."

"Go on." I leaned in closer. A tub filled with Martian Breezes and a team of scantily clad cheerleaders couldn't have pried me away from him at that moment.

Well, probably not.

"The first layer consists of simple beacons," Caesar continued. "Six hours out from Obsidian, you'll encounter these beacons. They're unarmed but still need to be bypassed. If this isn't done properly, they will signal the base of your approach."

"Do you have remote access to bypass the beacons?" Bog asked.

"Yes."

At least that would help. "Okay, go on," I said. "What's the second security layer?"

"This is where it becomes more dangerous. About an hour from Merk, orbiting Obsidian, are a complex series of mines."

I moaned inwardly. I hated minefields. They were cowardly and far too often harmed innocents instead of their intended targets.

"How do we disable the mines?" Bog asked.

"Not so fast, big boy."

Bog stood up, towering over the old man like an oak tree. I had to place my hand on Bog's jagged black forearm to prevent him from going too far.

"The mines in that field are shaded, meaning they're invisible to eyes and most forms of spatial attenuators," Caesar said. "I will have to register the right frequency into *Orbital*'s spatial attenuators just to view them."

"And then what?" I asked, all the more anxious from this talk of minefields.

"And then we test your courage, Captain. The first mine must be deactivated manually, in person."

"To hell with that!" Bog exclaimed, flaring up again. "Who would be crazy enough to jump out of *Orbital* and strap himself to a drifting mine with nothing but a tether between him and death?"

I cleared my throat and Bog looked at me. He sighed sheepishly as he realized it wasn't so long ago that I'd done exactly that.

"In this case, I think, we'll have to bring the mine aboard and deactivate it in the cargo bay," Caesar suggested.

Bog growled. "That sounds like a piss-poor idea!"

"I agree," I said. "*Orbital* may have its difficulties, but a giant hole in the side of its hull isn't one of them. I would like to keep it that way."

"Captain of Militia I don't think you have any other choice."

"What about remote access?" I asked, sceptical.

"Remote access is available…" He trailed off and I was about to cut in when he held up his hand. "…but this is a trap. The mine cannot be manipulated remotely. Any attempts to do so will immediately trigger the warhead."

"That sounds unfortunate," I said, half to myself.

"It gets worse."

"It always does, doesn't it?"

He ignored my comment. "The mines are located just close enough that when one detonates, an area of one hundred thousand cubic kilometres will go up in flames. Shortly after, the vast expanse of undetonated mines will fill the void and make the problem worse."

"And what the hell do we do with the mine if we manage to bring it on board?" Bog asked.

"Well, let's just say the process is physically demanding."

Caesar took the next ten minutes to describe the complicated process of deactivating the mine.

"You have got to be shitting me!" Bog exclaimed.

I ignored the outburst and chose to carry on. "So what is the third layer of security?"

Caesar leaned forward in his chair, peering into my eyes. His grey irises were intense, and for a moment I thought I saw a flicker of gold flash in them.

Note to Brant Zenith: maybe lay off the Martian Breezes for a while. You're starting to see things.

"What do you know of Society Sentinel Drones?" Caesar asked quietly.

Bog winced. "Aww, shit!"

"I see you've heard of them." But Caesar didn't show whether he was surprised to hear that.

"I thought all of them were destroyed in the Moridian uprising twenty-five years ago," I said, racking my brains for the history lesson I had learned back at the Prime Academy about a decade ago.

"Officially, that's true."

"And unofficially?" I asked.

"Of the one thousand and one Society Sentinel Drones created, only three remain unaccounted for. This is one of those three."

I frowned. "Wait a minute. Correct me if I'm wrong, but there were only nine hundred Society Sentinel Drones created to help withstand the slave uprising in the Moridian system. Where did the extra one hundred and one come from?"

"It was a last-ditch effort by the Sonnen overlords to restore order."

"From what I hear, the Society Sentinel Drones were a catastrophe," I continued, recalling more of the details. "Many of them failed to accept orders after they were deployed. They began indiscriminately attacking settlements on both sides of the conflict. If it weren't for the fully functioning drones being deployed to overcome the malfunctioning drones, the whole system would have ended in a violent eruption—"

"Hold on just a moment," Mara interrupted. "What exactly is a Society Sentinel Drone?"

It was nice to realize that I finally knew something she did not.

"They're often referred to as the most devastating weapons built in the past one hundred years," I explained, the sentence coming back to me almost verbatim from my military history course. I wasn't sure how or why I remembered it now, but I was grateful. "The drones were automated, early-generation war machines that sported every known defensive shielding and more than enough of an arsenal to wipe out a whole fleet of ships... or so I remember."

I knew they weren't large, though. Perhaps three times the size of *Orbital*'s own escape capsules... or a large outhouse.

Mara looked perplexed. "And they stopped being used? Why?"

"Because they led to such a horrifying disaster," Bog said.

"Well, that's true," I said, turning towards Stairn. "Can I see the digital specs on file for the drones?"

Using the digital pad he always had on him, Stairn pulled up all information our computer had on Society Sentinel Drones, which unfortunately wasn't much better than a couple of drawings sketched on a napkin. I did my best to ignore the poor state of affairs Militia's military intelligence was in.

"How can the situation get worse than an automated drone that's capable of destroying entire armadas?" Bog asked pessimistically.

Caesar sighed. "Because when those one hundred and one final ships were deployed, they were the most advanced models, accounting for every possible improvement learned from the first nine hundred. They were superior in every way."

"Oh," Mara said, not really wishing to hear more.

"Plus, these drones are shaded," the informant added. "But it's not all bad news. There's only one drone around Merk's perimeter and I know how to read its signature. I believe we may be able to move on Obsidian safely before we're detected."

"How long of a time window will we have?" I asked.

"About twenty minutes."

Bog snorted derisively.

I wasn't convinced it would work. "How do we get past the drone, arrive at the base, find the Dirge, talk to or capture him, and make our escape in under twenty minutes?"

"Zenith, the complex isn't very big," Caesar assured me. "You can walk it end to end in minutes. Besides, that's what the ETT is for. You'll be able to speak with the Dirge with minutes to spare. We'll just need to approach the moon's orbit carefully. I'm confident we can do it."

"About the ETTs…" I said. "They may not be in working order. We may need to use the shuttle. But it's very possible to land the shuttle within a minute or two."

Or so I hoped.

Once more I felt that familiar sinking feeling somewhere between my heart and my gut, but I swallowed it down.

"Wait a minute," Bog said sharply. "How can we even know for sure that the Dirge is there?"

"He'll be there," Caesar said. "Of this I'm certain."

I found it odd that he would offer up such a certainty, given how difficult he had been with us so far. And I didn't like the look of that curious smirk at the corner of his mouth. Was he even aware of it?

"I don't feel that we have much choice," I said, looking towards Bog to gauge his opinion.

Bog turned to Caesar. "If you betray us, I will break every bone in your body."

And on that light note, our meeting with Caesar concluded.

"Captain, we're approaching the first beacon," Sparling reported twelve hours later. We were sitting at our stations in the control hub.

"Good." I stood up from my chair. "Put it on the viewscreen."

The beacon was almost indistinguishable from random space junk. If our attenuators hadn't been set to such high sensitivity, it would have been easy to overlook.

In fact, the beacon was smaller than an average-sized dog and looked like a squat metallic cylinder. It didn't seem to have any lights to draw attention to it. It was well designed in that sense. Only a few surface ridges gave any indication that this was anything other than a chunk of debris.

I looked over at Caesar and pointed to him, giving him the cue to enter the remote deactivation sequence. I didn't trust him, but Bog was towering over his shoulder, watching every move to ensure he didn't do something to screw us.

I sat back down. "I want feedback."

"Yes, Captain of Militia," Caesar replied with a hint of annoyance. His name for me was irksome but I shrugged it off.

I stared down at my chair's armrest and touched the screen, receiving a slight jolt of electricity for my trouble. It was good to know my personal equipment was as reliable as ever.

However, I had a trump card up my sleeve. Without anyone's knowledge, I activated one of my own spatial attenuators, so small that it was barely larger than a single human cell. From my armrest panel, I was able to force it up to the side of the beacon, getting close enough to relay accurate information about the beacon's configuration. The details appeared on my control panel. In moments I could tell the ambient temperature within the device, how it was wired, and even read the scribbling of some disheartened factory shopworker who had apparently thought someone named Jofu could suck one his, uh, appendages...

I chose not to think too much about this and continued to monitor the work being performed by Caesar. I looked up at Bog, who nodded his approval of the man's work. But something in my mind still screamed for us to be careful. I didn't ignore that voice, even though I couldn't see any reason to be so concerned.

Suddenly, my attenuator detected a quick pulse of energy—and then the beacon went dead. I frowned. What had just happened?

"Success, Captain," Caesar said with satisfaction.

I checked with Bog first, who nodded.

"Good," I said, still feeling distrustful. "How long before we reach the minefield?"

Caesar looked down at his screen. "Five hours and two minutes."

"Okay. Agent Sparling, let us know when we're one hundred thousand kilometres from the nearest mine. Until then, we have some practicing to attend to."

Bog escorted Caesar to the control hub's doorway. I followed them out.

We made our way down to the cargo bay, the only areas on the ship large enough for practical demonstrations—and not lined with shag carpeting or plants.

The fake mine was held in place by one of the dilaxan grapplers that the Prime technicians had been nice enough to gift us. They were of a better quality and much longer length than the ones *Orbital* had employed. I suspected we could snag a Telnian cow from kilometres away—if that cow was floating in space, that was.

As we got down to business, Caesar began assembling a mock-up of one of the mines. With Simbden's and Bog's help, and the use of several banks of equipment, it took them the better part of two hours.

I had reluctantly agreed that it would be best to defuse the mine inside *Orbital* herself. I had argued passionately that I didn't want to bring a warhead like that into the ship, but the alternative was that the men would have to work on the mine while in space. That would make completing the task much more difficult—and should something go wrong, none of them would survive the blast. At least aboard *Orbital* they would have gravity, an atmosphere, and the option of calling for help.

By the end of the process, we had a proportionally accurate mine.

"Good work, gentlemen," Caesar said enthusiastically. "Final tests check out. Now, let's get to work."

I watched as he leaned down towards the mock-up.

"Hold on a second," I said. "If there's no warhead, how will we know if we've succeeded in disarming it?"

Caesar's reply was quick. "We have this covered, Captain Militia." I noticed that the name he gave me was shortening.

Simbden then took over with the explanation. "My captain, I've used some integrated circuitry to rig up a panel that will trigger an alarm in case of failure."

"Sounds good to me." But something struck me as being off about the whole operation. "Where off *Orbital* did you usurp this integrated circuitry, exactly?"

"Nowhere important, Brant," Bog said a little too quickly for my liking.

That made me tense up in suspicion. He rarely called me by my first name.

"Yeah, I recognize that tone in your voice," I said. "Last time you used it was when you slept with my third cousin's cousin—in my bed, no less. You even spilled a tankard of Warvian ale on my pillowcase. So I want answers, now."

They all looked around sheepishly as I became more annoyed. A sensation of doom crept over me and their aloofness didn't help the situation.

"Er, we got it off the resistor assembly running along the support column in Common Room 2A," Bog said. "Its use wasn't critical."

I scratched my chin in deep thought, wondering why that particular common room sounded so familiar.

Then it struck me. "Hold on. Which system or device did that circuitry contribute to?"

"Well, nothing critical to our safety," Bog said offhandedly. "It was on the BodyBake 75."

"What!" I exclaimed. "That's my personal tanning bed. Is nothing at all sacred to you guys?!"

Perhaps I was letting my personal concerns overrun my decision-making process, but I was startled.

"I'm sorry, my captain," Simbden said. "I looked thoroughly around the ship, and this was the only component that I knew for certain would work in the small time I had to put this together."

"Well, can I get it reinstalled when we're done?"

"Of course, Captain Militia," Caesar assured me.

I sighed a deep breath of relief.

"Unless the primary resistors backsurge," Simbden added, to which Caesar gave him a dark look.

I felt the tears well up in my soul. "And how likely is that?"

"About fifty percent, my captain."

The look of guilt on Simbden's face was the only reason I didn't personally tear that circuitry off the mock-up and head back to my quarters for a Martian Breeze.

Well, that and I had absolutely no idea which specific bit of circuitry it was or how to reinstall it in the tanning bed. My hands shook as I clenched them.

"Let's just fucking start already," I said in frustration. "If my BodyBake 75 isn't operational by the end of the week, I'll have you three lifting Queel goo from the shag carpeting."

Bog replied a little too quickly: "I can handle th—"

"And you'll be using only your tongues to do so," I interrupted.

That shut him up completely. He could only nod and look very intently on the now life-and-death struggle with the mocked-up mine.

After a couple of tense moments, I remembered why we were here.

"Okay, let's get this wagon rolling, shall we?" I paused. "What do we have to do?"

"Well, it's a long process," Caesar explained. "There are forty-three steps—"

"Forty-three steps? Seriously! We'll be here all day on one trial."

"That's only to shut down the mine's shaded functions," Bog said. "There are another one hundred twenty-two steps to shut the mine down completely."

"Holy fuck," I stated with dismay.

"Exactly," my big friend responded. "I zoned out after they began describing the first twenty-six."

"Can we get started already?" Caesar asked testily.

I could swear I saw his eyes flash gold again, but I didn't have the time to ponder it any further. Before I could say anything, Simbden flipped the on-switch, which simulated the approach of a ship equipped with a power source like ours.

I watched the fake mine carefully. Its hull had a string of lights that flashed several different colours. I could surmise that the lights we had chosen probably wouldn't be identical to the ones on the real mine. It almost looked like these lights had come from my Christmas tree decorations, the ones I'd lost five years ago.

Nevertheless, they served their purpose and twinkled prettily.

Note to Brant Zenith: reinstate holiday gift-giving. It looks like I may need another BodyBake 75.

"Now, pay attention, big man." Caesar was hunched over the mine, but his comment was directed at Bog.

I thought Bog was going to lift the frail little man into the air and force him down onto the mine's tiny protrusions. Luckily for us all, the Nova Martian managed to contain his anger.

Caesar began his explanation of the mine. "It's been many, many years since I last saw one of these, so my memory may be a little rusty. But not all the steps are dangerous. Most are relatively simple. There are only a few very difficult parts…"

He began going through the process, point by point. It wasn't as bad as I had expected it to be, for the most part. Caesar spoke truly, as many of the steps were paint-by-numbers: "Turn control switch ninety degrees, cut green wire, attach green wire to red wire," etc. But there would definitely be some harrowing moments along the way.

Caesar then turned to the finer details in defusing the warhead. Bog, although often exhibiting signs of childishness, was keen to understand everything the old, wispy-haired man had to say when it involved weaponry. My Nova Martian brother had always been talented that way. That didn't, however, mean that Bog was perfect in each of his attempts to defuse the warhead.

When the first mistake occurred, we were all caught off-guard. We braced ourselves for the sensation of shock, dismay, and death… instead the mine, being a mock-up, gave off a noise that sounded more like a Telnian cow: "Mmmmmoooooooo!" But the alarm was deafening. I put my hands to my ears and wondered if the worm Daisee had put in my ear might burrow its way out to escape.

The infernal mooing continued for what felt like forever. It didn't even have the good grace to sound like an Earth cow but rather the underlying gurgle of the gaudier Telnian variety.

"What the hell is that?" I yelled at no one in particular. Everyone had their hands to their ears like I did.

I looked around the cargo bay and thought I could feel the walls sway with the rumbling moo. In fact, the mooing continued to blare in our ears for two more minutes, and I swore I could feel myself growing an udder and slew of teats.

"Would someone shut that freakin' thing off already?" I exclaimed over the device's gurgling protestations.

"I am very sorry, my captain," Simbden said, sheepishly clasping his hands in stress. "I accidentally set the alarm for thirty minutes, not thirty seconds."

I shouted directly into the young engineer's ears. "Aww, fuck. Well, isn't there a way to alter it now?"

"Not without permanently damaging the mine and all its components. Did you want me to try?"

"Fuck no!" I yelled in response. I didn't need my hearing that badly. "Well, I for one am coming back in half an hour."

I turned to exit the bay.

"Zenith, we can't leave!" Caesar grabbed my arm, much too firmly than I would have expected. I looked at him with surprise. "If any of us leave the cargo bay, we may inadvertently set the mine to self-destruct!"

"What?" I said, shocked. "You told me it wasn't armed."

"Not with a warhead of colossal destruction, but the energy source used to power this demonstration can still cause quite a blast," Caesar said. "I'm afraid we're all stuck right here for the next little while."

"Hell," I murmured under my breath.

And so we endured the racket for another twenty-eight minutes. Eventually the mooing died down, although the noise didn't entirely disappear. It transitioned into the morning wakeup call of a rooster.

I looked over at Bog peevishly, but he shrugged off his irritation.

When the alarm finally ended, blessed silence cascaded over my ears.

"Finally. Thank the Mackmian gods of fate!" I exclaimed, forgetting that there was a Mackmian standing right next to me.

"Well, now that that's over, let's get back into it, shall we?" Caesar said.

I nodded and the informant opened his mouth to continue his explanation of how to proceed. But first I had Simbden reset the alarm's duration to five seconds. I double-checked the readout and was satisfied that it was done.

After a few more trials, all of which were successful, we decided that we had more or less mastered the process. All was going well… until an argument broke out.

"So why the green shit do I have to handle this next part?" Bog asked defiantly, his horns and tusked flashing red in annoyance. He was referring to the upcoming step where he was to use his body as an insulator to disconnect a power relay and reconnect it elsewhere. I could tell he didn't like cowering for long periods of time over the complicated mine. He was growing more frustrated with each passing moment.

"Because you are the chief of security," I reminded him blandly.

Bog sighed. "Yes, but I have agreed to disarm the warhead. From there on out, the rest is an engineering puzzle."

It was Caesar who answered. "Simbden doesn't have the necessary attributes to succeed at—"

"What? Mackmians aren't good enough?"

"Well, quite honestly, no," Caesar said, turning to Simbden. He placed a hand on the slim young Mackmian's forearm. I think the old man genuinely liked him. "No offence to you, my young friend."

"So what 'attribute' is he missing?" Bog asked.

"A fat ass." Caesar looked back to Simbden and added genuinely, "No offence again, my young friend."

Apparently that was the wrong thing to say to both Bog *and* Simbden. Simbden seemed quite sad to hear that his ass wasn't fat enough, but Bog of course was upset to learn his ass was sufficiently fat.

I hadn't been aware Bog was so touchy about his weight! He pushed forward to crumple the old man and I had to step in to prevent geriatric bloodshed.

We were running out of valuable time, and I wouldn't put up with another word of contention between them.

Caesar took a couple of moments to think through his next response. "New Martian, after the circuitry is disconnected, the mine will attempt to pass energy through it anyway. We will need a barrier to withstand those attempts, and unfortunately the only workable type of barrier is organic. In other words, your…" He paused, looking at Big, and considered his words carefully. "…ample posterior."

"Can't we use something else instead?" I asked, concerned. "I don't really like the idea of my chief of security being used as nothing more than an insulator."

"I'm afraid not."

"Aww, shit," Bog muttered. "I knew I shouldn't have eaten that second nugget of lava for breakfast."

The session finally came to an end, just a minute or so before we heard the staticky intercom fire up.

"Captain, we're one hundred thousand kilometres from the minefield," Sparling reported from her station in the control hub.

"Good, I'll be there momentarily." I turned to the others. "It's up to you fine men now. We have a lot riding on this, so be careful. Watch out for each other." I paused for dramatic effect. "And don't fuck it up."

I said this last bit with a smile. I thought a little humour may help lift their spirits.

I left them in the cargo bay as they began suiting up using the new batch of spacesuits we'd picked up at Prime Station Alpha.

When I got to the control hub, I sat in the captain's chair and looked up at the live feed of the minefield on the viewscreen. The mines were flashing a bright warning to all who would disturb their long slumber. They were almost mesmerizing, and I dimmed the lights in the control hub to accentuate the beauty of one of the most fantastic sights I'd ever seen.

"Black mamba," I whispered to myself, forcing myself to remember that we were potentially only minutes away from our deaths. "Send word to our Brunken friends following us to stay back until we deal with the mine." I ordered and Mara obeyed.

"Message sent." She replied. After a few moments she spoke up again. "The Brunken have confirmed that they will not move forward until instructed to do so."

"Good." I did not wish for them to get caught up in this anymore than was necessary. I looked out towards the field again.

As Caesar had explained, the mines would remain unshaded until an approaching ship came within a thousand kilometres of them. But from here, I could make out the beams of energy crisscrossing between them, forming a deadly grid.

No doubt most visitors would choose not to venture too close. Most were either less desperate or more intelligent than I was.

"Okay, Stairn, give me a report," I said, never taking my eyes off the screen.

"Approximately thirty-two million mines in orbit around Obsidian. Obsidian is only ten million kilometres past the minefield."

Mara let out a long exhalation. "Wow."

"Agent Sparling, hold position here for a while."

I stood up and stepped closer to Stairn. I handed him the diagnostic pad with the record of what my spatial attenuator had picked up when we had first approached Obsidian several hours ago. I still wanted to know what was behind that brief pulse of energy I'd detected before the beacon went dead.

When I spoke to him, my voice was soft and quiet so as not to alert or surprise the others. "What do you know?"

Stairn's eyes lit up, and from his reaction I could tell he knew something was up. "Very curious, Captain."

"Can you elaborate?"

"I don't think the energy pulse was either imaginary or accidental."

"Anything else?"

"I don't know enough. There could be so many reasons for the pulse, only some of which are suspicious. I'm sorry." He paused. "Nevertheless, we should be prepared."

I had hoped he could shed some light on the situation, but I would have to make do. The main problem weighing on me was that Caesar hadn't wanted to guide us here. Then, when we had reached the beacon, he had deactivated it… and then I had noticed that brief pulse of energy. What had caused it?

I decided to let my nagging suspicions roam freely a while longer.

"Agent Sparling, bring us in." I tapped on my wristband communicator and spoke to the officers down in the cargo bay. "All right, gentlemen. Showtime."

Sparling brought us within two thousand kilometres of the nearest mine. We got to within scant metres of triggering it and consequently letting all thirty-two million other mines know of our existence.

I drew a deep breath. "Now, Agent."

I watched Sparling reach for the newly installed dilaxan grappler controls, then let out my breath as I saw the grappler cable snake away from the ship and strike true. The ultra-thin line, at least as thin as fishing wire, was impossible to see even with our viewscreen centred directly on it. But they had a high tensile strength from what I understood of them.

Stairn proceeded to fire a modified sonic pulse through the grappler, detaching the mine from its attached communications array. Now it couldn't warn the other mines of *Orbital*'s proximity.

If we had failed, several dozen nearby mines would have locked on to it, tracked us down, and blown our pretty little asses halfway across the universe.

But we hadn't failed, and it was now safe to pull the mine into the cargo bay. Well, as safe as it could be to bring aboard a hundred-kilogram weapon of colossal destruction!

I watched on the screen as the cargo bay doors opened and the mine disappeared inside. I switched the view to an internal camera showing a wide angle of the cargo bay. Already my crew was busy with their efforts to deactivate the mine.

"My captain, the mine is properly secured," Simbden reported over the intercom.

I exhaled deeply. "Good work."

Stage two. All I could do was wait. I couldn't leave the control hub to check on my crew's progress, since if anything went wrong I would need to be in command to help fend off the other thirty-two million mines. Letting others do the dirty work was the hardest part of this stage of the mission. I hated feeling helpless.

"My captain, we are dismantling the outer shell," said Simbden in a shaky voice.

"Good. Be careful."

Clang! The sound reverberated out of the cargo bay and into my ears like I was sitting inside a giant bell. Holy fuck, that had been deafening.

At least we weren't dead yet.

"Report!" I demanded tersely. "What happened?"

"It's okay," Bog called over the com channel.

I leaned forward. "Is the warhead intact?"

"Yeah. I just dropped the god-damned cover panel on my toe."

"How's the mine?"

Bog paused, but only for a moment. "How's my toe?"

"I have a bottle of EZ-Heal to help you with that," I replied. "But it won't do any good if we're all dead. Now report."

"The warhead is fine. I'm beginning to dismantle it now."

I stared tensely at the viewscreen, watching their progress. But the screen didn't offer the high-definition views I would have liked; it was static-filled and showed no colour. I supposed it was better than nothing.

I saw Bog proceed exactly as we had practiced for the past several hours. Sweat formed on my forehead as my friend pulled the warhead away from the casing. Then Bog used a smaller version of the ship's dilaxan grappler and attached it electromagnetically to the warhead's arm. It hung there, momentarily out of the way.

After twenty minutes, I breathed a huge sigh of relief as the mine shut down, deactivated. Theoretically, the worst was over.

That's when everything turned into a sour pile of Telnian cow shit. We hadn't known, couldn't have known, that each mine had a security feature that fired up when the warhead was disconnected from the rest of the mine.

As I watched, a bright jolt of electricity arced up from the inner circuitry and hammered into the communications array. Bog was no longer standing between the two; if he had, his body would have absorbed the electrical current and prevented the mine from activating. At what cost to his health, I would never know.

The communications array on the mine came back to life and sent out proximity signals to the neighbouring mines. I looked to the control hub's main viewscreen in time to see the nearest mines light up like fireflies. They shot forth beams of light as they began closing in on us.

Before I could call out an order, they all turned invisible. Death was about to rain down on our heads.

"Report!" I called.

"Six mines have shaded," Stairn stated calmly. I envied his ability to do so. "They seem to be homing in on our position."

I mashed my hand into my wristband communicator. "Zenith to Bog."

"Go for Bog."

"Six nearby mines have locked onto us. We're being targeted."

"Fuck me."

I couldn't have said it better myself.

"My captain, the warhead is deactivated," Simbden said. "Can we jettison the mine away from the ship and leave the others to chase it instead of us?"

Good question. I was surprised he had thought of it before me.

"That won't work," Caesar interrupted, clearly panicked too. "These six mines are no longer chasing the location beacon on this mine, but rather our unique signature."

If I had suspected him of causing this, those suspicions fell fast away. I understood and recognized true fear when I heard it.

"What if we jettison our communication array?" I suggested.

"Would the mines go after it?"

Caesar thought about it for a moment. "That could work. But we wouldn't have long before their sensors reoriented to us. Even so, how would we escape the mines? They have very high-speed capabilities."

I could feel time slipping away, like the droplets of sweat running down my face. We only had moments, not minutes, before the mines detonated on us.

"I have another idea," I said. "If this mine were to explode, might the others assume we had been destroyed as well?"

"You're smarter than I would have guessed, Captain Militia," Caesar said quickly. I couldn't tell if the compliment outweighed the implied insult. I didn't care. "We've discovered the exact carrier wave of this mine, so we may be able to use it to trick the other mines into registering us as a neutralized target."

"Well, theoretically," Stairn cut in.

"Yes, theoretically. But we have no other options right now." I turned to Sparling. "Veer us as far from the incoming mines as possible. I know we can't track them, but make your best guess as to where they are and head away."

"Yes, sir."

The seconds of that minute were very trying as they ticked slowly by. Facing a life-threatening situation was difficult, but the pumping of adrenaline made it bearable; this, on the other hand, was torture.

"My captain, it's ready!" Simbden shouted.

At that moment, the ship veered so heavily to starboard that our atmospheric stabilizers failed to compensate. I had to grab hold of my armrests to stay in the chair.

I looked first at the viewscreen, then up at the large domed window over my head in time to see the rematerialized mine whip by our hull. We had missed it by less than a metre.

"Jettison the mine's warhead *now!*" I screamed through the crackling intercom.

Using my armrest controls, I brought up *Orbital*'s rear view on the viewscreen—just in time to see another mine whiz right by us. Thank the Mackmian gods of fate for Sparling's incredible piloting skills!

Even so, we had only seconds to live.

On the screen, I saw the guts of the mine launch out of the cargo bay doors. As it fell away from us, the warhead detonated in a bright explosion and I held tight to my chair as the impact rocked *Orbital*.

"Did it work?" I demanded aloud.

Just as the words left my mouth, the other six mines unshaded and shut down with a sound reminiscent of a whistle.

"The mines have disengaged," Stairn said calmly.

"Zenith to the cargo bay," I shouted, less calmly. "How is everyone down there?"

The answer came from Simbden. "All is well."

"Good. Return to your stations."

I breathed a sigh of relief, but the relief gave way quickly as the next wave of sheer panic rolled over me.

"Captain, the Society Sentinel Drone has detected us," Stairn reported. "It's ten million kilometres away and closing."

"Sparling, how long do we have?" I asked.

"Forty-five seconds, s–sir…"

"Shit."

Suddenly, Bog's voice came in on the communication channel.

"Caesar vanished from the cargo bay," Bog said. "I've looked everywhere, but I think he used black rift transport."

Fuck! I swore to myself.

"Keep looking for him!" I shouted, panicked, furious. That dick Caesar! My mind fumed.

I realized that he must have had the black rift transport on him the whole time. I gave him credit for not using it while being "trapped" in the lavatory. That had demonstrated some extreme restraint.

But I had to focus on the more dangerous situation: the drone. I quickly went to work on my armrest screen, bringing up weapons control. But I doubted any of our shitty armaments would be nearly powerful enough to save us. Propulsion cannons would attack the drone too late and the ballistic space torpedoes were probably much too slow and ungainly to take it down.

"Incoming!" Sparling warned.

The drone filled the viewscreen, but it was misleadingly small and careened right by us at what felt like lightspeed. The lights began to flicker and waver across all our computer monitors. What the hell? I hadn't even seen an attack.

The drone drifted out of view.

Before I could contemplate it further, though, it swung around and came at us a second time. We had an agile, thinking weapon hunting us down.

I had to trust my experience and gut. "Sparling, I need our bow facing the drone."

"Captain, an escape pod has just been launched," Stairn reported behind me. "It's on course for Obsidian."

"Bog!" I yelled, slamming on my wristband communicator.

The device gave me a jolt. I wondered if I had hit it too hard... or had the drone messed that up for us too? Regardless, it was at the shittiest of timing.

"Sparling, fire the dilaxan cable!"

She had used the dilaxan cable on the mine, so I hoped she could use it again on the escape pod.

"Captain..." She hesitated, her screens blinking on and off. "...I can't access it."

Desperate, I swivelled to face Stairn and my expression must have conveyed the emotions coursing through me. I don't know how he knew what I was thinking, but he shot up out of his chair and hurried out of the control hub, disappearing faster than a cupcake in a room full of Mackmians.

I didn't know if the computers in the cargo bay were suffering from the same inconvenient troubles we were having up here, but I knew the cargo bay was well engineered. Perhaps it had a chance...

The seconds ticked by like an uphill-flowing avalanche, impossibly slow. I wondered if Stairn was already in the cargo bay. I had no way of knowing.

Suddenly, our screen flared to life.

"Fantastic!" I shouted. "Sparling, try your dilaxan cable!"

"I *am* trying. Controls are still unresponsive…"

I knew we were on the moon base's doorstep now, so I no longer had any time to ponder Caesar's betrayal. The drone had swooped up from below, its immense weapons glowing blue with raw power. I could practically feel the air molecules around me vibrate in anticipation.

But at least we were regaining control of the ship. Using the buttons on my armrest, I locked in on the fast-moving drone as well as I could and let loose *Orbital*'s full complement of weapons. They were nothing more than propulsion blasts, but at least we were in very close proximity.

I couldn't see anything on the viewscreen. Not knowing whether it had worked, I fired again and again, barely taking a moment to check whether the drone was still intact and on approach.

When I stopped firing, I saw that the drone had powered down its weapons. It changed course, turned away from us, and shaded.

My crew and I awaited another attack, but seconds went by and nothing happened. Was it possible? Had my attack struck true? The propulsion guns couldn't have damaged the drone, could they? I hadn't hit any specifically critical system as far as I could tell.

Instead I had worked off a hunch. Back during a previous visit to Prime Station Alpha, years ago, I had encountered a drone that was so finetuned against powerful weapons that it hadn't responded at all to propulsion blasts that fell beneath its detection threshold. If it didn't recognize a target as a threat, it ceased to engage that target.

Perhaps these Society Sentinel Drones had been programmed with the same flaw? Still, I wasn't sure of that. Was there something more at play here?

In the meantime, I didn't know where the drone had gone. I hoped it wouldn't be quick to return.

My mind flashed back to the problem of Caesar Roman. We couldn't let him get away.

"Stairn, what's your status!"

I hoped that Stairn could hear me and that he'd met with greater success in the cargo bay than we had here.

I pulled up the live feed on our viewscreen from the cargo bay just as the logistics officer hurtled into the room at inhuman speeds. How had he managed to get all the way down there in just thirty seconds?

Stairn flew past the remaining escape pods, only recently replenished since the visit to Prime Station Alpha, his legs pumping almost frictionlessly against the metal flooring. He practically crashed into the mounted dilaxan cable grappler.

It only took him a handful of seconds to load the grappler and fishing-wire-thin cable into the mount. He activated it and found his target through the open cargo bay door. He pulled up the computer monitor for aiming and firing.

As I watched, Stairn hit the trigger.

A normal officer, I suspected, would have had less than a five percent chance, give or take, of successfully reeling in the escape pod. But Stairn was no normal officer, as I'd discovered over and over in the course of recent events.

I switched to an external view to see the grappler loose itself toward the pod, the attached cable unspooling behind it; I just hoped the cable was long enough…

With all but a few centimetres of cable remaining, the grappler struck the side of the escape pod, sticking into the hull with a steadfast electromagnetic pull.

And just like that, Caesar's attempt to escape was over.

"Captain, this is Stairn," he reported back. "We have the escape pod tethered. Unless he's willing to jettison himself from the pod, he isn't going anywhere."

"Good work, Stairn," I exclaimed in a hushed manner, surprised by and thankful for the feat.

I finally began to allow myself to relax—

"My captain, what is happening?" I knew it was Simbden over the intercom, of course. And he sounded tense.

"Everything's okay for now, Simbden."

But the Mackmian's voice was still nervous. "Something is happening to the ship…"

My own nerves once again flickered like a candle. "What do you mean?"

"Can you feel it?" he asked. "The ship isn't right, my captain. I can't explain. The internal spatial attenuators are motionless."

I looked down at the internal readouts from the millions of microscopic spatial attenuators inside the ship. They were always on the move, but Simbden had told the truth; they were completely still. What the hell was going on? Perhaps it was a latent malfunction from all the damage and stress *Orbital* kept taking?

"What the shit is that!" Bog shouted from his station.

Mara replied with shock and dismay. "It can't be!"

"What can't be?" I asked impatiently. The viewscreen showed nothing.

Then I thought to look up through the domed glass ceiling, and there I saw something impossible: a pink-coloured haze floating down towards us. Whatever this substance was, it surrounded us very quickly. It permeated itself right through to our interior, as if *Orbital*'s hull were nothing more than a cheese cloth.

How had it done so?

That's when things turned truly strange. I could feel my body slowing down, the blood in my veins pumping less quickly, and my thoughts beginning to dawdle. I gazed at each member of my crew, but my eyes were sluggish to respond. Even the light seemed to be hitting my irises in a delayed manner. I could see that everyone had a hugely bewildered look on their face.

Time itself crept slower and slower. I felt like I was being overtaken by a glacier, but of course there was no cold. Or heat, for that matter. Just a deadly stillness in the air.

The haze grew heavier, and I struggled to keep my eyes open… and finally I couldn't help it anymore. My body fell limp, my eyes closed, and the world went black.

CHAPTER TWENTY

Haze of Lies

My eyes reopened to the hazy aftermath of whatever had happened to me. It took several long minutes to understand that my face was planted on the floor. As my senses snapped into alignment, I felt the scratchy texture of the shag carpet and smelled the putrid sour milk aroma wafting off it.

As quickly as I could, I pushed myself onto my hands and knees. The situation didn't look favourable. My entire crew remained sprawled on the floor, much like I had been moments ago. I could only guess why I had been the first to awaken, but it might have had something to do with my high tolerance for narcotics.

My movements were difficult at first. With my hands numb and shaking, I struggled to pull myself up from my chair. It took a few moments to get my feet under me and move again with any certainty.

It took me another several moments to remember what had transpired just before we'd all blacked out. Then a certain thought hit my muddled mind: *Caesar!*

Remembering his betrayal, I hurried to Stairn's controls and confirmed that the escape pod and grappler were still attached to *Orbital*. And upon inspection I could tell there was still one lifeform inside. That was a good sign.

But whatever had affected us had also affected the escape pod, since it too was in a state of hibernation.

That's when I noticed the date on the screen and the realization hit me, with the force of an avalanche of Telnian cow dung, that we'd lost three days. Three days! Fuck!

I got down to the business of awakening my troops. Since Sparling was closest to me, I started with her. She was groggy and disoriented but otherwise seemed unharmed. After a few minutes, she retook her post.

"Keep us steady and moving away from this hellhole," I commanded.

She didn't need to be told twice.

I continued waking the others, although I decided not to bother running down to the infirmary to check on Daisee. For now, I would just assume she was all right. Brunken were built like tanks and I felt confident that she was fine like the rest of the crew.

The doors opened and Stairn stumbled into the control hub. A moment later, Bog followed in; he too looked a little woozy on his feet.

"Captain, the escape pod doesn't have enough power to sustain its atmospheric stabilizers much longer," Agent Sparling said. "What are your orders?"

"Just leave it the hell out there," Bog rumbled. "Or better yet, let me shoot it down."

Bog went so far as to reach for his weapons controls.

"No," I said, ice filling my veins. I didn't feel merciful, but revenge would do me no good. "Pull him in."

"Really?!" Bog's large mouth frowned at me, the lava-like saliva hanging dangerously from one of his lower tusks. I noticed at that moment that Bog did not appear to be suffering from the three consecutive days of below ideal temperatures he was susceptible to.

I had to guess this was a good sign that the haze that engulfed us somehow excluded him from the temperature difference.

"Really." I responded. "And bring him up here. I'm done with his games. It's time he answered for his actions."

That made Bog feel a little better as he lumbered out of the control hub and made his way down to the cargo bay.

I truly doubted we had the time to meet the Dirge anymore, not after all this lost time. If we rushed into Obsidian, could we still pull it off? The viewscreen showed the cloud of pinkish haze we had just passed through. It was almost pretty to the eyes.

"Sparling, where is the Brunken ship?"

Her fingers danced over the controls for a moment before bringing up some readings of the Brunken warship, which had been following close behind us ever since it had left Daisee in our care and departed. It appeared they were several hours or longer in our wake, drifting in the middle of the pink haze.

"What shall we do to help them?" Mara asked.

"Nothing," I said. "They appear to be unharmed, just as we are. They'll exit that pink expanse soon enough, and I'm not going to risk re-entering it."

I didn't like leaving them on their own, but we couldn't afford to fall even further behind schedule and fail to get to Mondo 4 on time. As it was, we were going to be cutting it close.

The intercom crackled to life.

"My captain," Simbden spoke from the engine room, "can you please tell me what's going on?"

"I don't know yet. How are the engines?"

He didn't hesitate. "Engines are beginning to function normally again, my captain. I expect them to be back to eighty percent in the next fifteen minutes."

"That's good." I felt greatly relieved. The last thing we needed at this point in our mission was to be dead in space.

The intercom continued to crackle. "My captain, can I see you in private?"

"Can it wait, Simbden? I have a certain informant I need to deal with right now."

"Well, it's about Caesar Roman, sir."

That caught my immediate attention. My response was equally quick. "I'll come to you."

I looked over at Stairn. "When Bog returns with our *guest*, make sure he stays put here. I will return soon."

"Of course, Captain."

I flew out of the control hub, not having realized just how full of angst and frustration I was. After ten seconds of walking, I broke into a run. My legs were still wobbly so I couldn't quite move at full speed and I managed to bump into a couple of walls, thankful for the first time ever that they were covered in shag carpet.

Something was definitely wrong; I could feel it. As timid as he was, Simbden would not have called me down without a very good reason.

By the time I reached the engine room, I was short of breath. "Simbden. You have something important to say. Tell me now."

Given a hundred guesses as to what he might say, I would never have gotten it right. "My captain, Caesar Roman does not smell right."

I listened intently as Simbden continued his very surprising story.

"Captain Zenith, things did not go as planned," Caesar stated omitting his nickname for me this time. His eyes afire and his body completely erect—more than I may have expected from someone who looked to be about three hundred solar cycles in age.

Only minutes ago, he had been slumped over in his chair, his eyes hazy. The strange suspension we'd been trapped in for the past three days had hit him even harder in the escape pod than it had us in *Orbital*.

But he had recovered remarkably quickly after we pulled him out.

"Oh, it sure as hell came close, though, didn't it, Caesar?" I said.

We had once again gathered in the dank, dreary conference room since I didn't trust Caesar to be anywhere near the control hub. Flanking the prisoner were Stairn and Bog.

I couldn't have been more pissed off at anyone than I was at Caesar at that moment. It was one thing to screw with me, my ship, and my crew. But it was unforgivable to have risked the lives of hundreds of millions of innocent Mondorians.

His old, wrinkly face contorted in thought. I think he knew he was screwed.

"Captain Zenith, I couldn't betray the Dirge," he said. "He's my friend. I hope you understand."

And I did understand. I understood very well, for the first time since I'd met him. It had taken me several long minutes while walking back from my talk with Simbden to piece it all together. At last, I had the final piece of the puzzle that had been eluding me for the past several days.

"What are you?" I asked, stepping in close. I stared into his grey eyes and the prominent lines surrounding them.

He stood up and took a defensive posture, his hands raised in front of him. "Captain, I don't know what you mean."

My patience, hanging by a thread, finally snapped. I grabbed him by the throat and slammed his wrinkly, sagging frame up against the wall.

"That was a deceptive question," I said in a deadly whisper that only Caesar could hear. "I was simply giving you the chance to finally tell me the truth. I know what you are."

His eyes widened as he began to comprehend that I wasn't bluffing.

I placed the tip of my propulsion gun to his forehead. "Now, Dirge, if you don't wish to breathe through your forehead, end this whole irritating act."

"How could you know?" he asked as the seconds ticked by. His wrinkled eyes were no longer wide in surprise. He seemed to have recovered quickly from my assertion.

"There were clues. You aren't quite as clever and cautious as you believe," I said. He looked sceptical. "Twice I grabbed your arm and twice it felt like that of a much younger man. I believe it's time to drop the disguise, don't you think?"

I almost missed his briefest of nods. The wrinkles on his face began to tighten and his pale skin turned golden and tanned. Next, his white, wispy hair grew out to shoulder-length, dark and thick. Most surprisingly, his eyes went from light grey to intense gold. His shape remained humanoid, but his posture corrected itself and he grew several centimetres taller. He looked human enough, except for his eyes and earlobes, which were pointed downward and slightly forward.

All of this happened in seconds. And if I hadn't felt inclined to perforate his entire body with propulsion blasts, I would have admitted that he had transformed into a damned handsome young man.

Doppelgangers were extremely rare, even in a galaxy as immense as this one. I had only heard of them in drunken legends spoken in out of the way drinking dens in the seedier corners of dangerous solar systems. But I'd learned a long time ago never to doubt the existence of anything; the universe had a way of surprising us all.

From my peripheral vision, I saw Bog and Stairn step closer, their arms raised, each with a weapon in hand. Bog's breathing intensified into louder, shallower breaths. Knowing him as well as I did told me that Caesar's transformation had caught him by surprise.

Stairn, on the other hand, seemed to be more relaxed. I guess he felt confident dealing with the Dirge as he was now brandishing his weapon.

I continued watching the final moments of Caesar's transformation. Not only had his physical appearance changed, but so had his clothing. I found that odd. Instead of baggy, worn clothes, the man now sported a form-fitting flight suit in black and red. The sleeves covered his arms and hands completely, only leaving his fingers to poke free.

"First things first," I said. "Caesar, or Dirge, or whatever the hell you call yourself, what was that hazy effect we just passed through?"

I pointed at the image of the Brunken ship on the screen built into the conference room table. At the speed they were drifting, they were perhaps a few more days back.

When Caesar spoke again, his voice sounded young and exotic—almost musical. "Yes, that was my trump card in case I ever fell in with someone who wouldn't be easily dissuaded from causing me harm."

"Explain," I demanded.

"It's a rare technology I stumbled upon some time back."

I raised my weapon again and pressed it to his forehead. I got the sense he didn't like how it felt.

"Captain, please, can we keep this more relaxed?" he asked.

I stepped back but kept my arm raised. The pistol never ventured further than a metre from his head. After a few seconds, he understood that this was all the courtesy I was willing to lend.

"I thought I told you to explain."

He sighed. "It's known as the miasma, and it's harmless. It's a suspension barrier that serves as the last line of defence for my home here."

"Well, it worked great, except you failed in your escape." I wasn't sure if I should feel impressed or insulted by the man's action. I felt that I deserved more for having saved his life.

"*Orbital* and the Brunken ship were supposed to be stranded for the better part of a week." He seemed to get visibly angry. I didn't think he was used to having his defences work so imperfectly. "Zenith, your ship is unusual."

"That's one way to describe it."

"You mock her, but the miasma should have penetrated all of *Orbital*'s systems much more quickly and for much longer."

Bog snarled. "Well, I'm glad your escape plan got screwed."

"My plan was good, but yes, the escape was... imperfect. I was delayed by your new medic. She is a forceful creature! I was through the hallway and halfway to the escape pod when I was grabbed from behind and dragged into the infirmary for an impromptu examination." He blushed. "It was very embarrassing. And it prevented me from getting away in time."

I smiled inwardly as I realized just how useful Daisee could be. It seemed she had intervened by pure luck.

Note to Brant Zenith: promote Daisee to chief medical... ah, screw it. We don't have any other medical officers anyway...

"Embarrassing?" I said. "I'm sure it was."

I peered out the window and noticed the stars skimming by more quickly than before. *Orbital* was pushing its engines to reach Mondo 4. And it was a good thing; we had only one day before that mysterious grey void released the system from its grip. I had wanted nothing more than to get there early, but I just had to let it go.

I looked down at Caesar's wrists and even beneath the clothing I noticed something that hadn't drawn my attention before. Just below the fabric on his wrist, something left a slight bulge. I pointed to his right forearm and the circlet held tightly around it.

"I would like to see that," I said, feeling a hunch coming on.

It took him a moment to understand what I meant and another to appreciate that I understood the very thing he had been trying to hide. He eventually smiled and pulled up his right sleeve.

I heard Bog whistle in surprise. Even Stairn, normally implacable, showed renewed signs of interest at the almost unheard-of sight.

Caesar had a Militon chain, and it glowed a pale blue. The chain looked more like tendrils of a vine, intertwining and disappearing up Caesar's forearm. The power radiating through the chain was almost palpable.

I couldn't disguise my admiration. "It's been some time since I saw one of these…"

"You've seen one before, Zenith?" Caesar seemed to doubt me.

"I have. But that's not important right now."

"You're wondering whether you can remove it from me."

"Not at all." But it came out so quickly that even I was taken aback. I knew that a Militon chain couldn't be removed from its owner by force. Even death couldn't part an owner from his chain; when the wearer died, the chain simply ceased to exist or so I had learned.

As far as I knew, an owner couldn't even give away a Militon chain once it had been worn.

Every Militon chain was a bit different, but one thing always remained the same: they were impossible to fully understand.

"What is it you want with me, Zenith?" His posture was still fully erect, and his golden eyes shone like embers. I detected great intelligence within him, and his eyes looked aflame.

I gave his question some consideration and decided to set aside the issue of the Militon chain. What we really needed was information before we arrived at the Mondo system.

"I want to know everything you can tell me about what's happening to Mondo 4."

I knew this could take some time and pointed to the seat next to mine, giving him permission to sit. I then pressed the intercom control on the table and called for Mara to join us.

When Mara stepped in, she froze at the sight of Caesar and his greatly transformed appearance. I had to give her credit, though, for she only hesitated for a moment before taking the seat on the other side of me. The small surprise she showed, I thought, might have had more to do with the Militon chain than anything else. Besides, the chain itself is what might have given Caesar his shapeshifting ability.

"Now, Dirge, tell me what I want to know." My eyes flicked over to Mara when I called him the Dirge, watching as she put the pieces together.

"Please, Zenith, call me Caesar." He paused. "Mondo 4 is the fourth planet orbiting Mondo in the Mondo system—"

"Yes, of that much I am aware," I cut in. "Explain what's happening there."

"What do you mean?"

"What I mean is this: why the devil was Mondo's sun, and then its planets, swallowed up by a grey void?"

"Grey void? Mondo has been consumed by a grey void?" Now he appeared to be growing agitated.

"We've been periodically losing contact with the entire system," Mara said.

Caesar stood up in a panic. "That's impossible!"

I had to stand as well, and raise my gun in response. Caesar's face was contorted in shock and dismay. The fire in his eyes burned intently and it took a few seconds before he realized that he was staring once again at the barrel of my propulsion gun.

"It is quite possible," I said, "and happening as we speak."

"Why didn't you tell me before?" he asked quickly.

"Tell you what?"

"Tell me about Mondo 4, about Mondo, about this grey void."

"Right," Bog interjected. "Because you've been so trustworthy this far."

Caesar sat down again. I watched him intently, looking for some clue as to what he knew and why he seemed so shaken. According to everything we'd learned, he had escaped from the

Dawnstar immediately after the grey void had taken hold in the Mondo system.

I decided that it might be best to take the direct approach. "You escaped from the *Dawnstar* not too long ago. Don't you remember?"

"Of course I remember. But it was hardly an escape. I simply convinced the crew that I was nothing more than a traveller trying to get home to Saladan Prime. They never doubted me. There was no real security issue. They gave me a shuttle ride to a small asteroid base near Hayken. Shortly after, I was picked up by a Warvian trader who was happy for the company and dropped me off at Docentric."

"And you know nothing about the disappearance of the *Dawnstar* or what happened to the Mondo system?" I asked, not really believing the man. I could often tell when someone was lying, but it was difficult when the truth was so skilfully intermingled with untruth.

Which seemed to be the case every time the Dirge spoke.

"I don't know anything more about the *Dawnstar*," Caesar said. "I swear. I left them near Mondo 4."

I could believe only part of that story, and only because he was visibly shaken by what I'd told him about the grey void.

"Caesar, this would be so much easier if you would just stop being so damned suspicious." I paused, trying to figure out how to best phrase the thoughts swirling through my mind. "You know more than you're telling me. I'm not sure what it is, but you should know that we're on our way to help the Mondorians."

"Why you, Zenith?" he asked sceptically.

"Because Mondo 4 is located in Militia Space Fleet territory."

"That's not true. The Mondo system is in Prime space."

Bog shook his head. "Only a small portion."

"Yes," I said. "Only about five percent of the Mondo system is Prime. Mondo 4 and the star itself belong to the Militia, which is why we've been sent to help the Mondorians. But I can't help them effectively if you keep holding back critical information."

He paused to think about this. To grant him more space, I lowered my gun onto the table. I still had it in hand, but I didn't grip it or toy with the trigger. His internal conflict was obvious. He was a very good actor, but at the moment his true emotions seemed to be getting the better of him.

"You're right, Zenith," he finally said. "I know a great deal about Mondo 4, but I need to see some technical data about this grey void. Do you have any?"

Stairn had been listening intently to our conversation, his eyes hardly leaving Caesar's face. I wondered what he thought of the situation.

Looking down at the digital pad in his hand, I nodded to my logistics officer my approval.

Stairn handed Caesar the pad, and when the man read from it a look of shock and frustration rippled across his fiery eyes.

When he spoke next, his voice was subdued. "Zenith, I fear we must hurry."

"Our speed is already at maximum," Stairn replied plaintively.

"That's not quick enough!" Caesar snapped, catching even me off-guard.

Bog clamped a hand down on Caesar's shoulder. "Too damned bad, Dirge. If we hadn't spent the last three days in that useless fog, maybe we wouldn't be in this mess. Thank you very much."

"Zenith, if you had told me why you wanted the Dirge... I mean, me... then I wouldn't have been so elusive."

"You mean you wouldn't have been such a big pain in all our asses?" Bog cut in sarcastically.

"Be that as it may, if we don't get there more quickly, I worry that there won't be a planet left to save."

My stomach lurched at the sound of that.

"We're moving as fast as we can considering all the damage we've sustained," Stairn said. Could I detect a hint of frustration in his voice?

"What are we walking into?" I asked. "A cataclysmic planetary destruction?"

"If I'm right, I'm afraid it could be much worse."

Well, that sounded like the shits to me. "We're a day's travel from Mondo 4 now. There's nothing more we can do."

"That may not be exactly true," Caesar conceded after a moment. "I know a way to get us there in less than two hours."

"And how dangerous is that going to be?" My question was mixed with equal parts sarcasm and scepticism. Everything this man had gotten me involved in so far had proved to be a life-threatening situation.

"Oh, I don't think it will be so bad. There's someone who can help us, a man I've dealt with many times. It will be easier than breathing." Caesar's eyes burned with enthusiasm. "Trust me."

CHAPTER TWENTY-ONE

Crumpled Space

It took about an hour to arrive at the asteroid where Darfus the Dwuvian lived. The little outhouse of a facility turned my stomach. The place was only one street over from hell itself. The steamy, putrid-smelling corridors were framed by rusty pipes and jagged metal walls that made me wonder when I'd gotten my last tetanus shot. Dank fumes rose up from the grates on the floor, nearly searing my feet despite my trusty woollen socks.

When I'd agreed to Caesar's plan, he hadn't indicated just how squirmy and visibly untrustworthy his man Darfus really was. My nostrils were debased by the deep stench of unnatural decay of what could have been any four-legged carcass from any unknown planet in this system.

Within seconds of our arrival inside the building, the Dwuvian had wrapped his three tendril-like arms around my body, searching for weapons, space quids, and God only knew what.

I pushed back from the embrace and was rewarded for my defiance by a sonic blast to my gonads.

"Captain of Militia," he growled as I keeled over. "You kneel now and honour Darfus." It seemed to be a growing trend of disrespect that particular name for me.

He pulled a piece of meat off the rotting carcass on a plate near where he stood and shoved it into his slimly little mouth, then glowered over me in what I could only guess was arrogant contempt. His face, like all others of his race, was a jagged cliff of weathered skin. Creepier yet was the oily residue that flowed out of what could be called pores and trickled down his parched cheeks.

But worse than the Dwuvian himself—so much worse, so unbelievably, ridiculously worse—was the method he offered for getting us to Mondo 4 on time.

The plan would require the use of this derelict little station whose only purpose had been to test a highly questionable method of transportation formally known as "inert spatial compression," and much more informally known as "space crumpling."

The process, which involved squeezing down a region of space like an empty box and then passing through it, had always been dangerous and controversial. Developed more than a century ago, it had also been seen at first as a scientific breakthrough, a technological marvel that would change the galaxy.

Unfortunately, after ten years and several very serious disasters, crumpling had been banned by most species due to the risk of damaging the fabric of space itself. The test vessels were often disintegrated, scattering their miniscule particles over many parsecs of space so that they became impossible to find after the fact.

Crumpling would require a vessel like ours to depart from a predetermined departure point—in this case, Darfus the Dwuvian's derelict station. In addition to the likelihood of us meeting our demise, it would also be really difficult to aim us in exactly the right direction…

Well, let's just say I didn't like the whole idea of space crumpling. I didn't trust space crumpling. And I sure as shit didn't want to use space crumpling to get to Mondo 4.

I suppose Caesar had suspected this, which is why he had been vague about how his friend would get us there. I had assumed we'd been talking about an engine upgrade or a new type of fuel.

So I didn't feel particularly good about the plan laid out by the unscrupulous Dwuvian. But I didn't feel that we had much of a choice, given the urgent stakes.

The only thing that gave me hope was the fact that Caesar seemed to have been here many times before and lived to tell the tale. Maybe Darfus really did know what he was doing?

For our excursion to Darfus's asteroid, Caesar had once again taken the appearance of a three-hundred-year-old human man. He'd explained that he used a different guise every time he came to Darfus. I suspected there was a lot more to the story than Caesar was telling me, of course.

As I contemplated the details of the insane plan, Darfus ate his lunch, taking a long slurp of a piece of disgusting intestine; the juices dripped down his parched chin onto a so-called "shirt" that only haphazardly covered his lean and equally disgusting torso.

"To crumple space for a voyage to the Mondo system... it will cost you ten thousand space quids," Darfus pronounced when he'd finished eating.

Before I could respond, Caesar grabbed hold of my arm.

"Come with me, Captain Militia," the Dirge said to me, his voice filled with contempt at the quoted price. "It would appear that greasy entrails aren't the only nasty thing coming out of this Dwuvian's mouth today."

We turned and made it look like we were going to leave.

Darfus clicked his thin fingers, the signal for a pair of robust Handrian bodyguards to drop their heavy hammers near the door in front of us. If I stepped even a centimetre closer to the exit, I knew we would be attacked.

Caesar and I remained motionless as Darfus stepped around us and placed himself between us and his guards. They stood with their arms crossed, staring down at us. They were humanoid in shape but had cartoonish-looking faces with big beady eyes, large pointy ears, and bulbous teeth that barely fit inside their oversized mouths. Their clothing was minimalistic, like Darfus's. Their powerfully built arms and shoulders squeezed out of their clothing like toothpaste from its tube.

I couldn't look away from their expressions. They looked like psychos! But then I came to realize that this was their natural resting visage. They gave me the urge to grab back my not-so-trusty propulsion gun and start blasting holes...

"Space crumpling is expensive," Darfus said. "You would be well advised to pay the price."

"And if we don't?" I asked, holding back my anger. I was unarmed now that the Dwuvian had lifted my propulsion gun at the door.

"Then you will be asked to leave."

"Gladly."

"Through the airlock."

I did not like Darfus and I sure as shit didn't trust him to get us where we were going, so I abruptly made the decision to forget this whole thing.

I glanced at my propulsion gun, hanging from the end of Darfus's belt, and calculated whether I could wrestle it free. He was overconfident and might eventually step close enough for me to do so. I would put the gun up one of his greasy nostrils and see what came out the top of his head when I pulled the trigger...

Caesar may have been a mind reader, because he pulled several bills of lithium paper from his jacket. He unfolded and flipped through the currency, then counted out ten thousand space quids. I couldn't say I was surprised that he had brought so much cash along with him.

"On one condition." He pulled back the money from the overeager Dwuvian's greedy fingers. "We leave immediately."

Darfus snatched the money, and I snatched back my weapon. His guards didn't take well to this, but Darfus held up a hand to halt them.

I guess he realized that if his guards made their move towards me and Caesar, the greasy entrails of that godawful creature he'd slurped down wouldn't be the only slimy substance coating the walls. I would be all too happy to explode that wiry man all over the room.

"You play a dangerous game," Darfus said. A dribble of grease slid down his chin and landed on the metal grates that made up the floor. I heard it sizzle as it dripped below and plopped into something probably equally as disturbing.

The large Handrian guards looked like they could jump out of their skin at any moment. I knew for certain that Darfus would be a goner if they did. I wasn't so certain whether I would have the time to press my trigger four more times, misfires included. One shot each probably wouldn't be enough.

"The way I see it, Darfus, it's only dangerous if the wrong choices are made," I said slowly.

Darfus left his hand raised to keep the Handrians at bay. His dull grey-green eyes seemed to come to life; the irises actually swirled as he spoke. It reminded me of efflorescent sewage circling down a toilet bowl.

"Captain, the danger falls upon you…" He left that statement to hang there without a further word.

"Do tell," I said, glancing around the chamber where pipes still steamed and hissed, puddles of goo and putridity wafted, and the lights shone just brightly enough to make all this garbage visible.

"Your weapon is less dangerous than your outcome."

I didn't really understand what he meant, but I was disconcerted by that strange swirling activity in his eyes. I was beginning to understand that his eyes could be a telltale sign of his emotional state. I realized that I had sparked his ire.

"Captain Militia," Caesar whispered to me.

With the noise of the pipes hissing and puddles dripping, I didn't believe anyone else would be able to hear him. Even I could barely hear his voice. I had to concentrate hard to make out his next words.

"You're signing our doom." His voice was steady, but I could hear the desperation. "We can't help the Mondorians in time because we can't use crumpled space now. Even if he agrees to send us across crumpled space, he may just decide to use his equipment to destroy us."

He was right. Fuck! I had let my anger over losing another weapon cloud my reasoning… again. Maybe Mara was right about my temper. How had this not been obvious to me? We could never trust Darfus now.

Caesar read the situation quickly, and he read it better than I had. He stepped in front of me, looked Darfus in the eyes, and raised his hands beseechingly.

"You're correct," Caesar said to Darfus. "We are your guest here and it's not our place to demand or threaten."

I looked over Caesar's shoulder to observe the leathery Dwuvian's reaction. It was hard to know for sure, but I thought I saw him ease up a bit.

"You're smarter than your friend." Darfus lowered his hand, but his Handrian bodyguards didn't back down.

They also didn't make any further threatening moves.

"We simply wish to get to the Mondo 4 without any trouble," Caesar said.

"Trouble is inevitable for you, my friends," Darfus remarked as smoothly as he could—which is to say that it reminded me of sandpaper rubbing onto cardboard.

"What do you mean?" I asked, careful to remove any trace of contempt from my voice.

"You showed Darfus disrespect and contempt, Captain of Militia," he said. It seemed he sometimes liked to refer to himself in the third person. "You threaten Darfus in his own place? There is no walking away for you now."

Well, that sealed it.

"Then the only way forward is through you," I said, resigning myself to the fact that we were screwed every which way from Sunday.

I pulled Caesar back by the shoulder as I edged in front of him. Then I raised my weapon from Darfus's chest to his head.

The Handrians stepped forward, ready to drop the proverbial hammer of doom, but I noticed that they hadn't yet pulled their weapons on me. They knew what I did—that they couldn't kill me before I exterminated their boss.

Darfus smiled and showed no outward signs of fear. "If you pull the trigger, that will be the end of you."

"Not before you." I had to believe that I'd just undone all of Caesar's attempts to generate some good will. I seemed to be pretty good at that.

"If I fall to my enemy, my ally will avenge my death."

I found his words cryptic. And I doubted that this pathetic little man had any allies.

"We are only as strong as the allies who support us," Caesar agreed. "True strength rests with us."

This was such a strange exchange of words that I couldn't figure out what to think of it.

Without a discernible reason, Darfus's grey-green irises began to swirl violently. His leathery jaw dropped, exposing his rotting, cavernous teeth.

"What is that you say?" Darfus asked, his voice subdued.

"You've heard that before, have you not, Darfus?" Caesar asked.

"I'm not certain what you say."

I wasn't keeping up with the conversation, but something inside me said that a very important or dangerous turn had just happened. I couldn't be sure what it was, though, and my only option at the moment was to keep my questions to myself.

"Perhaps there is one on Barrier Void who could explain it to you better," Caesar said.

I don't know how to explain the sudden drop in the room's emotional temperature at that precise moment. It felt almost as though the slimy shit dripping down the walls would freeze on contact with the air.

Darfus remained motionless. He didn't even dare to blink.

I looked over at his Handrian guards again and wondered if my eyes deceived me. Did they seem to shrink back from Caesar?

"Barrier Void?" Darfus said.

"Perhaps a message to the Cadvarious would alter your perspective."

Now I *really* had no damned idea what was being said. They were speaking in English—of this I was mostly sure.

Even though I held the only raised pistol in the room, I felt more anxious than ever.

"You know of the Cadvarious?" Darfus whispered. He sounded small and weak.

"More importantly, they know I'm here, Darfus." Caesar glared down on the Dwuvian.

How the hell was Caesar doing this? I pointed my weapon at Darfus, his death only a sneeze away, and he showed me nothing but contempt. Caesar tossed out a few words and the man nearly had to pick up his greasy jawbone off the floor.

"They're following our progress, Darfus. They're keeping very close track of my movements. Do you think they wouldn't look into my disappearance if it should happen here and by your hands?"

Darfus stepped back a couple of steps. He bumped into his bodyguards and nearly jumped from the light impact. He raised his hands peaceably.

It was weird to see his right hand shake and not his left. Almost as if his wiry wrist was having difficulty keeping it attached.

"What do you need from Darfus?" the greasy Dwuvian asked, his voice shaky.

"We *need* nothing from you." Caesar kept his voice steady, but he raised his posture to emphasize his next point. "All we want from you is to satisfy our transaction here today. Do so, and I'll make sure the Cadvarious remain unaware of your presence."

"I can do that," Darfus allowed, his voice soft.

"And Darfus, when I said that the Cadvarious knows where I am, I want to make sure you're absolutely clear on the fact that they have our ship tracked. Think very hard about how well you program our voyage through crumpled space. Wouldn't want anything… unfortunate… to befall us…"

The unpleasant man shrunk back at the implications of Caesar's words. "Agreed. If you board your ship now, you will be safely in the Mondo system within minutes."

Darfus turned towards his guards and nodded. With that, they promptly led us back to the airlock that would return us to *Orbital*.

We left that shithole of an asteroid station as quickly as my stride would allow us. I didn't understand what had just happened, but I felt the need to get the hell out of there.

"One day I would love to hear an explanation," I said to Caesar.

I felt that I was well-versed in many matters in this section of the Gambit Galaxy, but I had never heard of the Cadvarious. But anything that could terrify a greasy slug like Darfus must be truly dreadful. Fear like that wasn't easily faked.

"Perhaps," Caesar replied, as cryptic as ever. "One day."

He didn't seem inclined to delve into it just now, however, and I chose not to press the issue any further. I had enough on my mind.

As we finished our short journey, I took us by the engine room to fill Simbden in on our impending attempt to travel by crumpled space. I didn't want to tell the rest of the crew, but our engineer couldn't be left in the dark.

Caesar and I stepped into the engine room and immediately approached the young Mackmian. I watched his face closely as we walked him through the space-crumpling procedure.

"My captain, the Mackmians have no trust in this technology," he said when we had finished. "Can't we find another way?"

He looked at Caesar to see if the other man would agree with him. Caesar remained silent.

"I shouldn't have to remind you of the doom about to descend on Mondo 4," I said. "This is our only option."

That seemed to satisfy him. He still looked worried, of course. Any sane man would.

"I'll do my best to keep *Orbital* together," he said. He sounded hopeful… but not quite certain.

With that errand complete, we returned to the control hub. My thoughts dwelled on crumpled space. Even I had never been crazy enough to try anything like this before. The horrific accidents I'd read about had caused me to swear to those same Mackmian gods of fate never to try.

But I didn't have a long time to ponder my fear, since I soon found myself back in the captain's chair.

The looks I received from the crew over the next few seconds were hard to decipher. I could tell they were eager to learn about whatever was about to transpire.

I wasn't surprised when Mara was the first to speak.

"Brant, what exactly are we about to attempt?" she asked.

Glancing up at the domed ceiling, I watched as we rounded Darfus the Dwuvian's asteroid. Which meant, of course, that we were already taxiing towards our departure point. Caesar was handling the details from his position behind me.

"We will be travelling to Mondo 4," I said after a few moments. "Caesar has informed me of a method we can use to get there in minutes."

"Okay…" Mara frowned. "What's this method called? And how does it work?"

She was all questions, and I had a hard time deflecting them.

Before I could reply, Caesar spoke up on my behalf. "It's called crumpled space. I've travelled this way dozens of times. Haven't had any issues."

I looked quickly at Bog, and then at Stairn. Bog seemed not to recognize the term. From Stairn, though, I saw a flash of recollection. He looked concerned and seemed about to voice his opinion—

—and then chose not to.

I glanced around my shoulder just in time to see Daisee step into the control hub. I was happy to see that she hadn't appeared to have suffered much from the miasma attack. This suggested that the other Brunken aboard their ship were most likely recovering just as well.

"Oh," Mara said. Had she heard of crumpled space before? Maybe she had but couldn't quite place it. "Well, I'm not familiar with it. But if it's tried and tested, I suppose that's perfectly acceptable. I trust your judgment, Brant."

Shit. That was harder to endure than any scathing rebuke.

Orbital was soon directed via flashing lights to the launch zone in orbit around the asteroid, a circle of space surrounded by bright beacons.

We were about a minute away from our target when something in my mind snapped.

Fuck!

"I can't do this to you," I said softly, catching everyone by surprise. "I need to tell you… everything. Crumpled space is quick, yes, and we are in some ways fortunate to have the option…"

I stood up from the chair and began to pace.

"But you should understand the risks."

It was hard to admit the truth now that I had more or less already decided to throw my crew to the proverbial wolves. It sure would have been easier to keep my mouth shut. But Mara's declaration of faith in me couldn't go unacknowledged. It was wrong to betray that trust.

"Crumpled space has an extremely sketchy past," I told them. "In fact, it's outlawed in many solar systems. The truth is, it's possible that I've let my desperation get the better of me. But make no mistake… this situation is as desperate as they come."

Mara turned to Caesar. "But you've done it so many times before?"

Her face was flushed, meaning she must be angry. But how angry?

"I have," Caesar said calmly.

"But that doesn't change the fact that our journey is risky," I said. "If anything goes wrong, *Orbital* could be destroyed. That's why if any of you aren't willing to take the risks, you have the option of taking our shuttle and heading to Tartius 3. It's a planet about two days away with a large population and a small Prime outpost in orbit."

I watched my crew intently, feeling the clock tick down. We would enter the launch point soon. On the viewscreen, I could see a large ring just ahead of us.

"You must make the choice now."

"I'll stay," Mara said a moment later. Her eyes were on her computer, and I could tell she had quickly pulled up some information on the procedure.

I looked into her eyes and tried to read any emotion there. Too many were visible for me to decipher them all. But one of them was unmistakable: courage.

"This is too important to back away now," she added.

As if on cue, the rest of the crew quickly fell in line behind her.

I don't know if I was more relieved or worried over their collective decision. Perhaps all I could do was hope that fate, that fickle mistress, would smile down upon us.

We were almost at the launch point now. Currently the indicator lights were solid red, but they began to flash as *Orbital* ventured closer, indicating that we were to stop within the aperture of the ring. The ring seemed to be set to accommodate the largest allowable size of ship; anything larger would be deemed unsafe for travel.

Feeling hopeful I looked over at my closest friend and brother. Bog stood at the weapons console, showing no discernible expression except his usual glowering discontent. It was both a terrifying look and one I'd grown to love.

I couldn't see Sparling's face, since she was facing away from me at the pilot's console.

The expression I saw on Caesar's face was intense and I didn't know him nearly well enough to read it. I was glad he was here where I could keep an eye on him, even though I felt more and more certain that I wouldn't be able to control him.

The lights around the ring flashed yellow. It would only be another few seconds now.

I used those seconds to focus on Mara. God, she was beautiful. I wanted to step closer and hold her. I wanted to tell her that everything would be okay, and we would be safe.

But I couldn't bring myself to be dishonest with her again.

The lights shone green. The time had come.

The next several moments felt bizarre, for lack of a better word. We were caught in a tumultuous glare of strange lights, pitch darkness, and an indescribable pressure that manifested itself in my vision and sense of inertia. The interior of *Orbital* remained undisturbed, but the sound was eerie… like the strange, dull emptiness of being underwater.

I dared not move for fear that any motion could cause this untrustworthy technology to malfunction and send us spinning fragmented into oblivion.

I felt like I was riding an elevator that moved so smoothly that it almost didn't seem to be moving at all. Interestingly, the stars on the viewscreen didn't so much speed by us as bleed through the dark blanket of space and merge into one another.

I hoped it was just an optical illusion.

The starlight continued to blend and swirl until the ship seemed to be surrounded by a surreal puddle of paint. Goosebumps raised disconcertingly on my neck and arms and my fear grew stronger. I had to swallow a lump down.

I closed my eyes for a brief moment, hoping it would be over soon.

Then I opened my eyes, startled. It seemed that all the light in the universe suddenly flashed in our eyes—and we went blind.

The darkness permeated every part of my being. My eyes couldn't detect light—this was apparent to me immediately—and something within me screamed that everything was terribly wrong.

And the darkness persisted.

Can anyone hear me? Is anyone there? I spoke the words aloud, I was certain, but no actual sound came from my mouth.

Fear began to take over. I typically wasn't prone to the sensation, but alone in the dark not knowing if I were even still living or what had befallen my crew? It knocked me down to a level I hadn't experienced in a very long time.

Deep within my mind, I began to panic. I moved my hands and feet in the dark, not even feeling certain whether they were there. I bade my right hand to reach out to my left and the action left me terrified. I couldn't touch one hand to another.

I tried touching my torso, desperate for any concrete sign that I still lived. I screamed in frustration and fear, all the while losing hope that existence for me and possibly everyone I cared for had come to a quick and ignoble end.

At the height of my dread, I looked down—or so I thought—and I began to see a glow. Quickly after, a second glow formed.

They were my hands! At last, something real. Something that definitely *existed*. I hadn't felt elation quite like this in years.

Next, a kind of indistinct bluish-silver light radiated from around my hands. As I watched, the effect extended to my wrists and continued up towards my elbows.

I moved my hands around and noticed now that the right one glowed more powerfully than the left. I couldn't understand what this meant. I couldn't understand anything at the moment.

Still trapped in darkness, I tried to move but it wasn't clear to me whether I was successful. My hands could move, that was certain, but I couldn't yet pick up any meaningful sensations from the rest of my body.

Seconds or hours later (I couldn't accurately decipher which), my eyes picked up another light source. And then another one.

"Is anyone else there?" a voice called out in the darkness.

I recognized it. Agent Stairn was calling to me from… somewhere. I'd never once been so happy to hear that voice.

"Stairn, it's me, Zenith."

"Captain, are you okay?"

"I seem to be intact." I hesitated, unsure how else to summarize the situation I found myself in. "What about you?"

"Likewise. I can see your hands glow."

"I'm not the only one, it would appear." I looked in the direction his voice came from and saw the outline of his shadowy figure. A deep red tendril of light had wrapped itself around his neck and partially down his torso.

"You two are here?" someone else spoke.

I looked around for the unexpected presence. It sounded not altogether familiar, but not totally unfamiliar either.

A moment later, a third light did indeed begin to glow in the darkness. And there around the speaker's wrist was a light blue circlet.

That circlet looked very familiar.

"Caesar?" I asked, recognizing the unmistakable shape of the Militon chain, which wrapped around his wrist like a vine.

"It is I," he said. His voice sounded different than it ever had before, yet similar enough to what I remembered of the young, handsome form of the Dirge.

I wondered what was causing the difference but didn't have time to ponder the question. Without warning, the ethereal looking lights glowing from our bodies strengthened and began to cut through the terminal darkness. I looked over at Stairn and for the first time ever witnessed an expression of bewilderment on his face. I wondered if he knew something more than me about what was happening.

Where was the rest of the crew? The thought crossed my mind, but it was the last thought I would have for a while.

Suddenly, I felt my body being thrown around through an invisible yet unambiguously cylindrical tunnel. I watched as my colleagues were treated to the same. We spun within that invisible cylinder as if a tornado were pulling us up and pinning us down all at the same time. It didn't feel like any wind I'd ever known; rather, it felt as if all of gravity had been turned sideways and decided to spin like a top.

We were moving fast and my only point of reference was the glow from our bodies. It was breathtaking. And terrifying. I smelled no scents, heard no sounds, and felt no pain.

But that didn't last.

Before my very eyes, the constituent elements of my body began to tear themselves away, the particles moving in the opposite direction around that invisible cylinder. The effect was eerie and utterly inexplicable.

Caught in that gravity tunnel, or whatever it was, I spotted a glimpse of the face I had thought to belong to Caesar. But what I saw was not how I remembered him. His face was still tanned, his hair long and dark, and his ears appeared to have the same general shape as far as I could focus on them. His eyes even shone gold, as they had earlier.

But there was something different about his face. It wasn't quite the same handsome visage I remembered. Similar, but much plainer.

None of this mattered. The swirling vortex of gravity continued to tear at my body, increasing its ferocity.

That's when the pain kicked in. First, a pinprick on my upper arm. Then another on my neck, and on my chest. Then more and more. I felt every agonizing second of it but didn't understand. What the hell was happening?

More and more pieces of myself swirled away into the dark tempest, dissolving as they disappeared from view.

"Caesar, what the hell is going on!" I demanded in a panic.

Despite the tortuous pain and visual frenzy, the vortex was silent—aside from my screams and the indistinct howls of Caesar and Stairn.

"Speak!" I yelled.

And then Caesar's voice cried back: "I don't want to say."

"No more of your accursed games! Tell me the truth!"

Suddenly, my body—what remained of it—flew past the one belonging to Caesar. It was hard to make out, as the surrounding darkness permeated everything. And as quickly as I saw him, he was gone again, having rolled away as though trapped in a metal barrel pitching uncontrollably down a steep hill.

The only light in our vicinity came from us. In addition to the light emanating from my hands and lower arms, the darkness was somewhat offset by the glows representing Caesar and Stairn.

And those glows were continuing to intensify over time—outside of my control, and I had no reason to think it was any different for the others.

Finally, the sides of the vortex began to show some signs of turning visible. I felt it before I actually saw it... some sort of recognizable shape...

Was that the dome of *Orbital*'s control hub spinning around us? What the hell?

"Caesar, what the flying fuck is going on!"

"We should be dead," I heard him say, the words sounding like an admission of defeat. He seemed deeply afraid. "Crumpled space... it failed... we should be torn to subatomic particles... scattered to the cosmos..."

That sounded like a truly piss-poor end.

"Fucking Darfus," I swore to myself. "Why the hell aren't we dead...?"

Somehow Caesar had heard me. "I truly don't know."

I tried to close my eyes as we continued to swirl downward. Although, now that I paid attention to the movement around me, it did seem as though our speed might be levelling off. The pain... was it become more tolerable? Were the particles tearing loose from my body slowing down?

"It's because of *Orbital*," Stairn called.

As he spoke, I saw him slowly pass by my position in this swirling cocoon; I could tell he was as helpless as I seemed to be.

"*Orbital* is a strange ship," I said, repeating Caesar's earlier sentiment, the one he had expressed after the miasma had failed to hold *Orbital* as long as it should have.

All around me, the image of the domed control hub grew in clarity... and eventually even the spinning ceased. I closed my eyes as my feet landed upon the familiar floor at the base of the captain's chair. Whatever had happened within that swirling vortex of crumpled-space doom had finally run its course.

And we were alive.

CHAPTER TWENTY-TWO

Mondo

O*rbital* landed on the edge of the Mondo system, the voyage through crumpled space having ended in a gradually deescalating shock for everyone concerned. Well, at least physically. The mental strain left on my mind was another story altogether.

I looked around the control hub, trying desperately to process what the airborne shit had just happened to Stairn, Caesar, and myself. Where had the others been throughout all this? Why exactly were we not all dead? And how had we ended up where we intended?

The crew were all standing or sitting in the positions they had been in when we'd begun our launch through crumpled space. They looked exactly as they had been moments before the journey. It looked like nothing had even happened to them or the ship. Had the whole thing been a surreal dream?

I had not a single answer to any of these questions. I didn't even have time to ponder them, since what I saw next shook me on a whole new level.

I was utterly dismayed by the sight on the viewscreen. Instead of the star and its many orbiting planets, all we saw was the enormous grey void. I knew we had been told to expect the void, of course, but it was a terrible sight to behold. And were we too late? It had already swallowed up the whole damned system!

We were a scant thousand kilometres from the edge of the void, the effect of which was hard to discern. No matter which angles our viewscreen showed, it looked the same—hazy and confusing.

I immediately sent out array after array of spatial attenuators to bring in more data, but we received no immediate feedback—except for one conclusion: the void was shrinking, pulling the system in with it.

"Report!" I called to anyone and everyone.

The order met with silence for a few moments. They seemed to need some time to take in what had just happened in crumpled space, not to mention what was transpiring in front of us now.

"Spatial attenuators are sending back readings." Mara's voice sounded shaken.

I punched on my computer screen and information began to pop up. Trying to make sense of spatial attenuator readings could be a little like divining the weather with a stick. The readouts were extremely confusing, and practice was needed in order to quickly assess them.

Our current readings were awash with conflicting information.

"All planets and moons read as present," Sparling said, bringing up the same information.

The control hub suddenly glowed with the three-dimensional holographic display that only intermittently worked. The lights of it reflected off every glistening surface in the room. It felt a little like New Year's Eve on the party planet Camdian where the food tasted like heaven, the alcohol flowed freely, the loving came easily and the only thing you couldn't do was remember how you'd made it to your bed in the morning and what the hell had happened the four days previous…

I took note of the three-dimensional planetary orbs of various sizes drifting around the Mondo system's sun. Each moon and planet was visible and countable. Just as Sparling had assured us, every celestial body seemed to be accounted for.

However, I could see through the actual domed window above that nothing of the kind was actually visible. Mondo's most distant planet should have been within easy eyeshot of our location, but there was nothing there but grey void.

The data coming in from the spatial attenuators were conflicting. Most likely, the grey void was screwing up our equipment.

I again sent out array after array of spatial attenuators to try bringing in even more data.

"The void is shrinking further," Bog rumbled from his corner. "But the attenuators aren't clear as to the velocity of that reduction."

I focused my attention on what I could actually see. The edge of the void did appear to be clearing, like steam escaping a shower stall. Tendrils of its grey substance trailed off at the point where the void's density waned. Without a doubt, it was thinning and pulling inwards on itself.

As far as I was aware, this was unprecedented. I simply didn't know how to proceed.

"Spatial attenuators are showing some indication of the constitution of the void," Mara cut in. From my vantage point, she seemed to be perusing through a mountain of digital data, trying to source it out.

"Bring the info up on the main screen, Mara."

When the data filled the viewscreen, it became a little easier to get a handle on what was going on.

"It seems to be a mixture of dark energy, dark matter, and some other unknown energy, compound, or element," Mara stated.

I couldn't recall her many qualifications including astrophysics, but she was spot on with her assessment. I hadn't seen a composition like this in all my years in space.

I looked across the control hub to Caesar and attempted to gauge his reaction. His appearance had returned to his youthful, striking, gold-eyed form. He was more handsome than ever and he stood still as a statue, his eyes burning with intensity. His arms were crossed in front of his chest.

"It's not what I expected," I said quietly, in awe of the spectacle.

Caesar remained motionless. "And it's exactly what I feared."

"What's going on, Caesar? No more lies."

"Captain Militia, we need to raise our defences."

I couldn't argue with his logic. "Bog, are any of our weapons working right now?"

I feared the answer even before the words left my mouth.

"Hull propulsion cannons are…" Bog acted like his computer screen had frozen. He wound up and gave it a solid bang with his cement-like forearm. The resultant *gooooong* reverberated through the control hub, nearly rattling the eardrums right out of my head.

Satisfied that the maneuver had worked as intended, Bog continued his explanation. "Hull propulsion cannons are operational. Controls for ballistic space torpedoes are actually responding!"

"Holy shit," I said more to myself than my colleagues. I hadn't expected anything to work. I'd suspected that the only offensive weapon at my disposal was going to be my middle finger…

"Sparling, how is the helm responding?" I asked, wondering if it wasn't too much to hope for her controls to be as functional as our weaponry.

"No problems here, Captain."

Her voice sounded a little rattled, but I could tell she was doing her best to hold her emotions in check.

"Energy barriers?" I asked next.

"Functional too, by god!" Bog stated enthusiastically.

I tapped on my wristband communicator to connect with the engine room. "Simbden, how are we doing down there?"

"Everything is returning to normal, my captain." His young voice came through loud and clear.

"Good," I said.

Maybe our luck was taking a turn for the better.

But just a like a toilet backing up, that's when everything changed.

"Captain, we're being pulled in," Sparling suddenly announced through the quiet room.

I looked down at my armrest controls and saw that she was entirely correct. We were spiralling slowly in the direction of the void. As the void contracted, we were being drawn closer.

Orbital's orientation shifted unexpectedly. Our vantage and trajectory began to tilt, going all cockeyed.

I searched around the room for clues as to what was transpiring. At first my eyes fixed on the holographic projection, trying to read the information it displayed. When that failed to give me what I so desperately sought, I opted to concentrate on the window above.

Our vessel was right on the edge of the contracting grey quagmire. I wasn't sure what would happen if we were pulled in more quickly than the strange grey void was shrinking. Thankfully, it appeared that *Orbital*'s motion had matched the anomaly's gradual speed of contraction. And we were maintaining some distance between ourselves and the edge of the void.

The bad news, of course, was that the odds of us managing to break free didn't look promising.

"Agent Sparling, full power to engines. Keep us back!"

Her fingers flew over her controls. I could see upon my own control screen, the systems' status of our engines and the power output readings. We appeared to be at maximum output. So no matter what Sparling attempted, we continued to be pulled closer.

To my dismay, even with her efforts, I could see that we were speeding up. At the current rate of acceleration, what originally would have been a trip of several hours to the centre of the system would take only minutes. We were fortunate not to have been placed on a collision course with a planet or other form of space debris.

The void had already shrunk to a fraction of its initial size when we'd first entered the system.

I watched closely, my stomach feeling sick as we raced towards the heart of the Mondo system, as though mimicking the journey of a paddleless rowboat over the edge of an epic waterfall.

As the void pulled back towards its ultimate epicentre, somewhere inside the star itself, the sun and all its planets pulled back into focus. They had been entirely invisible one moment, and the very next they wavered into existence like a mirage on a smouldering hot desert horizon.

I gripped the armrest of my chair, my knuckles turning white from exertion. Our momentum was going to carry us right into the star!

"Everyone, brace for collision!"

I felt the ship's atmospheric stabilizers struggle to keep up as *Orbital* agitated around us like a pair of maracas. The ship was being pulled apart as we crashed towards the star, its radiance beating down on us with the heat and intensity of a supernova.

I knew of course that the star itself wasn't actually getting larger, but it sure seemed that way as we approached. The solar flares became sickeningly clear on the static-filled viewscreen. I had to hold my hand in front of my eyes to prevent its brightness from scarring my retinas. Sweat formed on my brow and the palms of my hands, whether from the heat or from stress I couldn't tell.

Abruptly, *Orbital* slowed—and then came to a stop. I swayed with queasiness, my stomach and head churning from disorientation. I presumed the void must have collapsed entirely, releasing its pull on us. And miraculously it seemed that our protective shields had been successful at holding back the worst of the scorch damage.

The star's light in the control hub was unbearable at first. It took a few seconds for the auto-dim feature to kick in. It was a good thing, too, since we were about to go blind—for real, this time.

The heat was another story altogether. It felt like someone had cranked the dial to maximum and then thrown firewood, coal, and gasoline on the blazing bonfire which I felt was burning under my seat.

I knew *Orbital* and the crew wouldn't withstand this mind-boggling heat for long.

"Sparling, back us out of here!" I commanded.

"I'm trying, Captain. Thrusters aren't responding. My controls tell me they should be. I don't know what's—"

"Keep at it, Agent!"

I looked over at Caesar. His hands were gripping the handrail just as hard as mine did the captain's chair.

"What is going on here?" I asked him.

"I believe the pull from the void is releasing us. It will be up to your crew to correct our position… and I suggest you do it quickly."

Thanks a buttload, I thought sarcastically.

"Agent?" I called over to Sparling, hoping for some sign that *Orbital* was moving in the correct direction: away from the damned star.

I watched Sparling for several more tense moments, her controls lit up like a Christmas tree. It looked to me like she was trying every trick she knew to coax *Orbital* back into motion.

And finally, thankfully, albeit like a mule, we started to move again, our thrusters backing us off from the star's corona.

The glow surrounding us began to drop off and the temperature soon followed suit, thank the Mackmian gods.

Sparling set us on a heading for Mondo 4. It was surreal to fly through the space again under our own power.

As we approached the fourth planet, its atmosphere glowed greenish-blue. That's when it struck me that there would normally be a fleet of manmade satellites in orbit, and yet I couldn't see a single one.

I hammered on my control screen, looking for any clue to determine whether the satellites still existed.

"Bring me up readings from the planet's surface," I said.

"On screen," Stairn replied. "What the...?"

It probably wasn't a good sign that Stairn would sound so confused and concerned. And surely, he appeared to have a good reason. In keeping with the missing satellites, the planet was devoid of all lifesigns.

Mara choked back a gasp. "Where did everything go?"

It was a terrifying realization. This had been a planet with more than six hundred million inhabitants... and they'd all vanished. We appeared to be alone in the solar system.

The view of the planet seemed eerily, deceptively peaceful. Its atmosphere seemed intact, its orbit unaffected by the effects of the mysterious void that had passed through. Under any other circumstance, I would probably have been able to appreciate the natural beauty below.

"What the hell has happened to everyone... everything?" Bog asked. His normally deep grumble of a voice sounded frail.

"Mara?" I asked, hoping she had found an explanation.

She didn't reply, so I used my controls to scan the surface again. Before the void, Mondo 4's surface had been habitable to most humanoid physiologies. I wondered if it were still so. Skimming through the readouts, I saw that the topography and atmospheric composition was intact. The planet's three very large oceans were exactly where they ought to be. The continents were in their right places.

All was calm. Too calm.

I looked over at Caesar and studied his expression, contorted in dismay. His face looked like he'd just witnessed his best friend being dropped off a building. He didn't even notice me staring at him from several paces away. If he had, he probably would have worked harder to suppress the tears that were beginning to form…

Oh fuck. That scared me more than almost anything could at that moment.

"Caesar?" I asked, keeping my tone respectful. I didn't feel the need to bark demands. True, I was desperate for answers and he was the closest thing to an authority on what was going on here, but he seemed distraught.

I got up from my chair and took a half-step towards him.

He looked over and quickly wiped the moisture from his tanned face. His eyes shone an even more intense shade of gold than usual.

"Caesar, what's happened?"

"Devastation," he said quietly.

"What does that mean?" I asked, my heart racing.

He chose not to speak. Maybe he didn't know how to answer.

I waited a little longer, taking a moment to absorb the mental abrasion I felt we had all just received.

But the moment passed.

Without warning, quicker than a flash of lightning, our proximity alarm began to blare. I looked at my controls and saw that *Orbital* had been instantaneously surrounded by a host of alien spacecraft. In less than a blink of an eye, they were everywhere!

It was an enormous armada! So tightly packed were the ships that if we even tried to move, we would have scraped the paint off the nearest one.

"What the fuck!" Bog exclaimed, matching my thoughts exactly. "Where the hell did they come from?!"

Our viewscreen continued to show an overview of the solar system—and there we were, right in the middle of a swarm of countless alien ships.

Nonetheless, Sparling managed to turn *Orbital* to face the nearest ship head-on.

My jaw dropped about as quickly as my hopes. I had seen ships like these before—during the battle for Quazar. All the luck in the universe wouldn't be able to save us now, at least not if they chose this moment to end us.

I ground my teeth and felt my stomach heave. We had come all this way, enduring so much danger, for nothing.

If I had known what was about to happen next, I may have opted for a fiery, flaming death within the Mondo star. I sighed, the knowledge settling in that we were about to face a far less pleasant doom.

Manufactured by Amazon.ca
Acheson, AB

10872086R00243